FEJ

KU-717-559

SWALLOWS
·AND·
AMAZONS

B000 000 019 3763

ABERDEEN LIBRARIES

DESPATCHES

SWALLOWS AND AMAZONS

by

ARTHUR RANSOME

SWALLOWS·AND·AMAZONS·FOR·EVER!

Illustrated by the Author
with help from Miss Nancy Blackett

RED FOX

RED FOX

UK | USA | Canada | Ireland | Australia
India | New Zealand | South Africa

Red Fox is part of the Penguin Random House group of companies
whose addresses can be found at global.penguinrandomhouse.com.

www.penguin.co.uk
www.puffin.co.uk
www.ladybird.co.uk

Penguin
Random House
UK

First published Jonathan Cape 1930
Published by Red Fox 1993
This edition published 2016

002

Text copyright © Arthur Ransome, 1930
Front cover artwork copyright © STUDIOCANAL Limited, 2016

The moral right of the author has been asserted

Printed in Great Britain by Clays Ltd, St Ives plc

A CIP catalogue record for this book is available from the British Library

ISBN: 978-1-782-95739-3

All correspondence to
Red Fox
Penguin Random House Children's
80 Strand, London WC2R ORL

MIX
Paper from
responsible sources
FSC® C018179

Penguin Random House is committed to a
sustainable future for our business, our readers
and our planet. This book is made from Forest
Stewardship Council® certified paper.

CONTENTS

CONTENTS

LIST OF ILLUSTRATIONS

LIST OF ILLUSTRATIONS

MAPS (BY STEVEN SPURRIER)

TO

THE SIX FOR WHOM IT WAS WRITTEN

IN EXCHANGE FOR

A PAIR OF SLIPPERS

AUTHOR'S NOTE

I have often been asked how I came to write *Swallows and Amazons*. The answer is that it had its beginning long, long ago when, as children, my brother, my sisters and I spent most of our holidays on a farm at the south end of Coniston. We played in or on the lake or on the hills above it, finding friends in the farmers and shepherds and charcoal-burners whose smoke rose from the coppice woods along the shore. We adored the place. Coming to it, we used to run down to the lake, dip our hands in and wish, as if we had just seen the new moon. Going away from it, we were half drowned in tears. While away from it, as children and as grown-ups, we dreamt about it. No matter where I was, wandering about the world, I used at night to look for the North Star and, in my mind's eye, could see the beloved skyline of great hills beneath it. Swallows and Amazons grew out of those old memories. I could not help writing it. It almost wrote itself.

A.R.

Haverthwaite
May 19th, 1958

Wild Cat Island.

CHAPTER I

THE PEAK IN DARIEN

> "Or like stout Cortez, when with eagle eyes
> He stared at the Pacific – and all his men
> Looked at each other with a wild surmise –
> Silent, upon a peak in Darien."

Roger, aged seven, and no longer the youngest of the family, ran in wide zigzags, to and fro, across the steep field that sloped up from the lake to Holly Howe, the farm where they were staying for part of the summer holidays. He ran until he nearly reached the hedge by the footpath, then turned and ran until he nearly reached the hedge on the other side of the field. Then he turned and crossed the field again. Each crossing of the field brought him nearer to the farm. The wind was against him, and he was tacking up against it to the farm, where at the gate his patient mother was awaiting him. He could not run straight against the wind because he was a sailing vessel, a tea-clipper, the *Cutty Sark*. His elder brother John had said only that morning that steamships were just engines in tin boxes. Sail was the thing, and so, though it took rather longer, Roger made his way up the field in broad tacks.

When he came near his mother, he saw that she had in her hand a red envelope and a small piece of white paper, a telegram. He knew at once what it was. For a moment he was tempted to run straight to her. He knew that telegrams came only from his father, and that this one must be the answer to a letter from his mother, and letters from John, Susan, Titty, and himself, all asking the same thing, but asking it in different ways. His own letter had been very short. "Please, Daddy, may I, too? With love. Roger." Titty's had been much longer, longer even than John's. Susan, though she was older than Titty, had not written a letter of her own. She had put her name with John's at the end of his, so that these two had sent one letter between them. Mother's letter had been the longest of all, but Roger did not know what she had said in it. All the letters had gone together, a very long way, to his father, whose ship was at Malta but under orders for Hong Kong. And there, in his mother's hand, was the red envelope that had brought the answer. For a moment Roger wanted to run straight to her. But sail was the thing, not steam, so he tacked on, heading, perhaps, a little closer to the wind. At last he headed straight into the wind, moved slower and slower, came to a stop at his mother's side, began to move backwards, and presently brought up with a little jerk, anchored, and in harbour.

"Is it the answer?" he panted, out of breath after all that beating up against the wind. "Does he say Yes?"

Mother smiled, and read the telegram aloud:

BETTER DROWNED THAN DUFFERS IF NOT DUFFERS WONT DROWN.

"Does that mean Yes?" asked Roger.

"I think so."

"Does it mean me, too?"

"Yes, if John and Susan will take you, and if you promise to do whatever they tell you."

"Hurrah," shouted Roger, and capered about, forgetting for a moment that he was a ship, and anchored in a quiet harbour.

"Where are the others?" asked Mother.

"In Darien," said Roger.

"Where?"

"On the peak, you know. Titty called it that. We can see the island from there."

Below the farm at Holly Howe the field sloped steeply to a little bay where there was a boathouse and a jetty. But there was little of the lake to be seen, because on each side of the bay there were high promontories. A path ran down the field from the farm to the boathouse. Half-way down the field there was a gate, and from that gate another path ran into the pinewoods that covered the southern and higher promontory. The path soon faded away into nothing, but on the very evening of their first coming, a fortnight before, the children had found their way through the trees to the far end of the promontory, where it dropped, like a cliff, into the lake. From the top of it they had looked out over the broad sheet of water winding away among the low hills to the south and winding away into the hills high to the north, where they could not see so much of it. And it was then, when they first stood on the cliff and looked out over mile upon mile of water, that Titty had given the place its name. She had heard the sonnet read aloud at school, and forgotten everything in it except the picture of the explorers looking at the Pacific Ocean for the first time. She had called the promontory Darien. On the highest point of it they had made their camping place, and there Roger had left them when he had come through the trees to the field and, seeing his mother at the gate, had begun his voyage home.

"Would you like to take them the answer?"

"And tell them it's Yes for me too?"

"Yes. You must give the telegram to John. It's he who has to see that you are not duffers."

Mother put the telegram in its red envelope, and gave it to Roger. She kissed him, anchored as he was, and said, "Supper at half-past seven, and not a minute later, and mind you don't wake Vicky when you come in."

"Aye, aye, sir," said Roger, pulling in his anchor hand over hand. He turned round, and began tacking back down the field, thinking of how he should bring the news.

Mother laughed.

"Ship ahoy!" she said.

Roger stopped, and looked back.

"You had the wind against you coming up the field," she said. "It's a fair wind now. You needn't tack both ways."

"So it is," said Roger, "it's dead aft. I'm a schooner. I can sail goosewinged, with a sail on each side." He spread out his arms for sails, and ran straight down the field to the gate into the pinewood.

When he came out of the field into the wood he stopped being a sailing vessel. No one can sail through a pinewood. He became an explorer, left behind by the main body, following their trail through the forest, and keeping a sharp look-out lest he should be shot by a savage with a poisoned arrow from behind a tree. He climbed up through the trees to the top of the promontory. At last he came out of the trees on a small open space of bare rock and heather. This was the Peak of Darien. There were trees all round it, but through them could be seen the bright glimmer of the lake. In a hollow of rock a small fire was burning. John was stoking the fire. Susan was spreading bread and marmalade. Titty, with her chin on her hunched-up knees, was sitting between two trees on the edge of the cliff above the lake, keeping watch and looking at the island.

John looked up and saw the telegram. He jumped up from the fire.

"Despatches?" he said.

"It's the answer," said Roger. "It's Yes, and it's Yes for me too, if I obey orders, and you and Susan take me. And if it's Yes for me it must be Yes for Titty."

John took the telegram. Titty scrambled up and came, running. Susan held the knife with the marmalade on it over the bread so as not to lose any, but stopped spreading. John opened the envelope, and took out the white paper.

"Read it aloud," said Susan.

John read:

BETTER DROWNED THAN DUFFERS IF NOT DUFFERS WONT DROWN.

"Hurrah for Daddy!" he shouted.

"What does it mean?" asked Susan.

"It means Yes," said Titty.

"It means that Daddy thinks we shall none of us get drowned and that if any of us do get drowned it's a good riddance," said John.

"But what are duffers if not duffers?" asked Susan.

"It doesn't say that," said Titty. "It says that if we were duffers we might as well be drowned. Then it stops and starts again, and says that as we aren't duffers . . ."

"If," said John.

"If we aren't duffers we shan't be drowned."

"Daddy put that in to comfort Mother," said Susan. She went on spreading the marmalade.

"Let's start at once," said Roger, but at that moment the kettle changed its tune. It had been bubbling for some time, but now it hissed quietly and steadily, and a long jet of steam poured from its spout. The water was boiling. Susan took the kettle from the fire, and emptied into it a small packet of tea.

"We can't start tonight anyhow," she said. "Let's have tea, and then we'll make a list of the things we shall want."

"Let's have tea where we can see the island," said Titty.

They carried their mugs and the kettle and the tin plate piled with thick slabs of brown bread and marmalade to the edge of the cliff. The island lay about a mile away towards the lower, southern end of the lake, its trees reflected in the glassy water. They had been looking at it for ten days, but the telegram had made it much more real than ever it had been before. Looking down from Titty's Peak in the evening of the day on which they had come to the farmhouse where their mother had taken lodgings, they had seen the lake like an inland sea. And on the lake they had seen the island. All four of them had been filled at once with the same idea. It was not just an island. It was *the* island, waiting for them. It was their island. With an island like that within sight, who could be content to live on the mainland and sleep in a bed at night? They had gone back and told their mother of their discovery, and begged that the whole family should leave the farmhouse the next day, and camp on the island for ever. But there was little Vicky, a fat baby, like the pictures of Queen Victoria in old age, full of all sorts of needs. Mother could not take Vicky and the nurse to camp even on the best of uninhabited islands. Nor, without leave from Daddy, could she let them go alone. And though John and Susan were both well able to manage a sailing boat, Titty and Roger had only begun to learn how to sail when their father had been home on leave a year before. In the boathouse below the farm there was the *Swallow*, a sailing boat, a very little one, and there was also a big, heavy rowing boat. But no one wants to row who has ever sailed. If there had been no island, no sailing boat, and if the lake had not been so large, the children, no doubt, would have been happy enough to paddle about with oars in the bay by the boathouse. But with a lake as big as a small sea, a fourteen-foot dinghy with a brown sail waiting in the boathouse, and the little wooded island waiting for explorers, nothing but a sailing voyage of discovery seemed worth thinking about.

So the letters had been written and posted, and day after day the children had been camping on the Peak of Darien by day, and sleeping in the farmhouse by night. They had been out in the rowing boat with their mother, but they had always rowed the other way so as not to spoil the voyage of discovery by going to the island first. But with each day after the sending of the letters it had somehow seemed less and less likely that there would ever be an answer. The island had come to seem one of those places seen from the train that belong to a life in which we shall never take part. And now, suddenly, it was real. It was to be their island after all. They were to be allowed to use the sailing boat by themselves. They were to be allowed to sail out from the little sheltered bay, and round the point, and down the lake to the island. They were to be allowed to land on the island, and to live there until it was time to pack up again and go home to town and school and lessons. The news was so good that it made them solemn. They ate their bread and marmalade in silence. The prospect before them was too vast for chatter. John was thinking of the sailing, wondering whether he really remembered all that he had learnt last year. Susan was thinking of the stores and the cooking. Titty was thinking of the island itself, of coral, treasure and footprints in the sand. Roger was thinking of the fact that he was not to be left behind. He saw for the first time that it was a good thing to be no longer the baby of the family. Vicky was youngest now. Vicky would stay at home, and Roger, one of the crew of a ship, was to sail away into the unknown world.

At last John took a sheet of paper and a pencil from his pocket.

"Let's make the Ship's Articles," he said.

The bread and marmalade had all been eaten, so he turned

the plate upside down, and put the paper on the back of it, and lay on his stomach on the rock. He wrote:

"Sailing Vessel *Swallow*. Port: Holly Howe. Owners . . ."

"Who are the owners?"

"She belongs to us for the rest of these holidays anyhow," said Susan.

"I shall put 'Walkers Limited' to do for all of us."

He wrote, "Owners: Walkers Limited." Underneath that he wrote:

> "Master: John Walker.
> Mate: Susan Walker.
> Able-seaman: Titty Walker.
> Ship's Boy: Roger."

"Now," he said, "you all have to sign opposite your names." They all signed.

"Well, Mister Mate," said John.

"Sir," replied Susan smartly.

"How soon do you think we shall be ready to put to sea?"

"With the first breath of wind."

"What do you think of your crew?"

"The best I ever shipped."

"Can they swim?"

"Able-seaman Titty can. The Boy Roger still keeps one foot on the bottom."

"He must learn."

"I don't keep a foot on the bottom all the time," said Roger.

"You must learn as soon as possible not to keep it on the bottom at all."

"All right," said Roger.

"That's all wrong, Roger," said Titty. "You ought to have said, 'Aye, aye, sir!'"

"I nearly always do," said Roger, "I said it to Mother."

MAKING SHIP'S PAPERS

"You must say it to the captain and to the mate. Perhaps you ought to say it even to me, but as there are only two in the crew it won't do for them to be saying sir to each other."

"Have you got any more paper?" said Susan.

"Only the back of the telegram," said John.

"Mother won't mind our using it," said Susan. "You know we can't really sail with the first breath of wind, not until everything is ready. Let's make a list of the things."

"Compass," said John.

"Kettle," said Susan.

"A flag," said Titty. "I'll make one with a swallow on it."

"Tents," said Roger.

"Telescope," said John.

"Saucepan, mugs, knives, forks, tea, sugar, milk," said Susan, writing as hard as she could go.

"Spoons," said Roger.

They kept remembering things and then getting stuck, and then remembering some more until there was no more room on the back of the telegram.

"I haven't got another scrap of paper," said John. "Even the Ship's Articles have got sums on the other side. Bother the list. Let's go and ask Mother if we can have the key of the boat-house."

But when they came to Holly Howe Farm, Mother met them in the doorway with her finger on her lips.

"Vicky's asleep," she said. "Don't make a noise coming in. Supper's just ready."

CHAPTER II

MAKING READY

"What care I for a goose-feather bed,
    With the sheet turned down so bravely, O?
For tonight I shall sleep in the cold open field
    Along with the wraggle-taggle gipsies, O!"

Sʜɪᴘ's Articles, though important, are but a small part of
making ready for a voyage of discovery. There was a great
deal more to do. Luckily, Mother had nearly finished making
the tents. She had decided as soon as they had sent off the
letters that tents would be wanted if the expedition to the island
was allowed, and that if it was not allowed, the next best thing
would be a camp on shore. So she had bought the thin canvas
and had been working at tent-making every day, while fat Vicky
was sleeping and the others were fishing by the boathouse or
camping on the Peak of Darien. That night, after Captain
John and Mate Susan had followed their crew to bed, Mother
had finished both tents.

Next morning, after breakfast, John and Susan, with Mother
to help them, Titty to watch, and Roger to get in the way, had
put up one of the tents between two trees in the Holly Howe
garden. The tents were of the simplest kind. Each tent had a
three-cornered piece for the back. The back was sewn to the
sides, and a piece of stout rope was stitched to the canvas inside
to make the ridge of the roof. The ends of this rope were
fastened to two trees, and so held the tent up. No tent poles
were needed. Along the bottom edges of the back and sides
there were big pockets, to be filled with stones. On rocky ground,

where you cannot drive in tent pegs, this is a good plan. At the front of the tent there were loose flaps, joined to the sides, so that they could be rolled up and tied out of the way with two pairs of tapes that worked like the reef points in a sail.

"Properly," said John, "we ought not to take tents with us. We ought to make a tent out of a sail by hanging it across the yard for a ridge pole, and we ought to hold it up with two pairs of oars, a pair at each end. But one tent would not be big enough and to make two we should want eight oars and two sails, big ones. *Swallow* has only got one small sail, and two oars. So these tents are much better."

"They are good enough tents except in a high wind," said Mother. "Father and I often slept in one when we were young."

Titty looked gravely at Mother.

"Are you really old?" she said.

"Well, not very," said Mother, "but I was younger then."

Mother had bought two square waterproof groundsheets, one for each tent. One of them was spread inside the tent that was being tried.

"You be careful," said Mother, "to keep the edges of the groundsheet inside the tent, or if it rains you'll find yourselves sleeping in a puddle."

Everybody crowded into the tent and sat down. Titty borrowed fat Vicky from Nurse, and brought her in too. Susan shut the flaps of the tent from inside.

"We might be anywhere," Titty said.

"Next time we put the tent up we shall be on the island," said John.

"What about mattresses?" said Mother.

"Rugs," said Captain John.

"Not enough," said Mother, "unless you want to be like the lady who ran away with the wraggle-taggle gipsies and caught her death of cold."

"The song doesn't say so," said Titty. "It only says she didn't care."

"Well, and what happened to Don't Care?"

"Came to a bad end," said Roger.

"A cold is a bad end when you are camping, especially on a desert island," said Mother. "No, we must get some haybags filled for you to sleep on. If you put them on the groundsheets and lie on the top of them, and roll yourselves up in rugs and blankets, you'll come to no harm."

Captain John was in a hurry to try the *Swallow* under sail.

"Let's go down to the harbour and overhaul the ship," he said. "We can take her out now, can't we, Mother?"

"Yes. But I'd like to come with you the first time."

"Come along. Do. You can be Queen Elizabeth going aboard the ships at Greenwich that were sailing to the Indies."

Mother laughed.

"It doesn't matter a bit about your not having red hair," said Titty.

"All right," said Mother, "but I think we must leave Vicky with Nurse."

So they all crawled out of the tent. Fat Vicky was given back to Nurse, and Queen Elizabeth walked down to the boathouse with Captain John of the sailing ship *Swallow*, Mate Susan, Able-seaman Titty, and the Boy Roger, who ran on ahead with the big key to get the boathouse open.

The boathouse was a stone one, with a narrow quay along each wall inside, and a small jetty sticking out beyond it into the lake.

Roger had got the door open by the time they came to it, though he had had a tough struggle with the rusty lock. He was already inside, looking down on the *Swallow*. The *Swallow* was a sailing dinghy built for sailing on a shallow estuary, where the sands were uncovered at low tide. Most sailing

27

dinghies have centreboards, plates which can be let down through their keels, to make them sail better against the wind. *Swallow* had none, but she had a rather deeper keel than most small boats. She was between thirteen and fourteen feet long, and fairly broad. Her mast lay in her, and beside it, neatly rolled up, were boom, yard, and sail, and a pair of short oars. Her name, *Swallow*, was painted on her stern.

Captain John and his crew looked at her lovingly. She was already their own ship.

"Better bring her outside and make fast to the jetty while you step the mast," said Queen Elizabeth. "You won't be able to get her out if you step the mast while she's in the boathouse. That beam is too low."

Captain John went aboard his ship. Mate Susan untied the painter, and between them they brought the *Swallow* out of the boathouse. Then Susan fastened the painter to an iron ring on the end of the jetty. She too climbed down into *Swallow*.

"Can I come too?" asked Roger.

"You and Titty and I will wait till they have the sail up," said Queen Elizabeth. "Give them plenty of room and a free hand. We should only be in the way if we went aboard now."

"Hullo," said John, "she's got a little flagstaff, and there are flag halyards on the mast to hoist it by." He held up a tiny flagstaff with a three-cornered blue flag on it.

"I'm going to make her a much better flag than that," said Titty.

"Better take this one to make sure you make yours the same size," said Queen Elizabeth.

John and Susan had done plenty of sailing, but there is always something to learn about a boat that you have not sailed before. They stepped the mast the wrong way round, but that was set right in a moment.

"She doesn't seem to have a forestay," said John. "And there isn't a place to lead the halyard to in the bows to make it do instead."

"Let me have a look," said Queen Elizabeth. "These little boats often do without stays at all. Is there a cleat under the thwart where the mast is stepped?"

"Two," said John, feeling. The mast fitted in a hole in the forward thwart, the seat near the bows of the boat. It had a square foot, which rested in a slot cut to fit it in the kelson.

"Get the sail ready and hoist it, and make fast there and see how she does," said Queen Elizabeth.

"I wonder whether the real Queen Elizabeth knew much about ships," said Titty.

"That Queen Elizabeth was not brought up close to Sydney Harbour," said Mother.

Susan had got the sail ready. On the yard there was a strop (which is really a loop) that hooked on a hook on one side of an iron ring called the traveller, because it moved up and down the mast. The halyard ran from the traveller up to the top of the mast, through a sheave (which is a hole with a little wheel in it), and then down again. John hooked the strop on the traveller and hauled away on the halyard. Up went the brown sail until the traveller was nearly at the top of the mast. Then John made the halyard fast on the cleats, which were simply pegs, underneath the thwart which served to hold the mast up.

"That looks all right," said Queen Elizabeth from the jetty. "But to make the sail set properly you must pull the boom down. That'll take those cross wrinkles out."

"Is that what those blocks (pulleys) are for hooked to a ring in the kelson close to where the mast is stepped? But they are all muddled up."

"Isn't there another ring under the boom, close to the mast?" asked Queen Elizabeth.

"Got it," said Captain John. "One block hooks to the ring

29

under the boom, and one to the ring in the bottom of the boat. Then it's as easy as anything to haul the boom down. How's that?"

"The crinkles in the sail go up and down now, and not across," said Mate Susan.

"That's right," said Queen Elizabeth. "The wind will flatten them out as soon as we start sailing. Can I come aboard, Captain Drake?"

"Please," said John, "but never mind about being Queen Elizabeth just now." He was just going to sail *Swallow* for the first time, and he had quite enough to think about without queens.

Titty, Roger, and Mother climbed down from the jetty into *Swallow*, as she lay there with flapping sail, ready to start.

"Will you take the tiller, Mother, while I cast off?" said Captain John.

"Not I," said Mother. "Queen or no queen, I'm a passenger, and I want to see how you manage by yourselves."

"Right," said Captain John. "Mister Mate, will you come forward to cast off. Send the crew below to keep their heads out of the way of the boom."

"Aye, aye, sir," said Mate Susan. "Get down on the bottom, you two." The boy and the able-seaman crouched in the bottom of the boat with their heads below the gunwale. John took the tiller. Susan untied the painter from the ring on the pier, put the end of it through the ring, and held it.

"Ready," she said.

"Cast off," said the captain, and a moment later *Swallow* was moving.

"Are we going to the island?" asked the boy.

"No," said Mother. "It would take too long to go there and back. There's a lot to be done if you are to start tomorrow morning. Just sail her a little way up against the wind, and then we must run back to deal with haybags and stores, and all the other things you'll want for the voyage."

So *Swallow*'s trial trip was a short one. John sailed her up against the wind, tacking from side to side, and making a little every time, just as Roger had done when he had tacked up the field the day before. Then they turned round for the run home, and raced back with the water creaming round her.

"Your ship is all right, Captain John," said Mother, when they were once more moored to the jetty, and Susan and John were stowing the sail, and taking the mast down to take the *Swallow* into the boathouse.

"She's a beauty," said John.

The rest of that day was full of business. Mother was stitching haybags out of sacking. Titty had taken the little flagstaff up to the farm, and had cut a triangular flag out of some of the canvas left over from the tents. Mother had drawn a swallow on a bit of paper, and Titty had cut one out of some blue serge that had once been part of a pair of knickerbockers. Then she had put the pattern on the white flag, and cut out a place to fit it. Then she had sewn the edge of the blue swallow all the way round into the place for it in the white flag. When she had done there was a fine white flag with a blue swallow flying across it, and it looked the same from both sides. Then she had fastened it on the little wire flagstaff where the blue flag had been, so that it was ready to hoist to the masthead.

Captain John and the mate were getting together the really important stores and deciding what they could do without. The list had grown very much last night after supper. Roger was kept busy running up and down to the boathouse with all sorts of things that everybody agreed could not be left behind.

The mate's chief task was fitting out the galley, with the help of Mrs. Jackson, the farmer's wife, who was lending the things.

"You'll want a kettle first and foremost," said Mrs. Jackson.

"And a saucepan and a frying-pan," said Mate Susan, looking at her list. "I'm best at buttered eggs."

"And are you really?" said Mrs. Jackson. "Most folk are best at boiled."

"Oh, well, I don't count boiled," said Susan.

Then there were the knives and forks and plates and mugs and spoons to be thought of, and biscuit tins, big ones to keep the food in, and smaller tins for tea and salt and sugar.

"We'll want rather a big one for sugar, won't we?" said Roger, who had come in and was waiting for something else to carry down to the boathouse.

"You won't bake, I don't suppose," said Mrs. Jackson.

"I think not," said Mate Susan.

The pile of things on the kitchen table grew and grew as Susan crossed off the items on her list.

John and Titty came in to show her the new flag and to see how she was getting on.

"Who is going to be doctor?" she asked.

"Surgeon," said Titty. "It's always surgeon on board ship."

"You are," said John. "You're the mate. It's the mate's job. He comes dancing on to the scene, 'And well,' says he, 'and how are your arms and legs and liver and lungs and bones afeeling now?' Don't you remember?"

"Then I ought to take some bandages and medicines and things."

"Oh, no," said Titty. "On desert islands they cure everything with herbs. We'll have all sorts of diseases, plagues, and fevers and things that no medicine is any good for and we'll cure them with herbs that the natives show us."

At this point Mother came in and settled the question. "No medicines," she said. "Anyone who wants doctoring is invalided home."

"If it's really serious," said Titty, "but we can have a plague or a fever or two by ourselves."

John said, "What about a chart?"

Titty said that as the ocean had never been explored, there could not be any charts.

"But all the most exciting charts and maps have places on them that are marked 'Unexplored'."

"Well, they won't be much good for those places," said Titty.

"We ought to have a chart of some kind," said John. "It'll probably be all wrong, and it won't have the right names. We'll make our own names, of course."

They found a good map that showed the lake in a local guide-book. Titty said it wasn't really a chart. John said it would do. And Mrs. Jackson said they could take it, but must keep it as dry as they could. That meant another tin box for things that had to be kept dry. They put in besides the guide-book some exercise books for logs and some paper for letters home. They also put in the ship's library. Titty had found on the shelves in the parlour a German Dictionary left by some former visitor. "It's full of foreign language," she said, "and we shall want it for talking with the natives." In the end it was left behind, because it was large and heavy, and also it might be the wrong language. Instead, Titty took *Robinson Crusoe*. "It tells you just what to do on an island," she said. John took *The Seaman's Handybook*, and Part Three of *The Baltic Pilot*. Both books had belonged to his father, but John took them with him even on holidays. Mate Susan took *Simple Cooking for Small Households*.

At last, when almost everything was piled in the boathouse, just before it was time for Roger and Titty to go to bed, the whole crew went up the path into the pinewood to the Peak of Darien to look once more at the island. The sun was sinking over the western hills. There was a dead calm. Far away they saw the island and the still lake, without a ripple on it, stretching away into the distance.

"I can't believe we're really going to land on it," said Titty.

"We aren't unless there's wind tomorrow," said Captain John. "We'll have to whistle for a wind."

Titty and Roger, by agreement, whistled one tune after another all the way home. As they came to the farm the leaves of the beech trees shivered overhead.

"You see," said Titty, "we've got some wind. Wake up early, and we'll go out and do some more whistling before breakfast."

CHAPTER III

THE VOYAGE TO THE ISLAND

"There were three sailors of Bristol City
    Who took a boat and went to sea;
    But first with beef and captain's biscuits
    And pickled pork they loaded she."

                                    THACKERAY.

THERE was very little room in the *Swallow* when they had
finished loading her at the little jetty by the boathouse. Under
the main thwart was a big tin box with the books and writing
paper and other things that had to be kept dry, like night-
clothes. In this box was also a small aneroid barometer. John
had won it as a prize at school and never went anywhere without
it. Underneath the forward thwart, on each side of the mast,
were large biscuit tins, with bread, tea, sugar, salt, biscuits, tins
of corned beef, tins of sardines, a lot of eggs, each one wrapped
separately for fear of smashes, and a big seed-cake. Right
forward, in front of the mast, was a long coil of stout grass
rope and the anchor, but it had been found by trying that there
was room for the Boy Roger here in the bows as look-out man.
Then there were the two groundsheets in which were rolled up
the tents, each with the rope that belonged to it. These were
stowed just aft of the mast. The whole of the space that was
left in the bottom of the boat was filled by two big sacks stuffed
with blankets and rugs. Besides all these there were the things
that could not be packed at all, but had to go loose, wedged in
anyhow, things like the saucepan and frying-pan and kettle, and
a big farm lantern. Then there was a basket full of mugs, plates,

spoons, forks and knives. There was no room for anything else big except the crew and there on the jetty were four great hay-bags, stuffed with hay by Mr. Jackson, the farmer, which were to serve as beds and mattresses.

"We shall have to make two trips of it," said Captain John.

"Or three," said Mate Susan. "Even with *Swallow* empty we shall never be able to get more than three of the haybags into her at once."

Able-seaman Titty had an idea. "Couldn't we get a native to bring them in a native rowing boat?" she said.

John looked back into the boathouse at the big rowing boat belonging to the farm. He knew, because it had been privately arranged, that Mother was to pay them a visit before night to see that all was well. He knew, too, that it had been arranged that Mr. Jackson, the farmer, should row her. Mr. Jackson was as good a native as anyone could wish.

Mother and Nurse, carrying Vicky, were coming down the field.

John went to meet them. It was agreed that the natives would bring the haybags in a rowing boat.

"Are you sure you haven't forgotten anything?" Mother asked, looking down from the jetty into the loaded *Swallow*. "It's very seldom people go on a long voyage without forgetting something."

"We've got everything that was on my list," said Mate Susan.

"Everything?" said Mother.

"Mother, what are you holding behind your back?" asked Titty, and Mother held out a packet of a dozen boxes of matches.

"One might almost say 'By Gum'," said John. "We could never have lit the fire without them."

They said their farewells on the jetty.

"If you are ready, you'd better start," said Mother.

THE START OF THE VOYAGE

"Now, Mister Mate," said Captain John.

"All aboard," cried Mate Susan.

Roger took his place in the bows. Titty sat on the middle thwart. John hooked the yard to the traveller on the mast, and hauled up the little brown sail and made the halyard fast. Titty's flag, with the dark blue swallow on a white ground, was already at the masthead. Titty had hoisted it herself as soon as they had stepped the mast after breakfast. John went aft to the tiller. Susan pulled down the boom until the sail was setting properly, when she too made fast.

There was a very light north-westerly wind, brought, no doubt, by the urgent whistling of the crew. Mother held the end of the painter, and then, when the little sail filled, she threw it to Roger who coiled it down, and stuffed it away under his feet. Very slowly the *Swallow* slid away from the jetty.

"Goodbye, Mother. Goodbye, Vicky. Goodbye, Nurse."

"Goodbye, goodbye," came from the jetty.

Mother waved her handkerchief. Nurse waved hers, and Vicky waved a fat hand.

The crew of the *Swallow* waved back.

"Three cheers for the stay-at-homes," called Captain John. They cheered.

"We ought to sing 'Spanish Ladies'," said Titty. So they sang:

"Farewell and adieu to you, fair Spanish ladies,
   Adieu and farewell to you, ladies of Spain,
   For we're under orders for to sail to old England,
   And we may never see you fair ladies again.

"So we'll rant and we'll roar, like true British sailors,
   We'll range and we'll roam over all the salt seas,
   Until we strike soundings in the channel of old England,
   From Ushant to Scilly 'tis thirty-five leagues."

"Of course, really, we're going the other way," said Susan, "but it doesn't matter."

The *Swallow* slipped slowly out towards the mouth of the bay. She made at first no noise and hardly any wake. Then, as she came clear of the northerly side of the bay, she found a little more wind, and the cheerful lapping noise began under her forefoot, while her wake lengthened out and bubbled astern of her.

Darien, the promontory on the southern side of the Holly Howe bay, was longer than the promontory on the northern side. Also Captain John was taking no risks. At the end of Darien there might be rocks. He held on straight out of the bay until he could see into the bay on the other side of the point. Far away down the lake the island showed. It seemed further than it had from the top of Darien. At last John let out the mainsheet, and put the helm up. The boom swung out, the *Swallow* swung round and, with the wind aft, John steered straight for the island.

Mother and Nurse, with Vicky, were still on the jetty. They gave a last wave. The whole crew of the *Swallow* waved back, and then in a moment they could see into the bay no longer. The bay was hidden behind Darien. Above them was the Peak from which they had first seen the island. The Peak itself seemed lower than it had. Everything had grown smaller except the lake, and that had never seemed so large before.

"Are we all right about jibing?" asked Mate Susan, remembering a sad day the year before when, running before the wind in another small boat, the boom had jibed over with sudden decision, and given her a bump that had lasted for a long time.

"Look at the flag," said Captain John. "It's blowing well over on the same side as the sail. There's no fear of a jibe so long as it's doing that."

The wind was steady, though light, and on the whole John was glad that there was no more of it on this first voyage to the island with the heavily laden *Swallow*. Reefing would have been a terrible nuisance, with the boat so full of tents and biscuit boxes and cooking things. Besides, there was so much to see that looked different now that it was seen from the water instead of from the Peak of Darien.

The island was not in the middle of the lake, but much nearer to the eastern shore, on the same side of the lake as Holly Howe and Darien. Along that shore was one little promontory after another. Here and there was a field by the water's edge, but mostly there were thick woods. Here and there among the trees were houses, but not many of them, and above the trees were the heather-covered slopes of the hills.

As they passed the second cape beyond Darien, Roger, the look-out, reported a ship, and pointed towards the shore. The sail was on that side, so that Roger saw it before the others. In the bay beyond the cape lay a strange-looking dark blue vessel. She was a long narrow craft with a high raised cabin roof, and a row of glass windows along her side. Her bows were like the bows of an old-time clipper. Her stern was like that of a steamship. She had nothing that could properly be called a mast, though there was a little flagstaff, where a mast might have been, stepped just forward of the glass-windowed cabin. There was an awning over her after-deck, and under it a big fat man was sitting writing in a deck-chair. The vessel was moored to a large buoy.

"It's a houseboat," said John.

"What is a houseboat?" asked Titty.

"It's a boat used instead of a house. There was one at Falmouth, where people used to live all the year round."

"I wish we lived in a boat all the year round," said Susan.

"I shall some day," said John, "and so will Roger. Father does."

"Yes, but that's different. A destroyer isn't a houseboat."

"You live in it just the same."

"Yes, but you don't stay in one place. A houseboat sticks in one place like a boathouse. I remember the houseboat at Falmouth too," said Susan. "There was a whole family living in it, and we used to see them rowing ashore for milk in the mornings. The butcher and the baker used to call there, just as if it was a house. They used to come to the shore and shout 'Houseboat ahoy!' and then the man or the woman used to row ashore to buy meat and bread from them. Look out what you're doing, John!"

Captain John, with his mind on the houseboat, had not been thinking about his steering, and the little white flag with the blue swallow on it was fluttering on the side of the mast away from the sail. The boom was just going to swing over when Susan called, but John, putting the helm down instantly, just saved a jibe. After that he looked at the houseboat only out of the corner of his eye. The wind was so light that a jibe would not have mattered much, except perhaps to bumped heads, but it would hardly have done for the captain of the ship to have set an example of such bad steering to his crew.

Able-seaman Titty had wedged herself in the bottom of the boat between the tent bundles with a basket of small crockery in her arms for safety's sake. She could just see over the gunwale.

"I wonder," she said, "if the man on the houseboat has his family with him."

"He's all alone," said Roger.

"The others may be cooking in the cabin," said Susan.

"He's probably a retired pirate," said Titty.

Just then a harsh squawk sounded over the water, and a large green bird which they had not noticed shook itself where it stood perched on the rail that ran round the stern of the house-boat.

"He *is* a pirate," said Roger. "There's his parrot."

Before they could see any more the next little cape hid the houseboat from them. This was perhaps lucky, because even Captain John wanted to see the parrot, and good steering is impossible when you are looking two ways at once.

"Steamship coming up astern," said Mate Susan.

A long steamship had come into sight beside the promontory of Darien, far astern, one of the steamships that ran from end to end of the lake two or three times a day, calling on the way at the little town a mile higher up the lake than Holly Howe, and at one or two landing stages. The little town is known in guide-books by another name, but the crew of the *Swallow* had long ago given it the name of Rio Grande. After calling at Rio, the steamers ran directly to the foot of the lake, stopping only sometimes to put a passenger ashore at a jetty or to pick one up if he was signalling that he wanted to come aboard. The steamer track ran close by the island, but at this point was nearer the further shore. The steamship quickly overhauled them and passed them. Her wake, spreading across the lake, rocked the little *Swallow* so that kettle and saucepan and frying-pan rattled on the bottom boards and Able-seaman Titty had to hold tight to the crockery basket. Soon the steamer was no more than a blob with a feather of white smoke far away beyond the island.

Then there was a roar in the distance, getting rapidly louder. A splash of white showed beyond the island near the steamer. The splash seemed to slide over the water nearer and nearer. It was a fast motor boat, much faster than the steamship and hundreds of times as loud. It roared up the lake, passed the *Swallow* a hundred yards away, and had soon disappeared astern of her beyond Darien. Here and there, close to the shore, there were rowing boats with fishermen. But after all there was no need to notice any of these things if one did not want to, and the *Swallow* and her crew moved steadily southward over a desolate ocean sailed for the first time by white seamen.

They were getting near the island.

"Keep a look-out for a good landing-place," said Captain John.

"And keep a look-out for savages," said Titty. "We don't know yet that it is uninhabited, and you can't be too careful."

"I'll sail between the island and this shore and then beat up again on the other side, so that we can choose the best place," said Captain John.

The island was covered with trees and among them there was one tall pine which stood out high above the oaks, hazels, beeches, and rowans. They had often looked at it through the telescope from Darien. The tall pine was near the north end of the island. Below it was a little cliff, dropping to the water. Rocks showed a few yards out from the shore. There was no place to land there.

"Now, Mister Mate," said Captain John, "we must keep a good look-out."

"Sing out like anything if you see any rocks under water, Roger," said the mate.

John steered to pass between the island and the mainland, not too near the island so as not to lose the wind. In a moment or two *Swallow* was slipping through smooth water, though there was still enough wind to keep her slowly moving. A little more than a third of the way along the eastern shore of the island there was a bay, a very small one, with a pebbly beach. Behind it there seemed to be a clearer space among the trees.

"What a place for a camp," said Susan.

"Good landing too," said John, "but no good if the wind came from this side. We'll sail right round the island first to see if there is anything better."

"Rocks ahead," sang out Roger, pointing to some that were

43

just showing above water. John steered a little further from the shore.

The sides of the island were steep and rocky. That little bay seemed to be the only place where it would be possible to land a boat. There were rocky cliffs, like the Peak in Darien, only much smaller, with heather on them and little struggling trees. At the south end of the island the rocks grew smaller and then suddenly rose again into a promontory of almost bare stone. At this southern end the island seemed to have been broken up into a lot of little islands. John sailed on till he was well beyond the last of them and then began hauling in the sheet, putting the helm down and bringing *Swallow* round below the island.

"That first place is the only good one on that side," said Susan.

"We'll sail up this side in short tacks, to have a good look at it," said Captain John. He hauled the sheet closer in and brought *Swallow* nearer to the wind. He sailed her so till she was about forty yards from the island, standing out on the starboard tack. Then:

"Ready about."

Susan ducked her head. Titty, sitting on the bottom boards, was low enough already, but she ducked too. Roger was well out of the way, before the mast.

John put the helm down. *Swallow* shot up into the wind. The boom and the brown sail swung over and filled again on the other tack and *Swallow*, with the water rustling under her bows, sailed in towards the island's western shore. Here there were no outlying rocks, but the island itself dropped steeply, like a wall, into the water.

"Sing out when you see the bottom, Roger," called Mate Susan.

"Aye, aye, sir," said Roger, looking as hard as he could into the green depths.

"We ought to have brought a lead for sounding," said Susan.

"It wouldn't have been much good here," said John.

They sailed on and on till they were within five yards of the shore and the water was still dark beneath them. John dared go no nearer.

"Ready about," he called.

It was not until they were already swinging round, close under the wall of rock, that Roger shouted, "I can see the bottom." On this side, it was clear, the island rose sharply up out of deep water.

Down went Susan's head and down went Titty's, though she had no need. Round swung the little *Swallow* and off again on the other tack out into the lake. John did not take her far before it was "Ready about" once more and she slipped in again towards the island. Backwards and forwards they went, each time a little further north along the island's shore.

All this western shore was the same, a steep, rocky wall, dropping into deep water, with no bay in which it would be possible to land.

"That place on the other side is the only one," said Susan.

"It's not much of a harbour," said Captain John, "but if it's the only one it'll have to do. We can haul the ship well up."

With the next tack John took the *Swallow* further out into the lake and went about for the last time when he was well clear of the northern end of the island. He sailed past it and as soon as he was clear of all its rocks he called:

"Jibe O!"

Mate Susan hauled in the sheet as fast as she could. John put the helm up. *Swallow* turned south once more, the boom swung over their heads, Susan paying out the sheet as soon as it had passed over, and they were once more sailing down the inside, eastern shore. Just before they were opposite the little bay with the pebbly beach, John called out:

"Stand by to take in sail. Lower away!"

Mate Susan was all ready with the halyard in her hand. She slackened the halyard without letting go of it. Down came the sail.

"Grab the yard, Roger!" and Roger grabbed it.

Susan unhooked the traveller and she and Roger together brought down the sail and the yard. Titty with the crockery basket was well out of the way under the folds of the sail. All this happened much quicker than I can tell it, and when the sail was down *Swallow* still had enough way on her to slide in towards the beach.

"Look out, Roger," said Mate Susan, and she too looked anxiously over the bows.

"Rock on the starboard bow," she shouted.

John shifted the tiller a very little.

The *Swallow*, in quite smooth water, slipped on and on.

"Now," said Susan, and scrambled to the stern again over the top of Titty, who had just pushed her head out from under the sail. Susan had gone to the stern to lighten the bows of the boat, and just as she got there, there was a gentle grumble and scrunch, and *Swallow*'s nose was on the pebbly beach. She had hardly touched before Roger had jumped ashore with the painter.

CHAPTER IV

THE HIDDEN HARBOUR

Susan was ashore next. Then Titty with her basket of crockery. John stayed in the *Swallow* to hand out the stores. First went the loose cooking things that had been tucked in anywhere. Then went the two tents, each rolled in its groundsheet, then the biscuit tins, and then the heavy tin box with the books and barometer and the things that had to be kept dry. That lightened the ship, and Mate Susan and the able-seaman pulled her a little further up, which made it easier to bring ashore the big sacks full of rugs and blankets. Everything was piled together on the dry pebbly beach.

"Now, Mister Mate," said Captain John, "let's go and explore."

"The first thing to do," said Susan, "is to find the best place for our camp."

"Not too easily seen from anywhere," said Titty.

"We want a flat bit of ground with trees to hold the tents up," said John.

"And a good place for a fire," said Susan.

"Is it safe to leave the things here?" said Titty. "There might be a tidal wave, forty feet high, washing over everything."

"Not as big as that," said John. "That would cover the island."

"Hullo, where's that boy?" said the mate. The Boy Roger was exploring already. Just then he shouted from close to them, behind some bushes.

"Someone's had a fire here before."

The others ran up from the little beach. Between the landing-place and the high part of the island where the big pine tree was, there was a round, open space of mossy ground. There were trees round the edge of it, and in the middle of it there was a round place where the turf had been scraped away. Roger was there, looking at a neat ring of stones, making a fireplace with the ashes of an old fire in it. At opposite sides of the ring two stout forked sticks had been driven into the ground and built round with heavy stones, and another long stick was lying across the fireplace in the forks of the two upright sticks, so that a kettle could be hung on it over the fire. Close by the fireplace there was a neat pile of dry sticks all broken to about the same length. Someone had had a fire here, and someone was meaning to have a fire again.

"Natives," said Titty.

"Perhaps they are still here," said Roger.

"Come on," said Captain John. "We'll go all over it."

There was really not very much of the island to explore. It did not take the crew of the *Swallow* very long to make sure that, though someone had been on the island sometime, there was nobody but themselves on the island today. They went up to the northern end of the island, and looked out over the lake from the high part of the island by the big tree. Then they went to the southern part of the island, but found it rocky and covered with heather and small stunted bushes, growing so thickly that it was not easy to push one's way through them. There were trees, too, but not so tall as those at the northern end. But there were no signs of human beings, and no place where it would be safe to have a fire. They came back to the fireplace.

"The natives knew how to choose the right place," said Susan, "and it's a fine fireplace."

"There are no natives on the island now," said Roger.

"They may have been killed and eaten by other natives," said Titty.

"Anyhow, this is the best place for a camp," said John. "Let's put the tents up at once."

So they set about making their camp. They brought the tent bundles up from the landing-place and unrolled them. They chose four trees on the side of the fireplace nearest to the big pine. "The high ground will shelter them from the north," said John. Then he climbed about seven feet up the trunk of a tree, and fastened one end of one of the tent ropes. Susan held the other end until he had climbed up another tree, when he fastened it at about the same height. The rope, of course, sagged in the middle, so that the tent was only about five feet high. The rope was not made too taut, because the dew at night would make it shrink. The tent now hung down on both sides of the rope like a sheet put to dry. The next thing to do was to fill its pockets with stones. As soon as there were a few stones in the pockets that were at the bottom of each side of the tent, it was easy to keep the walls apart. But to make sure that the tent was firmly set up they carried a great many stones from the beach, besides the stones they picked up under the trees, so that all round the two sides and back of the tent there was a row of stones in the pockets keeping the tent walls properly stretched.

"It's a good thing Mother made this sort of tent," said Susan. "The rock is close under the ground everywhere, and we could never have driven any pegs in."

The next thing was to drag the groundsheet into the tent and spread it. As soon as that was done, they all crowded in.

"Good," said Susan. "You can just see the fireplace from inside."

The second tent was set up in the same way, and then all

the rest of the stores were brought up from the beach. Mate Susan began to think about dinner. Able-seaman Titty and the Boy Roger were sent to gather firewood. There were a lot of dry branches scattered about under the trees. Somehow, no one wanted to use the neat little pile of wood that had been left by the last users of the fireplace. And really there was no need. Presently a fire was burning in the blackened ring of stones. Susan found a place by the landing beach where it was easy to stand on two rocks and dip a kettle full of clean water. She came back with the kettle, and slung it on the cross stick over the fire.

"Everything is all right," said Captain John, "except the landing-place. Everybody can see it from the mainland, and if it comes on to blow from the east it's a very bad place for the *Swallow*. I'm going to look for a better place."

"There isn't one," said Susan. "We've sailed all round."

"I'm going to have another look, anyway," said Captain John.

"But we've just been all over the island," said Susan.

"We didn't go to the very end of it," said John.

"But it's all rocks there," said Susan.

"Well, I'm going to look," said Captain John, and leaving the mate and the crew to their cooking, he went off to the southern end of the island.

He knew there was nothing that would do for a harbour on the north end of the island, or on the west, because there the rock dropped down like a wall of stone into the water. On the eastern side, except for the landing-place, it was much the same. But there was just a chance that he might find what he wanted at the south end where the island broke up into smaller islands, bare rocks sticking up out of the water, some of them lying so far out that he had not thought it was safe to come very near when they had been sailing round in *Swallow*.

He took the easiest way through the undergrowth and the small trees. Almost it seemed to him that someone had been that way before. He walked straight into the thing he was looking for. He had been within a yard or two of seeing it when they had first explored the island. Yet it was so well hidden that he had turned back without seeing it. This time he almost fell into it. It was a little strip of beach curving round a tiny bay at the end of the island. A thick growth of hazels overhung it, and hid it from anyone who had not actually pushed his way through them. Beyond it the south-west corner of the island ran out nearly twenty yards into the water, a narrow rock seven or eight feet high, rising higher and then dropping gradually. Rocks sheltered it also from the south-east. There was a big rock that was part of the island, and then a chain of smaller ones beyond it. It was no wonder that they had thought that there was nothing but rocks there when they had sailed past outside.

"It may be only a puddle with no way into it," said John to himself.

He climbed out on the top of the big rock. There was heather on the top of this rock, and John crawled out on it, looking down into the little pool below him. Further out on the far side of the pool he could see that there were big stones under water, but on this side it seemed clear. The water in there was perfectly smooth, because it was sheltered by the island itself from the wind which was still blowing lightly from the north-west. It looked as if you could bring a boat in from outside through a narrow channel between the rocks, but of course under water there might be rocks out there which he could not see.

He climbed back and hurried to the camp.

"I've found the very place," he shouted. "At least I think I have."

"Found what?" said Susan.

51

"A real harbour for *Swallow*. I don't know yet. I'm going to take her round to see if there is a way in. Will you come?"

"Can't leave the cooking," said Susan.

"Well, I must have one of the crew," said John. "Can you spare the able-seaman?"

"Go along, Titty," said the mate.

"Me too," said Roger.

"Only one," said John, "but if we get her in, we'll whistle. Then you can come. Will you lend me your whistle, Mister Mate?"

Susan gave him her whistle, and John and Titty hurried off to the landing-place, and launched *Swallow*.

"I'll row her round," he said. "It's no good putting the sail up just to take it down again."

Titty sat in the stern while he rowed. *Swallow* was a hard boat to row, because of her keel and the ballast that made her so good a boat to sail. But very soon they had passed the end of the island. John rowed her round outside the furthest of the rocks.

"Now," he said, "we'll try to go in. I'll paddle her in sculling over the stern, and you go forward with the other oar ready to fend off if there are rocks under water."

"I'd better get in front of the mast, like Roger does," said Titty.

"All right, if there's room."

In the stern of *Swallow* there was a half-circle cut out of the transom, like a bite out of the edge of a bit of bread and butter. There was just room for an oar to lie loosely in it, so that the boat could be moved along by one oar worked from side to side, and twisted this way and that so that it always pushes against the water. A lot of people do not know how to scull over the stern of a boat, but it is easy enough if you do know, and John had been taught by his father long ago in Falmouth harbour.

FEELING THEIR WAY IN

The only trouble is that the nose of the boat waggles a bit from side to side.

Captain John unshipped the rudder, and put it in the bottom of the boat. Then he began sculling over the stern, gently, enough to make *Swallow* move slowly in towards the lines of rocks. Titty, with the other oar, was ready in the bows.

"There are rocks on each side under water," said Titty.

"Sing out if there are any right ahead," said John. "Don't let her bump one if you can help it."

He sculled on. Slowly *Swallow* moved in among rocks awash. Then, besides the rocks awash, there were rocks showing above water. These grew bigger. Then there were high rocks that hid the eastern side of the lake, while the western side was hidden by a long rocky point sticking out from the island. It was almost like being between two walls. Remembering what he had seen when he had climbed out on the big rock above the pool, John kept the *Swallow* as near as he could to the eastern wall, Titty with her oar fending off when the rock seemed too close. If they had been rowing in the ordinary way their oars would have touched the rocks on either side. Still *Swallow* moved on with the water clear under her keel.

At last the green trees were close ahead, and *Swallow* was safe in the pool and ran her nose up the beach in the tiny bay, sheltered by the trees from the north, and by the walls of rock from any other wind.

"What a place," said the able-seaman. "I expect somebody hid on the island hundreds of years ago, and kept his boat here."

"It's a perfect harbour," said John. "Shall we blow the whistle for the others?"

He blew the whistle as loud as he could. He put the oars neatly in their place, and climbed ashore with the painter. Titty was already ashore, and was struggling through the hazels to meet the others. Presently they came.

"Well," said Captain John, "what about this for a harbour?"

"However was it that we never saw it when we sailed past?" said Susan.

"The rocks go so far out."

"No one will find her in here," said Susan.

"And if we are overpowered by enemies we could escape here," said Titty. "You can't see it from anywhere, even from the island. It's the finest harbour anybody ever had."

"We can fasten the painter to that stump of a tree," said Captain John, "and then take a line from her stern to that bush on the rock and then we can keep her afloat. Far better than hauling her half out of the water."

"May I tie her up?" said Roger.

John gave him the painter.

"What did you put the cross on the tree for?" said Roger.

"What cross?" said John.

"This one."

Nearly at the top of the tree stump, which was about four feet high, a white cross had been painted on the side nearest to the water. It had been painted some time ago, and had faded, and neither John nor Titty had noticed it. They had been thinking of rocks more than of trees.

"I didn't put it there," said John. "It must have been there already."

"Natives again," said Titty sadly. "That means that somebody else knows even about the harbour."

"I expect it's the same people who made the fireplace," said Susan.

At this moment Mate Susan remembered that she was also cook.

"The kettle will be boiling," she cried. "It'll be putting the fire out. And I had the eggs just ready when you whistled."

She ran off back to the camp.

The others pushed off *Swallow* till she floated. Captain John fastened one end of a length of spare rope to a cleat in the stern, and Able-seaman Titty climbed out on the rock with the other end of it. Roger held the painter. Then John came ashore. Titty pulled in on the stern rope and made it fast round a little rowan bush that was growing on the rock. Roger and John made the painter fast round the stump with the white cross on it, and the *Swallow* lay in the middle of the little harbour in two or three feet of water, moored fore and aft, and sheltered on every side.

Captain John looked at his ship with pride.

"I don't believe there is a better harbour in the world," he said.

"If only somebody else didn't know about it," said Titty.

Then they hurried back to the camp.

The camp now began to look really like a camp. There were the two tents slung between the two pairs of trees. The mate and the able-seaman were to sleep in one, and the captain and the boy in the other. Then in the open space under the trees the fire was burning merrily. The kettle had boiled, and was standing steaming on the ground. Susan was melting a big pat of butter in the frying-pan. In a pudding-basin beside her she had six raw eggs. She had cracked the eggs on the edge of a mug and broken them into the basin. Their empty shells were crackling in the fire. Four mugs stood in a row on the ground.

"No plates today," said Mate Susan. "We all eat out of the common dish."

"But it isn't a common dish," said Roger. "It's a frying-pan."

"Well, we eat out of it anyway. Egg's awful stuff for sticking to plates."

She had now emptied the raw eggs into the sizzling butter, and was stirring the eggs and the butter together after shaking the pepper pot over them, and putting in a lot of salt.

"They're beginning to curdle," said Titty, who was watching carefully. "When they begin to flake, you have to keep scraping them off the bottom of the pan. I saw Mrs. Jackson do it."

"They're flaking now," said Susan. "Come on and scrape away."

She put the frying-pan on the ground, and gave everyone a spoon. The captain, mate, and the crew of the *Swallow* squatted round the frying-pan, and began eating as soon as the scrambled eggs, which were very hot, would let them. Mate Susan had already cut four huge slices of brown bread and butter to eat with the eggs. Then she poured out four mugs of tea, and filled them up with milk from a bottle. "There'll be enough milk in the bottle for today," Mother had said, "but for tomorrow we must try to find you milk from a farm a little nearer than Holly Howe." Then there was a big rice pudding, which had been brought with them on the top of the things in one of the big biscuit tins. It too became a common dish, like the frying-pan. Then there were four big slabs of seed-cake. Then there were apples all round.

CHAPTER V

FIRST NIGHT ON THE ISLAND

AFTER they had finished the eggs and the rice pudding and the brown bread and butter and the seed-cake and the apples, the mate and the able-seaman did some washing up. The spoons had to be cleaned and the frying-pan scraped, and the mugs and pudding-basin swilled in the lake. The captain and the boy took the telescope, and found a good place on the high ground above the camp at the northern end of the island, where they could lie in a hollow of the rocks and look out between tufts of heather without being seen by anyone. Close behind them was the tall pine tree that they had seen when they looked at the island from the Peak in Darien.

Captain John lay on his back in the heather, and looked up into the tree.

"Properly," he said, "we ought to have a flagstaff on the top of it."

"What for?" said Roger.

"So that we could hoist a flag there as a signal. Supposing Susan and Titty were here alone, while you and I had gone fishing . . ."

"We've forgotten our fishing rods," said Roger.

"We'll get them tomorrow," said John. "But supposing we were away fishing, and the natives came back, the ones that made the fireplace, then if we saw the flag hoisted we should know something was the matter, and come back to help. And it would make a fine lighthouse too. If any of us were sailing

58

home after dark, whoever was left on the island could hoist the lantern, and make the tree into a lighthouse, so that we could find the island however dark it was."

"But Susan and Titty and I could never climb the tree. It's got no sticky-out branches."

Like most pines, the tree was bare of branches for the first fifteen or twenty feet of its height.

"If I can swarm up it as far as the bottom branch I could hang a rope over it so that both ends came to the ground. Then no one would have to climb it again. Anybody could tie the lantern to the rope and pull it up. One end would have to be tied to the ring on the top of the lantern, and the other to the bottom so that we could pull it either up or down, and keep it from swinging about."

"Have we got enough rope?" said Roger.

"We haven't any small enough. The anchor rope is much too thick, and the spare rope isn't long enough. I'll have to get some small rope tomorrow. It's a good thing I had a birthday just before we came here. We can get plenty of rope with five shillings."

Just then Mate Susan and Able-seaman Titty joined them, and threw themselves down in the heather.

"Everything's ready for the night," said Susan, "except the beds, and we can't make them till the native brings the hay-bags."

Titty jumped up. "There's a boat coming now," she said. "Roger, you must be sleepy, or you'd have seen it."

"I'm not sleepy," said Roger. "I wasn't looking. You can be wide awake, and not see a thing when you aren't looking."

Captain John sat up, and put the telescope to his eye.

"It is the native," he said, "and he's got Mother with him."

"Do let me have the telescope," said Titty. John gave it her, and she stared through it.

59

"Mother is a native too," she said at last.

"Let me have it," said Roger.

He fixed the telescope to his eye, and pointed it the right way. "I can't see anything at all," he said. "It's all black."

"You've got the cover over the eye-place," said Titty, who knew all about telescopes. "Twist it round, and it'll come open again."

"I can see them now," said Roger.

The native, who was Mr. Jackson from the Holly Howe Farm, was rowing his boat with long steady strokes. It looked like a water spider far away. But through the telescope it was easy to see that it was a boat, and to see the big lumps of the haybags and to see that Mother was sitting in the stern.

Roger and Titty took turns with the telescope as the boat came nearer. The captain and the mate went down to the camp to make sure that everything was ready to show the visitors. The captain put his tin box, the big one, against the back of his tent in the middle. He took the little barometer out of it and hung it on the fastener in front of the box. There was nothing else in the tent, so that it was very neat indeed. Titty and the mate had made their tent much more home-like. In the middle of it were the biscuit tins, with the food in them. These tins made two seats. Then at each side of the tent, where their beds were going to be, they had spread out their blankets and folded in the tops of them. The cooking things were neatly arranged in one corner, just inside the tent. Outside the tent, on the rope on which the tent was hung, two towels were drying. Captain John looked in and then went back to his own tent and spread his and Roger's blankets in the same way. They certainly made the tent look more as if it had been lived in. And, after all, it would be no bother to put the haybags under them when they came. Mate Susan put a few more sticks on the fire, to make a cheerful blaze. Then they went back to the others.

"The natives will soon be here," said Titty. "Shall we show them the harbour?"

"No," said Captain John, "you never know with natives, even friendly ones. We'll keep *Swallow* hid. It isn't as if Mother were by herself."

"Besides," said Susan, "they are bringing the haybags, and the landing-place is close to the camp. It'll be much easier to carry them from there than through the thicket at the low end of the island."

All the crew of the *Swallow* stood up and pointed to the east. Mother, the female native in the stern of the rowing boat, pointed between the island and the mainland on the eastern side, to show that she knew what they meant. She said something to the native at the oars, and he glanced over his shoulder, and, pulling strongly with his left for a stroke or two, altered his course.

They were passing the head of the island. Roger had already run to the landing-place. The others of the *Swallow* were close behind him and when the native ran his boat ashore, the whole ship's company were on the beach, ready to help him to pull the boat up.

"But what have you done with your ship?" asked Mother. "Where is the *Swallow*?"

"Allawallacallacacuklacaowlacaculla," said Titty. "That means that we can't possibly tell you because you're a native . . . a nice native, of course."

"Burroborromjeeboomding," said Mother. "That means that I don't care where she is so long as she is all right."

"She's in a splendid place," said Captain John.

"Shall I interpret for you?" said Titty gently.

"As a matter of fact," said Mother, the female native, "I've picked up quite a lot of English what with talking to you, but I'll wallacallawalla instead if you'd rather I did."

"If you know English there's no need," said John.

"Glook," said the female native. "That means, all right. Now I hope you are going to let the natives see your camp, so that we can help to carry up the haybags."

Mr. Jackson, the farmer from Holly Howe, had taken all four haybags out of the boat. He was a very powerful, strong native, and he picked up three of the haybags together and hove them up on his shoulders. John and Susan carried the fourth. Roger took the female native by the hand and Titty showed the way to the tents.

"Well, you have got a lovely camp," said the female native.

"Isn't it?" said Susan. "Would you like to come inside this tent?"

The female native stooped and went in. Mr. Jackson dumped down his haybags.

"Come on, Roger," said John, "let's get our tent all ready before she comes in."

John took hold of one end of a haybag. Roger helped, and between them they pulled first one and then another haybag into their tent. They put one on each side of the tent, punched them and shook them until they were fairly even and covered them with their folded blankets. Then they lay down, each on his bed.

Meanwhile Susan and the female native were making up the beds in the other tent. Mr. Jackson had gone back to his boat.

Presently the female native put her head into the captain's tent.

"You look comfortable enough in here," she said, "but what are you going to do when it gets dark?"

"We ought to have brought two lanterns," said John. "I forgot about that. We've only got the big lantern for the whole camp."

"I've brought you two small candle-lanterns, one for each

tent if you promise to be careful with them and not set the tents or yourselves on fire. Where is the oil for the big lantern?"

"Just outside the tent," said John.

"You ought to keep it in a safe place well away from the camp and from the fire."

Just then that powerful native, Mr. Jackson, came back with another load from the boat.

"Come along out," said the female native. "I am not going to stop here now, because Mr. Jackson must be getting back to his farm. But there are several things to be settled. First of all, about the milk. There are no cows on your island, so you will have to go to the mainland for milk. I have arranged with the farm over there, Dixon's Farm, to let you have a quart of milk every morning. If you want more in the evening, Mrs. Dixon will let you have it. But every morning you must row over there to bring your milk. You can see their landing-place by the big oak tree. Thank you, Mr. Jackson."

The powerful native had put down a big basket that he had brought up from the boat. In it was a milk-can and a lot of other things. The female native began taking them out as if she were digging the presents out of a bran pie.

"Here is the milk-can for you," she said, "and mind you keep the milk as cool as you can during the day. Keep it out of the sun and do remember to wash the can very clean before you take it up to the farm for more. Then, for tomorrow, I've brought you a meat pie Mrs. Jackson cooked today. You will soon get tired of living on corned beef. . . ."

"Pemmican," said Titty.

"Pemmican," said the female native. "So if I were you I should only open a pemmican tin when you haven't anything else that you can eat without cooking. By the way, Susan is the chief cook, isn't she?"

"Yes," said Captain John.

"Then I'll give the stores over to her. There is the pie. Then I've brought a box of Force for breakfast. Susan is going to have a busy time without having to cook porridge in the mornings."

"I like cooking," said Mate Susan.

"If you want to go on liking it," said the female native, "take my advice and make the others do the washing up."

Mr. Jackson came up again from the boat, carrying a big sack.

"Mrs. Jackson has been good enough to let you have your pillows here," said the female native. "You can sleep without them, I know, but a pillow makes such a lot of difference that I'm sure Christopher Columbus himself always took his own pillow with him."

The pillows were taken out and two were taken into each tent.

"Did you see the pirate with the parrot?" asked Titty when she came out after stowing her pillow.

"What pirate?" asked the female native.

"The one on the houseboat. We saw him. And his parrot."

Mr. Jackson laughed. "So that's what you call him," he said. "I dare say you're right."

"I saw the houseboat," said the female native.

"It's Mr. Turner," said the powerful native. "He usually lives on the houseboat in summer-time. This year he won't let anyone go near him. Last year those Blackett girls, nieces of his from the other side of the lake, were always with him. Not this year though. Keeps himself to himself this summer, does Mr. Turner. No one knows what he does there, but they do say he's got things in that houseboat worth a fortune."

"That's his treasure," said Titty. "I knew he was a retired pirate. Of course he can't let anybody go near it."

"Vicky will be wanting me," said the female native, "so I won't stay with you. And anyhow you don't want too many natives about, I'm sure. It's beginning to get dark and if I were you I should be early to sleep, for the sun will wake you in the morning, even if the birds don't."

"Thank you ever so much for bringing the things," said Susan.

"Specially the lanterns," said Titty.

"Glook, glook, glook," said the female native, as she began to walk down to the landing-place. "No, I think I won't have any tea, thank you. You've had yours and day is nearly over. Oh," she added, "there's one thing I'd forgotten." She went for a moment into the captain's tent and came out again smiling. Then, as she walked down to the boat she said to John, "I'm not going to keep on coming to bother you. . . ."

"You don't bother us, Mother," said John.

"I'm not going to anyhow, but I'm going to ask you to let me know every two or three days – or oftener if you like – that everything is all right. You'll be wanting provisions, you know, and we natives can always supply them. So you'll be calling now and then at Holly Howe, won't you?"

"I'll come tomorrow, if you like," said John.

"Yes, I'd like to know how the first night went."

"What did you do in my tent just now, Mother?" said John.

"You'll see when you get back."

The female native stepped into the boat and went to the stern and sat down. Mr. Jackson, that strong native, pushed the big boat off, kneeling on the gunwale of her as she slid away. He had the oars out in a moment and pulled away into the evening.

"Goodbye, goodbye, goodbye, Mother," shouted the *Swallow*'s crew. "Goodbye, Mr. Jackson."

"Good night to you," said Mr. Jackson.

"Drool," said the female native. "That means good night and sleep well."

"Drool, drool," they shouted back.

They ran to the head of the island, to the look-out place under the tall pine and waved as the boat with the natives rowed away into the dusk. Long after they could not see the boat they could see the white flashes as the oars lifted from the water. And long after they could not see them at all, they could hear the sound of rowing, growing fainter and fainter in the distance.

"We'd better be getting to sleep before it's quite dark," said Mate Susan.

"Lights out in half an hour," said Captain John.

"But we haven't lit our lights yet," said Roger.

"No, but we're just going to," said Captain John, opening his lantern and striking a match. There was still some light outside, though not much under the trees, but in the tents it was quite dark. John lit his lantern and took it into his tent and put it on the tin box, which he moved into the middle so that there should be no danger of setting fire to the tent walls. Then he remembered that the female native had done something in his tent just before she went away. He looked round to see what it was. Pinned to the tent wall near the head of his bed was a scrap of paper. On it was written, "If not duffers won't drown."

"Daddy knows we aren't duffers," said John to himself.

Susan had put her lantern on one of the two biscuit tins. She and Titty were making their beds comfortable.

The tents looked like big paper lanterns glowing under the trees. Shadows moved about inside them. It always takes some time to get comfortable on a haybag the first night. There were voices.

"Are you all right, Titty?"

"Aye, aye, sir."

"What about that boy?"

"He's all right, Mister Mate. Are you ready for lights out?"

"Yes."

"Lights out!"

FIRST NIGHT ON THE ISLAND

The two lanterns were blown out and the white tents were part of the darkness. There was no light now but the glow of the embers on the camp fire. "Good night! Good night! Good night!" There was no noise now but the lapping of the lake on the rocks. In a few moments the captain, the mate, the able-seaman, and the boy were fast asleep.

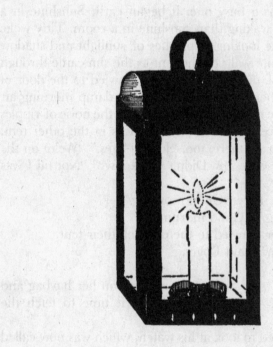

CHAPTER VI

ISLAND LIFE

THE next day was a busy one. It began early. Sunshine in a tent is even more waking than sunshine in a room. Titty woke first and lay awake looking at patches of sunlight and shadow playing on the white walls of the tent as the sun came through the waving tops of the trees. Then she crawled to the door of the tent and put her head out, sniffing the damp morning air and listening to the rustling of the leaves and the noise of ripples on the island shore. Then she heard voices in the other tent. They were waking up there, too. "John." "Yes." "We're on the island." "Of course we are. Didn't you know?" "Not till I was properly awake."

"Hullo," called Titty. "Good morning."

"Good morning." "Good morning."

John and Roger crawled to the door of their tent.

"Where's Susan?" said Roger.

"Still asleep."

"No, she isn't," said Susan, rolling over on her haybag and rubbing her eyes. "What time is it? Is it time to fetch the milk?"

John disappeared to look at his watch, which was now called a chronometer because John was the master of a ship.

"Three minutes to seven," he said. He had thought of putting it into ship's time, but it would have taken him a moment or two to be sure what it was.

"I wonder whether they'll have milked the cows," said Susan.

"I'll row over for the milk," said John.

"Wait a minute," said Susan. "Let's all go this time. Then we shall all know the way and they will know all of us, so that anybody can go for the milk on other days."

There was some dressing and some washing done at the landing-place, not very much, faces, hands, and teeth. Then the whole crew pushed their way through the undergrowth to the hidden harbour at the south end of the island. There was their ship, moored as they had left her. Her thwarts were still wet with dew, in spite of the morning sunshine, and they dried places to sit upon with their pocket handkerchiefs. They paddled her out through the rocks, hoisted the damp brown sail and sailed across to the landing-place by the oak tree. Here they pulled *Swallow*'s nose well up on the beach and tied the painter round a big stone. Then they walked up to Dixon's Farm together.

Dixon's Farm was not far from the lake, like the farm at Holly Howe, hidden among damson trees at the top of a steep green pasture. They were not sure how they would explain that they were the captain and crew of the *Swallow*, but Mrs. Dixon saved them that bother, for she said at once, "You'll be come for the milk. I see you've your own can. They're at the milking now." She went off with the can and brought it back bubbling and warm with new milk. "There it is," she said, "and mind now, if there's anything else you want, don't be afraid to come and ask for it." Mr. Dixon came in while they were there, a tall thin farmer. "Grand weather we're having," he said, but did not stop for an answer.

They sailed back to the landing-place this time and not to the harbour. "Wind's north-west," said Captain John, "and the landing-place is well sheltered from there." Then there was the fire to build and breakfast to cook. Mate Susan took charge of that, but the others were too hungry to go far from the fire while it was being got ready. Then there was breakfast. Then they went all over the island again, but made no new discoveries. Then, while Mate Susan and Able-seaman Titty were busy in the camp, the captain and the boy sailed away to Holly Howe with the mails. The mails were only one letter, a very short one, but Titty had not thought of writing it until they were nearly ready to set sail. She would not have had time to write even so much, if it had not been that the wind was blowing rather harder after breakfast and Captain John decided to take a reef in the sail. While he was giving the boy a lesson in how to do it, Titty wrote her letter. Here it is:

"My darling Mother,
        We send our love from a desert island and hope you are very well. So are we.
                        Your loving,
                                Titty Able-seaman."

"But Mother was here yesterday," said Captain John, "she won't want letters today."

"Well, I've written it anyway," said Titty.

And so the *Swallow* carried mails when she sailed for Holly Howe.

The wind was really hard and she made a roaring passage of it, heeling over till the water nearly came in over the gunwale and crashing into the little waves so that buckets of water flew up and were driven in wet spray over the boy and the captain. With the wind from the north-west, they had to beat against it going up the lake to Holly Howe. The little *Swallow* rushed from one side of the lake to the other and back again, going about at the end of each tack with a shiver and flap of her brown sail, lying down to it as the sail filled and then picking herself up as she gathered speed again and rushed once more across the slapping waves.

THE CAMP FIRE

On one tack John took her right into Houseboat Bay, close by the houseboat and out again. They went beyond the houseboat before going about and had a good look at her. Titty's pirate was sitting on the after-deck, sheltered from the wind by the cabin and the awning. They sailed close under the stern of the houseboat and saw him, sitting in his deck-chair, writing at something on his knees. The green parrot was perched on the railing and looked down on the *Swallow*, while the wind ruffled the green feathers on his back. The retired pirate looked up for a moment as they passed and then went on with his work.

"What's he doing?" said Roger.

"The parrot?" said John.

"No," said Roger, "the pirate."

"Probably making treasure charts," said John. "Look out. I'm going about now."

The *Swallow* swung round and headed out of the bay, to pass on the northern side of the huge buoy to which the houseboat was moored. The brown sail hid the houseboat from John and Roger until they were nearly past the buoy. Just for one moment, however, they had a good view of her bows, when they saw something that made the old blue launch that had been turned into a houseboat seem more pirate-like than ever.

Roger saw it first. John was too busy with the steering to look at much else beside the brown sail, to be kept full of wind but not too full, and to think of much else beside keeping the wind on his right cheek and nose as he looked forward. *Swallow* was sailing very fast and they saw the thing only for a moment. But there could be no doubt about what it was.

"He's got a cannon," said Roger. "Look, look!"

On the foredeck of the houseboat, on the starboard side, its round, shiny nose poking out above the blue planking, was a brightly polished little brass cannon. Once upon a time, perhaps, it had been used for starting yacht races. Now there it was, on a wooden gun carriage, ready for action. Even for Captain John it was proof that the houseboat was more than an ordinary houseboat. A brass cannon and a green parrot.

"Titty must have been right," said Captain John.

He glanced back over his shoulder to see if there was another cannon on the port side. That would have settled the question. There was not. But still, a cannon is a cannon and ships with no secrets do not usually carry even one.

Roger was ready to go on talking about the cannon. Captain John was not. You cannot talk about anything when you are sailing a little boat against a hard wind and you cannot listen to anyone who talks to you. You are watching the dark patches on the water that show you a harder puff is coming and you have to be ready at any moment to slacken the sheet or to luff up into the wind. So Roger presently stopped trying to talk.

At last they passed Darien and reached into the Holly Howe bay. They made the painter fast to a ring on the stone jetty by the boathouse and lowered the sail. Then they went up the field to the farm. Only three days before Roger, being a sailing ship, had tacked up that field against the wind to find his mother at the gate by Holly Howe with the telegram that had set them free for their adventure. Now he had no need to tack. He had no need to be a sailing ship. He was a real boy from a real ship, come ashore on business with his captain. Since yesterday the field path and the gate into the wood on the way to Darien and the farm at Holly Howe had all turned into foreign country. They were quite different places now that you came to them by water from an island of your own. They were not at all what they had been when you lived there and saw the island far away over the water. Coming back to them was almost the same thing as exploration. It was like exploring a place that you have seen in a dream, where everything is just where you expect it and yet everything is a surprise.

It seemed queer to walk straight in at the door of Holly Howe Farm. John had very nearly stopped and knocked at it. Inside, everything was as it used to be. Mother was sitting at the table writing to Father. Nurse was sitting in the armchair knitting. Fat Vicky was playing on the floor with a woolly sheep with a black nose.

"Hullo," said Mother, looking up, "did you have a good drool?"

"We all drooled like anything," said John, "and we didn't wake up as soon as you said. At least not quite as soon."

"And you got the milk at the farm all right?"

"Yes."

"I liked the native at the farm," said Roger.

"So did I," said Mother, "when I saw her yesterday."

Nurse somehow did not seem to feel that she was talking with seamen from another land. "You haven't caught your deaths of cold yet," she said. "It's quite a holiday to be without you. And tell me, Master Roger, did you remember to clean your teeth? I never packed a tooth glass for you."

"I used the whole lake," said Roger.

"We've brought the mail," said John. "It's a letter from Titty."

He pulled the letter out of his pocket and Mother opened it and read it. "I must write an answer to that," she said.

"We've come for a cargo," said Captain John. "We forgot to take our fishing rods."

"Of course, you'll want them," said Mother. "And there are your bathing things too. They were hanging out to dry yesterday when you sailed away and I never noticed them till this morning. You haven't bathed yet from the island?"

"We didn't this morning," said John.

"We will tomorrow," said Roger.

"Well, be sure you choose a good place with no weeds," said Mother, "and be sure you don't let Roger get out of his depth."

"Until I can swim," said Roger. "I very nearly can."

"Until you can swim on your back and on your front. As soon as you can do that you will be all right. But better keep within your depth even then until you are sure you can swim a long way. Now, you get your fishing things together, while I write a mail for you to take back."

They put all the fishing tackle together. They took the four rods to pieces and put each one in its own bag. They packed the floats and hooks and reels in a big coffee tin. Meanwhile Nurse made the bathing things into a bundle, tying them all up in a towel. Then Mother came out with two letters, one for Titty, saying, "Love from all the Stay-at-homes, and thank you for your nice letter"; and one for Susan, saying that she must ask Mrs. Dixon for some lettuces, because if they tried to do without green vegetables the crew might get scurvy. Also Mother gave them a big bag of peas. "Tell Susan just to boil them with some salt, and then put a pat of butter on them," she said. Also she had a big tin of chocolate biscuits. "I don't expect that mate of yours will manage much in the way of puddings," she said, "and these may help out." The captain and the boy ran into the farm again to say goodbye to Nurse and Vicky, and then Mother came down with them to the jetty, to help to carry the things.

"It's blowing a bit harder this morning," she said as they were going down the field.

"We reefed," said Roger.

"Did you?" said Mother.

"I helped," said Roger.

"Which pendant did you tie down first?" asked Mother.

"The one nearest the mast," said Roger, "then the one at

the end of the boom, and the reef points in the middle of the sail last of all."

"And which are you going to let go first when you shake your reef out?"

"Reef points first," said Roger, "then the one at the end of the boom, and then the one by the mast."

"That's right," said Mother. "No duffers in your crew."

They stowed the cargo, hoisted the sail, and were soon reaching out of the bay.

"The pirate on the houseboat's got a cannon," shouted Roger as they sailed away. He had forgotten all about it while on land.

"Has he?" called Mother. "Well, so long, you sailormen."

This time, with the wind aft, and a good one, the *Swallow* fairly raced to the island, with her wake creaming out astern of her. They sailed straight past well outside Houseboat Bay. They were too far out to see very much, but they saw the man on the houseboat get up and lean on the railing round his afterdeck and look at them through a pair of glasses. A moment later they had passed the promontory on the southern side of the bay, and the houseboat had disappeared behind it.

Soon they were nearing their island, and just as Holly Howe had seemed strange, so now the island seemed home. It was delightful to see it coming nearer, and to think of the tents and the camp, and to see smoke blowing away over the trees and to know that it came from the mate's fire.

"It must be nearly dinner-time," said Roger.

"Meat pie," said John. "Hullo, there's the able-seaman at the look-out." Titty was standing under the tall tree on Look-Out Point. She waved and disappeared.

"She's gone to tell Susan we're coming," said Roger.

Meanwhile the mate and the able-seaman had had a busy time on the island. They had built a little pier of big stones so that they could walk out on it when they wanted to dip some clean water from the lake. It was also very good for rinsing plates and cups. They had peeled potatoes and had been boiling them for a long time, prodding them with a fork to see if they were done, until every potato looked like a sponge. Then the mate had cut a great pile of bread and butter. Dinner was ready, and Titty came down to meet the *Swallow* at the landing-place.

"We've got mail for you," shouted Roger, "and mail for Susan, and your pirate has got a cannon. We saw it."

"A real cannon?" said Titty.

"Yes," said Captain John.

"I knew he was a pirate," said Titty.

Titty carried the bathing things up to the camp, Roger carried the fishing rods and tackle. John carried the tin of biscuits and the bag of peas. In a few minutes the four explorers were making short work of the meat pie. The pie was cold, but the potatoes were so hot that they got left behind. No one could eat them as quickly as cold meat pie. So they made a second course. Biscuits and apples made the pudding.

Susan read her letter. "Mother says I must give you plenty of lettuces and peas and things, or else you'll all get scurvy. What is scurvy?"

"Sailors die from it like flies," said Titty.

"We'll have peas for supper," said Susan. "You and Roger had better start shelling them."

They shelled half a saucepan full of peas while the mate washed up after dinner.

The wind had fallen light again, and John went down to the *Swallow*, and let out the reef in the sail. Then they pushed off, and sailed away beyond the island to the south, where the lake widened and then narrowed again. Far away in the distance, they could see the smoke of a steamer at the foot of the lake.

"There must be a harbour there too, like the harbour at Rio," said Titty, "and savages on the mainland all round it."

"It'll be years and years before we have been everywhere," said Roger.

"We'll make a chart of our own," said John, "and every year we'll put in the part we have explored until we know it all."

They took turns in steering the *Swallow*. Susan, of course, was nearly as good a steersman as Captain John. Able-seaman Titty was learning fast, and before they came home even the Boy Roger was allowed to take the tiller, though John sat by him ready to take charge if anything should go wrong.

It was while they were beating home again that they discovered another island. There were plenty of islands in the lake, but this was one they had not noticed, because it was very small, and so near the mainland that they had thought it was a promontory. Now, when they were near the western shore of the lake, tacking homewards, they saw the water clear between the island and the mainland. It was on the western shore, not quite opposite their own island, but a little further north. At once they made up their minds not to sail home, but to tack a little further up the lake to look at this new island.

"Let's sail through the strait between it and the shore," said Titty.

"There isn't room," said John, "not beating. We could run through it all right, if there's deep enough water, but it's probably rocky. I won't take her through under sail. But we'll sail right up to the island."

One long tack took them to their own island, and the next brought them to this new island that they had just discovered. It was very small. There was nothing on it but rocks and heather and two dead trees. One of the trees had fallen. The other was still standing. Many of its branches were broken and it had no leaves. But instead of leaves on the bare tree, there was something else. Three dark birds with long necks were perched on its branches. Titty watched them through the telescope.

"They've got indiarubber necks," she said.

"There's another," said Roger. "It's got something in its beak."

A fourth bird flew up from the lake, with a bright, gleaming fish in its beak. It perched on one of the boughs, and threw its head up, and swallowed the fish. The other birds were waving their long necks and yawning.

"What are they?" said Roger.

"Cormorants," said Captain John.

"Not really," said Titty. "Then perhaps we're near the coast of China. The Chinese have cormorants and train them to catch fish for them. I've seen a picture of them."

As the *Swallow* sailed nearer, they saw one of the cormorants fly down to the water, followed by the other three. They counted the four birds in the water. Suddenly there were only three. Then the fourth came up again. Then another disappeared. Then another. Then one came up with a fish and flew back to the bare tree.

"They're fishing," said Titty, "they're fishing now."

"On our chart," said Captain John, "we'll call this island Cormorant Island."

When the *Swallow* came nearer to the island, the bird on the tree flew away, a big, dark bird, with a splash of white under his chin. The other three that were in the water swam fast away with only their heads and necks showing. Then they too lifted themselves from the water and flew after the first.

"Shall we land?" said Roger.

"It's nothing but stones," said John.

"Let's get back and make tea," said the mate.

"Ready about!" called John, and *Swallow* swung round. He let the sheet out, and *Swallow* ran for the southern end of their

79

own island. As Captain John luffed up into the opening through the outer rocks, Susan brought the sail down, and they paddled *Swallow* safely through into her little sheltered harbour.

After supper they took the telescope up to the Look-Out Point. Until it grew too dark, they could just see the cormorants on the tree on Cormorant Island. But they would not have known what they were if they had not seen them from close to. They lay there, making plans as if they were going to be on the island all their lives.

"Properly," said Captain John, "we ought to shoot wild goats for our food."

"Only there aren't any," said Susan.

"And we haven't got a gun," said Roger.

"Of course," said John, "it's quite all right to have provisions, pemmican, and all that, especially biscuits. All explorers do that, but they get most of their food by shooting and fishing. Tomorrow we'll fish, and we'll live on the fish we catch."

"I wish we had a tame cormorant," said Titty.

"We've got fishing rods," said John.

CHAPTER VII

MORE ISLAND LIFE

Next morning the whole of *Swallow*'s ship's company bathed before breakfast. The landing-place, with its little beach, on the eastern side of the island was a good place for bathing. There was sand there, and though there were stones, they were not so sharp as elsewhere. Also the water did not go deep there very suddenly, and after Susan had walked out a good long way, she said that Roger might bathe too.

Roger, who had been waiting on the beach, pranced splashing into the water.

"You're to swim as well as splash," said Mate Susan.

"Aye, aye, sir," said Roger. He crouched in the water with only his head out. That, at least, felt very like swimming.

John and Susan swam races, first one way, and then the other.

Titty, privately, was being a cormorant.

This was not the sort of thing that she could very well talk of to John or Susan until she was sure that it was a success. So she said nothing about it. But she had seen that there were lots of minnows in the shallow water close to the shore. Perhaps there would be bigger ones further out, like the fish the cormorants had been catching yesterday. Titty had watched them carefully. The way they did it was to swim quietly and then suddenly to dive under water, humping their backs, keeping their wings close together, and going under head first. She tried, but she found that unless she used her arms, she did not get under water at all. Even when she used her arms she could not get right under without a long, splashing struggle on the surface.

"Why do you wave your legs in the air, Titty?" Roger asked after one of these dives. It was too true. Titty herself knew that long after she had put her head under and was swimming downwards as hard as she could her legs were kicking out of the water altogether.

She went further out, to be nearer the fish, and further from Roger. At last she found the trick of turning her hands so that her arm strokes pulled her down. She found that she could open her eyes easily enough, but that it was like trying to see in a bright green fog. There were no fish to be seen in it. With a great effort she got right down to the bottom. Still there were no fish. She came up puffing, then dived again and again. It was no good. She picked a stone off the bottom to make sure that she had really been there, and came to the top again in a hurry, spluttering and out of breath. There was no doubt about it. The fish could see her coming, and could swim faster than she could. There was nothing for it but fishing rods. She swam in towards the beach holding her stone.

"What have you got?" said Roger.

"A stone," said Titty. "I got it off the bottom."

"What sort of a stone?"

"Probably a pearl. Let's be pearl-divers."

Cormorants were forgotten, and the able-seaman and the boy were pearl-divers in a moment.

"Don't let Roger go far out," called the mate. "I'm off to look after the fire."

John, too, had left the water, and presently rowed past the pearl-divers on his way to fetch the milk.

"What are you doing?" he shouted to them.

"Diving for pearls."

PEARL DIVING

"Don't stay in too long. No breakfast for anybody who isn't dry and dressed by the time I'm back with the milk."

"Aye, aye, sir," said Titty.

Roger tried to say "Aye, aye, sir," with his mouth under water. He failed.

He could not open his eyes under water either with any ease, and, splashing about in two or three feet of water, he picked up his pearls by feeling for them. Able-seaman Titty swam about on the bottom with her eyes open, looking for the whitest stones. They were all rather big pearls, but no one really minds a pearl being big, and soon the pearl-divers had a pile of wet and shining jewels by the water-side. The worst of it was that as soon as the stones were dry – and they dried quickly in the sun – they stopped shining, and could not be counted as pearls any more.

Pearl-diving came to an end as soon as the divers saw Captain John coming laden down the field from Dixon's Farm. There was a sudden splashing rush for the shore, and towels, and long before Captain John came rowing in in *Swallow*, his crew, dry and dressed, were waiting for him on the beach. There was plenty for them to carry, two loaves of bread, a couple of big lettuces, a basket of eggs as well as the milk-can full of milk, and a small tobacco tin.

"What is there in that?" said Roger.

"Worms," said Captain John.

"Are we going fishing?" asked Roger.

"Yes," said Captain John. "Mr. Dixon gave me the worms. He says there are lots of perch between here and his landing-place. He says we'll do better with minnows than with worms, and he says we'll find the perch anywhere where there are weeds in the water."

Breakfast was soon over, and while Mate Susan was tidying up, the others took the saucepan for a bait-can, and half filled it with water. Then they fished for minnows in the shallows, and caught a good lot of them. Then they unstepped *Swallow*'s mast, and left it ashore with the boom and yard and sail, so that there would be more room in the boat. Susan joined them, and got her rod ready too. Then they rowed across from the island into the bay below Dixon's Farm. The Boy Roger was in the bows, keeping a look-out for weeds.

"Weeds," he shouted, soon after they came into the bay. "Lots of them." On either side of *Swallow* they could see the long green streamers of weeds under water.

"We ought to be just off the edge of them, and where it's not too deep. Are you ready to anchor?"

Mate Susan told the boy: "Have the anchor over the bows, and drop it the moment I say 'Let go!'"

John was rowing a stroke at a time, and then looking down into the water, then rowing another stroke. "Can you see the bottom, anybody?"

"I can, now," said Roger.

"All right. So can I. There's grass on it. That means sand. And it's close to the weeds. We couldn't have a better place."

"Let go!" sang out the mate.

Roger let go. *Swallow* swung slowly round. A moment later four red-topped floats were in the water, two on each side of the boat.

"How deep are you fishing, Susan?" said Titty.

"Very nearly as deep as my rod will let me," said Susan.

"Mine's only about three feet down. I can see the minnow easily."

"That's no good," said John. "It ought to be about a foot from the bottom. Bring it in, and I'll push your float up."

Susan's float bobbed first. She struck at once, and brought up her hook with nothing on it.

"He's gone off with my minnow," she said.

"You struck too soon," said John.

"I wish the boat didn't swing about so," said Titty. "Look out, Roger, your float's nearly touching mine. Now you're lifting my float as well as yours. They're both tangled."

John disentangled them, but when he had done it, he found the boat had swung the other way, and his own tackle was tangled in the same way with Susan's.

"This is no good," he said. "We must have an anchor at each end so that the boat won't swing. All rods in! Haul up the anchor, Roger. We'll get a big stone on the shore. There's plenty of anchor rope to spare."

So they rowed ashore, and fastened a big stone to the other end of the anchor rope. Then they rowed back to another place not far away. Roger let go the anchor, and Susan lowered the stone over the stern of the boat. This time *Swallow* rested broadside on to the wind, and did not swing at all. But they found it was no good fishing on the windward side, because the wind, even though there was so little of it, brought the floats in under the boat. So they all four fished on the same side. As the boat was not swinging, this did not matter, and everybody tried to watch all four floats at once.

"Whose float will go first?" said Roger.

"Mine," said Titty. "It's bobbing already."

"Look out, John," said Susan. "Your float isn't there."

John looked round. His float was gone. He pulled. The top of his rod bent and jerked, and up came a fat little perch with bright red fins and dark green bars on his sides.

"That's one, anyhow," said John, as he put on another minnow.

After that the perch came fast, one after another. Sometimes three floats bobbed together. There was soon a pile of perch in the bottom of the boat.

Roger was counting them "Twelve, thirteen, fourteen . . ."

"IT'S A SHARK!"

"Where's your float, Roger?" said the mate.

"And look at your rod," said Titty.

Roger jumped up and caught hold of his jerking rod, which he had put down while he was counting the catch. He felt a fish at the end of his line. Just as he was bringing it to the top there was a great swirl in the water, and his rod was suddenly pulled down again. Roger hung on as hard as he could, and his rod was bent almost into a circle.

"It's a shark! It's a shark!" he shouted.

Something huge was moving about in the water, deep down, pulling the rod this way and that.

"Let him have line off the reel," said John, but Roger held on.

Suddenly a mottled green fish, a yard long, with a dark back and white underneath, came to the top. It lifted an enormous head right out of the water, and opened a great white mouth, and shook itself. A little perch flew high into the air. Roger's rod straightened. For a moment the great fish lay close to the top of the water, looking wickedly at the crew of the *Swallow* as they looked at it. Then, with a twist of its tail that made a great twirling splash in the water, it was gone. Roger brought in the little perch. It was dead, and its sides were marked with deep gashes from the great teeth of the pike.

"I say," said Roger, "do you think it's really safe to bathe in this place?"

After that nobody caught any more perch. The pike had frightened them away. And when the perch were not biting, nobody but John wanted to go on fishing. At last Susan said that they had enough perch anyway, and if they were going to eat them they would all have to be cleaned. So they hauled up the stone and the anchor, and rowed back to the island.

The cleaning was a dreadful business. The mate did it, slitting up the perch with a sharp knife, and taking out their insides. The insides were burnt in the fire, and Roger took the perch down one by one to the landing-place to wash them in the lake. The mate tried to scrape the scales off the first of them, but soon gave it up. She fried them in butter in their scales, first putting a lot of salt in them. When they were cooked the skin with the scales came off quite easily, and there was the perch ready to be eaten. The mate said it was rather a waste of good butter, but the captain and the crew said it was worth it.

In the afternoon they careened *Swallow*. They took the ballast out of her, and pulled her high on the beach, and laid her over first on one side and then on the other while they scrubbed her bottom, though she did not need it. But you never know. She might have been covered with barnacles, or draped with long green weed. Anyhow, ships ought to be careened. So *Swallow* was. Then they launched her, and put the ballast in her again, and stepped the mast and took her round to the harbour.

After that the mate called for more firewood, and the whole ship's company set to work and brought all the really good driftwood from the island shores, and piled it in the camp, close by the other pile that had been left there. After that they were tired, and went up to the look-out place to watch the shipping on the lake, and to agree about the names for all the places on the island. There was Look-Out Point, of course, under the tall tree. Then there were the Landing-Place, the Harbour, the Western Shore, and the Camp. Then there were the places that could be seen from the island. There was Darien, Houseboat Bay, Dixon's Bay (this name was given up, and it was called Shark Bay instead after Roger's great fish), and Cormorant Island. Far away to the south there was the Antarctic. Far away to the north beyond Rio was the Arctic. As for their own island, they could not agree on a name for it. They thought of

Swallow Island, Walker Island, Big Tree Island, but were bothered by the thought of the fireplace which they had found there, and were using, and the neat pile of wood which, somehow, they did not like to use. Perhaps the island had a splendid name already. That did not matter for places like Darien or Rio, but for the island itself, they felt that it did.

Meanwhile they took turns with the telescope to watch the shipping on the lake. There were the big steamers going up and down. A steamer would pass, and they would watch the spreading waves of her wash and listen for them to break along the shores. Then there were the motor launches. Then there were people fishing in rowing boats. There were also sailing yachts, but not many. But all of these vessels, steamers, launches, yachts, and even rowing boats, were much bigger than *Swallow*, and were put down as native craft. It was not until the third day of their life on the island that they saw another vessel of their own size, tacking out from beyond Darien, and disappearing into Houseboat Bay.

CHAPTER VIII

SKULL AND CROSSBONES

IT must have been about eleven o'clock in the morning of that third day when all four of the ship's company were at the lookout place at the northern end of the island. The mate was sewing a button on the boy's shirt, and as the boy was inside it, she was finding it difficult. The captain was busy with some string, trying some of the knots in *The Seaman's Handybook*. Able-seaman Titty was lying on her stomach in the heather, now and then looking through the telescope at the woody point that hid Houseboat Bay and the houseboat of the retired pirate.

"It's still in there," she said.

There was a loud bang and a puff of smoke showed above the woody point. Everybody jumped up.

"It must be fighting the pirate," said Titty.

"I told you he had a cannon," said Roger, squirming in the hands of the mate.

"Let's go and help," said Titty.

Just then a small sailing boat, with one sail, shot out from behind the point. She was about the same size as *Swallow*, only with a white sail instead of a tanned one. She was sailing close-hauled against a south-westerly wind.

The little boat sailed right across the lake on the port tack, and then came about and headed almost directly for the island.

"There are two boys in her," said Titty.

"Girls," said John, who had the telescope.

When the little boat was on the other side of the lake, the crew of the *Swallow* could be sure of nothing, but they watched her as closely as they could, and took turns with the telescope. She was a little varnished sailing dinghy with a centreboard. They could see the centreboard case in the middle of the boat.

"That's why she sails closer to the wind than we do," said John, "though *Swallow* sails very close," he added, out of loyalty to his ship.

In the little boat were two girls, one steering, the other sitting on the middle thwart. The two were almost exactly alike. Both had red knitted caps, brown shirts, blue knicker-bockers, and no stockings. They were steering straight for the island.

"Lie down everybody," said Captain John. "We don't know whether they are friends or enemies."

Roger, the button now fixed to his shirt, dropped flat. So did Titty. So did Susan. Captain John rested the telescope on the edge of the rock so that he could see through it while his head was hidden by a clump of heather.

"I can read her name," he said. "AM am, AZ az, O . . . N . . . Amazon."

The others, hiding in the heather, looked out as much as they dared. The little boat came nearer and nearer. The girl who was steering (they could see now that she was the bigger of the two) pulled something from under the stern-sheets. The other reached aft to take it, and then went forward, and was busy with something about the mast.

Suddenly the *Amazon*, now only twenty yards from the island, went about. They heard the girl who was steering say, "Ready about," and saw the other duck to let the boom pass over, when she stood up again at once, holding some halyards in her hands. She began to haul downwards, hand over hand,

and a little flagstaff with a flag on it went bobbing and jerking up to the masthead.

"They're hoisting a flag," said John.

The little staff straightened itself at the top of the mast, and the flag, a three-cornered one, blew out in the wind.

Titty drew a long breath that nearly choked her.

"It is . . ." she said.

The flag blowing out in the wind at the masthead of the little boat was black and on it in white were a skull and two crossed bones.

The four on the island stared at each other.

Captain John was the first to speak.

"Roger stops here," he said. "The mate watches the landing-place. Titty watches the western shore. I watch the harbour. No one will show themselves. It's quite likely they haven't seen us. Wait till they're well away on that tack and then we'll get to our places. They could see us if we moved now."

The *Amazon*, sailing fast on the port tack, was soon half across the lake.

"Now," said John; and the three of them, leaving Roger, slipped down from the look-out place into the camp. Susan hid herself behind some bushes close to the landing-place. Titty crawled through the undergrowth till she could see out over the steep rock that ran along the western side of the island. John hurried through the trees until he came to the harbour. There he found a place from which he could look out without being seen. He unstepped the mast of the *Swallow* in case it could be seen over the rocks, and then hid himself and waited.

Titty saw more of what happened than any of the others, and she really saw very little. The *Amazon* went about once more, and sailed round the southern end of the island. Titty watched her until the trees at that end of the island hid her.

John saw her only for a moment as she passed across the opening in the rocks outside the harbour. Then he could not see her any more. Then he heard voices not far away but dared not move for fear of showing himself. Presently he heard the voices further away, near the landing-place. He hurried back through the trees to help Susan. But Susan had seen them as they passed, for a moment only, through the trees. They had not stopped at all. Sailing fast, with the wind with them, they had run through between the island and the mainland, and were already north of the island, sailing straight on towards Houseboat Bay and Darien. Susan and John hurried together to the look-out point, where Roger, his legs kicking with excitement, was lying in the heather watching the *Amazon* growing smaller and smaller.

"They hauled down the flag almost as soon as they were clear of the island," he said.

"Then they must have hoisted it only because they saw us," said John.

Titty joined them.

"If they were pirates," she said, "why did the pirate on the houseboat fire at them?"

"Perhaps he didn't," said Susan. "Watch if they run into Houseboat Bay again."

"They haven't got a cannon," said Roger, "and he has, a beauty. I know it was the pirate on the houseboat who fired."

The *Amazon* did not run into Houseboat Bay. The little boat, with her white sail well out, held on her course, leaving a long line of wake astern of her, as straight as if it had been laid off with a ruler.

"They know how to steer," said Captain John. One of *Swallow*'s weak points was that she was inclined to yaw about with a following wind. It was none too easy to leave a wake like that. And, as John could not admit that there might be

94

easier boats to steer than *Swallow*, he had to give all the credit for that straight line to the sailors of the *Amazon*.

They watched the little white sail grow smaller until at last it disappeared beyond the Peak of Darien.

"She must be going to Rio," said Susan.

"We'd better follow and see where they come from," said Captain John. "They can't get back here without our seeing them. Now we can't see them, and they can't see us. So even if they do see us afterwards, they won't know we have come from the island."

"Unless they have seen us already," said Susan.

"They didn't see *Swallow*, anyhow," said John. "I took her mast down. Let's have a pemmican day. Then we needn't wait to cook dinner. Don't let's waste a minute. A loaf of bread and a tin of pemmican and some apples, and we'll get four bottles of ginger beer, grog, I mean, in Rio. Then we needn't bother about anything but tea when we get back. Come on, Roger. We'll bring *Swallow* round to the landing-place. Will you be ready with the stores, Mister Mate?"

"Aye, aye, sir," said Mate Susan.

John and Roger ran to the harbour, cast off *Swallow*'s moorings, and scrambled in. John stepped the mast, paddled her out through the narrows, and then began rowing as soon as there was room to use the oars. You can't do much sculling over the stern against a south-west wind. He rowed round to the landing-place. Susan and Titty were waiting there with a tin of pemmican, a tin-opener, a knife, a loaf of bread, a hunk of butter wrapped up in a bit of paper, and four large apples. A moment later the brown sail was hoisted and set, and *Swallow*, with her whole crew aboard, was slipping out from behind the island.

All four were in the stern of the boat to give her her best chance with a following wind. John steered, and the other three sat in the bottom of the boat. The little *Swallow* foamed through the water. John did his best to keep her nose steadily on the outermost point of Darien, but, glancing back, he knew that he was not steering so well as the girl at the tiller of the *Amazon*. Still, he did his best, and the noise of the water boiling under *Swallow*'s forefoot showed that *Swallow* was doing her best too. The tops of the trees on the shores of the lake seemed to race across the purple slopes of the hills.

Houseboat Bay opened up. There was the houseboat and on the foredeck of her stood the fat man.

"He's very angry about something," said Titty.

He seemed to be shaking his fist at them, but they could not be sure, and presently they had passed the further point and could not see him.

Darien grew clearer and larger every moment.

"They'll have lost the wind the other side of Darien," said John, "and they won't get much until they get beyond the islands off Rio. They've a long start of us, but we may get a sight of them and see where they go."

The *Swallow* rounded the point of Darien. All her crew looked towards Holly Howe. Outside the farmhouse they could see two figures and a perambulator – Mother, Nurse, and Vicky. They seemed to belong to a different, distant life. There they were, placid in the sunshine. Vicky was probably asleep. And here, foaming through the water, ran the *Swallow*, carrying Vicky's brothers and sisters who, not an hour before, not half an hour before, had seen with their own eyes the black flag with the skull and crossbones upon it run to the masthead by a strange vessel which, so they thought, had actually been fired at by the retired pirate with the green parrot from the houseboat in Houseboat Bay.

For a moment or two no one said anything.

Then Susan said, "It's no use trying to tell Mother about

the pirates, not until it's all over, anyhow. But we must put it in the log and tell her afterwards."

"We'll tell her when she isn't a native any more," said Titty. "It's not the sort of thing you tell to natives."

The *Swallow* ran on. There were now more houses on the eastern shore of the lake. The further they went, the more houses there were. There were islands. One big one had houses on it. A long sandy spit ran out with boathouses on its further side. The houses, no longer scattered among trees, clustered on the side of the hill above the little town of Rio, inhabited entirely by natives who had no idea that this was its name. The *Swallow* ran on in sheltered water beyond the outer islands and the spit of land. Now they could see Rio Bay and the steamer pier. They were slipping slowly through a fleet of yachts at their moorings. Motor boats were moving about with cargoes of visitors. Captain John sent the Boy Roger forward, to the boy's delight, as a look-out man, and himself was kept very busy avoiding the rowing boats and canoes. Rio on this summer day was a busy place. A steamship hooted, left the pier, and steamed slowly out of the bay. Not one of all the passengers who looked down from the deck on the little brown-sailed *Swallow* knew that the four in her were living on a desert island, and that they were interested, not in the big steamer, or the yachts, or the motor boats, but only in another little vessel as small as their own. For the crew of the *Swallow* there was no other vessel on the water, except, of course, this mass of clumsy native craft which really did not count. Their eyes were only for the pirate vessel they were pursuing.

She was not in Rio Bay. Four pairs of eyes searched every little jetty. She might have tied up and lowered her sail, in which case she would be hard to see. She might have slipped in behind the islands that made the bay so good a sheltered anchorage for yachts and so suitable a playground for all these noisy natives with their rowing boats.

"We'll sail right through the bay," said Captain John, "and out into the open water, so that we can see right up towards the Arctic. If we can't see her then we'll turn back and cruise among the islands."

The *Swallow* slipped through the bay, and almost as soon as she was clear of the long island that lies in front of the town, there was an eager shout from Roger, "Sail Ho!"

"It's her," shouted Susan.

From the northern entrance of the bay, beyond the long island, it was possible to see far up the lake, a long blue sheet of water stretching away into bigger hills than those which rose from the wooded banks of the southern part.

Little over a mile away a small white sail was moving rapidly towards a promontory on the western shore. In a moment or two it disappeared.

"What shall we do now?" said Titty.

There was a short debate.

Roger was all for going on. John thought not.

"We know just where they are now," he said. "They may be trying to draw us away from the island. If we sail down there, and they come out again, we might have to race them back to our own island. If we stay here we can be sure of getting back there before they do. I think we'd better stay here and eat our pemmican and see whether they come out or not."

Susan said. "What about the grog?" And that made them all feel thirsty and hungry.

"But they might come out while we are buying grog in Rio," said John. "They might slip through behind the islands, and then when we come back from Rio we might be waiting here while they are capturing our camp."

Titty had an idea. There were plenty of small islets at this end of the big islands that sheltered Rio Bay. Why not put her ashore on one of them to watch while they sailed into Rio for the grog. Then at least they could be sure of knowing whether the pirates had come out again or not.

"Good for Titty," said Captain John.

There was a small islet with nothing on it but rocks and heather only a hundred yards away. They sailed to leeward of it, and then John put *Swallow*'s head up into the wind.

"Keep a look-out for rocks under water, Roger," said the mate.

Swallow slipped along with sail flapping, yard by yard nearer to the islet.

"Stand by to lower the sail, Mister Mate," said John, and Susan made ready to lower away in a hurry. But there was no need. The islet rose out of water deep enough to let the *Swallow* lie afloat close alongside it. There was the gentlest little bump, and Titty was over the side and ashore.

"The telescope," she said.

"Here it is," said the mate.

"Push her off," said John, putting the tiller hard aport.

Titty pushed. The *Swallow* moved backwards. Then her sail filled, she hesitated, heeled over a little, and began to move forward again. Titty waved her hand and climbed to the top of the islet, and sat there resting the telescope on her knees.

Three or four short tacks brought the *Swallow* to the nearest of the landing stages for rowing boats that run out from the shore in Rio Bay. Roger climbed on to the landing stage, took two turns round a bollard with the painter, and then sat himself on the top of it. To be on the safe side they lowered the sail. Then John and Susan hurried up the landing stage to the little store where you could buy anything from mouse-traps to peppermints.

"Four bottles of grog, please," said John without thinking.

"Ginger beer," said Susan gravely.

John was looking at a coil of rope in a corner of the shop.
"And twenty yards of this rope," he said.

The shopman measured off twenty yards and made a neat
coil of them. He put four bottles of ginger beer on the counter.
John put down his five shillings. He took the coil of rope and
two of the bottles. Susan took the other two.

"It's a grand day," said the shopman as he handed out the
change.

"Yes, isn't it?" said John.

This was the whole of their conversation with the natives of
Rio.

When they came back to the landing stage, Roger said, "One
of the natives came and said, 'That's a fine little ship you have
there.'"

"What did you say to him?" asked Susan sternly.

"I said 'Yes,'" said Roger. He, too, had been giving nothing
away.

They sailed back to the islet for Titty. She waved to them
when she saw them coming, and was at the water's edge ready
to climb in when John brought *Swallow* alongside.

"It's all right," she said. "They haven't come out. They must
be still in there behind that promontory."

"Well, I'm glad we know, anyway," said John.

"May I land on Titty's island?" said Roger.

"Why not all land and have dinner on it?" said Susan.

So they lowered the sail and landed, taking the anchor with
them and letting *Swallow* lie in the lee of the island at the end
of the anchor rope. A rock on the top of the islet made a table.
John opened the pemmican tin, and jerked it till the pemmican
came out all in one lump. Susan cut up the loaf and spread
the butter, so that no one slice should be thicker spread than
another. On the hunks of bread and butter they put hunks of

ROGER ON GUARD

pemmican, and washed them down with deep draughts of Rio grog out of the stone bottles. Then they ate the apples. All the time they kept a close watch on the promontory where the little white sail of the pirate ship had disappeared.

"They may never have seen us at all," said Susan.

"I'm sure they did or they would never have hoisted that flag," said John.

"Perhaps," said Titty, "there were more of them. Perhaps these ones showed their flag so as to draw us away from the island while some of their allies landed there and took our camp."

"I never thought of that," said John. "There may have been a whole fleet of them waiting for us to go."

"They may be on our island now," said Titty.

"Anyway, let's sail," said Roger, who was never happy unless he could hear the water under *Swallow*'s forefoot.

It was lively work sailing home, tacking through the native shipping in Rio bay, and then beating against the south-west wind which met them squarely once they had left the shelter of the islands. They thought of taking in a reef, but did not want to if they could help it. There were hardish squalls now and again, and Mate Susan stood by ready to slip the halyard and bring the sail down if it was necessary. Roger got so wet with the spray splashing in over the bows that Susan made him come aft and sit in the bottom of the boat. There was no time to think of anything but the sailing until they came in under the lee of their own island. In Houseboat Bay the man on the houseboat got up from his chair on the after-deck and looked at them through binoculars. But they hardly noticed him.

"Wind'll drop at sunset," said John. "We'll land at the old landing-place. *Swallow* will be in good shelter there, and I'll take her round to the harbour later on when it isn't blowing so hard."

So they landed at the old place. As soon as they landed they ran in a bunch up to their camp and looked into the tents. Then they went all over the island. Everything was just as they had left it. Nobody had been there. The pirates in the *Amazon* had had no allies.

They made a fire in the fireplace, and by the time they were sitting round it drinking their tea they had begun to think that they had been altogether wrong in thinking that the pirate flag had been hoisted on the *Amazon* for them to see. They began even not to be sure that they had heard the gun in Houseboat Bay.

"Why did the man on the houseboat shake his fist at us?" said Titty. "Something must have happened to make him."

"Perhaps he didn't really," said John.

"I don't suppose we shall ever see the pirates again," said Titty sadly.

"If they were pirates," said Susan.

CHAPTER IX

THE ARROW WITH THE GREEN FEATHER

In the morning John was the first to wake. It was already late. The sun was high overhead. The first days had gone by on which the beginning of the morning light had been enough to waken the explorers. They had grown used to sleeping in a tent. Besides, yesterday, so much had happened. John woke not very happy. Yesterday seemed unreal and wasted. Those pirates, the gun in Houseboat Bay, the chase up the lake to Rio were a sort of dream. He woke in ordinary life. Well, he thought, one could hardly expect that sort of thing to last, and it was almost a pity it had begun. After all, even if there were no pirates, the island was real enough and so was *Swallow*. He could do without the pirates. It was time to fetch the milk.

He looked at the lump of blanket on the other side of the tent and decided to let it sleep. He crawled out of his own blankets, put his sandshoes on, picked up the bundle of his clothes and a towel, and slipped out into the lonely sunlight. Taking the milk-can with him he ran down to the landing-place. He splashed out into the water and swam hard for a minute or two. This was better than washing. Then he floated in the sunshine with only his nose and mouth above water. Seagulls were picking minnows from the surface not far away. Perhaps one of them would swoop down on him by mistake. Could it tow him by flying while he clung to its black hanging legs? But the seagulls kept well away from him, and he turned on his side again and swam back to the landing-place. Then he ran through the trees to the harbour, put his clothes and the towel and the milk-can into *Swallow*, and pushed off.

He rowed hard for the beach by the oak tree below Dixon's Farm. The sunshine and the warm southerly wind had almost dried him before he reached it. He gave a dry polish with the towel to the bits of him that seemed damp, put his clothes on, and hurried up the field.

"You're not so early this morning," said Mrs. Dixon, the farmer's wife.

"No," said John.

"What would you say to a bit of toffee?" said Mrs. Dixon. "I'd nothing to do last night so I fettled you up a baking. Four of you, aren't there?"

"Thank you very much," said John.

She gave him a big bag of brown toffee when she brought back the milk-can after filling it with milk.

"Have you had breakfast?" she asked.

"Not yet."

"And you've been bathing already. I can see by your hair. You'd better put something into you. Stop a minute while I get you a bit of cake."

After swimming, a bit of cake is very welcome, and John saw no harm in eating it. But while he was eating it, Mrs. Dixon said, "Mr. Turner of the houseboat has been asking about you. You haven't been meddling with his houseboat, have you?"

"No," said John.

"Well, he seems to think you have," said Mrs. Dixon. "You'd better leave Mr. Turner and his parrot alone."

Yesterday suddenly became real once more. John remembered how he had thought he had seen the retired pirate on the houseboat shaking his fist at them. In a moment he was Captain John, responsible for his ship and his crew, and

Mrs. Dixon, the farmer's wife, was a native, not wholly to be trusted in spite of her toffee and cake.

He set out at once on his way back, thinking that he ought to have wakened the mate before coming to fetch the milk.

But he could see the island from the field below the farm, and smoke was already rising from among the trees. The mate was up and about, the fire was lit, everything was right, and the kettle would be boiling before he got back with the milk.

He hurried down to the shore. Able-seaman Titty and the Boy Roger were splashing about by the island. He saw the two white figures splash up out of the water, kicking it in fountains before them. They were still drying themselves when he brought the *Swallow* to the landing-place. They helped to pull her up.

"I've got some toffee from the natives as well as the milk," said Captain John.

"Real toffee?" said Roger.

"Molasses," said Titty. "Toffee is only the native name for it."

"And I have grave news," said Captain John. "Something has happened. I shall call a council as soon as we have had breakfast."

"Aye, aye, sir," said the able-seaman, and poked the boy, who said, "Aye, aye, sir," too.

The able-seaman and the boy ran up to the camp with the milk-can and the molasses. The captain followed them, thinking, with his hands in his pockets.

"Breakfast ready, sir," called the mate cheerfully.

"Thank you, Mister Mate," said John.

"Here's the milk," said Roger.

"And a whole bag of molasses," said Titty. "Do you know how to make rum punch? That's made out of molasses, isn't it?"

"I expect so," said the mate. "I've never tried."

Tea was ready. Eggs were boiling in the saucepan, and the mate was timing their boiling by the chronometer.

"Three minutes," she said, "and they'd been in a little before I began to count. They're done all right now." She fished the eggs out one by one with a spoon. For some minutes eggs and bread and butter and tea put a stop to talking. After that there was bread and marmalade. After that the mate served out a ration of molasses all round. "Molasses are very good anyhow," she said. "We'll make rum punch if there are any molasses we don't want."

At last breakfast was over and Captain John spoke. "Mister Mate," he said, "I call a council."

They were all sitting round the fire, which was now burning low. The saucepan full of water was standing among the embers, keeping hot for washing up the stickier things.

Mate Susan sat up and looked about her.

"The whole ship's company is here, sir," she said.

"We have an enemy," said Captain John.

"Who is it?" said Able-seaman Titty eagerly.

"It's the pirates in the *Amazon*," said Roger.

"Shut up," said the mate.

"You know the man on the houseboat," said Captain John.

"Yes," said the mate.

"He has been telling the natives that we have been meddling with his houseboat."

"But we've never touched it."

"I know we haven't, but he has been telling them that we have. He is trying to set the natives against us. I don't know why he hates us, but he does."

"Then he *was* shaking his fist at us yesterday," said the mate.

"I knew he was a retired pirate," said Titty. "He has a secret. They all have. Either it's dark deeds or else it's treasure.

Look at the way he fired at the pirate ship. He must have thought they were after his hoard."

"Yes, but why is he against us?" said John.

"Perhaps this is his island," said Titty. "You know someone had been here before us and made a fireplace."

"But if it was his island he would live on it instead of living in the houseboat."

"It would be much more comfortable for the parrot," said Titty.

"Anyway, it looks as if he wanted to get us turned off the island."

"We won't go," said Roger.

"Of course we won't," said Captain John, "but the question is, just what ought we to do?"

"Let's go and sink the houseboat," said Roger and Titty together.

At that moment something hit the saucepan with a loud ping, and ashes flew up out of the fire. A long arrow with a green feather stuck, quivering, among the embers.

The four explorers started to their feet.

"It's begun," said Titty.

Roger grabbed at the arrow and pulled it out of the fire.

Titty took it from him at once. "It may be poisoned," she said. "Don't touch the point of it."

"Listen," said Captain John.

They listened. There was not a sound to be heard but the quiet lapping of the water against the western shore of the island.

"It's him," said Titty. "He's winged his arrow with a feather from his green parrot."

"Listen," said Captain John again.

"Shut up, just for a minute," said Mate Susan.

UNSEEN ENEMY

There was the sharp crack of a dead stick breaking somewhere in the middle of the island.

"We must scout," said Captain John. "I'll take one end of the line, the mate the other. Titty and Roger go in the middle. Spread out. As soon as one of us sees him, the others close in to help."

They spread out across the island, and began to move forward. But they had not gone ten yards when John gave a shout.

"*Swallow* has gone," he shouted. He was on the left of the line, and as soon as he came out of the camping ground he saw the landing-place where he had left *Swallow* when he came back with the milk. No *Swallow* was there. The others ran together to the landing-place. There was not a sign of *Swallow*. She had simply disappeared.

"Spread out again. Spread out again," said John. "We'll comb the whole island. Keep a look-out, Mister Mate, from your shore. She can't have drifted away. He's taken her, but he's still on the island. We heard him."

"Roger and I pulled her right up," said Titty. "She couldn't have drifted off."

"Spread out again," said Captain John. "Then listen. Advance as soon as the mate blows her whistle. A hoot like an owl means all right. Three hoots means something's up. Blow as soon as you're ready, Mister Mate."

The mate crossed the island nearly to the western shore. She looked out through the trees. Not a sail was to be seen on the lake. Far away there was the smoke of the morning steamer, but that did not count. Roger and Titty, half a dozen yards apart, were in the middle of the island. Captain John moved a little way inland, but not so far that anyone could be between him and the shore without being seen. They listened. There was not a sound.

Then, over on the western side of the island, the mate blew her whistle.

The four began moving again through the trees and the undergrowth.

"Roger," called Titty, "have you got a weapon?"

"No," said Roger. "Have you?"

"I've got two sticks, pikes, I mean. You'd better have one." She threw one of her sticks to Roger.

An owl hooted away to her left.

"That must be the captain," she said. She hooted back. Susan away on the right hooted in reply. And again they all listened. Then they moved forward again.

"Hullo," cried Roger, "someone's been here."

Titty ran to him. There was a round place where the grass and ferns were pressed flat as if someone had been lying there.

"He's left his knife," said Roger, holding up a big clasp knife that he had found in the grass.

Titty hooted like an owl three times.

The captain and the mate came running.

"He must be quite close to," said Titty.

"We've got his knife, anyway," said Roger.

Captain John bent down and felt the flattened grass with his hand.

"It's not warm," he said.

"Well, it wouldn't stay warm very long," said the mate.

"Spread out again and go on," said Captain John. "We mustn't let him get away with *Swallow*. He can't be far away, because we heard him. If he had taken *Swallow* to sea we should have seen her. He must have her here, somewhere, close along the shore."

At that moment there was a wild yell, "Hurrah, Hurrah." But the yelling did not come from in front of them. It came from behind them, from the direction of the camp.

"Come on," said Captain John, "keep together. Charge!"

The whole party rushed back through the trees towards the camp.

Just as they came to the edge of the clearing there was a shout, but they could see no one.

"Hands up! Halt!"

The voice came from immediately in front of them.

"Hands up!" it came again.

"Flat on your faces," cried Captain John, throwing himself on the ground.

Susan, Titty, and Roger were full length on the ground in a moment. An arrow passed harmlessly over their heads.

They looked at their own camp, and did not at first see what Captain John had seen. In the middle of the camp a tall stick was stuck in the ground with a black pirate flag blowing from the top of it. But there seemed to be nobody there. Then, inside their own tents, they saw two figures, kneeling, one with a bow ready to shoot, the other fitting an arrow.

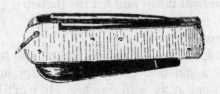

CHAPTER X

THE PARLEY

"I rs not the houseboat man," said Titty. "It's the pirates from the pirate ship."

"And in our tents," said Susan.

"Let's take them prisoners," said Roger.

"Hands up," said the pirate girl from the *Amazon*, who was in the captain's tent.

"Hands up yourselves," cried Captain John, and made as if to leap to his feet. Both the pirates shot off their arrows.

"Now," shouted John, "before they load again. Swallows for ever!"

The four Swallows were up and half-way across the open space in a moment.

The red-capped Amazons leapt up out of the tents to meet them.

But they pointed their bows to the ground.

"A parley," shouted the one who seemed to be the leader.

"Halt!" called Captain John.

The four explorers of the *Swallow* stood facing the two pirate girls from the *Amazon*. The Amazons were bigger than most of the Swallows. One of them was bigger than Captain John. The other was about the same size. If it had come to a fight, it might have been a very near thing.

But it did not come to a fight.

"Let's parley first and fight afterwards," said the leader of the Amazons.

"It's no good our parleying with you if the houseboat man has got *Swallow*," said John.

"The man from the houseboat?" said the younger Amazon. "But he's got nothing to do with it. He's a native, and very unfriendly."

"Well, he's unfriendly to us too," said John.

Susan pulled John by the sleeve. "If the houseboat man isn't with them," she whispered, "they must have taken *Swallow* themselves, and the only place they could put her is the harbour. Their own ship must be there too. So if they have got our tents we can take both ships."

"If he's unfriendly to you too, we had better parley at once," said the elder Amazon.

"Where is *Swallow*?"

"She is a prize, and we have taken her into our harbour."

"It's our harbour," said John. "And anyhow that's not much good to you. You can't get out from this end of the island against the four of us. The harbour end of the island is in our hands, so that really it's the *Amazon* that's a prize, and we've got both ships. You've only got our tents."

Titty spoke. "Why have your arrows got green feathers? The pirate on the houseboat must have given them to you. You must be on his side."

The younger Amazon exclaimed, "But the green feathers are our trophies. We took them ourselves. He was keeping them to clean his pipes and we boarded his ship and took them."

The elder Amazon said, "We are all on the same side, and I don't see the good of fighting."

John said, "But why did you come to our island . . . ?"

"Our island," said the Amazons together.

"How can it be your island? This is our camp."

"It's been our island for years and years," said the Amazons. "Who built the fireplace? Who marked the harbour?"

"How marked the harbour?" said John. "You mean putting a cross on a tree there. Anyone could put a cross on a tree."

The elder Amazon laughed. "That just shows it's our island," she said. "You don't even know how the harbour is marked."

"We do," said Roger.

John was silent. He knew that they did not.

At last he said, "Right, we'll parley. But you must put down your weapons, and so will we. You must take down your flag, because ours is in *Swallow*, so that we can't put it up beside it."

The elder Amazon said, "It seems a pity to take down the flag when there is such a good wind blowing it out. It isn't as if it was just hanging. One of you go to the harbour to get your flag from your ship, and then we can have both flags flying during the parley and everything will be proper."

"No fighting while one of us is going for it?"

"No. Peace. We'll put our weapons down now."

The Amazons put their bows on the ground. Roger and Titty put down their pikes. John and Susan had no weapons to put down.

"Mister Mate," said John, "will you send one of your men to the harbour to bring our flag from *Swallow*?"

"Skip along, Roger," said Mate Susan, and then, turning to the Amazons, "You swear the houseboat man is not there to take him prisoner?"

"Of course," said the Amazons. "But will you swear he does not do anything to our ship? We were very careful with yours, and we haven't done anything to your tents. We could have burnt them easily or razed them to the ground."

"We swear," said Captain John.

"Why not scuttle their ship and keep them prisoners?" said Titty.

"Until the parley is over it is peace," said Captain John. "Skip along, Roger, and get the *Swallow*'s flag, but don't touch anything else."

Roger ran off. "I've got their knife anyway," he shouted.

The elder Amazon turned to the other.

"Peggy, you donkey," she said. "Where's the ship's knife?"

Peggy, the younger Amazon, felt in the pocket of her breeches.

"Gone," she said. "We must have left it when we were in hiding in the bush."

"We don't want to take their knife," whispered Susan to John.

"We'll give you back your knife," said John to the Amazons. "As soon as our man comes back from the harbour he shall put it with the other weapons. We don't really want your knife. We have three knives on our ship."

"Besides the knives for cutting pemmican and bread and butter," said Susan.

"This knife was given us by Uncle Jim last year for polishing the cannon on the houseboat," said the elder Amazon.

"Is the man on the houseboat your uncle?" asked Titty. "I thought you said he was your enemy too."

"He is only our uncle sometimes," said the younger Amazon. "He was last year, but this year he is in league with the natives, and the natives are very unfriendly."

"Our natives are friendly," said Titty. "Everybody is friendly except the houseboat man . . . and you," she added. "And if he's your uncle you must be in league with him."

"We jolly well aren't," said the elder Amazon.

"Shut up, Titty, and wait for the parley," said Captain John.

Roger came back with Titty's flag from the *Swallow*.

"They've got a lovely boat," he whispered to Mate Susan.

"Hand over that knife," said John.

Roger handed it over and John cut a tall sapling from a hazel on the edge of the clearing. He made a sharp point at one end of it to stick in the ground. Then he fastened Titty's flag to the top of it, found a soft place, and planted his flagstaff firmly beside the pirate flag of the Amazons. Then he wiped the knife on the grass, shut it up, and put it with the bows and the pikes.

"Now for the parley," said he. He walked towards the Amazons and held out his hand.

"My name is John Walker," he said, "master of the ship *Swallow*. This is Susan Walker, mate of the *Swallow*. This is Titty, able-seaman. This is Roger, ship's boy. Who are you?"

The elder Amazon shook hands with him.

"I am Nancy Blackett, master and part owner of the *Amazon*, the terror of the seas. This is Peggy Blackett, mate and part owner of the same."

"Her real name isn't Nancy," said Peggy. "Her name is Ruth, but Uncle Jim said that Amazons were ruthless, and as our ship is the *Amazon*, and we are Amazon pirates from the Amazon River, we had to change her name. Uncle Jim gave us the ship last year. We only had a rowing boat before that."

Nancy Blackett scowled ferociously. "I'll shiver your timbers for you if you don't stop chattering, Peggy."

"They must be in league with the houseboat pirate," said Titty. "Didn't you hear how she said he gave them their ship?"

"That was last year," said Nancy. "He was friendly last year. This year he's worse than the natives."

"Hadn't we better sit down?" said Susan. "Shall I put a stick or two on our fire and warm up the kettle? It's still got some tea in it."

"We don't want any tea, thank you," said Nancy. "But use our fireplace if you want to."

"It's our camp," said Roger.

"Let's sit down," said Mate Susan.

The two parties sat on the ground by the fireplace where the fire was still smouldering. Susan was right. It is much more difficult to be fierce sitting down than standing up.

"First of all," said Nancy Blackett. "When did you come to these seas?"

"We discovered this ocean nearly a month ago."

"When did you first come to this island?"

"We have been on the island for days and days."

"Well," said Nancy Blackett. "We were born on the shores of the Amazon River, which flows into this ocean. We have been coming to this island for years and years."

"We used to come in a rowing galley until Uncle Jim gave us the *Amazon*," said Peggy. "We used to land at the place where we found your ship, until we discovered the harbour. We have made our camp here every year."

"Look here," said Nancy Blackett. "What is the name of the island?"

"We haven't yet given it a name," said John.

"It is called Wild Cat Island. Uncle Jim called it that, because it belonged to us. That shows you whose island it is."

"But it's our island now," said John. "It was uninhabited when we came and we put our tents up here, and you can't turn us out."

Titty broke in.

"Is your Uncle Jim a retired pirate?" she asked. "I said he was as soon as we saw him."

Nancy Blackett thought for a moment. "It's quite a good thing for him to be," she said at last.

"But," said Titty, "you are pirates too."

"That's why he hates us. He must be Captain Flint. He knows what pirates are. He knows the day will come when he will walk the plank off the deck of his own ship when we have captured it."

"We'll help," said Roger.

"He hates us," said Captain John. "He has been stirring up the natives against us."

"Let's be allies," said Nancy Blackett, "then it won't matter who the island belongs to. We will be allies against Captain Flint and all the natives in the world."

"Except our friendlies," said Titty.

"Let's be allies," said Peggy. "Really we wanted to be allies as soon as we saw your smoke on the island yesterday. We are sick of natives. And we wanted to be allies at once, if only we hadn't promised to be home for lunch. That was why we just sailed round the island and defied you with our flag. There wasn't time for anything else. Then we went home."

"We watched you from beyond the big islands by Rio," said Susan.

"Rio?" said Nancy. "Rio? Oh, well, if you'll agree to let the island go on being called Wild Cat Island, we'll agree to Rio. It's a good name."

"Wild Cat Island's a good name too," said John politely.

"But how could you see us beyond the islands by Rio when we left you here," asked Peggy.

"We manned the *Swallow* and gave chase," said John.

"Thunder and lightning," said Nancy Blackett, "what a chance we missed. If we'd only known we'd have given you broadside for broadside till one of us sank, even if it had made us late for lunch."

Peggy Blackett went on. "We came here today to look at you again. We got up at sunrise and sailed close by the island, and there was no smoke and we thought you had gone. Probably you were all asleep. Then we saw your ship at the landing-place. We sailed on to Tea Bay and had our second breakfast there, a real one with tea. The first was only cold porridge and sandwiches we got from Cook last night. Then we crawled along the shore and saw one of you coming back from somewhere in your ship. The others were bathing. Then we saw you all disappear, and we crawled back to our ship and sailed straight into the harbour. There was nobody there. Then we came through the bush on the island, scouting, and saw you round your camp fire. We took away your ship and put her in the harbour. Then we came back and made a surprise attack. When you found your ship was gone and you all ran down to the landing-place we slipped past and took the camp, and Nancy was saying that somehow it was going to be difficult to be allies. . . ."

"Avast there, Peggy, you goat," said Nancy Blackett. "Excuse my mate," she said to Captain John. "She does chatter so."

"Well, Nancy was saying that our surprise attack was such a good one that we'd have to go on being enemies, and I said I was sick of enemies, what with our natives and Uncle Jim being no good this year. . . ."

"He's Captain Flint," said Nancy.

"Anyway, if she hadn't remembered about parleys you would have been natives too, for ever and ever," said Peggy.

"We couldn't be that," said Titty.

"Of course not," said Nancy Blackett, "it's much more fun being sea-dogs and timber shiverers. I propose an alliance."

"I don't see why not," said Captain John.

"My idea," said Nancy Blackett, "is an alliance against all enemies, especially Uncle Jim – Captain Flint, I mean. But we want the sort of alliance that will let us fight each other if we want to."

"That's not an alliance," said Titty, "that's a treaty, a treaty of offence and defence. There are lots in the history book."

"Yes," said Nancy Blackett, "defence against our enemies and all sorts of desperate battles between ourselves whenever we want."

"Right," said Captain John.

"Have you got a bit of paper and a pencil?" asked Nancy.

"I have," said Titty, and ran into the mate's tent and brought out a leaf from her log and a pencil.

Nancy took it and wrote:

"I, Captain John of the ship *Swallow*, and I, Captain Nancy of the ship *Amazon*, do hereby make a treaty of offence and defence on behalf of our ships and our ships' companies. Signed and sealed at this place of Wild Cat Island in the month of August 1929."

She passed the paper to the others.

"It looks all right," said Captain John.

"It ought to be 'this month', not 'the'," said Titty, "And you haven't put in the lat. and long. They always put them in all over the place."

Nancy Blackett took the paper, crossed out "the" in front of the word "month" and put "this" instead, and after the word "Island" wrote in "Lat. 7 Long. 200."

"We ought to sign it in our blood," she said, "but pencil will do."

John took the paper and signed, "John Walker, Master."

Nancy signed it, "Nancy Blackett, Amazon Pirate."

The two captains shook hands.

Peggy said, "Well, it's peace today, anyhow."

Susan said, "Perhaps you would like some of our toffee?"

"Molasses," said Titty.

Peggy said, "We did see it when we took the camp, but we

did not like to take any. We'd like some very much, if you're sure you can spare it."

Nancy said, "Let's broach a puncheon of Jamaica rum. We've got a beauty in the *Amazon*. Let's go to the harbour and get it. It's really good stuff. Sometimes our cook is quite friendly, for a native. She calls it lemonade."

CHAPTER XI

IN ALLIANCE

THE Swallows and the Amazons went together to the harbour at the southern end of the island. The path was now well trodden, though they had to stoop under boughs and step over brambles and push branches out of the way. In the little basin the two ships lay together with their noses drawn up on the beach. The *Amazon* was a fine little ship, with varnished pine planking. She was a much newer boat than the *Swallow*, of the same length, but not quite so roomy. Close by the foot of the mast, between the mast and the centreboard case, there was a small barrel of polished oak.

The centreboard case puzzled Roger.

"What's that big thing sticking up all down the middle of the boat?" he asked.

"That's the case for the centreboard," said Peggy.

"But what is the centreboard?"

"It's an iron keel that we can lower into the water when we are beating against the wind. When we are running before the wind or when we are in shallow water we can haul the keel up into that case," said Nancy. "How do you manage to sail against the wind without one?"

"*Swallow* sails very well to windward," said Captain John. "She has a keel about six inches deep, but it's there all the time, so that we don't have to have any centreboard case to get in the way inside her."

"Uncle Jim – Captain Flint – says you can't do anything to windward without a centreboard," said Nancy.

"That only shows he doesn't know *Swallow*," said Captain John.

"What's the barrel for?" asked Roger.

"It was meant as a water breaker, because our natives thought the water in the lake wasn't fit to drink," said Peggy. "But we always drink it, not straight out of the lake, but boiled for tea, and so we use the water breaker as a puncheon for feastable drinks. It's got some lovely stuff in it just now."

"We'll carry it back to the camp," said Nancy Blackett.

"It'll be rather heavy, won't it?" said Susan.

"Not the way we carry it," said Nancy. "We sling it on an oar for portage. That's the proper way. Come on, Peggy, lend a hand."

The Amazons climbed into their ship. Nancy took a length of rope from the stern and made a noose at one end of it. Then she and Peggy hove up the barrel till it rested on the gunwale in the bows. John and Susan held it there, while the Amazons came ashore with the rope and one of the oars. Nancy fixed the noose round one end of the barrel and made it fast so that it could not slip. Then she took two turns of the rope round the oar and brought the rope down and through the loop, then along the top of the barrel and round it, to make another noose at the other end, then twice round the oar and down again, and made it fast.

"Ready, Peggy?" she said.

"Ready," said Peggy.

"Heave ho," said Captain Nancy. They lifted the oar so that each of them had one end of the oar on her shoulder. The barrel hung steady below the oar between them.

"March!" said Nancy, and the Amazon pirates marched up out of the harbour and along the path through the trees.

CARRYING UP THE PUNCHEON

"It doesn't weigh anything when you carry it like this," said Peggy. "This is the way all pirates carry their barrels and their treasure, or anything else that they take ashore from their ships."

Susan, Titty, and Roger went with them. Captain John waited in the harbour. He was still thinking about what the Amazons had said about the harbour being marked. What did they mean, exactly? He had seen the cross painted on the stump of a tree just by the shore, and when he had said that anyone could put a cross on a tree Nancy Blackett had told him that that showed that he did not know how the harbour was marked. Well, how was it marked? He looked about him. There was the stump with the white cross on it. But he could see nothing else that looked at all like a mark. There were no marks on the rocks and he could not see any more marks on trees. His respect for these Amazons grew. They seemed to know everything, besides being very good sailors. He would have to ask them, and yet, as a captain, it wasn't the sort of thing he liked to ask. He took a last look round and then hurried after the others.

He caught them up just as they were coming into the camp. The Amazons lowered the oar from their shoulders and set the barrel by the two flags. Then they wedged a few stones under it at each side to bring its tap well off the ground.

"We forgot the mugs," said Peggy.

"We've got plenty," said Susan, and she and Titty brought the mugs from their tent.

"We brought six mugs when we sailed out from home," said Titty, "for fear of breakages, and luckily we haven't broken any yet."

"We've got flagons in our ship," said Peggy. "They are just like these."

She filled all the mugs from the barrel. Nancy Blackett,

meanwhile, was sitting by herself, thinking hard. She took a mug when it was brought to her by Roger, and she took a hunk of molasses from the bag when it was offered to her by Titty, but, for a moment or two, she hardly seemed to see them.

At last she said, "The proper thing is to drink to the Jolly Roger, skull and crossbones, death and glory and a hundred thousand pieces of eight. But you aren't pirates, so we can't all drink to that. Really we ought to drink confusion to our enemies. . . ."

"The pirate with the parrot," said Titty.

"The houseboat man," said Captain John.

"Right," said Nancy, "I've got it. Swallows and Amazons for ever, and death to Captain Flint!"

"Swallows and Amazons for ever," repeated Peggy, "and death to Uncle Jim!"

"Captain Flint, you chump-headed galoot," said Captain Nancy.

The others said it all right, even Roger.

"Now swig," said Captain Nancy.

It was certainly the finest lemonade that pirate or explorer ever swigged.

"I never tasted better rum," said Able-seaman Titty.

"It is good," said Captain Nancy. "And so are your molasses."

Toffee does not help talking, and for a little time no one said anything.

At last Titty asked, "Where did Captain Flint get his parrot?"

Peggy Blackett swallowed a lump of molasses and began at once: "He brought the parrot from Zanzibar. He's been all over the world. Mother says he was the black sheep of the family when he was young, so he was sent to South America.

But he didn't stay there. He went everywhere. Last year he came home and said he'd gathered enough moss and meant to settle down. Mother's his sister, you know. But he always liked being at sea. So he bought the houseboat, and last year we were often in it. Last year he was one of us and we used to sail with him in *Amazon*. Then he gave us *Amazon* and went off again before the winter. And this year when he came back he said he had a contract and was going to write a book, and all through the summer he's been living in the houseboat, but instead of sailing with us he's in league with the natives. We've done everything we could to wake him up. But it's no good. He even asked Mother to make us leave him alone. So Mother told us he was writing a book and had to be left alone. But we thought it wasn't his fault to be writing a book, and that we would show him we didn't think any worse of him for it. But he wasn't pleased at all, even when we offered to come and live on the houseboat with him. It ended by his forbidding us to come near him."

"That's why we watched till he went ashore and boarded the houseboat and took the green feathers for our arrows," said Nancy, "just to show him. He had them in a pot for pipe-cleaners."

"It's such a pity, too," said Peggy. "We were teaching the parrot to say 'Pieces of Eight', so that it would be a good pirate parrot to take with us to Wild Cat Island. It only says 'Pretty Polly'. That's no use to anyone. But they say green parrots don't talk as well as grey ones."

"You said you thought he was a *retired* pirate, didn't you?" said Nancy to Titty.

"Yes," said Titty.

"Then perhaps it's all right for him to have a parrot that only says 'Pretty Polly'. One of the other sort would give him away."

"Did he really fire at you yesterday?" asked Captain John. "We saw the smoke and heard the bang."

"That wasn't him; that was us," said Captain Nancy. "We sailed into the bay and round the houseboat and looked in through the cabin windows. Uncle . . . Captain Flint was asleep. We saw him. So we took one of those big Roman candles that fizz and then go off with a bang, and we put it on the cabin roof and lit it and sailed away We were just clearing the point when it banged. We had saved it from last fifth of November, but it hadn't gone bad at all. It couldn't have banged better."

"We heard it here," said Roger. "It was a good bang."

"I bet it made him savage," said Nancy.

"He was standing on deck shaking his fist when we were sailing up to Rio after you," said John, "and that was long after."

"Well, we are all at war with him now," said Nancy. "Some day we'll capture the houseboat. We could easily do it all together. *Swallow* on one side and *Amazon* on the other. He couldn't be both sides of the deck at once. Then we'll give him his choice. He must throw in his lot with us like last summer, or else he must walk the plank."

"It'll be best for him to walk the plank," said Able-seaman Titty. "Then we'll take his treasure and buy a big ship, and live in her for ever and ever and sail all over the world."

"We could go to the China Seas to see Daddy," said Susan.

"We could discover new continents," said Titty. "America can't fill everything. There must be lots that haven't been found yet."

"We'd go to Zanzibar and bring back a whole shipload of parrots, grey ones, talking like fun," said Peggy.

"And monkeys," said Roger.

"I like green parrots best," said Titty.

"Look here," said Nancy Blackett, "we are forgetting all about this parley. We can't fight Captain Flint all the time. But we can practise. We mustn't sink each other's ships . . ."

"Nobody shall sink *Swallow*," said Roger fiercely.

"All right," said Nancy, "nobody's going to. But it'll be very good practice for us to try to capture *Swallow*, and for you to try to capture *Amazon*. The one who wins shall be flagship. There's always a flagship in a fleet. If you capture *Amazon*, then *Swallow* will be flagship and Captain John will be commodore. If we capture *Swallow*, then *Amazon* will be flagship and I'll be commodore. Beginning from tomorrow."

"And when that's settled, we'll go and take the houseboat," said Titty.

"But," said John, "you know where we keep *Swallow*, because you know we are here. If we don't guard her, you can easily take her. But we don't know where you keep *Amazon*."

"You saw where we went yesterday."

"We saw you go behind a promontory on the western coast."

"Well, if you go beyond that promontory you'll find the mouth of a river. That's the Amazon River. Not far up it on the right bank, that's the left bank as you sail up from the lake, there's a boathouse. It's a stone boathouse, with a big wooden skull and crossbones that we made fastened over the front of it. In it there's a motor launch that you mustn't touch because it belongs to the natives, and there's a rowing boat and also *Amazon* when she's at home. Now you know."

"Half a minute," said John, "I've got a chart here."

He got the guide-book and opened it at the map which showed the whole length of the lake. Nancy Blackett showed him the river Amazon. It had another name on the map. John gave her the pencil.

"You mark where the boathouse is," he said.

Captain Nancy made a mark with the pencil in the right place.

"It'll be a cutting-out expedition only," she said. "It's agreed that whoever wins is to be as careful with the other boat as with their own."

"That'll be us," said Peggy. "Nancy always does a thing if she says she will."

"We'll see about that," said Captain John.

"Beginning from tomorrow," said Captain Nancy.

"Look here," said Susan, "hadn't we better have dinner before all the lemonade has gone."

"Jamaica rum," said Titty, with reproach.

"We've got a lot of sandwiches," said Peggy.

"We've got pemmican," said Susan, "and sardines. We finished the meat pie and the next one doesn't come till tomorrow."

"What a pity we haven't been fishing," said Titty. "We might have been able to give you some fried shark."

"We like sardines just as well," said Peggy.

There was a stir in the camp. Peggy, the mate of the *Amazon*, seemed to be in charge of the ship's food, like Susan, the mate of the *Swallow*. With Titty and Roger to help them, they set about making ready a meal. They put fresh wood on the fire and blew up the embers to boil the kettle. They agreed that it was best to have boiling water for washing up and for making tea in case the little barrel did not hold out. Then there were sardine tins and a tin of pemmican to open, and sandwiches and a cake to be brought from the *Amazon*.

The two captains did not move at first, but watched the business of their crews.

At last John said, "Look here, Captain Nancy, I wish you'd tell me about the marking of the harbour."

"It's quite simple, Captain John," said Nancy. "Come

along and I'll show you while our tars are rigging the meal."

They walked together to the harbour, meeting Peggy with the basket full of cake and sandwiches on the way. When they came to the harbour they were alone, for which Captain John was glad. He went straight to the stump of a tree with a cross on it.

"I found this at once," he said.

"And you didn't find anything else," said Captain Nancy. "That's because we are Amazon pirates and keep our marks secret. One of them is no good without the other, and the other isn't marked at all."

"How is it a mark then?" said John.

Captain Nancy squatted on the beach and drew a half circle. "Suppose this is the harbour," she said, "and these are the rocks outside." She put some big stones in about the position of the rocks outside the harbour. "You want to come in. Well, a straight line like that brings you clean through the rocks without touching any of them. Draw the line a bit longer, right into the harbour and up on the beach. Your marks must be on that line. Take this for your first mark." She planted a twig. "That's the stump with the cross on it. Now you find anything else that you can see over the first mark and also on the same straight line. It can be anything. There's no need to mark it if you know it. Then when you want to come into the harbour from outside all you have to do is to keep the two marks one behind the other. So long as you do that you will be on the straight line that brings you safe through between the rocks. Even if the lake – the sea – is high, so that some of the rocks are under water, you can sail in without looking at them if you keep your two marks one behind the other."

"'Um," said Captain John.

"Hop into *Amazon*, and I'll take her out and show you."

John stepped into *Amazon*. Nancy Blackett shoved off and took her right outside the rocks, so that they were in the open sea. Then, sculling with an oar over the stern, she brought her round so that she was headed towards the island.

"Now," she said, "do you see the stump with the cross on it?"

"Yes," said John. "I can see the cross all right. The stump is hard to see against the beach. It's the same colour."

"That's why we had to paint the cross," said Nancy. "Now, look above it to the right and you'll see the fork of a tree with a big patch of bark off it just below the fork. Got it?"

"Yes."

"That's the other mark. As it is now there are rocks between us and the harbour. But, if I bring her up a bit, you'll see that fork of a tree come nearer to the marked stump until it's exactly over it. Then we can go straight in. Sing out as soon as the two are in a straight line."

"They're in a straight line now," said Captain John.

"Right," said Captain Nancy. "Now, I'm not going to look at anything again. I'll simply scull and keep my eyes looking at the bottom of the boat. You watch those two marks and tell me the moment they are not one above another."

She began sculling fast over the stern, and the *Amazon* moved in towards the rocks.

"The fork is to the right of the stump," sang out John.

Nancy sculled away, slightly altering her direction. "How is it now?" she said.

"In line."

She went on sculling.

"Fork showing on the left ... in line again ... showing on the left ... in line ... fork showing on the right ... in line."

Nancy never looked up, but altered the direction of the boat a little every time John said that the marks were out of line. The *Amazon* moved on between the rocks and came at last into the harbour.

"We're through," said John. "That was jolly good work."

"It's quite simple," said Captain Nancy. "Captain Flint taught us, last year when he was Uncle Jim, before he went bad. That's the way all harbours are marked, with two marks, showing how to steer into them. Really, of course, they ought to have lanterns on them, for coming in at night. With lanterns on the marks you could come in through the rocks even if it was perfectly dark."

"Is that what the pilot books mean by leading lights?" asked John.

"What are pilot books?" asked Nancy, and John was pleased to find that there were things that even Captain Nancy did not know.

They pulled up the *Amazon* and went back to the camp to take part in the feast. It was a very good feast. The sandwiches and sardines went well with the pemmican and the lemonade. By the time that was done the big kettle was boiling like anything, and it seemed a pity not to have tea with the cake.

Time went fast as the six mariners sat round the fire planning voyages. At last Captain Nancy looked up at the sun.

"We'd better be sailing," she said, "or there'll be more trouble with the natives. We've been late for supper twice this week already. This wind always goes and drops about sunset, and it's a tremendous way to row. Stir your stumps, Peggy."

"One of them's asleep," said Peggy.

"It'll wake up if you stir them both," said Captain Nancy. "Come on, lend a hand with that puncheon."

The empty barrel was easy to carry, but, to do the thing properly, they slung it on the oar as before. Titty carried the pirate flag for them. Roger carried the basket. The whole

crew of the *Swallow* went down to the harbour to see the
Amazons off.

The Amazons worked out of harbour, set their sail and, with
the fair wind that was still blowing, were soon slipping past the
northern end of the island. The Swallows had run back to the
look-out place to wave to them.

"War beginning tomorrow," shouted Captain Nancy.

"All right," shouted Captain John.

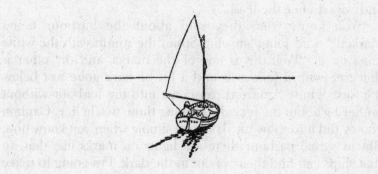

CHAPTER XII

LEADING LIGHTS

THAT night the Swallows were very late to bed. Soon after the *Amazon*'s little white sail had vanished beyond the Peak of Darien, Captain John took the hammer and a few nails and the two candle-lanterns and went to the harbour, with Mate Susan to help him, while the able-seaman and the boy washed and wiped after the feast.

"You know what they said about the harbour being marked?" said John, showing Susan the stump with the white cross on it. "Well this is one of the marks, and the other is that tree with a fork in it and a bit of bark gone just below the fork. Those Amazons can come into the harbour without bothering about the rocks by keeping those two in line. Captain Nancy did it to show me. It's quite simple when you know how. But in a real harbour there are lights on marks like that, so that ships can find their way in in the dark. I'm going to make the marks into leading lights, so that we can make a night attack on the Amazon and then find our way back, however dark it is."

He drove a nail into the middle of the white cross on the stump and hung one of the lanterns on it. Then he and Susan went to the foot of the forked tree. The fork was high above their reach.

"Are you going to climb up and put the lantern in the fork?" asked Susan.

"No, Mister Mate. It's no good doing that, for then only

you and I would be able to climb up and light it. We must have it somewhere where we can all light it. . . ."

"Except Roger," said the mate. "He isn't allowed to use matches."

"That's true," said Captain John. "We needn't make it lower than the highest Titty can reach. But if we make it too low it will be no good. We must be able to see it above the bushes. You go down the harbour and stand behind the stump and as near to the water as you can."

Susan went back and stood behind the stump, which was about ten yards from the water's edge. She stood on the edge of the water.

"Can you see the fork of the tree?" John called out to her.

"Yes," said Susan.

He put his hand on the trunk of the forked tree, as high up as he could reach.

"Can you see my hand?"

"Yes."

"Can you still see it?" He moved his hand slowly down the trunk of the tree.

"Now I can't," said Susan.

He raised it a few inches.

"I can see it now," said Susan.

"Blow your whistle for Titty," said Captain John, and Mate Susan blew her whistle. Titty and Roger came running. John held his hand where it was until they came. Then he asked Titty to try if she could reach it. She just could.

"Good," said Captain John.

"What for?" said Titty.

Captain John did not answer. He drove in a nail just above the place where his hand had been. Then he hung the second lantern on it.

"Now see if you can open the lantern."

Able-seaman Titty stood on tiptoe and opened the lantern.
"But what's it for?" she asked.

"You'll see as soon as it's dark," said Captain John.

"I can't reach it," said Roger, after trying.

"You won't have to," said Captain John.

"Not until you are allowed to use matches," said the mate,
"and by then you'll be tall enough."

As soon as it began to grow dark the whole crew of *Swallow*
were at the harbour again. John gave the able-seaman the
matches and she lit both lanterns, while the boy watched. Then
all four of them embarked.

"Roger ought to be in bed," said the mate.

"It won't take long," said Captain John, "and we can't leave
him alone."

"Anyway, I'm not sleepy," said Roger.

They rowed away down the lake. The dark came fast overhead. Stars shone out. Owls were calling. The edges of the lake
disappeared under the hills. They could see the outlines of the
hills, great black masses, pressing up into the starry sky. Then
clouds came up over the stars and they could not even see where
the hills ended and the sky began.

Suddenly high in the darkness they saw a flicker of bright
flame. There was another and then another, and then a pale
blaze lighting a cloud of smoke. They all looked up towards it
as if they were looking at a little window, high up in a black
wall. As they watched, the figure of a man jumped into the
middle of the smoke, a black, active figure, beating at the flames.
The flames died down, and it was as if a dark blind were drawn
over the little window. Then a new flame leapt up and again
the man was there, and then that flame died like the others
and there was nothing but the dark.

"It's savages," said Titty. "I was sure there must be some
somewhere in those woods."

LEADING LIGHTS

"It's the charcoal-burners," said John. "The natives at the farm were asking if we'd seen them. We'd have seen them before if we'd been sailing this way."

"They look like savages," said Titty. "Let's go and see them."

"We can't now, anyhow," said Mate Susan.

"How are we going to get home?" said Roger. "I can't see anything at all."

Captain John was also wondering the same thing. He could not be sure where they were. He could not see the lanterns on the marks behind the harbour, but that was natural enough, because they would be hidden by the high rocks unless the *Swallow* was opposite the entry. And, of course, he could not be quite sure that he could get in even if he could see the lights. He knew he ought to be able to. But, after all, he had never tried. It is one thing to row in using marks in daylight, when if anything goes wrong you can look about and see where you are, but quite another thing when you are wrapped up in darkness and have nothing to count on but the lights. Anyhow, the first thing to do was to find them. The sight of the charcoal-burners up on the hillside had shown him more or less where he was and which way the boat was pointing, but there were no stars to help him, and he was glad he had brought the compass.

He took a match and lit it and looked at the little compass, moving it round until the line marked at one side of it was opposite the dark end of the needle. That showed him where the north was. Happily, it was just where he had expected it to be. He pulled *Swallow* round and lit another match and had another look at the compass to make sure. Then he began rowing again, taking *Swallow* northwards up the lake.

"This isn't proper compass steering," he said. "We ought to have the compass fixed and a light shining on it all the time. What we really need is an electric torch. I wish I'd thought of getting one for a birthday present. Anyhow, all hands keep a look-out and sing out, anybody, as soon as our lanterns show."

A minute or two later Titty saw them, flickering among the trees and then disappearing again as they were hidden by the big rocks south of the island.

John paddled slowly on.

"There they are again," said Susan.

"Close together," said Titty.

John turned round from his rowing and had a good look at the two small stars twinkling over the water.

"Right," he said, and then, remembering Captain Nancy, "Now, I'm going to do nothing but row if you'll keep your eyes on the lights."

"We can't see anything else, anyhow," said Titty.

"Are they still close together?" asked John.

"Fairly close," said Susan.

"Which light is which side of which?" said John.

"What?" said Susan.

"Where is the top light?" asked Captain John.

"A bit to the left of the low one," said Susan.

John pulled a stroke or two, pulling a little harder with his right. "Sing out as soon as it is just above it."

"It's above it now. Now it's a bit to the right of it."

John pulled his left.

"Above it."

"Tell me the moment it is one side or the other."

He rowed on. Mate Susan, Able-seaman Titty, and the Boy Roger watched the lights and sang out the moment the top one showed a little to left or right of the lower one. With so many look-out men Captain John might have been content, but just once he looked round for himself and saw the two lights one above the other like the stop called a colon, which I am just going to make : there, like that. At last John just grazed a rock with his starboard oar.

"We must be close in now," he said. "I'm going to scull over the stern."

"The lights are exactly one above another," said Susan.

John had shipped his oars and was now sculling over the stern. Susan and Titty had wriggled out of the way. The boat moved on in the darkness.

"The lights are quite close to us," said Roger, and as he said it there was a gentle scrunch as the *Swallow*'s nose touched the soft, pebbly beach of the little harbour.

Captain John had used his leading lights for the first time, and had made his harbour in pitch dark.

"That is going to win us the war with the Amazons," he said with great delight. "It's the one thing they think we can't do, and we can. They think they are safe from us at night."

They scrambled ashore and unhooked the lanterns from the nails, moored *Swallow* by lantern-light, and by lantern-light found their way through the brambles and bushes back to the camp. Ten minutes later the lanterns were blown out, one in each tent, and about half a minute after that the whole camp was asleep.

CHAPTER XIII

THE CHARCOAL-BURNERS

NEXT day there was a dead calm, most unfit for war. Captain John turned over on his haybag and looked at the barometer, which was steady. He crawled out of his tent and looked at the sky. It was without a cloud. He went up to the look-out post and looked at the lake, which reflected the hills and the woods and the faraway farmhouses on the sides of the hills so closely that, as he found, if you looked at them through your own legs you could really hardly be sure which was real and which was reflection in the water. He went back to the camp and found the others getting up.

"Buck up, Titty," Roger was saying. "Remember the war's begun and the Amazons may be here at any minute."

"There's no wind," said Captain John, "and it looks as if it's going to be like this all day. They'll never come if there's no wind. And we can't try to do anything ourselves. It's too far to row. Today we needn't bother about the war. No wind, no war. It's an awful pity."

"May I row ashore for the milk with Titty?" asked Roger. "You said we might the first calm day." If there was to be no war, at least there were plenty of other things to do.

"All right," said Captain John, "but be careful not to bump her on a stone when you are landing."

"Of course," said the able-seaman.

So the able-seaman and the boy paddled *Swallow* out of harbour and rowed ashore in her. They rowed with one oar each, sitting side by side on the middle thwart. Then Roger rowed with both oars while Titty steered. Then Titty rowed with both oars while Roger steered. Their course was not a very straight one, but at last Captain John, who was swimming at the bathing-place but a little nervous about his ship, saw them going up the field carrying the milk-can.

When they came back the able-seaman rowed the whole way as hard as she could while the boy steered. Titty was in a hurry and had a good deal to say.

"Those were charcoal-burners we saw last night," she said. "I asked Mrs. Dixon if they were savages, and she said some people would say so. She says they live in huts they make themselves out of poles. She says they keep a serpent in a box. She says they would show it us if we went up the wood to see them. Do let's go."

"Mrs. Dixon says they won't be staying long in one place. They've nearly done where they are," said Roger. "We'd better go today."

"I'm sure they're better savages than any of our other natives," said Titty.

Susan looked up from her fire. "I don't see why we shouldn't go," she said. "The Amazons won't be coming. And we shall be taking *Swallow* with us, anyhow."

"Very good, Mister Mate," said Captain John. "If there is any wind we must come back, but while it's calm like this there'll be no war to bother about, and we may as well be explorers."

Soon after breakfast they took the mast and sails out of *Swallow* and rowed away. Roger was at his chosen post in the bows keeping a look-out. Captain John rowed, and Susan and Titty sat in the stern-sheets. They had the kettle and a knapsack of provisions stowed in the bottom of the boat, because if the calm weather held they meant to stay away most of the day and to bring back a fresh store of firewood. Firewood was getting difficult to find on the island and there was plenty of it along the high-water mark on the shores of the lake, and in calm weather they could put in anywhere to pick it up.

They rowed south from the island down the lake, where they had been last night in the dark. It looked very different in daylight. A great wood ran up the hillside on the eastern shore of the lake. Far up it they could see smoke curling slowly above the trees, a thin trickle of smoke climbing straight up. There, they knew, must be the savages they had seen in the night prancing in the smoke and beating down the flames. Today in the bright sunlight no flames were to be seen. There was the little trickle of smoke climbing into a tiny cloud above the trees. There was a faraway noise of wood-chopping. But that was all.

They found a good place to beach the *Swallow*, ran her nose ashore, pulled her well up and made her painter fast to a young oak tree growing near the water's edge.

"We won't take the kettle or the knapsack with us," said Mate Susan. "It's always better to make a fire on the shore than among the trees. We'll make a fire here when we come back, and we'll have dinner before getting the firewood, so that we shan't have to think about getting at the kettle and things while we are loading the ship."

"Oughtn't we to leave someone to keep guard?" asked Able-seaman Titty.

"You can stay if you want to," said Captain John, "but when we are high up on the hill we shall be able to see right up the lake. If we see the Amazons coming we can get back here quicker than they could get here rowing."

Titty, thinking of the savages she had come to see, hurriedly agreed that there was no need for a guard.

Then the whole party began scrambling up through the trees. They had not gone very far before they came to a road.

They crossed that and then the forest became much steeper. Sometimes it was a wonder how the little trees themselves clung on among the rocks. There were all sorts of trees. Here and there was a tall pine, but most of the trees were oaks and beeches and hazels and mountain ash. There was no path and the brambles on the ground and the long strings of honeysuckle twisting from branch to branch made it hard work pushing through the undergrowth.

"We'd better keep together," said Mate Susan, when Titty tried to take a line of her own.

"It's a real forest," said Roger.

"A jungle almost," said Titty.

"We ought to have an axe to blaze the trees so that we can be sure of finding our way back," said John, "but we can't go far wrong if we keep going straight down on the way back. That will bring us to the lake, anyhow, and once we're on the shore it'll be easy."

"What if we don't find the charcoal-burners?" asked Titty.

"Listen," said Captain John. They listened and could hear the steady plunk, plunk of an axe somewhere far above them. "We can't very well miss them, so long as they are making a noise like that."

They climbed on and on through the wood. Captain John went first, then Roger and Titty, then Mate Susan, to see that there were no stragglers. Rabbits showed their white scuts as they scampered away among the bushes. A squirrel chattered at them out of a pine tree. Roger chattered back at it.

"It's almost as good as a monkey," said Titty. "If only there were some parrots."

Just then there was a loud raucous squawking close in front of them and a tremendous flapping among the leaves, and a pair of jays flashed through the tops of the trees, showing for a moment white and black and pinky-grey and the bright blue bands on their wings.

"There are the parrots," said Roger. "Talking ones. Listen to them saying 'Pretty Polly', only it's in savage language, not ours."

At last they came to a track in the wood. It seemed to lead upwards towards the noise of the wood-chopping.

"Now we must make a blaze," said Captain John, "to show the place where we came into this track. Then we'll know where to turn off on our way down."

Titty pulled out her knife and cut a blaze on the side of a hazel. It was not a very big one.

"We might easily miss that," said the captain. "We must have something easier to see." He bent down two branches of the hazel and tied the ends of them to the tree, so that they made two big hoops at the side of the track.

"We're sure to see those," said Roger.

"We'll have a patteran as well," said Captain John.

"What's that?" asked Titty.

"It's what gipsies make to show each other which way they have gone. You take a long stick and a short one and put them in the road across each other, so that the long stick shows the way."

He cut two sticks and put the long one in the middle of the track pointing towards the hazel with the two bent boughs. The short stick he laid on the other, so that they made a cross.

"That's a patteran," he said.

"But suppose somebody kicks them away?" said Roger.

"Nobody would do it on purpose," said Susan.

"And if they did, there would still be John's hoops and my blaze," said Titty.

They got on much faster when they were walking along the track which wound up the side of the hill than they had when they were clambering through the bushes and trees. Presently the track came out into a clearing at a patch of flat ground. In the middle of the clearing was a big circle of black burnt earth.

"This is where the savages have had a corroboree," said Titty. "They cooked their prisoners on the fire and danced round them."

"Yelling like mad," said Roger.

On the other side of the clearing they found the track again. The noise of the chopping was now close at hand. A keen smell of smouldering wood tickled their nostrils. Suddenly they came out of the trees again on the open hillside. There were still plenty of larger trees, but the smaller ones and the undergrowth had been cut away. There were long piles of branches cut all of a length and neatly stacked, ready for the fire. There was one pile that made a complete circle with a hole in the middle of it. Forty or fifty yards away there was a great mound of earth with little jets of blue wood smoke spirting from it. A man with a spade was patting the mound and putting a spadeful of earth wherever the smoke showed. Sometimes he climbed on the mound itself to smother a jet of smoke near the top of it. As soon as he closed one hole another jet of smoke would show itself somewhere else. The noise of chopping had stopped just before the explorers came into the open.

"Look, look," cried Titty.

At the edge of the wood, not far from the smoking mound, there was a hut shaped like a round tent, but made not of canvas but of larch poles set up on end and all sloping together so that the longer poles crossed each other at the top. On the side of it nearest to the mound there was a doorway covered with a hanging flap made of an old sack. The sack was pulled aside from within and a little, bent old man, as wrinkled as a walnut and as brown, with long, bare arms covered with muscles, came out. He blinked at the explorers in the sunlight.

Roger took Titty's hand.

"Hullo, you!" said the little old man. "Come to have a look, have you? Glad to see you."

"Good morning," said Captain John.

"It is that," said the little old man, "it's a grand day."

"Good morning," said the rest of the Swallows.

"Same to you," said the old man. He seemed a very friendly savage. Roger let go of Titty's hand.

All the Swallows were staring at the hut.

"It's a Red Indian wigwam," said Titty.

"Like to look inside?" said the old man. "Folk generally what do," he added, almost to himself.

"May we?" said Titty, partly to the old man and partly to Mate Susan.

"Aye," said the old man, and as for Susan, she was as keen as Titty to see inside.

The old man took a corner of the flap of sacking and hooked it up on a nail on the outside of the wigwam.

"Come in," he said. "You'll get used to the dark in a minute."

The doorway was so low that Captain John had to bend. It was so low that in spite of the sunlight outside it was very dark in the hut. The Swallows went in one by one and stood together inside the doorway. The old man had gone in first, but they could hardly see him. They heard him chuckle.

"You'll see better than bats in a minute. Sit you down on yon bed."

Gradually their eyes grew accustomed to the darkness, and they saw that on each side of the hut a stout log divided off a place where there were rugs and blankets. Between the two logs there was an open space, where it looked as if there had been a small fire. The only light came through the doorhole. Not a speck of light came from between the poles of which the wigwam was made. Every chink had been well stuffed with moss. Overhead there hung a lantern, like their own camp lantern, from a hook at the end of a bit of wire. But it was not lit. High above them was pitch darkness, where the poles met each other at the pointed top of the hut. The old man was squatting on the log that shut off one of the bed-places. The Swallows sat in a row along the other.

"Do you live here always?" asked Susan.

"While we're burning," replied the old man.

"While you're burning the charcoal," said Susan.

"Aye," said the old man. "Someone has to be with the fire night and day, to keep him down like."

"Have you really got a serpent?" asked Titty.

"An adder? Aye," said the old man. "Like to see him?"

"Oh yes, please," said all the Swallows.

"Well, you're sitting on him," said the old man.

All the Swallows, even Captain John, jumped up as if they had sat on a pin. The old man laughed. He came across the hut and rummaged under the blankets and pulled out an old cigar-box.

"It's young Billy's adder," he said, "we'll take it out to him. Hi, Billy," he shouted from the doorhole, "let them have a look at your adder."

He carried the little box out of the hut and the Swallows followed. Young Billy gave a last pat or two to the smoking mound, and came to them. He was another old man, but not quite so old as the first.

"Dad been showing you round?" he said to the Swallows.

"Is he your son?" Roger asked the first old man.

"He is that, and got sons and grandsons of his own, too. You wouldn't think I was as old as all that. But I'm Old Billy and he's Young Billy."

THE SERPENT

"He doesn't look like a son," said Roger.

Young Billy laughed. "Let's have the box, Dad," he said, and Old Billy gave him the cigar-box. He put the box on the ground and knelt beside it. He undid the catch and lifted the lid. There was nothing to be seen but a lump of greenish moss. He took a twig and gently stirred the lump. There was a loud hiss, and the brown head of a snake shot out of the moss and over the side of the box. Its forked tongue darted in and out. Young Billy touched it gently with his twig. It hissed again and suddenly seemed to pour itself in a long, brown stream over the edge of the box. Young Billy dropped his twig and took a stick and picked the snake up on the stick and lifted it off the ground. Its tail hung down on one side of the stick and its head on the other. Its head swayed from side to side as it swung there, hissing and darting out its tongue. The Swallows shrank back from it but could not look away. Suddenly it began sliding over the stick. Young Billy was ready for it, and before it dropped on the ground he caught it on another stick.

"Is it safe to touch it?" asked Susan.

"Look," said Young Billy. He lowered the snake to the ground and put the stick in front of it. Instantly the snake struck at it open-mouthed.

"Never you go near an adder," said Young Billy. "There's plenty of them about. And you mind where you're stepping in the woods or up on the fell. They'll get out of your way if they see you, but if you happen to step on one, he'll bite, just as he did that stick. A bad bite it is too. There's many a one has died of it."

"What do you keep him for?" asked John.

"Luck," said Young Billy. "Always had one in the hut, ever since I can remember, and Dad, that's Old Billy here, can remember longer than me."

"Aye, we've always had an adder," said Old Billy, "and so

had my Dad, when he was at the burning, and he was burning on these fells a hundred years ago."

Young Billy neatly dropped the snake in its box and shut the lid on it. He held the box for the children to listen. They could hear the snake hissing inside. Then he gave the box back to Old Billy, who went off with it back into the hut.

A big puff of smoke rolled from the burning mound.

"Look there," said Young Billy. "Can't leave him a minute but he's out. Like the adder is fire. Just a bit of a hole and out he comes." He picked up his spade and went to the mound, where a small tongue of flame was licking a hole from inside. He put a spadeful of earth on the hole and patted it down.

"Why don't you let it burn, if you're burning?" said Titty. "We always want our fires to burn and sometimes they won't."

"We want ours to burn good and slow," said Young Billy. "If he burns fast he leaves nowt but ash. The slower the fire the better the charcoal."

Susan was watching carefully.

"Why doesn't it go out?" she asked.

"Got too good a hold," said Young Billy. "Once he's got a good hold you can cover a fire up and the better you cover him the hotter he is and the slower he burns. But if you let him have plenty of air there's no holding him."

"Could we do it with a little fire?" asked Susan. "If I cover it with earth will my camp fire burn all night?"

"Aye," said Young Billy, "if you want a fire to last, cover him with clods of earth and pour some water on them to damp them. He'll be alight in the morning, and he'll boil your kettle for you when you take the clods off him."

"I'll try it tonight," said Susan.

"Let me have the telescope," said Roger.

Captain John was looking through the telescope at the lake which lay far below them. From those high woods where the charcoal-burners had their fire and their wigwam of larch poles, the whole length of the lake could be seen. Far beyond Rio and its islands, the blue lake under the clear summer sky stretched away into the big hills. Away to the south the lake narrowed and narrowed until it became a winding river through green lowlands. A little cloud of white steam where the lake ended and river began showed where one of the lake steamers was resting by the pier there. Another steamer was moving down the lake by Darien. On this windless day the water was smooth and blue but astern of the steamer were two long, spreading waves, like a huge V moving down the lake and stretching from one shore to the other.

"Let me have the telescope," said Roger again, "I want to see our island."

"Wait a minute," said Captain John, "there's a boat close to it."

"It's not the Amazons, is it," said Titty, "coming to make a surprise attack?"

"No," said Captain John, "there's only a man in it. One of the natives probably, fishing. But we ought to be going down all the same. We've left *Swallow* all alone."

He gave Roger the telescope.

"You can't see the whole of our island," he said. "Part of it is hidden by the trees down there. But watch where that man goes to."

"Are you the children camping on the island below?" asked Young Billy. "I thought you were. You had those Blackett lasses with you yesterday, hadn't you? We saw their little boat. Hi! Dad!"

Old Billy came back from the wigwam.

"Dad," said Young Billy, "they're the young ones that have been camping on the island. Blackett's lasses were with them yesterday."

"Aye," said Old Billy, "I mind well when Mrs. Blackett, little Miss Turner she was then, came to see my fire and my hut when she was no bigger than what you are now, miss." He looked at Susan measuringly. "She and Master Jim. Eh! Eh! And now she's a grown woman with two lasses of her own."

"It's Master Jim I'm thinking of," said Young Billy. "It 'ud be a good thing to let him know what folk are saying."

"It would that," said Old Billy.

Young Billy turned again to John and Susan.

"Shall you be seeing those lasses again?" he asked.

"Yes," said John, "as soon as ever there's a wind for sailing. But we can't do anything in a calm like this."

"Well, you tell them to tell their Uncle Jim . . ."

"They can't," Titty broke in, "they're at war with him."

"They'll tell him right enough," said Young Billy. "You tell them to tell their Uncle Jim that Young Billy, that's me, sent him word to put a good padlock on that houseboat of his if he leaves it at nights. Down in the pub at Bigland yonder there was a deal too much talk going about that houseboat and what he has in it. Nobody in these parts would touch it, but when talk gets going as far as Bigland, you never know who hears it. There's more than plenty of wild young lads that are up to anything without thinking twice.

"Maybe nowt'll come of it," he went on, "but if anything did happen, I wouldn't like to think we hadn't told him. I was going down to see him myself, but I can't leave the fire for a day or two yet, and if you'll tell the lasses, that's as good."

"We'll tell them," said John.

"You won't forget?" said Young Billy.

"No," said Susan, pulling out her handkerchief. "Not with this." She tied a big knot in one corner of it.

"I can't see the boat with the man in it any more, because of the trees," said Roger.

John took the telescope. "We ought to be going down, anyway," he said.

Susan turned politely to the old men. "Thank you very much for letting us come to see you. We have enjoyed ourselves very much."

"And thank you for showing us the serpent," said Titty.

They said "Goodbye," and the Billies, the two old men, one very old and the other older still, said, "Goodbye to you all."

The Swallows started on their way back into the steep woods.

"Don't forget to tell them lasses about their Uncle Jim," Young Billy called after them.

"We won't forget," shouted Susan, and waved her handkerchief with the knot on the end of it.

CHAPTER XIV

THE LETTER FROM CAPTAIN FLINT

THE Swallows were back in real life, almost before they were
out of sight of the charcoal-burners.

"They're the finest savages we ever met," said Titty. "I
expect the serpent is for witchcraft. Medicine men, I should
think they are. They're so old. Medicine men from a wandering tribe from beyond the ranges."

For a minute or two she was silent. Then suddenly she
exclaimed, "Bother the Amazons!"

"Why?" asked Susan.

"Because the Amazons discovered them too. They discovered our island. There's nothing left for us to discover for
ourselves."

"Well, we did discover them," said Susan, "and they showed
us their adder."

Titty was cheered by this. "Perhaps they never let the
Amazons into their tribal secrets. Perhaps the Amazons have
never seen their serpent. Perhaps it's all right and we really are
the proper discoverers. Just seeing a person is nothing."

"Let's galumph," said Roger.

"Come on," said Titty.

Galumphing, which is partly jumping and partly galloping,
is a quick way of going downhill.

It was such a quick way that Able-seaman Titty and the Boy
Roger passed the patteran and the bent and tied hazel branches
without seeing them. Captain John passed them too. He was

wondering what he ought to do about warning the retired pirate about putting a padlock on his houseboat. What would the Amazons say about it? If Captain Nancy wanted to seize the houseboat by a surprise attack when the pirate was somewhere ashore, she would certainly rather it were not locked up. Captain John galumphed half-heartedly. Ought he to have told the two Billies that they were talking not to friends but to enemies of the houseboat man, who, for the present at least, was not the Blackett lasses' Uncle Jim, but Captain Flint, against whom Amazons and Swallows had concluded a solemn alliance. He galumphed half-heartedly. But even though he was not galumphing with heart and soul, when it is easy to get so giddy that you can see nothing at all and to go so fast downhill that you can hardly stop yourself, he never noticed his own patteran. Susan, however, saw it. She had begun looking out for it as soon as she was in the path through the trees, and on that account her galumphing could hardly be called galumphing at all.

She came last down the track and found that the galumphing feet of the others had kicked the patteran aside. She would not have been sure of it herself if she had not seen the two hazel branches bent into hoops and then Titty's blaze in the side of the hazel tree.

"John!" she called.

There was no answer but the sound of galumphing feet far away down the winding path.

She took out her whistle and blew it as loud as she could.

The noise of galumphing stopped. She blew it again.

She heard John shout, "Hi! Titty! Roger!"

She blew it again three times.

John came slowly back up the path and after him the able-seaman and the boy, all three of them out of breath.

"You passed your own patteran," said Susan. "It's here."

"So I did," said Captain John. "I was thinking of something else. It's a good thing you saw it."

"That path might have taken us anywhere," said Titty.

"Where is the patteran?" said Roger. "Somebody has kicked it away. Perhaps it was me. Let's put it right again."

"No, of course not," said Captain John. "We put it there for ourselves to find our own way back. If we were to leave it now it would show the savages the way we had gone. We must unfasten these boughs too." He cut the strings and the boughs sprang up again. "Now there's nothing but the blaze, and it's a very little one. No one will know where we left the path."

"If they were good trackers," said Titty, "they could follow our footprints."

"It's a good thing really that we went further than the patteran," said Susan. "Our footprints will throw them off the scent. They'll go on and on down the path."

"On and on," said Roger.

"To the end of the world," said Titty.

"We mustn't make any marks when we turn off the path," said Susan, "that might show them."

"The proper way is to jump," said John. He took a flying leap off the path and into the wood. "Now, you three, all jump off the path at different places."

They all jumped and, having thus thrown off the pursuit of all possible enemies, they came together and began climbing down through the steep wood. They slipped and stumbled and saved themselves from falling by holding to the stems of the trees.

Roger spoke privately to Titty.

"But were the charcoal-burners enemies?" he said.

"No. Not just then," said Titty, "but, of course, they might be."

"I liked them," said Roger.

"So did I," said Titty, "especially the serpent. But they were savages all the same. The serpent showed it. Besides, they're no good if they aren't savages."

"But they don't really eat people," said Roger.

"They may have eaten hundreds of thousands," said Titty. They came to the road and crossed it.

"I see water," said John.

"The sea," shouted Titty.

A moment later they came out of the trees on the shore of the great lake. They looked round for *Swallow* and saw her where they had left her, about a hundred yards away.

"Properly," said Captain John, "we ought to have made marks all the way up, so that we could have come out exactly at the same place. But we've done it near enough."

"Hullo," said Susan, "there's one of the native boats close to our island."

John pulled out the telescope and looked through it.

"It's all right," he said, "it's going the other way. Probably a fisherman. When it's calm like this they just row along the shore and tow a spinner to catch pike."

"Sharks," said Roger.

"The first thing to do," said Mate Susan, "is to make a fire on the shore and have our grub. Then we can gather firewood and stow it in *Swallow*."

"Right, Mister Mate," said Captain John. "All hands to gather firewood. We can get enough for the fire and then go on gathering firewood while the mate is boiling the kettle."

Mate Susan built a small fireplace of stones on the beach close by *Swallow*. The others gathered dry sticks that had been left all along the high-water mark. Susan took a few handfuls of dry leaves and moss. She put them in the middle of her fireplace and built a little wigwam over them with bits of dried reeds from last year. It was like a little copy of the charcoal-burners' hut. Then she lit the moss and the reeds blazed up, while she built another wigwam over the reeds, this time of small sticks, all meeting at the middle over the blaze. When they caught fire and began to crackle she piled bigger sticks against the small ones. In a few minutes she had a strong fire. At one side of the fireplace she had put two big stones, and on these she balanced the kettle so that most of it was over the flames. She stayed by the fire, putting more and more sticks on it and keeping the flames as much under the kettle as possible, while the others, scattering along the beach, gathered as much firewood as they could carry. It lay there, ready for picking up. There was no need to look for it, and soon the pile of firewood was growing much faster than Susan used it up for the boiling of her kettle.

It was very hot, and the smoke of the fire went straight up. Even so some of it got into her eyes, and the sharp smell of it got into her nose and mouth. But it was not such hot work boiling the kettle as it was gathering firewood, and presently Roger said, "It must be boiling now." Titty threw a bundle of firewood on the growing pile. "It's boiling now, isn't it?" she said. "I'm too hot to gather any more."

"It'll change its tune in a minute," said the mate.

"Like the cuckoo," said Titty, "except that kettles change their tune as soon as they boil, and don't wait till June."

Just then the kettle did change its tune. Susan blew her whistle to let Captain John know that grub was ready. "Sit down, you fo'c'sle hands," she said to the able-seaman and the boy. They sat down. Captain John came back, very hot, with a huge bundle of firewood on his back. He had doubled a long piece of string and brought it round the sticks to keep them together.

After dinner they went on gathering firewood. The captain and the able-seaman and the boy gathered it, and Susan sorted it and packed it in *Swallow*. It is always the mate's business to see to the stowage of cargo. Presently, when they had gathered all the best firewood on that stretch of beach, they embarked, and rowed along the shore and brought her in again in a bay, the shores of which were brown with dry sticks. *Swallow* was soon so full of firewood that there was hardly room for her crew.

"She won't hold much more," said the mate.

"She's down to her load line already," said the captain.

"That'll do, then," said the mate, but just then came Titty, dragging after her the whole of a small dead tree that had been blown down in the great storm of the last winter. It was quite dry and fine for firewood, and nobody wanted to leave it behind.

"We'll have to carry it as deck cargo," said Captain John.

Swallow was already so laden that they could hardly push her off. The mate ordered Titty and Roger aboard, and sent them to the stern. Then he and the captain took their shoes and stockings off, and, one each side, pulled *Swallow* out until she floated. It was very unpleasant walking without shoes and stockings on the stones, but pleasant to feel the water.

"I want to take my shoes and stockings off," said Roger.

"You can't now," said the mate.

"Wait till we get back to Wild Cat Island," said the captain, splashing ashore to fetch Titty's tree. "Then you can take your shoes and stockings off, and help to discharge cargo. And then we'll all bathe before supper."

Meanwhile, Titty and Roger were clambering over the cargo to settle themselves in the bows. John brought the tree, and with Susan's help balanced it amidships, sticking out on either side. Then he and Susan came aboard. Rowing was impossible, because of the deck cargo. Captain John carefully pulled out one oar, and paddled with it over the stern.

"It's a good thing it's so calm," said the mate, looking at the water, which was not very far below the gunwale.

LOADING FIREWOOD

Sculling over the stern is slower than rowing, but in the dead calm *Swallow* moved easily, heavily loaded though she was, and no water came aboard, though some nearly did when Roger suddenly changed his mind about the side of the boat that he liked best.

"We'll take her to the old landing-place," said Captain John. "That's a good place for landing a cargo, and we want the wood handy for the camp."

"It would be a dreadful business carrying it all the way from the harbour," said the mate.

So *Swallow* was carefully sculled up the lake to the island, and beached at the old landing-place. Titty and Roger had pulled off their shoes and stockings before they arrived there, and two pairs of shoes and two pairs of rolled-up stockings went flying ashore as soon as the ship touched the ground. A moment later the whole ship's company was in the water, pulling up the ship and discharging her cargo. The mate settled down to make a neat stack of the wood like the long piles they had seen by the wigwam of the charcoal-burners. Titty's tree was laid aside to be broken up later. Then, when all the sizeable sticks had been taken out, Captain John went aboard the *Swallow* to pick up all the small bits and chips and broken twigs and dead leaves that were lying all over the bottom boards. It is surprising what a mess a ship is in after carrying a cargo of any kind, and small firewood is as untidy a cargo as you can have. It was a long time before *Swallow* looked as neat and trim as she had done when they had rowed away that morning. When at last there was not a dead leaf or a twig as big as a match to be seen in her, John pushed her off, and paddled her round to the harbour. He took the mast from where it had been hidden in the bushes, and stepped it again. He put the sails aboard, and tried the halyards to see that the traveller on the mast was working properly. It would never do for the wind to get up and the *Swallow* not to be ready to put to sea at a moment's notice. Then he walked through the trees to join his crew at the other end of the island.

They had already stacked the wood, and close beside the fireplace Susan had heaped up a lot of pieces of turf.

"What's that for?"

"That's to keep the fire in, like the charcoal-burners do," said Susan. "I'm going to try it tonight."

John walked on to his tent.

He stopped suddenly.

"Someone's been here."

In the middle of the doorway of his tent a stick had been stuck into the ground, and in a cleft at the top of the stick there was a small folded piece of white paper.

The others came running. John opened the piece of paper. On it was written in big plain letters:

"Called to tell you that you had jolly well better leave my houseboat alone. Once is quite enough. No joking.

James Turner."

"But we've never touched his houseboat," said Susan.

"Of course we haven't," said John.

"He's a beast," said Roger.

"That must have been his boat we saw," said John, "the one I thought was a fisherman. First he goes and tells the natives we've been bothering him. And now he creeps into our camp when we're not there. . . ."

"We ought to have gone with the Amazons and sunk him at once," said Titty. "It's the proper thing to do. You take the treasure out and sink the galleon or burn it to the water's edge. We could have saved the parrot."

"What are we to do about it?" asked Susan.

"We must hold a council with the Amazon pirates," said Captain John. "They know him. He's their enemy as well as ours."

"Let's go and row round him and shout, 'Death to Captain Flint,'" said Titty. "That'll show him what we think of him."

"We were doing nothing to him at all," said John. "We were even bringing a message for him from the charcoal-burners . . . the one they gave us for the Amazons. I wish there was a wind. We can't go to them and they can't come to us. I don't know what we ought to do."

He read the letter again. Then Susan and Titty read it.

"He doesn't even sign his real name," said Titty. "That shows he's up to no good." She ran into the other tent and came out with a pencil. "Let's put his proper name on it," she said. Susan gave her the letter and Titty wrote after the words "James Turner" "Captain Flint" in even larger letters.

"We can't do anything about it now," said Captain John gloomily. "Let's bathe."

In two minutes all *Swallow*'s ship's company were splashing about by the landing-place. Captain Flint's letter was forgotten in the water, but Captain John remembered it long before he was dry. He hardly listened at supper while the others were talking of the snake and the charcoal-burners. Last thing at night he went up to the look-out station. The sun set in a clear sky behind the sharp edges of the western hills. The stars as they came out were reflected in still water. There was not a sign of wind. He went down to the camp, undressed and wriggled into the blankets on his haybag. Roger in the blankets on the other haybag was already asleep. John heard Susan say, "Half a minute before lights out. I want to damp the earth over my fire." He heard the hiss of water on hot ashes. He heard Susan come back into her tent. "Ready now," she called. "Right. Good night. Lights out," he replied, and blew out his lantern. For a long time he could not sleep, and when at last he did disturbing thoughts of Captain Flint bothered him even in his dreams.

CHAPTER XV

CAPTAIN JOHN VISITS CAPTAIN FLINT

THE first thing John did when he woke in the morning was to listen. He could hear Roger's breathing somewhere in the blankets on the other haybag. He could hear a wren quarrelling with some other bird on the island. But he could not hear any rustling of leaves. He could not hear any noise of water on the shores. It was another day of absolute calm. He rolled over and looked at the barometer. It had hardly moved. No, it was another calm day, and the Swallows and Amazons were held apart by long miles of windless, useless water. What was he to do about Captain Flint? But just then he heard one noise that puzzled him, a little noise, surprising, uncertain. It was the crackle of fire. He sniffed. He could smell the fire, too, the same sharp, pleasant smell that had hung about the charcoal-burners' camp. He crawled out of his blankets, and walked out of the tent, rubbing the sleep from his eyes. The mound of earth that was the mate's fire was smoking. Some of the clods on it had fallen in. Some were blackened. But in the middle of them the fire was still alight, and making little noises like a waking bird.

"Hullo, Mister Mate," called Captain John. "Your fire's still burning."

"What?" came sleepily from Susan's tent.

"Rouse up, and come and look at your fire. It's burned all night."

"Has it? Good," said Susan. "I was afraid I'd damped the earth too much."

"Come out and look at it."

"In a minute," said the mate. "What about filling the kettle? I used all the water last night to damp the fire."

John picked up the kettle, and went down to the landing-place. He dipped the spout of the kettle under, so that water came into the kettle through the spout instead of through the hole at the top where the lid is. If he had simply dipped the whole kettle, the water would have poured in, bringing with it any scum that might be floating about. By dipping the spout, he drew his water from below the surface. By the time he came back with the full kettle, Susan was already busy at her fire, pulling aside what was left of the earth clods, and putting new sticks on the red fire that was underneath.

Titty was looking out of her tent.

"Let's keep it alight for ever and ever," she said. "We will keep it burning, all our lives, and then our children, and then their children. It'll be like the fire in a savage temple that never goes out at all."

"Probably in temples they have oil lamps," said Susan. "They have them in some churches. This is a real fire."

"Well, it hasn't gone out either," said Titty, half asleep.

The fire blazed up well, and Susan hung the kettle over it.

"I think I can leave it while I bathe," she said.

"Come on, Roger," said Captain John, reaching into his tent and pulling the blankets off the boy, "let's see you swim with both feet on the bottom."

"One," said Roger, "and not all the time."

Two minutes later all the Swallows were in the water.

"Try swimming on your back," said John.

"Can't," said Roger.

"It's easy. Stand like this in the water, leaning back. Then put your ears under."

Roger leant back.

"Ears right under," said John.

"They are," said Roger.

Even as he said it, there was a wild splashing, and Roger disappeared. He was up again at once, spluttering.

"I couldn't keep my feet on the bottom," he said. "They came up of themselves."

"I knew they would," said John. "If you hadn't doubled up you'd have floated."

Titty was swimming round them like a dog, paddling with her arms and legs, not in pairs, but one after another. "Try it again, Roger," she said.

"I'll put a hand under the back of your neck so that your mouth won't go under," said John.

Roger lent back once more, and rested his head on John's hand. He pressed his ears under, and again his feet floated up.

"Kick," said John. "Kick like a frog. Kick again. You're swimming. Well done."

"You really did swim on your back," said Titty, as Roger struggled to his feet again.

"I know I did," said Roger. "Watch now." He leant back towards the shore, put his ears under, and kicked hard. He got three good kicks in before he ran aground. He had swum three yards at least.

But Mate Susan had not seen him. She had just had a few minutes' good hard swim, and then had run up to the camp again to dry and dress, and see to her fire and the kettle at the same time. There were eggs to boil, and bread and butter to cut. The mate's job is not an easy one, with a hungry crew to feed. Roger looked round for her, splashed out of the water, and ran, prancing, up to the camp to tell her that he had swum on his back.

"Did you really swim?" said the mate.

"Aye, aye, sir," said the boy. "Three kicks, not touching anything. Come down, and I'll show you."

"Can't now," said the mate. "You dry yourself and help to get the breakfast. We'll bathe again in the middle of the day, and you can show me then. Now skip, and get the captain's chronometer out of his tent." He got it. "Hi!" she called, as he capered off again. "Take the milk-can down to the *Swallow*. It's time someone went across to the farm."

John and Titty went across to the mainland to fetch the milk from Mrs. Dixon's. Roger and the mate between them had breakfast ready when they got back.

After breakfast John called a council for a second time.

"It's about Captain Flint again," he said.

"Do let's go and sink him," said Titty.

"Shut up, you fo'c'sle hands," said the mate.

"It's not altogether about his letter," said Captain John, "it's about what the charcoal-burners said. You see, there's no wind. We shan't see the Amazons today, so we can't give them the message. That means that the houseboat man . . ."

"Captain Flint . . ." said Titty.

"Able-seaman Titty, will you shut up?" said the mate.

"It means that he won't know what the charcoal-burners wanted him to know. Don't you think we ought to tell him without waiting for the Amazons? You see," he went on, "it's all native business. It's got nothing to do with us, even if he is a beast, and thinks we've been touching his houseboat. We haven't and we've got an alliance against him with the Amazons, but all the same, about this native business, it wouldn't do not to tell him. We were to have told the Amazons. They're not here, so I think we'd better tell him ourselves."

"Would the Amazons tell him?" asked Susan.

"I'm sure they would. They wouldn't like anyone else to break into his houseboat, specially when they're going to break into it themselves. They've broken into it before, when they took the green feathers. I've been thinking about it, and I'm sure they wouldn't like natives breaking into it. I'm going to tell him."

"You could declare war on him at the same time."

Captain John cheered up. "Yes," he said, "so I could. The Amazons couldn't help being pleased with that. Yes. I'll tell him what the charcoal-burners said. That's got nothing to do with us. It's native business. Then I'll tell him we haven't ever been near his boat. Then I'll tell him that we declare war on him and are going to do everything we can against him."

"Let him look to himself," said Titty. "That's the proper thing to say."

"We ought to give the message, anyhow," said Susan. "We promised we would, and I tied a knot in my handkerchief and showed it to the charcoal-burners. That's a double promise. Shall we all go?"

"I'll go by myself," said Captain John, "then he can't think it's an attack. He'll know it's only a parley."

And so it happened that on the second day of the calm Captain John once more took the mast and the sail out of *Swallow*. Only this time he rowed north instead of south, and he rowed alone. He did not like going, because he was worried about what the Amazons would think, and after all it was their message. Also he did not like going to deliver a message to an enemy who had stirred up the natives against them so unjustly. He remembered what Mrs. Dixon had said. Further, he held the houseboat man for a bad kind of enemy because he had come to the camp while the Swallows were all away. Still, there was the message, a native message. It would be more uncomfortable not to deliver it than to deliver it. It would soon be done anyway. Captain John waved as he passed the camp, and then settled down to work, rowing steadily, navy stroke, with a smart jerk as he lifted his oars from the water.

It did not take him long to reach the southern point of Houseboat Bay. He rounded it, looked over his shoulder to see that he was heading straight for the houseboat, and then looked over the stern of *Swallow* to the opposite shore of the lake. Directly over the stern on the far side of the lake there was a white cottage. On the hillside above the cottage was a group of tall pines. He chose the one that seemed exactly over the chimney of the white cottage. The cottage and the tree would be like the marks leading into the harbour on Wild Cat Island. So long as the tree was directly over the cottage and over the stern of the *Swallow*, he knew he would be heading as he was, straight for the houseboat. He made it a point of honour not to have a look round to make sure of his direction.

He plugged away at the oars again, navy stroke, not hurrying but keeping his timing as regular as a clock. It was another point of honour that the oars should not splash when they went into the water. Yes, he was rowing quite well. But meanwhile he was thinking of what he should say to the houseboat man. The message was native business, not real, so that it would not do to call the houseboat man Captain Flint. That would come afterwards with the declaration of war. He would have to begin by calling him Mr. Turner. Then there was that beastly note. That would come in the Captain Flint part of the talk. Yes. The first thing to do would be to give the message from the charcoal-burners. Then, when the native business was done with, he could talk about the note, and declare war.

Suddenly he heard the squawk of a parrot and a shout, quite close to him.

"Look out! Where are you going to?"

Captain John backwatered sharply, and looked round. He was a dozen yards or so from the houseboat. He pulled with his right, and backwatered with his left, so as to turn *Swallow* round. Then, backwatering gently with both oars he brought her, stern first, nearer to the houseboat.

The houseboat man was on deck, lowering a large suitcase into a rowing boat that lay alongside. In the bows of the rowing boat was a large cage with the green parrot in it. The houseboat man, in very towny clothes, was lowering his suitcase into the stern. A motor car was waiting on the road which ran close to the shore at the head of the little bay. It was clear that the parrot and the houseboat man were presently going away.

John was just going to say "Good morning," or something like that, but the houseboat man spoke first.

"Look here," he said, "did you find a note I left in your camp yesterday?"

"Yes," said John.

"Can you read?"

"Yes."

"Did you read it?"

"Yes."

"Well, I meant what I said in it. I told you to leave the houseboat alone, and here you come the very next morning. Once is quite enough. Just you lay to your oars and clear out. Fast. And don't come here again."

"But . . ." said John.

"And if you've got any more of those fireworks, the best thing you can do with them is to drop them in the lake. If you must let them off, let them off in a field."

"But I haven't," said John.

"That was the last one, was it? Well, it did enough damage. How would you like someone to come and let off a firework

CAPTAIN JOHN BACKWATERED

in your boat and set fire to the sail or something? Look at the mess you made of my cabin roof."

There was a large burnt patch on the top of the curved cabin roof. The houseboat man pointed to it indignantly.

"But I've never had any fireworks," said John, "at least not since last November."

"Oh, look here," said the houseboat man, "that won't do."

"And I've never been near your boat before, never as near as I am now."

"Listen," said the houseboat man. "When you came and lit that beastly thing that made such a mess of my cabin roof, you cleared off round the point. I came up and put the fire out, and guessed at once what you had done. But you may not know that about half an hour afterwards I came on deck again, and saw you sailing across the mouth of the bay. Think I can't recognise a boat when I see it? You've the mast out of her today, but I'd seen her several times before, and you in her."

"We saw you that day. You were shaking your fist."

"Ah. You saw that, did you?"

"But I didn't set fire to your boat. I never touched your boat. This is the first time I've been near her, except once sailing to Rio, when you were sitting on the deck, and saw us too."

"Who did set fire to her, then?" said the houseboat man.

John said nothing. It would never do to give the Amazons away.

"There were four of you in the boat," said the houseboat man. "But you were the biggest. You ought to know better than to let the others do a thing like that, even if you didn't do it yourself."

"We didn't do it at all," said John.

"Clear out," said the houseboat man. "I've nothing more to say to you."

"But I came to tell you . . ."

"Clear out," said the houseboat man. "I don't like talking to liars."

"But . . ."

"Clear out, and don't come near the houseboat again."

John choked. He went very red and stood up in the boat.

"Go away," said the houseboat man. "I'm busy."

John sat down and rowed away out of the bay. He rowed much harder than before, and his rowing was not so regular. He even forgot about navy style. He was out of breath and very hot when he brought the *Swallow* back to the landing-place at Wild Cat Island.

The others met him there.

"Did you see the parrot?" asked Titty.

"What did he say when you gave him the message?" asked Susan.

"Did you go aboard the houseboat?" asked Roger.

"I didn't give him the message," said John. "He wouldn't let me."

"Did you declare war on him?" asked Titty.

"No," said John. He pulled *Swallow* up on the beach.

"He called me a liar," he said, and went off by himself to the look-out place. The others looked at each other, but did not follow him.

"I always said we ought to sink the houseboat," said Titty.

CHAPTER XVI

THE BIRTHDAY PARTY

AFTER about half an hour at the look-out place, Captain John felt himself again. After all, nothing could be done about Captain Flint without the help of the Amazons. He was their uncle, not the uncle of the Swallows. If the Swallows had had an uncle, he would have been different. John had thought of writing a letter to the houseboat man, but he was no good at writing. Susan was even worse. Titty was the one for that, and Titty would not write the sort of letter that was needed. Bother the calm. If only there had been a wind and a chance of meeting the Amazons he would never have had to go by himself to give Captain Flint his message, and the thing would never have happened. But the big hills far up the lake helped to make him feel that the houseboat man did not matter. The hills had been there before Captain Flint. They would be there for ever. That, somehow, was comforting. John cheered up, and decided that it was a good day for swimming round the island.

He went down to the camp.

"Susan," he said, "it's a lovely day for swimming round the island."

"Are you sure you can?" said Susan.

"I'm going to try," said John. "I can come ashore if I get too tired."

The others came down to the landing-place to see him start. He swam at first with the side-stroke, fast and splashy. It was easy work to swim to the rocks at the low end of the island.

Titty and Roger ran to the harbour, and climbed on a high rock to see him swimming round well outside the rocks that guarded the passage. "Hurrah," they shouted as they saw him go by. Then they ran to the western side of the island, where the rock dropped straight down like a wall into deep water. John came swimming along, using breast stroke now for a change, quietly and not hurrying. He began to feel that it was a very long way down that western side.

"Stick to it," shouted Titty.

"Go it," shouted Roger.

Susan came up from the camp to the tall pine at the northern end of the island, and looked down from the high rocky wall. John had almost reached the look-out place. He was moving very slowly.

"You can get ashore just here if you're done," she called, "then you can rest and go on again."

John tried to wave his hand, and got a lot of water into his mouth in doing so. He turned on his back and floated, blowing like a whale.

"You're nearly round," shouted Titty, who had run up to the look-out place and joined Susan.

John began again, kicking with his legs and using his arms only a little. He was round the head of the island. He went on swimming on his back. He turned over and lifted his head. For one moment he saw the landing-place, and *Swallow* lying there pulled up on the beach. His head went down, and he got more water in his mouth. He blew and spluttered. Still the landing-place was really not so very far off. He turned on his side and swam on. Somehow his arms would not pull, and his legs would not gather up and kick as hard as they ought to.

"You've done it," shouted Titty.

"Come on," shouted Roger.

Again John caught a glimpse of the landing-place. He must

do it now. Suddenly he felt stronger again. He swam in towards the beach. He had started from this side of *Swallow*. Well, he would not touch bottom until he was on the other side. Another two strokes and he gripped *Swallow*'s port gunwale, touched the bottom, and crawled ashore, coughing, spitting, shivering, spluttering, and triumphant. Titty and Roger cheered. John was too much out of breath to speak.

"Here's a towel," said Susan. "I've hotted it by the fire."

He put it round his shoulders. He rubbed first one arm and then the other. He felt much better.

"Well, I thought I could do it," he said at last. The day was a good day after all, in spite of Captain Flint.

Susan was just thinking of getting dinner ready when there was a shout from Titty, who had taken the telescope up to the look-out place just in case of cormorants, pirates, or anything else worth looking at.

"A native boat," she shouted. "It's Mother. It's the female native. She's got her little native with her, and the nurse belonging to it."

The Swallows all ran to the look-out point. The female native herself was rowing. She had already passed Houseboat Bay. Vicky and Nurse were sitting in the stern of the rowing boat. The Swallows had one look and then rushed back to tidy their tents and put the camp in order. They spread their blankets neatly over their haybags, and turned down the tops of them. Susan put a lot of fresh wood on the fire. There was not much else to do. Then they ran back to the look-out place. The female native was already quite near. They waved. Nurse and Vicky waved back. The female native couldn't wave, because she was rowing. She passed the head of the island, and a moment later was pulling in to the landing-place. The Swallows were there before her.

"Sit still, Nurse, till I get ashore," said the female native.

The Swallows had already seized the boat and pulled it up. There was a big hamper in the boat just forward of the rowing thwart. The female native climbed round it.

"Welcome to Wild Cat Island," said Titty.

"Welcome, welcome," shouted the others.

There was a general scramble. Mother might be a native, but it was all right to kiss her none the less.

The female native counted the Swallows after she had kissed them. "One, two, three, four," she said. "No one drowned yet. That's a good thing, because it's somebody's birthday."

"Whose? Whose?" they shouted. "It can't be John's, because he's just had one."

"No, it isn't John's."

"Is it mine?" said Roger.

"No," said Mother.

"Is it mine?" said Titty.

"No."

"It can't be mine," said Susan, "because mine's on New Year's Day, and this is summer."

"Whose is it?" they asked.

"Vicky's, of course," said the female native. "She's two. Rather too young for a birthday, really, so I've brought a present for each of you."

"What about Vicky?" said Susan.

"Vicky's got a lamb and an elephant. I took her to the shop, and she chose them herself. Now then, help me out with the hamper, so that Nurse and Vicky can come ashore."

"It's a very heavy hamper," said Titty.

"The presents are not," said the female native. "The presents are very small."

"Then what's in the hamper?" said Roger.

"Birthday feast, of course," said the female native.

"Hurrah, no cooking," said Susan.

"Aha," laughed the female native. "I thought you'd get tired of that. But I must say you seem to have managed very well. No illness in the camp?"

"None at all," said Susan, "and I'm not sick of cooking, but it's jolly not to have to just for once."

"Of course we've had plague and yellow fever and Black Jack and all the other illnesses belonging to desert islands," said Titty. "But we cured them all at once."

"That's right," said the female native, "never let an illness linger about."

They carried the hamper up to the camp. Nurse brought Vicky ashore, and they all wished her many happy returns. Vicky had the elephant with her. She forgot her lamb in the boat, and it had to be fetched later. Vicky liked the elephant better than the lamb because it was smaller. The lamb was so large it was always being put down and forgotten.

The female native opened the hamper. On the top, well wrapped up in tissue paper, was a birthday cake, a huge one with Victoria written in pink sugar on the white icing and two large cherries in the middle, because Vicky was two years old. Then there was a cold chicken. Then there was a salad in a big pudding-basin. Then there was an enormous gooseberry tart. Then there was a melon. Then there was a really huge bunch of bananas which the female native tied in a tree as if it was growing there. "You can pick them just as you want them," she said.

Then there were more ordinary stores, a tin of golden syrup, two big pots of marmalade and a great tin of squashed-fly biscuits. Squashed-fly biscuits are those flat biscuits with currants in them, just the thing for explorers. Then there were three bunloaves and six bottles of ginger beer.

"Hurrah for the grog," said Titty.

"But where are the presents?" said Roger.

"I told you they were very little ones," said the female native. "Here they are."

She dug down at the bottom of the hamper and brought up four small brown paper parcels, each about as big as an ordinary envelope and as fat as a matchbox.

"The nights are getting very dark now," she said, "with no moon, so I thought perhaps you could do with some electric torches. You mustn't keep them lit for long at a time or they'll soon wear out. But for signalling, or looking for something in the dark. . . ."

"Mother," cried Captain John, "how did you guess we were wanting them? They've come exactly at the right moment."

The other were flashing their torches at once, but they were not much good in the sunlight. Roger and Titty went into the mate's tent and crawled under the groundsheet to get some darkness.

When they came back, rubbing the mud from their knees, for under the groundsheet it had been very damp and sticky, the female native said, "I've had a letter from Daddy, and he reminded me of something. Can Roger swim yet?"

"He swam on his back for the first time today," said John. "Three good strokes. Once he can do that he will be able to swim on his front quite easily."

"Shall I show you?" said Roger, and was for running down to the landing-place at once.

"Before we go home," said the female native. "Not this minute. Well, Daddy said that Roger was to have a knife of his own as soon as he could swim, and I brought it with me in case he could."

She dipped into the hamper for the last time and pulled out a knife with a good big blade. Roger was off with it at once, trying it on the trees. "Now I can make blazes, just like Titty," he shouted.

"If you can really swim three strokes both on your back and on your front, you can keep it," said the female native. "If not, I must take it back tonight and bring it again next time."

"I'm sure I can do it," said Roger, wiping the blade on his knickerbockers.

"You'll have to show me," said the female native. "No feet on the bottom, you know."

"Not even one toe," said Roger.

Then came the birthday feast. There is no need to say anything about that. It was a good one. No one had much time for talking. It ended after Roger had been sent to pick some bananas from the new banana tree.

"I hear you've had some visitors," said Mother.

The Swallows stared at her. It really was astonishing how news flew about among these natives.

"Mrs. Blackett called on me yesterday and told me her little girls met you on the island. She seemed very jolly. How did you get on with the girls?"

"Beautifully," said Susan. "One is called Nancy and the other is called Peggy."

"Really," said Mother. "I thought the elder one was called Ruth."

"That's only when she is with the natives," said Titty. "She is the captain of the Amazon pirates, and when she's a pirate her name is Nancy. We call her Nancy."

"I see," said Mother. "Mrs. Blackett said they were a couple of tomboys, and she was afraid they might be too wild for you."

"They aren't any wilder than we are," said Titty.

"I hope not," said Mother, laughing.

Then she said. "Their uncle lives during the summer in that houseboat we saw. You haven't been meddling with it, have you?"

"No," said John, gloomily. "But he thinks we have."

"I know," said Mother, "Mrs. Dixon told me. I said I was sure you hadn't."

"But he thinks we have. He's been here. He came when we were all away and left this." John pulled out the note and gave it to Mother.

Mother looked at it. "Who is Captain Flint?" she asked.

"He is," said Titty.

"Oh," said Mother.

Then John told her of what the charcoal-burners had said, and of how he had gone to give the message himself, because there was no wind and he could not give it to the Amazons.

"You did quite right," said Mother, "but Mrs. Dixon said he was going away for a night or two."

"He was just going when I saw him this morning," said John.

"Wasn't he pleased to get the message?" said Mother.

"He wouldn't listen to me," said John. "He called me a liar." The whole trouble of the morning loomed up again.

"He wouldn't have called you that if he knew you," said Mother. "It doesn't matter what people think or say if they don't know you. They may think anything. What did you do?"

"I came away," said John.

"Mrs. Blackett says he is very busy over some writing and wants to be let alone. She says she's afraid her tomboys lead him a terrible life."

There was silence. It was all right to talk to Mother about their own affairs. Mother was a friendly native. But nothing could be said about the affairs of the Amazons. Mother noticed the silence, and at once began to talk of something else. She really was the very best of natives.

The birthday party grew cheerful again. The female native told stories of old days before they had been born. She talked of Malta and Gibraltar, and of sailing in Sydney Harbour when she was a little girl.

Later on in the afternoon they bathed, and Mother came down to the landing-place to see Roger swim. He swam three strokes on his front and managed six good kicks on his back.

"If you have got as far as that," the female native said, "I think you can keep the knife. All you want now is practice."

John wanted to swim round the island again to show her that he could do it, but she said that once was quite enough for one day. Titty did some pearl-diving. Susan swam a short race with John and very nearly beat him.

Then there was tea.

At last it was time to take Vicky home.

The empty hamper was carried down to the landing-place.

"How soon are you going to get tired of your island?" asked the female native.

"Never, never," said the Swallows.

"You've been lucky to have good weather so far," she said. "And you seem to be doing yourselves no harm. But there's only another week before we must be going south. You can stay here until nearly the end of it, unless the weather breaks. If the weather breaks, I mean if the rainy season comes on, you'll have to come away. In the rainy season desert islands, even the best of them, are almost uninhabitable."

The Swallows looked at each other.

"A week's a long time," said Mother.

"But we want to stay for ever," said Roger.

"I dare say you do," said the female native.

She kissed them all round. They all kissed fat Vicky. Nurse and Vicky got into the boat and sat down in the stern.

Titty said, "Mother, you don't mind being a native, do you?"

"Not a bit," said Mother.

"Then just for one minute I'll be a native too. What about

rubbing noses? Like the natives you told us about in the Australian bush."

Titty and the female native rubbed noses, after which, of course, Roger had to do the same.

Then the female native kissed all the Swallows goodbye and took her place in the boat. The empty hamper was lifted in. John and Susan pushed the boat off, and Mother rowed away.

"Let's be a convoy," said Captain John.

In a moment *Swallow* was afloat, her crew was aboard, and Captain John was rowing as hard as he could. The female native waited, resting on her oars. Then they rowed side by side. It was much harder to row *Swallow* than to row the boat from Holly Howe, because *Swallow* was deep in the water and built for sailing, not rowing. But the female native did not hurry. At last, just before they came to Houseboat Bay, Captain John stopped. He did not want to see the houseboat again that day. He turned *Swallow* round.

"Goodbye, natives," called Titty.

"Goodbye, palefaces," called the female native. "Drool is the word, isn't it? Drool. Drool."

"Let me row," said Roger.

"Let me," said Titty.

Captain John gave them each an oar. He and Susan sat in the stern. Roger rowed in the bows. Titty rowed stroke. Susan steered.

Susan pulled out her handkerchief to wave to the boat with the natives, disappearing in the distance. The handkerchief still had a knot in it. She unfastened the knot, but did not say anything.

As they landed once more at Wild Cat Island, John said, "Titty and Roger had better do some whistling for a wind. We shall have to hurry up about the war."

CHAPTER XVII

A FAIR WIND

THEY spent that evening round the camp fire, making their plans. There would surely be a wind in the morning. But who could tell which way it might blow. A southerly wind would mean one plan and a northerly wind another, and, supposing there were to be one of those rare winds that made it possible to reach either way up or down the lake, neither of these plans would be much good. But such a wind would be the same for both sides, and it was little good making plans for it. Besides, such winds were very rare. No matter which way the clouds moved overhead the high hills on each side of the lake tended to make the winds blow up or down it. So they made two plans only, one for a southerly wind and one for a northerly. A northerly would make it easy for the Amazons to sail to Wild Cat Island. A southerly would make it easy for the Swallows to sail to Amazon River. Getting back mattered less. It would not matter how long that took.

So there were two plans made.

"In naval warfare," said John, remembering a well-known book, "two things are important; to know exactly what you want to do and to do it in the manner that your enemy least expects."

"Well," said Titty, "what is it we want to do?"

"We want to get hold of the *Amazon* when the Amazons are not aboard her, and we have to remember that they will be trying to capture *Swallow* in the same way. Whoever gets hold of the other one's ship wins. We settled that when they were here. The whole thing is that there's no time to lose. They'll be in a hurry too, so if the wind's from the north tomorrow they will make an attack on us and if it's from the south they will know that we shall make an attack on them."

"I don't see how we are going to capture *Amazon* if they come here in her," said Susan.

"This is the plan for that," said Captain John. "If there's a northerly wind, one of us takes *Swallow* out and hides her in the reeds where we were fishing. The other three hide on the island in ambush close to the harbour. The Amazons will sail into the harbour, and land and go to the camp. While they are at the camp, we shall take the *Amazon*, and they'll be marooned, and we shall have won. That's simple enough."

"And if it's a southerly wind?" said Titty.

"Then it'll be more difficult, for then they'll be expecting us, and they'll probably have a good plan of their own."

"I don't see how we can surprise them," said Susan.

"It's more difficult," said Captain John, "but we can do it. There's just one thing that we can do that they think we can't do. We can find Wild Cat Island in the dark, and bring our ship into harbour. They know about the marks, but they don't know that we have made them into leading lights. So they'll be sure that we shall make our attack early enough to get home by daylight. Well, we won't. A cutting-out expedition by day would only fail. The pirates' harbour may be within sight of their house."

"Stronghold," said Titty.

"There may be natives all over the place who would give the alarm. We must capture their ship while they are feasting ashore, or sleeping off their drunken orgies."

"They had a whole barrel in the boat. They must have tubs and tubs of rum on land."

This, then, was the plan for a southerly wind. *Swallow* was to sail to the islands by Rio as soon as she could, so that they could keep a look-out beyond them, and see if the Amazons sailed out of Amazon River. It would never do for the *Amazon* to be hiding among the islands, so that the Swallows would find her gone when they came to the river. If they did not see her, the Swallows would sail on at dusk, into the river, find the boathouse, cut out the *Amazon*, put aboard a prize crew (Susan) to sail her back, and return to Wild Cat Island in the dark. There was to be a lighthouse on Wild Cat Island, and the leading lights would be lit to make it safe to bring the ships into the harbour in the dark. Candles will not burn all day, so someone had to stay on the island to light them at the last minute, as well as to look after the lighthouse. That someone was to be Titty. For one thing, Roger could not be left alone, and John and Susan would both be needed for sailing the two ships. For another, Titty longed to have Wild Cat Island all to herself, to be a lonely lighthouse keeper, to be Robinson Crusoe, and to feel just what a really desert island was like. A blanket would do for a goatskin.

So that was settled. The making of a lighthouse had to be left till morning. The only question was, would there be a wind, and which way would it blow? There was a little whistling done at night, but it had no effect. John went up to the look-out place and lit a match, and held it pointing upwards. But there was not even a flicker in the flame to show where some wind might be coming from.

*

In the morning there was a fog on the lake. They could not see the mainland from the island. When John rowed across for the milk and a new supply of eggs and butter, Roger, who went with him, hooted like a foghorn, a long, hollow hoot, repeated again and again, like a big ship hooting its way through a fog in the Channel. Titty, who was very much looking forward to having the island all to herself, went up to the look-out place and whistled "Spanish Ladies" again and again, looking into the soft, white cloud that hid everything but a few yards of water. John and Roger very nearly missed the island on their way back. "If it goes on like this," said John, "not one of our plans will be any use."

But after breakfast a little ripple showed on the water under the fog. The fog moved and drifted through the trees, and began to lift from the lake. Now here, now there, the masses of the hills and the dark patches of the woods on the shores showed through the mist, disappeared, and showed again. The wind was southerly. It brought with it a light drizzle, but that passed and then the fog was gone, the wind strengthened, and the sun shone.

"It's a fair wind," said Captain John.

"Good," said Titty.

"We must hurry up," said John. "We must make sure of being in the islands off Rio before the Amazons could get there. Rations for three, Mister Mate. Dinner and supper. Come on, Able-seaman Titty, and you, Boy, and help to make the lighthouse."

Mate Susan set about making rations for the day. She emptied one of the big biscuit boxes, because it would be best to stow all the food in that, so that it would not be in the way in the boat. A biscuit box would fit comfortably under the thwart amidships.

Captain John went into his tent and brought out the coil of rope they had bought in Rio. Then, with the able-seaman and the boy, he went up to the look-out place.

The tree at the look-out place was a very tall pine. All its lower branches were gone, so that it had a long, bare trunk, and its first big bough was at a great height above the ground.

John tried his arms round it. It was just not too big at the bottom. Higher up he would be able to swarm it easily enough.

"The trouble is, I can't swarm up it if I've got anything in my hands."

He tied one end of the rope round his waist, and gave the rest of the coil to Titty.

"Now," he said, "you pay the rope out, and see that it doesn't catch on anything."

"Aye, aye, sir," said Titty.

Captain John spat on his hands, and rubbed them. This does not help much in climbing a rough-barked tree like a pine, but it seems to, so it is always worth doing.

Then he started. It was really not so difficult as it looked. The higher he got the easier it was, because the trunk was not so thick, and it was easier to get a good grip of it with his legs each time he wanted to move his hands up.

"Don't stand right underneath," he called down, and Titty moved a yard or two away.

"Don't stand on the rope, Roger," she said. She had the coil of rope on the ground, and was paying it out as John climbed.

The difficult moments were those when he had to pass one of the places where once upon a time there had been a bough. There was nearly always a sharp piece sticking out where the branch had been. It was easy to pass these sticking-out pieces with his arms, but not so easy to get his legs over them. They were strong enough to be awkward, but not strong enough to be used as footholds.

At last he came to the big bough. He rested for a moment with his head on a level with it. Then he got a good grip of the bough, let go of the tree with his legs and swung there.

"Take care," cried Titty.

But as she spoke John had done what he wanted. He pulled

THE LIGHTHOUSE TREE

up with his arms and kicked, and got one leg cocked over the bough. A swing and a jerk, and he was sitting astride.

"It's a fine place for a look-out," said Captain John. "I ought to have come up here before. But it's no good having the lantern as high as this. It would be half-hidden by the branches hanging down from above. It'll be better further down. The bough itself is a splendid thing to hang the rope over. Let's have more rope, Titty."

He hauled up more and more of the rope, unfastened the end that was tied round his waist, and dropped it to the ground on the other side of the bough.

Titty grabbed it.

"Hang on to both ends," called Captain John, "and keep them well away from the tree while I come down. Send Roger to get the big lantern."

Roger ran off for the lantern. Titty carried both ends of the rope to the edge of the look-out place, so that the rope did not hang near the tree, where it might have bothered John in coming down. John, astraddle on the bough, shifted himself till he was close to the main trunk of the tree. Then he got both his legs on the same side of the bough, and took a firm grip round the trunk. Then he slipped off the bough, and got a grip round the trunk with his legs. After that it was easy enough. He knew better than to slide down, but let himself down bit by bit, first moving his arms, and then his legs.

Before he came to the bottom, Roger was back with the lantern. Captain John tied one end of the rope to the handle on the top of the lantern. He tied the other end round the oil box at the bottom of the lantern. Then he hoisted away until the lantern was about three-quarters of the way up to the big bough. Then he looked round. "Now," he said, "if we make the downfall fast to this bush it won't hang against the lantern, so there will be no danger of burning it. Now then, Able-seaman, you're the lighthouse-keeper. Let's see you bring the lantern down, light it, hoist it up again, and make it fast. Here's a box of matches. You can steady the lantern with the other part of the rope."

Titty took hold of both parts of the rope, and paying out one and hauling on the other, she brought the lantern down. The rope slid easily over the bough. Then she opened the lantern and lit it, and began hauling it up.

"Is that the place for it?" she asked.

"About a foot higher."

"That right?"

"Couldn't be better. Now let's see you make fast."

Titty made fast the part of the rope that went over the bough to a little bush at the side of the look-out place, so that it was well out of the way. The other part, from the bottom of the lantern, she fastened round the trunk of the tree, so that the lantern hung straight. The spare rope lay on the ground between the tree and the bush.

"Fine," said Captain John. "Lower away, and put it out."

"Aye, aye, sir."

"That's that," said Captain John. "Light up the lantern for the lighthouse, and hoist it up just as soon as it begins to get dark. But it's no good lighting the candle-lanterns on the harbour marks until we are close to. Besides, you'll want them in the camp. You'd better not put them on the marks until you hear us give the owl call. Then you'll know it's us, and not an enemy. I say, Titty, do you think you really can manage by yourself?"

"Of course I can. But do hurry up, or they might slip past you in the islands, and I couldn't manage both the Amazons by myself."

"They won't have had time with the wind against them," said John, "but we ought to get away at once."

"Come along," said the boy.

They went back into the camp.

"Rations all ready, sir," said Mate Susan. "I'm taking a big bottle of milk for us. We'll put it in the bilge to keep cool. And I'm leaving a small bottle for the able-seaman. She'll be making tea for herself. Mind you don't let the fire go out, Titty," she added. "If you want to go to sleep, you cover it up with earth, like the charcoal-burners. It'll be cold at night."

"I'm not going to sleep," said Titty. "I shall watch by the camp fire, shrouded in my cloak."

"Roger," said Mate Susan, "go into your tent and put on two pairs of everything."

"Everything?" said Roger.

"Everything," said the mate. "Two vests, two pairs of drawers, two shirts, two pairs of knickerbockers, two pairs of stockings."

"I can't put on two pairs of shoes," said Roger.

"You won't have to. March. Put on two of everything else. Pretend you're going to the North Pole."

"Two ties?" said Roger, going into the tent.

"And jolly well buck up," said the captain. "There's no time to lose." He went off with Titty to step the mast, and get the sail ready. Susan came down to the landing-place with the stores.

"Isn't it a good thing we haven't got a centreboard, like the *Amazon*," she said, as she pushed the biscuit tin under the thwart.

"A centreboard's all right when you're sailing against the wind in a narrow place," said the captain, "but *Swallow* does very well without, and centreboards do take up a lot of room."

Susan went back for the milk. She brought both bottles, the big and the little.

"Look here, Titty," she said, "I'm putting your bottle in

the water here, to keep it cool. Don't go and forget where it is."

Just then the boy Roger strutted down to the landing-place. He was as round as a football, and his arms stuck out stiffly at each side.

The captain and the able-seaman laughed. But the mate looked at him critically.

"He ought to be warm enough like that," she said, "but we'll take a lot of blankets as well, in case."

She ran up to the tents for the last time, and came back laden with blankets.

"Have we got everything?" asked Captain John. "I've got the compass. What about your torches? I've got mine."

"Mine's in my pocket," said Susan.

"I've got mine," said the boy, "but I can't get at it. It's in the pocket of my underneath shirt."

"Never mind," said Captain John. "We'll get it out when we want it. Then there's the telescope."

"Oughtn't I to have the telescope, keeping watch?" said Titty.

John thought for a moment.

"Yes," he said, "I think you ought." He handed it over. He took a last look over the ship. "All aboard," he said, and the mate and the boy climbed in and went to the stern. The captain pushed, and as the *Swallow* floated off he set a knee on her bows and a moment later was busy with the sail. "You won't forget about the lights, Titty," he called. "Everything may depend on them if it's very dark. Lighthouse soon after dusk, and then when you hear us make owl calls, light the candle-lanterns on the harbour marks."

"Aye, aye, sir," said Titty. "Swallows for ever."

In another minute John hoisted up the sail and made fast. He hauled down the boom till the crinkle ran up the sail instead of across it. He made that fast too. They drifted out of the lee of the island. Then the wind caught them. With this fair wind the whole crew of the *Swallow* sat together in the stern. The mate was steering. The boom was well out on the starboard side, and the little ship with her brown sail slipped swiftly away in the sunshine.

"Hurrah," shouted Titty, running up to the look-out place, and standing under the tree that was now a lighthouse.

"Hurrah, hurrah," came back over the water from the *Swallow*.

The able-seaman watched them with the telescope until the brown sail disappeared behind the Peak of Darien. She then became Robinson Crusoe, and went down into the camp to take command of her island.

CHAPTER XVIII

ROBINSON CRUSOE AND MAN FRIDAY

S<small>HE</small> looked round the camp, and felt at once that there was something wrong. There were two tents, and a shipwrecked mariner on a desert island ought only to have one. For a moment she thought of taking down the captain's tent, but then she remembered that for part of the time she would not be a shipwrecked mariner, but would be in charge of an explorers' camp, while the main body had sailed away on a desperate expedition. During that part of the time the more tents there were the better. So she decided not to take down the captain's tent. "It's Man Friday's tent," she said to herself. "Of course I haven't discovered him yet. But it's ready for him when the time comes."

Then she went into the tent that belonged to her and to the mate. It was still a very Susanish tent. Susan had taken her blankets, but she had left her haybag. It was quite clear that it was a tent belonging to two people and not a tent belonging to a lonely shipwrecked sailor. So the able-seaman took Susan's haybag, and put it on the top of her own, and spread her blankets over the two of them. At once the tent became hers and hers alone, and it would be easy enough to put the mate's haybag back in its place when it was time to be on guard over a whole camp.

She lay down on the two haybags. The sun glowed through the white canvas of the tent, and through the doorway she could see smoke rising from the smouldering fire. She began to feel that she was really alone. Even the buzzing of the bees in the heather just behind the tent helped to make her feel that there was no one else on the island. She listened for other noises. Birds were not singing much, but a sandpiper was whistling somewhere near. There was the lapping of water against the western shore, and now and again the faint rustling of wind in the leaves. But there were no human noises at all. Nobody was clattering tins. Nobody was washing up plates. Roger was not there to be looked after. Susan was not there to be looking after both of them. John was not at the look-out place, or splicing ropes in *Swallow* at the other end of the island. Nothing was being done by anybody on the island. Nothing would be done if she did not do it herself. It was like being the only person in the world.

Suddenly she heard the chug, chug, chug of a steamer on its way down the lake. On ordinary days nobody bothered much about steamers except Roger, but today, on hearing it, Able-seaman Titty jumped up and ran out of the tent into the sunlight. Through the trees on the western shore she could see the steamer passing the island a long way off. She looked at it through the telescope. There were a lot of people on deck, and she could see one of the sailors at the wheel. Perhaps the people on the steamer were looking at the island. They did not know that there was nobody on the island except one able-seaman who had been wrecked there five-and-twenty years before. Of course, that was because she had not waved a flag to show that she was there, and waiting to be rescued. But who would wave a flag to be rescued if they had a desert island of their own? That was the thing that spoilt *Robinson Crusoe*. In the end he came home. There never ought to be an end.

The steamer hurried on down the lake, and Titty followed it through the trees on the high western shore of the island. The path to the harbour was turning into a regular beaten track. "It really looks as if I'd been here for years and years," said Titty, "but it's a pity I've got no goats. Goats would soon have nibbled off all these branches that hang across the path, and catch your hair if you try to run along it in a hurry." She took out her knife and began pruning the branches to make the path better. Every branch that hung across the path and was low enough to be in the way she broke or cut off until by working hard she had cleared the track the whole way to the harbour. Then she ran along it both ways, to the camp and back to the harbour again. Now it really was a path. What a funny thing it was that no one had thought of clearing it sooner. Somehow there was always more time to do things when you were alone.

At the harbour she reached up to the nail on the forked tree to make sure that she would be able to hang the lantern on it. She could not quite reach it, but that would be all right because she would be holding the lantern by the bottom part of it, and the ring that had to be hooked on the nail was at the top. The nail on the stump with the white cross on it was quite low. There would be no sort of difficulty about that.

She began to think that it was going to be a very long time till dark would come, and still longer till the *Swallow* and her crew would come sailing back. But it would be worth it if only they brought the *Amazon* with them as a prize. That would show the pirates. And then tomorrow the Swallows would sail up to the Amazon River to tell the pirates that they had lost the war, and to bring Nancy and Peggy back to Wild Cat Island as humble and respectful prisoners. For a moment Titty wished that she was with the others in the *Swallow*. Now they must be searching the islands by Rio, keeping a good look-out, waiting for dusk before going on to the mouth of the river. She wondered what the river was like. All the same you cannot have everything, and if she had not chosen to stay at home, and light the lighthouse lantern and the leading lights, she would never have had a chance of having a whole island to herself.

She took her shoes off, and paddled across to the big rock on one side of the harbour. She climbed to the top of it, and lay there, looking down to the foot of the lake and watching the steamer swing in towards the distant pier. And just then she saw the dipper. A round, stumpy little bird, with a short tail like a wren's, a brown back and a broad white waistcoat, was standing on a stone that showed above the water not a dozen feet away. It bobbed, as if it were making a bow, or a quick, careless kind of curtsey.

"What manners," said Titty to herself. She lay perfectly still, while the little brown and white bird bobbed on its stone.

Suddenly the dipper jumped feet first into the water. It did not dive like a cormorant, but dropped in, like someone who does not know how to dive jumping in at the deep end of a swimming-bath. A few moments later it flew up again out of the water, and perched on its stone, and bobbed again as if it were saying thank you for applause.

Again it flung itself from the stone, and dropped into the water. This time it dropped into quite smooth water sheltered by the big rock on which Titty was lying. Looking down she could see it under water, flying with its wings, as if it were in the air, fast along the bottom of the lake close under the rock. When it came up, it did not come up like a duck after a dive to rest on the surface, but simply went on flying with no difference at all when it left the water and came into the air, except that in the air its wings moved faster.

"Well, I've never seen a bird do that before," said Titty as the dipper perched on its stone and made two or three bobs. "It's the cleverest bird I've ever seen, as well as the most polite. I wish it would do it again." She lifted herself on her elbow to bow to the dipper when the dipper bowed to her. It's very hard not to bob to a dipper when a dipper bobs to you. But the dipper did not seem to like it, and flew away out of sight behind the other rocks, fast and low over the water.

For a long time Titty waited for it to come back. But it did not come. Perhaps it had gone back to the beck where it lived. Suddenly Titty remembered that she was guarding the island against all attack. She ought to be at the look-out place with the telescope, not here. So she climbed down the rock, paddled ashore, and put on her shoes. Instead of going back by the path she had cleared, she thought she would go by the other path, that was hardly a path at all, the track they had sometimes used between the harbour and the landing-place. Here the under-growth was thick, and the bushes were tangled with honey-suckle. It was like forcing your way through a jungle. Titty once more became Robinson Crusoe on his desert island.

She came out close by the landing-place, and stopped short. Something had happened while she was looking at the steamer and the polite dipper. She was no longer alone on the island. There was a rowing boat with its nose pulled up on the beach. A moment later she knew what boat it was. It was the rowing boat from Holly Howe. She ran up to the camp, and there was Mother looking at the empty tents.

"Hullo, Man Friday," said Titty joyfully.

"Hullo, Robinson Crusoe," said Mother. That was the best of Mother. She was different from other natives. You could always count on her to know things like that.

Robinson Crusoe and Man Friday then kissed each other as if they were pretending to be Titty and Mother.

"You didn't expect to see me so soon after yesterday," said Mother, "but I came to say something to John. I suppose he's with the rest of the crew in that secret harbour of yours that poor natives are not allowed to see."

"No. He isn't on the island just at present," said Titty. "No one is except me . . . and now you too."

"So you really are Robinson Crusoe," said Mother, "and I am Man Friday in earnest. If I'd known that I'd have made a good big footprint on the beach. But where are the others?"

"They're all right," said Titty. "They're coming back again. They've gone in *Swallow* on a cutting-out expedition." More than that she could not well say, because, after all, Man Friday might be Mother, but she was also a native, even if she was the best native in the world.

"I expect they've gone to meet the Blackett children," said Mother.

"Man Friday ought not to know anything about them," said Titty.

"Very well, I won't," said Mother. "But what are you doing all by yourself?"

"Properly I'm in charge of the camp," said Titty. "But while they're not here it doesn't make any difference if I'm Robinson Crusoe instead."

"I am sure it doesn't," said Mother. "Have they left you anything to eat?"

"I've got my rations in the tent," said Titty.

"Well, it's high time you ate them," said Mother. "Will you let Man Friday put some more wood on the fire, and make some tea? I can't stay very long, but perhaps they'll be back before I go."

"I don't think they will," said Titty. "They've sailed across the Pacific Ocean. Timbuctoo is nothing to where they've gone."

"Well, I'll make some tea, anyhow," said Mother. "Let's see what they've left you in the way of rations."

Titty brought out her rations, a good big hunk of pemmican, some brown bread, some biscuits, and a large fat slice of cake.

Man Friday did not think much of them. "Still," she said, "I think we shall be able to make a meal. What about butter? And potatoes? What if we were to make pemmican cakes?"

Man Friday rummaged in the store box, and found some butter which was rather soft. She sniffed at it, and said it ought to be eaten, anyhow, and more would have to be got from Mrs. Dixon's tomorrow. She found some potatoes and also the salt. Robinson Crusoe had the tea among her rations, rolled up in a screw of paper. She also had a tobacco box full of sugar.

Man Friday opened up the fire, and put sticks on it, and soon had it blazing up round the big kettle. She peeled some potatoes, and set them to boil in a saucepan at the edge of the fire. She chopped up the pemmican into very little bits like mince. Then, when the potatoes were soft, she took them out of the water, and broke them up, and mixed them with the chopped meat and made half a dozen round flat cakes of pemmican and potato. Then she put some butter in the frying-pan and melted it, and then she fried the pemmican cakes till they sizzled and bubbled all over them. Robinson Crusoe made the tea.

When they had eaten their meal, which was a very good one, Robinson Crusoe said, "Now, Man Friday, would you mind telling me some of your life before you came to this island?"

Man Friday began at once by telling how she had nearly been eaten by savages, and had only escaped by jumping out of the stew-pot at the last minute.

"Weren't you scalded?" said Robinson Crusoe.

"Badly," said Man Friday, "but I buttered the places that hurt most."

And then Man Friday forgot about being Man Friday, and became Mother again, and told about her own childhood on a sheep station in Australia, and about emus that laid eggs as big as a baby's head, and opossums that ran about with their young ones in a pocket in their fronts, and about kangaroos that could kill a man with a kick, and about snakes that hid in the dust. Here Robinson Crusoe, who had forgotten that she was Robinson Crusoe, and had turned into Titty again, talked about the snake that she had seen herself in the cigar-box that was kept in the charcoal-burners' wigwam. Then she told Mother about the dipper, and how it had bobbed at her, and flown under water. Then Mother talked about the great drought on the sheep stations, when there was no rain and no water in the wells, and the flocks had to be driven miles and miles to get a drink, and thousands and thousands of them died. Then she talked of the pony she had had when she was a little girl, and then of the little brown bears that her father caught in the bush, and that used to lick her fingers for her when she dipped them in honey.

Time went on very fast, much faster than when Robinson Crusoe had been alone. But suddenly Man Friday jumped up and said that she must go home.

"I can't wait any longer," she said. "I must go back to Vicky. But I'm sorry I haven't seen John. I saw he was worried yesterday about what this Mr. Turner had said to him, and I wanted to ask if he would like me to write to Mrs. Blackett to ask her to let her brother know that John had never touched his boat."

Titty was not sure. There were the Amazon pirates to think about. It would never do to get the natives mixed up in things. So she said she would tell John what Mother had said as soon as he came back.

"I wonder why they are so long," said Mother. "Are you sure you are all right here by yourself? Wouldn't you like to come home with me to Holly Howe? You could watch and shout to them when they come past, or you could come on a visit to me, and spend the night, and run along the road to Mrs. Dixon's in the morning to join the others when they come for the milk. We could leave a note here for John to say where you have gone."

For a moment Titty thought she would like to go. Somehow, with Mother going, the island seemed to be much lonelier than before she came. Then she remembered the leading lights and the lighthouse, and that she was in charge of the camp.

"No thank you," she said. "I'd rather stay here."

Mother took the frying-pan and saucepan and mugs and plates down to the landing-place, and washed them while Titty dried them. Then she brought them back to the camp, and put them neatly away. She filled the kettle and put it on one of the stones of the fireplace, half on and half off the fire. "It'll get hot there," she said, "and then it'll boil up quickly when they come back thirsty for their tea."

"I don't think they'll be back so soon," said Titty.

Mother looked at her.

"You'd better come along with me," she said. "The camp will look after itself all right."

"No thank you," said Titty firmly.

"Oh well," said Mother, "if you are quite sure you will be all right. But don't wait tea for them too long. The Blacketts might ask them to stay and have tea with them."

Titty said nothing.

Mother got into the boat, and pushed off with an oar.

"Goodbye, Robinson Crusoe," she said.

"Goodbye, Man Friday," said Titty. "It was very jolly having you here. I hope you liked my island."

"Very much indeed," said Mother.

She rowed slowly away. Titty ran up to the look-out point to wave. Mother rowed past below it. The island was suddenly very lonely indeed. Titty changed her mind.

"Mother," she called.

Mother stopped rowing.

"Want to come?" she called.

But in that moment Titty remembered again that she was not merely Robinson Crusoe, who had a right to be rescued by a passing ship, but was also Able-seaman Titty, who had to hoist the lantern on the big tree behind her, so that the others could find the island in the dark, and then to light the leading lights so that they could bring their prize into the harbour.

"No," she called. "Only goodbye."

"Goodbye," called Mother.

"Goodbye," called Titty. She lay down on the look-out point, and watched Mother through the telescope. Suddenly she found that she could not see her. She blinked, pulled out her handkerchief, and wiped first the telescope glass and then her eye.

"Duffer," she said. "That's with looking too hard. Try the other eye."

CHAPTER XIX

THE AMAZON RIVER

THE sun set behind the hills on the western shore of the lake. The belt of light along the tops of the hills on the eastern side narrowed and narrowed, and at last was gone. The wind dropped. The islands off Rio were reflected in still water.

"This will never do," said Captain John. "It may be dark before the wind comes again. We'd better slip across to the western shore and row along it. Even if they are watching they won't see us now if we keep close to the land."

"They'll take us for a fisherman," said Susan.

"Except for the mast," said John. "But we can take it down. Anyhow, we shall be sheltered nearly all the way if we come along that side of the lake. I bet they won't see us at all. And if the wind doesn't come again, we shall be too late to see things by the time we get into the river."

"Come on," said Susan.

"May I row?" said the Boy Roger.

*

It had been a long wait among the islands, and they were all glad to be moving again at last. In the morning the fair wind had brought them fast from Wild Cat Island down to Rio Bay. They had cruised in and out among the islands, and made sure that the Amazons were not lurking among them, waiting for their chance to capture the island once again. They had made sure that the *Amazon* was still in the Amazon River, so that the plan was working out just as they had hoped, and they would be able to sail in and capture her in the evening. They had anchored close under one of the islands north of Rio to wait till dusk. From there they had been able to look out over the northern part of the lake without being seen themselves, and all day long they had kept a close watch on the promontory behind which, they knew, lay the Amazon River and the stronghold of the Amazon pirates. But the afternoon had been very long, and at one time there had almost been a mutiny.

"Let's go straight on," Roger had said, and Susan had said, "Why not?"

Captain John had brought them to reason. Everything had been planned for an attack at dusk. There would be no chance at all of capturing the *Amazon* if they sailed up there in broad daylight. Besides, they had left Able-seaman Titty behind on Wild Cat Island to look after the lights for them so that they could come home in the dark. They could not leave Titty behind and then go and turn the day into an ordinary picnic. Susan had agreed. Roger had suggested swimming instead. The mutiny had thus been suppressed without bloodshed, as they say in the books.

The crew had been rewarded by getting permission from their captain to go ashore. They had landed on the island near which they were anchored. They had bathed from it, and made a fire on the shore, not for cooking, because they had brought no kettle, but because landing on an island without making a fire is waste of an island. They had drunk half their milk and eaten half their rations. Then while John stayed on the island he had sent the mate and the boy to sail in to Rio, to buy stores. They had bought a shilling's worth of the sort of chocolate that has almonds and raisins in it as well as the chocolate, and so is three sorts of food at once. They had come back. They had visited several other islands, and had an unpleasant meeting with some natives on one of them, who pointed to a notice-board and said that the island was private, and that no landing was allowed.

Only once Captain John had thought he had seen one of the Amazons moving in the heather on the promontory. But he could not be sure without the telescope. It might have been a sheep. The wait all through the afternoon and early evening had been long and tiring, and though there had been plenty to look at in the steamers and motor boats and rowing skiffs of the natives, they had seen no sails except those of large yachts far away up the lake. For the first time in their lives all three of them had wished to hurry the sinking sun upon its way.

*

Now, at last, the sun had set. Twilight was coming on. There was no wind, for the wind had gone with the sun as it so often does, and they were beginning to be afraid that the dark would come too soon for them. All was astir in the *Swallow*.

The mast was unstepped, and laid on the thwarts so that it stuck out over the bows. There was room for it in the ship, for it was a few inches shorter than *Swallow* was long. But to stow it all inside it had to lie straight down the middle, so that it was very uncomfortable for anybody who was rowing.

"Anyway, why shouldn't she have a bowsprit?" said John. "Besides, it's only for a short time."

Roger rowed. John was looking at the chart in the guide-book. Susan steered.

"Pull with your back," she said, "don't bend your arms till the end of the stroke."

"I'm pulling with all of me," said Roger, "but I've got too many clothes on."

"He's making a fair lot of noise and splash," said the captain.

"He'll be tired before we get near enough for it to matter," said the mate.

"No I won't," said Roger.

Slowly they moved across to the western shore. No one could row *Swallow* fast. It was growing dusk. Already the hills were dark, and you could not see the woods on them. It began to seem that after waiting so long because it was too light, they were going to fail after all because it would not be light enough.

"Look here, Susan," said John, "I think I'd better row."

But just then a line of ripples crept over the green and silver surface of the smooth water.

"Thank goodness," said Captain John. "Here's the wind again, and it's the same wind. Sometimes it changes after sunset, but this is still from the south."

The ripples grew as the south wind strengthened.

"It'll be against us on the way home," said the mate.

"There'll be no hurry then," said John.

"What about sailing?" said Roger. "But I'm not tired."

"It isn't as if *Swallow* had a white sail," said Captain John. "They'll never see the brown one in this light, especially if we hug the shore. And we can with this wind. Yes, Mister Mate. Tell the men to bring the sweeps aboard."

"Easy," said the mate. "Bring the sweeps in."

Roger stopped rowing and lifted first one oar and then the other from the rowlocks and laid them quietly down.

"Keep her heading as she is," said Captain John.

"As she is, sir," said the mate. In a calm things go anyway in a sailing ship, but a little wind sharpens them up at once.

John stepped the mast as quietly as he could. He hooked the yard to the traveller and set the sail. There was a little west in the wind and the boom swung out on the starboard side.

"She's moving now like anything," said the boy.

"I don't want to get there too soon," said John, "but I do

want to get into the river while it's still light enough to see but
late enough for the pirates to be off their guard and feasting
in their stronghold."

"Peggy said they had supper at half-past seven," said Susan.

"Well it's ages after that now," said John. "I should think we
are all right."

Here and there on the shores of the lake lights twinkled in
the houses of the natives. Astern of them, over the tops of the
islands, there was a huge cluster of lights in Rio Bay. But it was
not quite dark yet, though the first stars were showing.

Swallow was sailing fast and in a very little time they were
abreast of the promontory, and could see its great dark lump
close to them.

"We must lower sail now," said the captain.

He lowered the sail himself. He could not trust even Susan
to lower it without making a noise. Then he wetted the rowlocks
so that they would not squeak.

The *Swallow* drifted on past the point. Beyond the promontory was a wide bay with deep beds of rushes on either side
of it. Somewhere at the head of the bay was a house with lights
in its windows. The lights, reflected in the water, showed exactly
where was the opening of the river mouth between the reeds.
A moment later they lost sight of the reflections and knew that
they had drifted too far.

"Now, Mister Mate," whispered John. "Will you row, as
quietly as ever you can? Roger goes forward to keep a look-
out. Don't shout if you see anything. Just tell the mate under
your breath."

"What about the mast?" asked the mate.

"If they're watching, they'll see the ship and know her,
anyhow," said Captain John. "If they're not watching, the mast
doesn't matter. If they are in the house in those lighted rooms,
they won't be able to see anything at all out here. I'm sure

we've done them, if we can find the boathouse. They'd have challenged us long before this if they'd seen us."

The mate rowed with slow, steady strokes. Her oars made no noise at all. They slipped in and out of the water without a splash. *Swallow* was in smooth water now, sheltered by the high ground of the promontory. John steered till he could see the lights of the house reflected in the river. That was the opening in the reeds. He steered towards it. Presently there were tall reeds on either side of them. They were in the Amazon River.

"The boathouse is somewhere on the right bank," whispered John. "That's our left. Tell Roger to keep a look-out to port."

Suddenly there was a splash in the reed-beds, followed by a loud quack.

"What's that?" said Susan, startled.

"Duck," said the captain.

Susan rowed on.

There was a whisper from the look-out. "There it is. I see it."

"Where?" whispered the mate looking over her shoulder.

"There," said the boy.

High above the reeds, not far ahead of them, on the right bank of the river rose the black square shape of a large building.

"That's it," whispered the captain.

"The boathouse," said the mate.

"Quiet."

"'Sh."

The boathouse stood deep in an inlet among the reeds. Captain John steered towards it.

"Easy all!" he whispered. There was a dead silence on the river as the *Swallow* drifted on. There was a noise of music in the house with the lights in it.

"Captain Nancy said the boathouse had a skull and crossbones on it," whispered Captain John.

THE ENEMY'S BOATHOUSE

"I see it. I see it," cried Roger.

"Shut up. Be quiet," hissed the mate.

"That's it, all right," whispered Captain John.

On the front of the big open boathouse, high up over the entrance, cut out of wood and painted staring white were a huge skull and crossbones big enough to have belonged to an elephant.

"Can you see in," asked Captain John.

"There's a big boat in there," said Roger.

"They said there would be. That'll be the launch that belongs to the natives. Will our mast clear that beam? Gently now, gently."

Swallow slid into the big dark boathouse as Susan brought her oars in.

"There's a rowing boat," whispered Roger loudly.

"Look out. Don't bump the launch," whispered Susan.

"There's nothing else," said Roger. "The *Amazon* isn't here."

John was standing in the stern of the *Swallow*, holding on to the gunwale of the launch. He pulled out his pocket torch. "They won't be able to see the light from the house," he said, and pressed down the button.

The bright light wavered round the boathouse. It showed a rowing skiff and the big launch and an empty space on the further side. It was clear that a boat was usually moored there. Pinned to the wooden stage that ran along that wall of the boathouse there was a big envelope, white in the light of the torch.

Captain John pushed at the launch and *Swallow* moved across towards the wall. Roger grabbed the envelope.

"Give it to me," said the mate, and the boy obediently gave it.

The captain and the mate examined the envelope by the light of the torch. There was a skull and crossbones on it, done in red pencil. Under that, in blue pencil, was written, "To the Swallows." John tore the envelope open. Inside there was a sheet of paper with another skull and crossbones, done in blue. Under them in red were the words "Ha! Ha!" written very large, and under them were the words, "The Amazon Pirates," and two names, "Nancy Blackett, Captain" and "Peggy Blackett, Mate" also written in red.

Captain John thought for a moment.

"It's quite simple," he said. "They've hidden her up the river. It's an old pirate trick. We know they haven't put to sea, for we've been watching all day. Come on." He shut off the torch.

They pushed out.

Out of doors it seemed quite light after the darkness of the big boathouse.

"Now, Mister Mate, lay to your oars," said Captain John. "There's still light enough to find her if we're quick."

Mate Susan bent to her oars and *Swallow* moved fast up the river. John, staring as hard as he could into the dusk, kept her clear of the reeds. In another minute they were round a bend in the river.

*

Again there was a splash in the deep reed-beds at the river's mouth. Again a duck quacked loudly. It quacked two or three times, until a voice said sternly, "Stow it, you goat. Don't overdo things."

The nose of a boat pushed its way out from among the reeds. Just above the nose of the boat was the head of Captain Nancy Blackett. She watched for a moment and listened.

"All clear," she said. "They've gone up river. That'll give us a bit more start. Come on."

There was more splashing in the reeds as Peggy Blackett

poled over the stern. The boat came out of the reeds into the mouth of the river and drifted out towards the lake. Captain Nancy took the oars. She rowed hard for a minute or two.

"Safe enough now," she said. "I'm going to step the mast. Lucky we thought of taking it down, or they'd have seen it over the reeds. Hang on to the mainsheet, you son of a sea-cook," she said with great good temper and satisfaction. She hoisted the sail.

"Now then, my hearties," she said as she clambered aft. "Wild Cat Island and Amazons for ever! We've done them fairly brown."

CHAPTER XX

TITTY ALONE

AFTER Mother had gone, Able-seaman Titty thought it well to go all over her island. Everything was as it should be. The dipper had come back to a stone outside the harbour and bobbed to her again and again, and Able-seaman Titty bobbed to him in return, but this time was so far away that he did not fly off but stood on his stone, bobbing two or three times a minute. She watched him flop into the water and fly out again, and then she went on with her patrol. At last she came back to the camp and put some more wood on the fire.

Then she remembered that Robinson Crusoe kept a log, and that she had brought an exercise book in which to do the same. She sat down in the sunlight at the mouth of her tent and wrote "LOG" in capital letters at the top of a page. It was a pity that she had not been keeping count of the days by making notches on a stick, but as there was only one day to put in the log that did not really matter. So she wrote:

"Twenty-five years ago this day I was wrecked on this desolate place. Wind south-west. Sea slight. Fog at dawn. Met a polite bird. I saw him flying underwater. I found a native canoe on the shore. The native was friendly. Her name was Man Friday. In her country there are kangaroos. Also bears. It was a joy to me in my lonely state to hear a human voice, though savage. Man Friday cooked our dinner. Pemmican cakes with tea. She went away in her canoe to the mainland where the natives are. She . . ."

Able-seaman Titty could think of no more to say. She had caught up with herself. There was nothing else to say until something more happened. She began looking through *Robinson Crusoe*, not exactly reading, for she had read it all many times before, but looking from page to page. She came first on the bit about sleeping in a tree for fear of ravenous beasts.

"I went to the tree, and getting up into it, endeavoured to place myself so as that if I should sleep I might not fall; and having cut me a short stick like a truncheon for my defence, I took up my lodging, and having been excessively fatigued, I fell fast asleep, and slept as comfortably as, I believe, few could have done in my condition, and found myself the most refreshed with it that I think I ever was on such an occasion."

She wondered whether Robinson Crusoe had often slept in trees, and then whether there was any tree on the island that would be good for sleeping in. But then, there were no ravenous beasts.

Then she read the part about the footprint in the sand and remembered a number of things that she might have said to Man Friday.

Then, turning this way and that through the book she came on a passage which reminded her of Captain Flint.

"All the while I was at work," wrote Robinson Crusoe, "I diverted myself with talking to my parrot, and teaching him to speak; and I quickly learned him to know his own name, and at last to speak it out pretty loud . . . *Poll* . . . which was the first word I ever heard spoken in the island by any mouth but my own. . . ."

Of course, if only she had a parrot, the island would be

perfect. She thought of the green parrot on the rail of the houseboat. Then she remembered the jays that had flown chattering through the trees on the day when the Swallows had visited the charcoal-burners. The jays, like the green parrot, brought her mind back to Captain Flint, for she remembered the message that the old men had sent to the Amazons. She remembered the message, that the old men thought that someone was going to break into the houseboat and that Captain Flint ought to put a lock on it. Then she remembered that John had tried to give the message and that Captain Flint had been too cross to listen to it, besides calling John a liar. And now there was Mother wanting to send a message to Captain Flint by writing to the mother of the Amazons. And there was John gone to the Amazon River, not to see the Amazons, but to capture their ship. So the message would not be given to the Amazons until tomorrow.

"Bother Captain Flint," she said out loud, and put the book away and went up to the look-out place with the telescope to keep watch. There were plenty of boats on the lake and, looking through the telescope, she could see the cormorants on the bare tree on Cormorant Island. Time went very slowly in spite of them. Even making tea and boiling two eggs and eating them and a lot of bun loaf and marmalade did not seem to take as long as it does when there is something else that you are in a hurry to do next. It seemed that she was only in the camp and cooking and eating and washing up for a minute or two before she was back at the look-out, wondering what was happening to the Swallows. She knew they would not be back for a long time because of waiting for dusk to go into the Amazon River. Dusk seemed a long time coming, even longer for Able-seaman Titty on her island than for the captain, the boy, and the mate far away by Rio.

At last the sun went down. The last steamer, Roger's bedtime steamer, went down the lake. The last of the native fishermen rowed away into the twilight and disappeared. Titty became the keeper of a lighthouse on a lonely reef.

She lit the big lantern and hauled it up the tree and made fast. It gave a splendid light up there, high overhead, and she thought of swimming off to see what it looked like over the water. But that, she decided, was not quite what a lighthouse-keeper would do. He might be carried away by an ocean current, and then when the light burnt out there would be no one to put more oil in, and some great ship might run on the reef in the dark.

Before it was too dark to see what she was doing without a torch, Titty took one of the candle-lanterns and hooked it up on the nail on the forked tree. It would be easier to open it and light it up there than to light it and feel round for the nail to hang it on. Then she went back to the camp. "They may be capturing the *Amazon* at this very minute," she thought, and found it difficult to keep still. Once or twice she went up to the look-out place to see that the lighthouse lantern was burning properly, though she could see its glimmer through the trees without leaving the camp.

At last she made up her mind that there was really nothing to be done except to wait and to listen for the owl call, which would tell her that the Swallows were back and waiting for her to light the leading lights for them so that they could bring *Swallow* and *Amazon* into the harbour. "If only they've got her," she said.

She made up the fire well, with all the sticks pointing to the middle, and then covered it with the clods of earth that Susan had left ready. That made things very dark, so she uncovered it again. After all, there was plenty of firewood left from the cargo they had brought to the island two days before. She lit the other candle-lantern and tried to read by it, but reading

was not easy even with the candle-lantern, because of the fire
leaping up and flashing shadows across the pages. Then she
remembered that there was only a very short piece of candle
in the lantern, and it would be wanted at the harbour. She
blew it out. She was afraid to lie down on her bed for fear of
going to sleep and not hearing the signal when the Swallows
came back. So she took both her blankets from the tent. She
rolled herself up in one of them and made a hood and cloak
of the other and sat watching her fire, with the electric torch
and the candle-lantern close beside her. A box of matches was
in her pocket. She made sure of that. She could feel it through
the blanket. . . .

That was the last thing she remembered.

She was wakened with the wind in her face and the long
call of an owl. "Tu Whooooooooo. Tu Whooooooooo."

She sat up suddenly. Where was she? The fire had died
down to red embers. It was very dark, but there was a glimmer
high up in the trees behind her. The lighthouse, of course.
How long ago was it that she had heard that owl? Was it
before she fell asleep, or just now, or was it an owl heard in
a dream?

She tried to jump up, but had forgotten that she had rolled
herself up like a mummy. It must have been the owl call that
woke her up. John and Susan and Roger must be sailing about
in the dark with the two ships, wondering why the lights were
not lit. She scrambled to her feet and listened. For a moment
she could hear nothing, and then somewhere on the lake there
was the creak of a boom swinging over as a boat went about.

She felt about on the ground for the torch. She found it, and
the lantern close beside it. She lit the torch and ran out of the
camp and hurried, stumbling as she went, along the path to
the harbour. What a good thing that Mother had given them
torches for Vicky's birthday. It was hard enough to run even

with the torch. And what a good thing, too, that she had cleared the branches that hung over the track.

She found the forked tree and took out her box of matches, putting the torch in her pocket so as to have both hands free. Her first match blew out, and her second as she lifted it up to light the lantern. But the third match did it. She lit the other lantern easily and hung it on its nail on the stump with the white cross.

Well, John and Susan would see the lights now. But what if they had been waiting a long time? She, Titty, able-seaman, had fallen asleep just at the very time when she ought to have been most awake. What if they had tried to make the harbour in the dark and were wrecked on the rocks outside?

Suddenly a big owl flew by close over her head, between the two leading lights, puzzled by the glitter of them.

"Tu Whoooooooo. Tu Whooooooooo," she heard it as it swung away into the darkness.

Perhaps it had not been the owl signal she had heard. Perhaps all her fears were for nothing, and *Swallow* was still far away. And yet, that creak had sounded very like *Swallow*'s boom going over.

But just then, somewhere in the darkness in front of her, outside the harbour, she heard the noise of a sail coming down into a boat, and then the quick creak, creak that an oar makes when it is being used for sculling over the stern.

She was just going to call out joyfully to welcome the Swallows, when she heard a voice that was not John's, or Susan's, or Roger's.

The voice said, "Jolly good idea of theirs, putting lights on the marks."

For one moment Titty thought of blowing the lights out. But it was too late. The boat was close in. In another second it grounded in the harbour not six yards away.

Titty crouched down on the ground behind a rock. Why had she ever gone to sleep? It was a real owl she had heard and not the signal from the Swallows. If only she had been awake she would have known. And now, left on guard, she had lighted the Amazons into the harbour, and the Swallows would come back to find the island in the hands of the enemy. Would they ever forgive her?

Nancy Blackett was on the beach.

"What beats me," she was saying, "is how ever they managed to get here before us. I'm sure I heard them go up the river. They must have rowed like smoke. They couldn't do it sailing. And I would never have thought they could do it rowing, even though we were beating all the way. Funny we didn't see them or hear them on one tack or the other. Come on, Peggy, step lively, and show a light."

"Matches are damp," said Peggy, but just then there was a flicker in the boat, and a moment later she was coming ashore with a lantern in her hand.

"Why aren't they here?" she said.

"They just lit the lights for us and scooted back to camp," said Captain Nancy, "pretending they've been back for hours. Come along. Let's have that lantern."

The Amazon pirates passed so close to Able-seaman Titty that they could almost have touched her. They hurried on into the path.

Titty crouched trembling.

She heard Peggy say, "Wait for me. I can't see without the lantern."

Their steps sounded further and further away. Then there was silence except for the wind in the leaves. The Amazons had gone to the camp.

Titty did not know what to do. It was defeat, black and dreadful. Instead of the *Swallow* sailing home with the

Amazon a captured galleon, sailed by Susan as a prize crew, everything had gone wrong. The Swallows had not captured the *Amazon*, but the Amazons had landed on Wild Cat Island, and their pirate ship was snug in harbour. If only she had not lit the lights they could never have come in till dawn, and by then the Swallows would be back.

Just then she heard the loud shouting of the Amazons at the other end of the island. "Swallows ahoy! Captain John!"

The voices came nearer. The Amazons were coming back.

Just then Titty had her idea.

After all, it did not matter who of the Swallows captured the *Amazon*. And here was the *Amazon*, unprotected. Why not?

In a moment Titty was up and on the beach and a moment later she was afloat, clawing the *Amazon* stern first out of harbour along the edge of the big rocks. Then she pulled out her torch, and lit it for just long enough to find the oars. They were not quite like *Swallow*'s oars, but she could manage them. She stood in the stern of the *Amazon* to row, keeping her eyes on the two lights she had lit herself. She remembered that whatever happened she must keep the two lights in line, one above another. Now and then they would get askew in spite of all she did, but she managed pretty well, though the centreboard case and the lowered sail with its boom and yard were horribly in the way. She hit nothing at all hard, and had just paddled the pirate ship stern first clear of the rocks when the candle in one of the lanterns guttered and went out. "That's the one I had in camp," she thought. "It's lucky I didn't read any more." She went on rowing backwards for a bit to be sure she was clear. She knew the wind would be blowing her back towards the island, so she turned the *Amazon* round, sat down on the thwart with a leg on each side of the centreboard, and began to row properly, keeping the wind on her right cheek.

She lost sight of the other leading light. Then she saw it

again, and then a lantern flickered through the trees, the Amazons coming back to the harbour.

She rested on her oars and drifted, listening, but could hear nothing. Presently she saw another light, much higher up. That was the lighthouse, the lantern still burning high on the tree by the look-out place. She knew that the wind was driving her up the lake, past the island. She pulled hard with her left and brought *Amazon*'s head nearer to the wind. Then she rowed steadily.

It was very hard work. She could not keep on rowing like that all night. The best thing she could do would be to anchor in as safe a place as possible. She stopped rowing, pulled her oars in, turned on her torch, and scrambled forward. Yes, there was an anchor in the bows and a lot of rope. She remembered hearing John tell Susan never to let go the anchor without making sure that the end of the anchor rope was made fast. She burrowed down with the torch into the coils of rope. That was all right. The rope was made fast to a ring-bolt. She put the anchor where she could easily get at it, and then settled down again to the oars, rowing as hard as she could across and a little into the wind towards the western shore of the lake. She could see nothing now except the light of the lighthouse tree. She did not want to be anchored anywhere near the island when dawn came. Who knew how well these pirates could swim? The other side of the lake would be safe.

Suddenly she heard the splash of water on rocks, quite close to her. It would never do to run *Amazon* ashore in the dark. She stopped rowing, scrambled forward again, and lowered the anchor over the bows, letting out the rope hand over hand. Down it went, yard after yard. Deep water after all. Then it stopped being heavy. The anchor was on the ground. She let the rest of the rope go. The *Amazon* drifted back and brought up with a light jerk.

"Anyhow nothing more can happen till morning," said Able-seaman Titty to herself. "John won't try to land in the dark with one of the leading lights out. I've got *Amazon*, and *Swallow* will be flagship after all. Nothing more can happen now."

She was wrong. It is never safe to say that nothing more can happen.

Now that her prize was safely anchored, she did her best to make things ship-shape, but she could not do much in the dark, even with her little torch to help her. But she rolled up the sail as well as she could. She found a rug and wrapped herself up in it, for it was cold enough on the water now that she was not rowing. She also found a big hunk of chocolate. This she ate. "They always eat everything they find in a captured ship," she had said to herself when in doubt whether to eat it or not. She settled herself in the bottom of the boat, just aft of the centreboard case, so as to keep warm and get some shelter from the wind. She had eaten all the chocolate, and had begun to wonder how many hours it would be till dawn, when she stiffened suddenly, like a rabbit that has seen a man in a field.

She heard a new noise.

It was the noise of rowing, hard, fast rowing, the noise of two pairs of oars in a native boat, pin oars, and the slap, slap of a boat's bows into the short waves. She knew that noise well.

It came nearer and nearer. It passed close by her. Plunk, plunk. She could hear the splash of the oars so clearly that she almost thought she could see the boat in the dark.

Able-seaman Titty hardly breathed. These were not Swallows or Amazons, but natives. And what could they be doing in the middle of the night when everybody, except, of course, pirates and explorers, ought to be asleep?

"We must be near it now." A man's voice, loud in the wind, came to her out of the darkness.

"Not yet. Look at the light those kids have got on the other island. It must be another hundred yards at least."

"I can hear something. I bet it's not far now. Go a bit easier."

There was a crash somewhere close ahead.

"Told you, you blamed fool. You've blooming well smashed the blighted boat."

"Get out and pull her up, then."

"Take your hat off the lamp and let's have a bit of light."

There was a splash, and then the noise of a boat being pulled up over stones. Then there was a glimmer and a flash of a bicycle lamp.

"Boat's all right. Lost a bit of paint maybe. Lucky for us she isn't stove in."

"Give us a hand with the box, then. Nobody'll look for it here."

"They will if you keep flashing that lamp about. Much better take it with us."

"We can't carry that thing on a motor bicycle. Have to bring a car for it."

"Blast it. Why didn't you bring a chisel to smash it open?"

"Clever. Who'd have thought he'd keep the stuff in a thing like that. It'll take more than a chisel to get that open."

"It's a fool game, anyway."

"Well, we've done it now. And you can tell by the weight it's something worth having. He wouldn't keep it in a thing like this if it wasn't. Give a hand, then."

There was a noise of scrambling on stones, some curses, and then the noise of heavy stones being thrown down on something made of wood and metal.

Then voices again.

"We'll come out with fishing rods next time, and catch something worth having. Nobody'll find it now even if they do come looking. And you grumbling all the time. Wish I'd come by myself."

"Wish you had."

"Shove her off now. Sure she doesn't leak?"

"No, she won't leak. But it's not your fault she doesn't."

"Shove her off, then, and put your back into it. We've got to be far out of this before anyone's stirring."

The noise of rowing began again. This time it grew rapidly fainter.

"They didn't sound at all like friendly natives," thought Titty to herself. She listened, open-mouthed, till she could hear no more, staring into the darkness. Her eyes closed once or twice. She tried to keep them open with her fingers. "I'm going to sleep again," she said, "I know I am."

She was right.

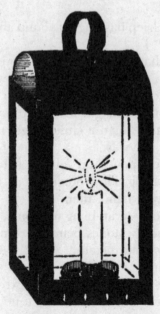

CHAPTER XXI

SWALLOWS IN THE DARK

With Mate Susan at the oars, Roger on the look-out in the bows, and Captain John at the tiller, the *Swallow* moved up the Amazon River in the rapidly gathering dusk. There were tall reeds on each side, then a bit of meadowland where they could see the shapes of trees against the darkening sky, then reeds again, shutting them in as if they were in a lane between high walls. Suddenly the river broadened into a wide, open pool, with tall reeds all round it, except where the river entered and left it.

"This must be what they called the lagoon," said Captain John. "It's the very place for them to hide their ship in. I wish it wasn't so dark."

He put the tiller hard over to starboard, so that the *Swallow* turned sharply to port.

"It's awful rowing if you steer with such a jerk," said Susan.

"Sorry," said John. "I want to keep close to the edge all round this place. I don't want to miss her."

"Something's pulling at my oar," said Susan, "I can't lift it."

The boat stopped moving.

John peered over the side.

"Water lilies," he said. "It's getting most awfully dark."

"They hang on to my oars like octopuses," said Susan.

"Perhaps they are octopuses," said Roger. "Titty read to me about how they put their arms out long, and grab people even out of a boat."

In Roger's voice there were clear signs of panic in the forecastle. Captain John took command at once.

"Rubbish, Roger," he said, "they aren't octopuses. They're only flowers." He leaned over and picked one, not without difficulty. "Here you are," he said. "Give it to him, Susan. Let him see for himself. They're only flowers. Only their stalks are horribly tough. Try to pull out into the middle, Mister Mate."

"All right. Only flowers," said Roger, fingering the water lily and letting his fingers run down its stout slippery stalk. "But I wouldn't mind even if they were octopuses."

Susan did her best. But the blades of the oars caught under the broad, flat leaves of the water lilies and swept them together. The long, fat, smooth stalks of the water lilies tangled together and held the oars like strong ropes. She lost an oar overboard. She picked it up again at once, feeling for it, for it was hard to see *Swallow*'s brown oars in the dark water. *Swallow* moved as if she were being driven against something springy, which gave a little and then gathered strength and pushed her back.

"Bother these flowers," said Roger.

"Let me row for a bit," said John.

The captain and the mate changed places. John tried rowing without feathering, keeping the blades of his oars on a slant downwards and forwards so that when he pulled they would not go deep in the water and could not catch under the flat leaves. That was better. Presently *Swallow* was clear of the lilies.

"I can't move the tiller," said Susan. "Only a little way."

"One of those lily stalks must be stuck between the rudder and the boat," said Captain John. "Let me get at it." He took off his coat, rolled up his sleeve, and plunged his arm into the water over the stern. Not one but half a dozen lily stalks were jammed together, wedging the rudder. He broke some of them and then pulled the bits through between the rudder and the keel.

"Clear now," he said, and put out the oars again. He rowed on, telling Susan not to steer too near to the reeds, where the lilies were, and yet not to go too far from the edge. The struggle with the lilies had taken time and it was getting darker and darker.

"I say," said Susan, "it's too dark to find the *Amazon* now. Hadn't we better give it up and go back?"

"If we waited till the morning we should find her all right," said Captain John.

"But what about Titty?" said Susan. "Besides, *Amazon* may not be here at all."

"She must be somewhere in the river," said John. "But I forgot about Titty. We'll go back."

He turned the *Swallow* round and went on rowing.

"It's no good steering," said Susan, "I can't see where to go."

John tugged sharply at one of his oars.

"More lilies," he said.

He pulled *Swallow* out of the lilies and she ran her nose into reeds.

"Do keep a look-out, Roger," said the mate.

"There's nothing to look at," said Roger, "until it's too late."

It was a long time before they found the place where the river left the pool. They had rowed right across the opening once, being afraid to go too near the reeds. At last they decided that even if anyone saw a light here he would not suspect what it was, and used their electric torches. Roger could not get at his, but he used John's, as John was rowing. Susan had her own. Even with the torches it was difficult. A pale light lit up, now here, now there, a patch of quivering reeds. But on either side of the patch of light was darkness. As they moved, the darkness turned to reeds when the round circle of light fell on it. At last they found a place where the lights showed a patch of reeds on each side, but nothing but darkness between them.

"This must be the opening," said John.

He pulled a stroke or two towards the darkness. There was still clear water round the *Swallow*, but the torches showed reeds on right and left. The reeds were all bent the same way and, though John was resting on his oars, the *Swallow* drifted on in the direction in which the reeds were sloping. She was in the river at last.

John let the stream take the *Swallow* with it, using the oars only when she touched the reeds on either side.

"Don't wave your torch in the air, Susan," he said, "or someone may see us. We must be getting near the house. Put yours out, Roger. We don't want to rouse the natives."

Once or twice they ran into the reeds at bends of the river, but they freed themselves without difficulty.

Presently they saw the lights of the big house, standing away from the water.

"We must be near the boathouse now," said John.

"Here it is," said Susan.

John backwatered. "We must look into it again," he said, "just to make sure."

Susan flashed her torch into the boathouse. A bat flew out almost into their faces. The big motor launch lay there as before and the rowing boat. The *Amazon*'s berth was still empty.

"They must have hidden her somewhere up the river," said John.

Just then the lights in the big house went out one by one.

"Dowse your glim, Mister Mate," said Captain John. "They

could see the light now if anyone were looking from those windows."

He pulled *Swallow* into the river again. She drifted on in the darkness.

No one spoke for some time. The plan had failed, and the cutting-out expedition had come to nothing.

Suddenly they began to feel a little more wind.

"We must have reached the open sea," said Captain John. "You can light up that torch, Mister Mate, and see what you can."

Susan flashed the torch all round them. There were no reeds to be seen. On every side there was nothing but rippled water.

"Hullo," cried Roger, "I can see lights far away."

"Rio lights," said John. "We're out. I'm going to hoist the sail. Hold the torch steady while I reef. Even Daddy used to say, 'Never be ashamed to reef a small boat in the dark.'"

Reefing in the dark, even with the help of a torch held by a willing mate, is not too easy, but it was done at last and John brought the *Swallow* head to wind and hoisted the sail, while Susan took the tiller and the mainsheet.

"Put her on the starboard tack," said John, as soon as she was sailing, "and keep her very full. We want to be sure that we are well clear of the rocks off the point."

Even with the reef down there was enough wind to send *Swallow* fast through the water with a steady rippling noise under her bows.

"We're sailing due east," said John presently.

"How do you know?" asked Susan.

"Look," said John.

A broad patch of clear sky showed overhead, and in it the larger stars.

"Look," said John, "there's the Saucepan. There's its

handle. There's its pot. And those two stars that make the front wall of the pot point to the North Star. There's the North Star. It's broad on our port beam, so we must be sailing east. And Rio lights are broad on the starboard beam away in the south."

"Why do the natives always call the Saucepan the Great Bear?" said Susan.

"I don't know," said John. "It isn't like a bear at all. It's more like a giraffe. But you couldn't have a better saucepan."

"She'd go a lot nearer the wind," said Mate Susan.

"Keep her full," said the captain, "Keep her sailing. But we must be well clear of the point now. I'm going to use the compass and chart."

The spirits of the *Swallow*'s crew had risen very much now that they were at sea once more and not fumbling in the dark with reed-beds and water lilies. There is nothing like sea-room to cheer a sailor's heart.

"Are you cold, Roger?" asked the mate.

"Rather," said the look-out.

"Get down below the gunwale and wrap yourself up in this blanket," said the mate, passing a blanket forward by way of the captain.

John, too, crouched in the bottom of the boat. He got out the guide-book, and found the chart in it with the help of his torch. Then he laid his compass on the middle thwart, so that the black line marked on the rim inside it was nearest to the bows. That was no good, because *Swallow* was heeling over and the compass was on a slant so that the compass card could not work. He had to hold it in his hand. Even then the card swung a good deal. He held the compass as steady as he could in one hand, while with the other he threw the light of the torch on it and watched to see what point on the card was

NIGHT SAILING

opposite the black line. It did not keep still, but swung first one way and then the other.

"Almost exactly east," he said at last. "Now bring her closer to the wind."

The mate put the tiller down a little at a time and *Swallow* pointed nearer and nearer to the wind.

"East, east by south, East-south-east, south-east by east, south-east," he said rapidly.

"She won't go much nearer than that," said the mate.

"Keep her so," said Captain John. "South-east it is, or jolly near it." He looked at the chart in the book. "That'll take her to about here and then she'll go perhaps a bit better than south-west on the other tack. But the trouble is, we don't know how far we go on a tack. We'll just have to sail fairly short tacks and try to keep them about the same length. Then we shan't be going near the shore on either side. We'll be able to see by the Rio lights when we are getting near the islands. I'm going to count a hundred, and then we'll go about. Then I'll count a hundred on the other tack before we go about again."

"Rio lights are going out," said Mate Susan.

They were. One by one the lights on the hill above Rio Bay disappeared.

"It must be awfully late," said Susan.

The clouds swept over the stars again. There were no lights to be seen anywhere. The little *Swallow* rushed along in the darkness, Susan keeping her close to the wind, facing directly forward and putting the tiller up a little when she felt the hint of a cold breath on her left cheek.

"Ninety-two, ninety-three, ninety-four, ninety-five, ninety-six, ninety-seven, ninety-eight, ninety-nine, a hundred. . . . Ready about," said John. Susan put the *Swallow* about. For a moment the water was silent under her keel, and then, as she gathered speed, the pleasant, galloping noise of the waves began again.

"You take the tiller, John," said the mate, "I want to get out some chocolate for that boy."

John took the tiller, counting steadily and slowly. He had the compass with him, and sometimes lit the torch and fixed it between his knees, and held the compass in its light. But it was really not much good, though he would have liked to think it was. The best he could do was to keep the ship sailing and to see that she sailed about the same distance on each tack. And then – what if the wind had shifted a little?

The mate got out the cake and the chocolate. She and the captain found that they could do with some just as well as the boy. The boy, warm in his two sets of clothes and his blanket, was enjoying himself enormously.

"Wouldn't Titty have liked it?" he said.

"Liked what?" said Susan.

"Sailing like this in the dark," said the boy.

Susan said nothing. She did not like thinking of Titty alone on the island for so long.

John said nothing. For one thing, he was counting to himself and getting near a hundred. For another, the light of Susan's torch in the bottom of the boat, where she was cutting hunks of cake and breaking up chocolate, and the light of his own torch, when he used it to look at the compass, made the darkness of the night even darker than it really was. It was better than being stuck in the river, much better, but Captain John knew very well that he could not really tell how near they might be to the shore. He was the captain of the *Swallow* and must not wreck his ship. Daddy had trusted him not to be a duffer and, sailing in this blackness, he did not feel so sure of not being a duffer as he did by day. And there were no lights in Rio to help him. Everything was black. He could only keep on tacking against the wind, and he was wondering what he should do when *Swallow* came near the islands off the bay. And how would he know when she was coming near them? It would not do to let his crew know that he was worried. So he said nothing, except that he went on with his counting. Perhaps he counted a little louder than before. He reached a hundred, put *Swallow* about, and began again: "One, two, three," as she went off on the other tack.

Backwards and forwards *Swallow* scurried across the lake in the dark. The islands could not be far away.

Suddenly John stopped counting.

"Listen," he said. "Trees. I can hear the wind in them. What's that?" He flashed his torch over the side. There was the white splash of water breaking on a rock. The noise of wind in trees was close ahead.

"Let go the halyard," called John. "Down with the sail. Grab the yard as it comes."

Susan was as quick as she could be. She knew by John's voice that there was no time to lose. The sail came down in a rush. She gathered it in as well as she could. Then she flashed her torch into the blackness ahead.

"There's something close here," she said.

Swallow drifted in smooth water. John put out the oars.

"It's here," said Susan. "Close here. Pull, pull your left. It's a landing stage."

Swallow bumped softly against wood.

"Hang on to it, whatever it is," called John. He shipped his oars. Then he scrambled forward. The torch showed the black damp wooden beams of one of the landing stages used by the natives for their rowing boats.

"Hold your torch up, Susan," he said. "I'm going ashore."

Susan held up her torch. John was on the landing stage in a moment.

"All right now," he said. "I've got the painter." He lit his torch, and Susan saw him, as *Swallow* drifted back, standing on the landing stage and making fast the painter round a post.

"We're all right here, anyhow," he said. "Lucky for us not to hit that rock we passed. I wonder which island this is."

He walked up the landing stage, lighting himself with his torch. Then he came back.

"There's a notice which says, 'Private. Landing Forbidden.'"

"What are we to do?" said Susan.

"Land," said Captain John. "At least, land if we want to. The natives are all asleep anyhow. We'll stay here until there's a little light. There's bound to be some light soon. Only duffers would try to get through the islands in dark as black as this."

"What about Titty?" said Susan.

"Titty's in camp. She's got a tent. She'll be all right. So are we now."

Captain John was extremely happy. Now that the danger was over, he knew very well that they had as nearly as possible been duffers after all, racing about in the dark. And instead of being smashed on a rock here was *Swallow* snugly tied up to a landing stage. Where they were did not matter. Dawn would show that.

*

Susan said, "Roger, you'd better go to sleep."

There was no answer. Roger was asleep already.

John came back into the boat.

"Look out you don't wake him," said Susan. John stepped carefully over the sleeping boy.

"There are two more blankets," said Susan.

"I'm not going to sleep," said John, making himself comfortable in the bottom of the boat. "You can."

"I say, John," whispered Susan a minute or two later.

Again there was no answer.

A few minutes after that she too was asleep.

*

The wind blew away the clouds and the stars shone out high over *Swallow* and her sleeping crew. The deep blue of the sky began to pale over the eastern hills. The islands clustered about Rio Bay became dark masses on a background no longer as dark as themselves. The colour of the water changed. It had been as black as the hills and the sky, and as these paled so did the lake. The dark islands were dull green and grey, and the rippled water was the colour of a pewter teapot.

*

When John woke it was still long before sunrise, but it was quite light enough for sailing. He woke with a start, and some shame at having slept. He was glad he had been the first to wake. He knew at once where they were, moored to the landing stage on one of the smaller islands at the northern end of Rio Bay. He tried to cast off and get the sail up without waking the others, but, as he moved, they stirred.

Roger yawned, and pulled himself up by the gunwale to look over the side. He just had one look and then, without saying anything, settled down to sleep again.

Susan woke as one wakes who has breakfast to get for a family.

"I say," she said, "we could have started ages ago. It's quite light."

"Come on, then," said John. "You take the mainsheet, while I set the sail. I didn't want to wake you . . . but I've only just waked myself, really. It's going to be another fine day, and the wind is the same."

He unfastened the painter and put it once round the post at

the end of the landing stage. Then he hoisted the sail. He had forgotten that it was reefed. It did not take a minute to shake out the reef. It was a great deal easier than tying it down in the dark. Then he hoisted the sail again and cast off. *Swallow* drifted backwards a few feet, and then gathered a breath of wind and began to sail. He came aft and took the tiller.

Susan blinked at the notice-board about landing being forbidden.

"We didn't exactly land," she said.

They tacked through between Rio and the islands. Rio Bay lay deserted as they had never seen it. No one was up. The houses had blinds in all their windows. Yachts lay at their moorings. The rowing boats of the natives lay drawn up on the beach. There was not a native to be seen.

"It won't be sunrise for some time yet," said John, looking up at the faint glow in the sky over the hills.

They sailed out into the open lake beyond the islands, and made a long board across to the farther side. Then, "Ready about," and back again. Their second tack beyond the islands let them see into the narrow bay below Holly Howe. There was Holly Howe itself, the farmhouse, white among its yew trees and hollies, up on the hillside at the top of the sloping field. Mother and Vicky and Nurse were in there asleep. John looked at Susan, and Susan looked at John. Both had the same thought, but neither said anything. It was not an altogether comfortable thought. Still, they would soon be back at the camp on Wild Cat Island.

At last Susan said, "I hope to goodness Titty had the sense to go to sleep."

"Bet she didn't," said John. "She wouldn't want to, any-how."

They left the Peak of Darien astern. John saw the houseboat moored to its big buoy in Houseboat Bay, but it reminded him of his meeting with Captain Flint, so he looked the other way.

They could see Wild Cat Island now, and suddenly Susan said, "Titty's awake. She's got a most tremendous fire."

A big column of smoke was lifting and blowing from the Island.

"Hullo," said John. "There's a boat. Why, it's the *Amazon*."

"Where?" said Susan.

"Over there. Starboard bow. By Cormorant Island. We shall fetch her on this tack."

"It's *Amazon* all right," said Susan. "But there's nobody in her. She must have broken loose from somewhere and drifted away."

John watched carefully.

"She's not drifting," he said. "She's at anchor. Perhaps the Amazons are asleep in her. Hurrah! Let's capture her after all. We'll get her anchor without waking them and tow her into harbour. Then when they wake they'll be prisoners."

"I don't believe there's anybody in her," said Susan.

"Rubbish," said John. "She couldn't have got there and anchored herself."

"Well, we'll see in a minute," said Susan.

John did not at first alter the *Swallow*'s course. That tack would bring her just to windward of the *Amazon*. Then he would be able to back down carefully with the oars to get hold of the anchor rope and take her in tow without waking the sleeping pirates. Then he changed his mind. It would be better to sail close under her stern to have a look into her. It would be silly to try to get their anchor if the Amazons were only pretending to be asleep.

"I'm sure there's no one in her," said Susan as they rushed towards the little anchored ship.

But just then a hand showed on the gunwale, and a moment

later, just as they were passing under *Amazon*'s stern, the white face and rather draggled hair of Able-seaman Titty appeared over the transom.

Able-seaman Titty had thought out the proper thing to say. Something about "Report", "Capture", "Enemies", and "Prize". But the words went out of her head at the last minute, and all she actually said was, "I've got her."

POINTS OF THE COMPASS

CHAPTER XXII

THE WHITE FLAG

CAPTAIN John let loose a hurrah that startled even himself and woke the sleeping Roger.

"Titty, Titty, how ever did you do it?" he said.

"Well done, Titty," said Susan.

Roger sat up in the bottom of the boat. "Hullo, Titty," he said, and then curled up and went to sleep again.

John jibed *Swallow* and then, bringing her to the wind, ran her alongside. Mate Susan scrambled forward and grabbed the gunwale of the *Amazon*.

"But where are the Amazons?" said John.

"They've got our camp. They've got Wild Cat Island," said Titty. "I couldn't help it. I was asleep, and there was an owl, and I thought it was you, and I lit the lights, and they came into the harbour. Then they went to the camp and I took *Amazon*."

"Who cares about the camp?" cried John. "It was whoever could capture the other's ship. And now we've got her. And I thought we'd failed. *Swallow* is flagship after all. Well done, Titty."

Titty tried to tell her story, how she had pushed out in the dark, how she had tried to anchor near the opposite shore and had found only when day came that she had anchored by Cormorant Island instead. Owls . . . the noise of rowing . . . men quarrelling . . . the leading light going out . . . it all seemed a muddle.

"The main thing," said Captain John, "is that *Amazon* is our prize. Now we'll sail over with the whole fleet. We'll make a landing in the face of the enemy and retake the island. Or we'll call upon them to surrender, and if they won't we'll keep the sea for days and days until they starve. But they'll have to give in. Hullo, what are they doing?"

Susan, Titty, and John stared at Wild Cat Island. Roger woke up again and stared too.

A large blanket, flapping heavily in the wind, was being slowly hoisted up the lighthouse tree. They could see the Amazons holding the ropes below it. It was a big, stout blanket and, though the wind was fresh, it could not blow it out square, but kept it flapping in slow, disheartened flaps.

"It's one of our blankets," said Susan.

"It's a white flag," said Titty. "They're surrendering."

"It isn't very white," said Roger sleepily.

"It's meant to be," said Titty. "I know it's a white flag."

"We'll soon find out," said Captain John. "I say, Mister Mate, will you sail the prize or shall I?"

"You'd better," said Susan, "because of the centre-board."

"Right," said the captain. "Roger stays with you in *Swallow*. Titty sails in *Amazon*. Look out, Titty, I'm coming aboard."

He climbed from one boat into the other.

"Hang on to *Swallow*'s painter while I get sail on *Amazon*," he said.

"Aye, aye, sir," said Titty.

Mate Susan let go of *Amazon*'s gunwale, and *Swallow* drifted astern at the end of her painter.

"Where's the pirate flag?" asked Captain John, looking up the mast to see that all was clear for setting sail.

"They'd left it at the masthead," said Titty. "I hauled it down as soon as it was light and I saw it. I didn't think of it before."

"You did quite right," said Captain John. "While she's a prize she mustn't fly her own flag. She ought to fly ours, but we haven't a spare one."

Amazon's sail was a standing lug, just the same as *Swallow*'s, so that John had no trouble in setting it. He began hauling in the anchor rope.

"Now then, Able-seaman, will you take the tiller to sail her across? She's your prize really, you know. Are you ready, Mister Mate? Shall we cast off *Swallow*?"

"Ready," said Susan. "Roger, run forward to coil down the painter."

Roger, fully awake now, hurried to the bows. Titty let go of *Swallow*'s painter. Roger hauled it in hand over hand and coiled it down. *Swallow*'s sail filled and she began to move. John hauled on the *Amazon*'s anchor rope until it was straight up and down.

"Ready, Titty?"

"Ready."

"She's sailing now. Keep her full." John hauled up the anchor as fast as he could. *Amazon* began to sail, but slipped away to leeward.

"Centreboard's not down," said John. "She'll sail all right as soon as it is. She hasn't got a keel like *Swallow*."

He lowered the centreboard and *Amazon* stopped slipping sideways and her wake lengthened astern of her.

"All right, Titty?" he asked.

"Fine," she said. "I mean, aye, aye, sir." With her mouth a little open and her eyes earnestly on the sail she was steering *Amazon* for the first time. It was no wonder that she used the wrong words.

In the fresh morning wind the fleet moved towards Wild Cat Island, *Swallow* a little ahead.

Mate Susan called across the water, "Shall I make straight for the harbour? I can do it easily on this tack."

"No," called Captain John. "We'd better sail to the look-out point, and ask them what they mean by that blanket."

"I'm certain it's a white flag," said Titty, without shifting her eyes from the sail.

"We'll make sure of it, anyway," said Captain John. "They might try to rush the *Amazon* as we bring her in."

At the look-out place, under the great flapping blanket that hung on the lighthouse tree where the lantern had hung last night, were the Amazon pirates. They were not standing still. They seemed to be dancing.

"What are they doing?" said Captain John.

"That's Captain Nancy, the one who's jumping up and down," said Titty. "Perhaps she's dancing with rage." Titty could not afford to take more than a short look out of the corner of her eye. She was sailing their ship, and she wanted them to see that she could do it. She wanted to leave a wake as straight as theirs.

Susan in the *Swallow* went about before reaching the island. *Amazon* passed under her stern.

"It's deep water right under the look-out place," said John. "You can sail her close to it. She'll lose the wind, but she'll find it again the other side. She's got enough way on her to carry her past."

"Aye, aye, sir," said Titty.

The Amazons on the look-out place seemed to be beckoning them on. "Hurry up," they shouted.

Titty sailed close under the point, and John shouted up to the Amazons, "Do you surrender?"

Nancy Blackett shouted back, "We do. We jolly well do. But buck up."

"Do be quick," shouted Peggy.

"No trickery," shouted John.

"Honest Pirate," shouted Nancy.

"Honest Injun too?" said John doubtfully.

"Honest Injun," shouted Nancy. "Honest anything you like. But don't waste any more time. Bring her to the landing-place."

"We'll take her into port," said Captain John.

"The landing-place is nearer."

"She's our prize," called John, "and we'll take her to the harbour."

Already *Amazon* had passed with flapping sail through the sheltered water under the point. Now she had the wind again, and was sailing fast across the channel between the island and the eastern shore of the lake.

"Close-hauled, Titty," said Captain John.

"Close-hauled it is," said Able-seaman Titty, bringing *Amazon* nearer to the wind. "But what are they in such a hurry about?"

"I don't know," said Captain John. "Don't stint her. We'll race Susan for the harbour. She's beating up the other side."

But *Swallow* had too good a start and was sailing in the open lake. When Titty brought her prize round the rocks at the southern end of the island, *Swallow* was already there. Susan had taken down her sail and was waiting with oars out, just outside the entrance to the harbour.

"It's all right," shouted John. "You can go in. They've surrendered. They're in an awful hurry about something. We'll go in together."

Susan pulled with one oar and backwatered with the other, turned *Swallow* round, and paddled her in towards the harbour.

"DO YOU SURRENDER?"

"Let me row *Amazon* in," said Titty. "I got her out in the dark last night."

"Look here, Titty, can you see the marks? The wind's exactly right. You can sail her in. I'll lower the sail at the right moment. You needn't think about anything but keeping the marks one behind the other."

"I'll try," said Titty, and steered straight in.

"Don't take any notice of me," said John. "Keep the marks together." Just as they shot in among the rocks he lowered the sail and pulled up the centreboard. "Keep your eye on the marks. That's right. Look out for *Swallow*. Well done!"

Just as *Swallow* grounded on the beach in the little harbour, *Amazon* slid quietly in and grounded close beside her.

The Amazons were waiting on the beach. They seemed altogether friendly. Peggy Blackett pulled *Swallow* up, and Nancy Blackett did the same for *Amazon*. But Captain John was taking no risks.

"Captain Nancy," he said, "which ship is flagship?"

Captain Nancy did not hesitate. "*Swallow* is. And earned it. But do buck up. No one knows we're here. We're supposed to be in bed. And we must get home in time to get up for breakfast when we're called."

"You'll never do it," said Captain John.

"Yes we will. The wind's getting stronger every minute, and the sun's only just rising. But do be quick. Let's help to carry the things. There's an awful lot to say."

Titty climbed out over *Amazon*'s bows, and Captain Nancy shook her by the hand and slapped her on the back. "By thunder, Able-seaman," said she, "I wish you were in my crew. This morning when I saw that you'd done us all by yourself, I could have swallowed the anchor. You did just exactly what we had planned to do."

Susan was unloading the blankets and things from *Swallow*.

Roger had run off to the camp. Everybody else took something to carry. Roger came running back.

"They've got a grand fire," he said, "and the kettle's boiling over."

"Who's for tea?" said Mate Susan.

"Well, there's hardly time," said Peggy.

"Come on, quick," said Nancy. "There's lots that's got to be said, and we can slop the tea down while we're saying it."

The Swallows and the Amazons trooped along the path to the camp. The Amazons did most of the talking.

"The real thing is," said Captain Nancy, "that we've got leave to come and camp on the island for a few days, beginning the day after tomorrow. . . ."

"That's tomorrow now," said Peggy.

"Mother had a party last night at home, and there are people coming today, you know, the sort of people we have to be best-frocked for. So the only thing was to have the war last night. We can't very well be at war with each other while we're living in the same camp. The wind wouldn't let us have it before. It had to be last night or never. And then the able-seaman did us. It was a noble feat of arms."

"I got in an awful row when we found *Amazon* had gone," Peggy broke in, "Captain Nancy thought she had drifted away, and when I said she couldn't drift against the wind . . ."

"You wait, Peggy," threatened Captain Nancy.

"Oh, well," said Peggy. "You know what you said. Anyhow, it wasn't till it got light that we knew what had happened to her. At least we didn't know at first, not even after we saw her. Not until Able-seaman Titty sat up and hauled our flag down."

"Well," said Captain Nancy, "yours was a great plan. Anybody might have been taken in by it. When we saw you at the boathouse . . ."

"Where were you?" asked Captain John.

"We were in the reeds at the mouth of the river."

"I never thought of that," said Captain John.

"When we saw you had gone up the river, I was sure you were all aboard. I knew you'd find nothing up the river, and I thought we should have time to get down to Wild Cat Island before it was quite dark. I thought you'd be going back there at once. But I never thought of your leaving a shore party and going up the river simply to trick us into our own trap. It really was a great plan."

"But it wasn't a plan, really," said Captain John. "At least I never thought of it. But what were you going to do?"

"Well, it worked, anyhow," said Captain Nancy. "Our plan was very simple. We were going to sail to Wild Cat Island. My mate was to put me ashore there and sail on and wait in the next bay. I was going to hide, and then, when you came back and went to the camp, I was going to collar *Swallow* and go off to look for Peggy and the rest of the fleet."

"What did happen?" said Susan.

"It took us much longer to get here than I had thought it would. It got dark so quickly, and we had a horrible time getting through the islands. And then, when we saw your lantern . . ."

"Lighthouse," said Titty.

"We thought you'd got back before us. Then we saw a light moving on the island."

"That was my torch," said Titty.

"And we thought we'd sail on and wait somewhere till dawn. Then we saw the two lights, and I guessed at once that they were on the marks. So I came in under oars to tell you about tomorrow. Then we went to the camp and found nobody. Then we shouted a bit, and came back to the harbour, and there was no *Amazon*. Titty did her part awfully well."

"Then what did you do?" asked Susan.

"We had a bit of an argument," said Nancy.

"A bit," said Peggy. "It was a whole one and a half."

"Then we found a seed-cake and ate it. I hope you don't mind."

"Not a bit," said Susan. "There's a new one coming today."

"I ate all your chocolate in *Amazon*," said Titty.

"You'd earned it," said Captain Nancy generously.

They came to the camp. The fire was blazing high and steam was pouring from the kettle.

"Shall I make the tea?" said Peggy Blackett.

"Avast there, Peggy," said Captain Nancy. "We've lost. Captain John is Commodore. Captain John, do you think your mate will give us some tea?"

"Mister Mate," said Captain John, "a round of tea would do us all a bit of good."

"But there's no milk," said Susan, "and it's too early to go to the farm."

"And there isn't time for that," said Captain Nancy. "Let's have it without."

"And call it hot grog," said Titty.

So hot grog it was and served in large tots. No tea with milk ever tasted better than this hot milkless tea on Wild Cat Island while the first sunlight was creeping down from the tops of the opposite hills. But it was so hot and the Amazons were in such a hurry to be off that Peggy was sent down to the landing-place for a bottle full of cold water to cool the grog with.

"Is the war over?" said Nancy. "It had better be, if we're coming tomorrow."

"Right. Peace," said Captain John.

"Skip off and haul down the white flag, then," commanded Nancy, and Peggy, putting her mug of hot grog on the ground, went up to the look-out place and hauled down the blanket from the lighthouse tree.

"The sun's really coming up now," said Peggy when she came back. "We ought to start or we shall never be back in time."

"Come on, then," said Nancy. "And tomorrow we'll set sail as early as ever we can, and we'll bring our tent, and then we'll make a raid on Captain Flint."

"I say," said Susan, "we nearly forgot to give you the message."

"What message?"

"From the savages," said Titty. "We went up into the forest, and saw them, and they showed us a serpent."

"You've been seeing the Billies, the charcoal-burners," said Nancy.

"Well, they live in a wigwam," said Titty.

"They gave us a message for you," said Susan. "We were to tell you to tell him . . ."

"Who?" said Captain Nancy.

"Captain Flint," said Titty.

"That old Billy, or young Billy, I forget which, said that he ought to put a good lock on his houseboat when he leaves her."

"But why?" said Nancy.

"Because of us?" said Peggy.

"No," said Susan. "Because of some talk he'd heard among the other natives."

John had said nothing. Now he spoke. "We couldn't give you the message, because there was no wind," he said, "and I did not know what to do about it. I tried to give him the message, but he wouldn't listen. Would you have told him it or not?"

"But if he locks up the houseboat we shan't be able to raid it for green feathers for our arrows," said Peggy.

"If he doesn't lock it up, it may be raided by someone else," said Nancy. "We ought not to let it be wasted on natives."

They were now hurrying towards the harbour. The point was debated from all sides. It was finally settled by Nancy.

"We'll tell him," she said. "Let him put a padlock on it. Let him put ten padlocks. We'll smash them with crowbars. I'll tell him now, on the way home."

"But you can't," said John. "He's gone away."

"Gone away?" said Nancy, as she pushed *Amazon* off.

"I saw him go. He took his parrot."

"Well, he's back then," said Nancy. "We saw his light in the houseboat on our way here last night. The cabin windows were all lit up."

"We can't tell him now," said Peggy.

"Why not?" said Nancy.

"Because we're at home in bed," said Peggy.

"Shiver my timbers, so we are," said Captain Nancy. "I'd forgotten that. Shove off. So long, Commodore."

As fast as they could, the Amazon pirates paddled their ship out of the harbour and set sail. There was no time to lose. The sunlight had almost reached the edge of the water on the far side of the lake. The Swallows went back to their camp. As they got there they heard a shout from the water, and John and Titty ran up to the look-out place. *Amazon* was sailing by, moving very fast with the fresh morning wind, her sail well out to starboard. At her masthead fluttered once more the pirate flag. Peggy held the flag halyards. Suddenly the flag dropped, and was lowered to half-mast. Then it rose again, and fluttered at the masthead as before.

"Hurrah for the Swallows," shouted Nancy and Peggy over the water.

"Hurrah for the Amazons," shouted Titty and John. Roger ran up just in time to shout, "Hurrah." Susan was busy dividing out the blankets between the two tents. Presently she came up to the others who were still watching the little white sail growing smaller and smaller in the distance.

"Roger," she said, "your watch below. Go to bed this minute."

"But it's tomorrow," said Roger.

"I don't care if it's the day before yesterday," said Susan. "March!"

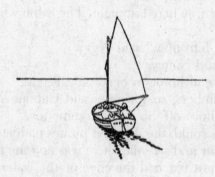

CHAPTER XXIII

TAKING BREATH

THAT day it was one o'clock before John and Roger rowed across and went up to Dixon's Farm for the milk and a new supply of eggs and butter. It had been nearly seven in the morning before Susan had hurried them to bed in broad daylight. No alarm clock could have stirred them, and they had no alarm clock on Wild Cat Island. The camp was roused at last by Roger, who was waked, some time after noon, by a strong desire for breakfast.

"You can't have breakfast till we've got the milk," Susan had said, waking up to find the boy pulling at her, and saying, "I want something to eat." She had given him a biscuit, but a biscuit does not go far.

Titty had waked with a great start just as Roger went out again. She had sat up suddenly, thinking she heard an owl, and that she was still watching by the camp fire. But on finding herself in the tent with Susan, and the hot sun pouring through the white canvas walls, she lay down again to pick up in her mind the threads of the night's adventure.

Roger went back to the captain's tent. The captain's feet stuck up temptingly under his blanket. Roger took hold of one of them in both hands, blanket and all, and gave a tug. The foot jerked suddenly away, and John woke up.

"Susan says, 'Go and fetch the milk,'" said Roger.

"I didn't. I said we couldn't have breakfast without it," called Susan from the other tent.

John yawned. "Come on, then. Where are our towels?"

"Let's swim afterwards," said Roger. "I'm empty."

John rolled over to look at the chronometer, which lay with the little aneroid on the tin box at the back of the tent. As soon as he saw what time it was, he threw his blankets off and jumped up.

"Come on," he said. "We'll go for the milk right away."

"Take a basket for the eggs," called Susan.

The captain and the boy went to the harbour, pushed off the *Swallow*, and worked her out with the oars. There was still a good wind blowing, and they decided that it would be quicker to sail than to row.

"What will we do to her to show that she's the flagship?" asked the boy.

"Why, nothing," said the captain.

"What is a flagship?" asked the boy.

"It's the chief ship of a fleet."

"But why flag?"

"Because the Admiral of the Fleet, or the Commodore (that's me), flies his flag on her."

"But you haven't got a flag, only the one Titty made."

"Well, that's a very good one," said the captain. "It's different from theirs. That's all that matters."

They landed, and hurried up the field with the milk-can.

"You're more than a bit late for the milk this morning," said Mrs. Dixon, who was scrubbing the slate floor in the dairy. "Morning," she said, "why, it's afternoon already. I was just saying to Dixon that I thought maybe he ought to run down to see if you were all right, or happen go along the road to Holly Howe to see if you were gone home."

These natives! Friendly though there were, there was never any knowing what mischief they might do. It was just that thought that had made John jump up in such a hurry when he saw the time. If Mr. Dixon had gone along to Holly Howe to ask what had happened, and whether the milk was wanted, Mother would have been bound to think that something had gone wrong. And nothing had gone wrong at all. Everything had gone right. John knew well enough that Mother counted on the regular morning visit to Dixon's Farm for the milk to keep her in touch with the Swallows. Mother knew that the Dixons would let her know at once if no one had come up from the island with the milk-can. Natives were like that, useful in a way, but sometimes a bother. They all held together, a huge network of gossip and scouting, through the meshes of which it was difficult for explorers and pirates to slip.

"I'd have run along myself, first thing," said Mrs. Dixon, "if I hadn't been that busy."

"Well," thought John, "it was a good thing that the natives had plenty to do."

"What was gone with you?" asked Mrs. Dixon, bustling round and pouring the milk out of a great bowl. "Did you sleep so hard you never wanted any breakfast?"

"I did," said Roger.

"We overslept," said John. "We were late in going to bed."

"You were that," said Mrs. Dixon. "We saw the light you had on the island when we were going to bed, and that was ten o'clock, for we were none too early ourselves."

"We were much later than that," said Roger, and was just going to say how they had captured the *Amazon* and not gone to bed till after sunrise, when he remembered, just in time, that Mrs. Dixon was a native.

"Better late than never," said Mrs. Dixon. "Here's your milk. And I've a dozen eggs to put into that basket, and there's a loaf of bread and a bunloaf, and the seed-cake they sent along yesterday evening from Holly Howe. I hope Miss Susan and Miss Titty are both well."

"Miss Susan and Miss Titty!" Mrs. Dixon could not have found a better way of showing how deep is the gulf that exists between native life and real life than by so describing the mate and the able-seaman.

"Quite well, thank you," said the captain.

"The seed-cake'll go in the basket on the top of the eggs," said Mrs. Dixon. "It's that light, it won't crack them. But where you'll put the bunloaf and the bread I'm sure I don't know."

"I'll carry them," said Roger.

They went down the field with the hearts of those who have had to cross some rather thin ice. The captain carried the milk-can in one hand, and the basket in the other. Roger had a loaf in each arm. They could see the smoke rising from the fire on the island and, by the time they had sailed across and beached *Swallow* at the landing-place, Susan had the kettle boiling, tea made, and was only waiting for the milk and the eggs.

Breakfast was a silent, hungry meal until it began to turn into dinner.

"We may as well go straight on," Susan said, and the others agreed, though they had eaten their eggs and had got as far as bread and marmalade. John opened a pemmican tin.

"Why don't the natives ever have pemmican after bread and marmalade?" said Roger. "It's very good. May I have marmalade *on* my pemmican?"

"No," said Susan.

"Why not?" said Roger.

"You'll be ill, like you were on your last birthday."

Roger thought for a minute. "I don't think so," he said.

"Well, you're not going to try," said Susan.

Susan was in a very native mood that day, as Able-seaman Titty observed. Perhaps the adventures of the night were heavier on her conscience than on those of the other Swallows.

Perhaps she needed sleep. Her mood showed itself in not allowing Roger and Titty to bathe the moment they had finished their breakfast-dinner meal of Grape Nuts, eggs, bread and marmalade, bread and pemmican, bunloaf and marmalade, bananas fresh from the tree (the Amazons had only eaten two each, and there were still plenty on the bunch), seed-cake and tea. Also washing up had to be done at once in a very native manner. And when that was done there were buttons to sew on.

"How you manage to lose such a lot of buttons, I can't think," she said to Roger.

"Well, you would make me put on two of everything," said Roger, "and there wasn't room in one of them for both."

There had been little time for talk in the early morning when the captain, the mate, and the boy had come sailing home to find the able-seaman with her prize anchored by Cormorant Island and the Amazons marooned on Wild Cat Island and in a dreadful hurry to get back. And now, of course, Titty wanted to hear all about the Amazon River, and Roger had plenty to say about the lagoon that was full of octopuses that turned into flowers when you took hold of them. Then she had to hear the whole story of the wild sail down the lake in pitch dark and how nearly they had been wrecked off the Rio Islands, and how they had waited there until the beginnings of daylight. And then John wanted to hear the whole story of the watch on the island and the way in which the able-seaman had been able to capture the enemy ship. And Titty told of the dipper, and of the coming of the Amazons, and of how she fell asleep and was wakened by a real owl and mistook it for the Swallows' signal. Then she told of how she had been Robinson Crusoe and had found a strange boat at the landing-place and had been visited by Man Friday. It was not until she came to talk of Man Friday that she remembered that she had a message for John.

"Oh yes," she said. "I promised to tell you. Mother came

here really to see you, not me. It was about Captain Flint being so beastly. She wanted to know if you'd like her to write to Mrs. Blackett to ask her to tell Captain Flint that he was a liar, not you, and that you'd never touched his boat."

"What did you say?" asked John quickly.

"I said I didn't know. I said I'd ask you."

John jumped up and went into his tent to look at the chronometer.

"I'm going to Holly Howe to talk to Mother," he said, when he came back.

"Native talk?" asked Titty.

"Yes," said John. "I must tell her she'd better not write."

"Can I come too?" said Roger.

"You stay here," said Titty. "It's native talk he's going for. You'd only be in the way. Besides I've got a plan for us."

"What plan?"

"A tremendous one."

"What's it about?"

"Treasure," said Titty. "Come on and see the captain off. Then we'll go to a secret place while the mate goes on with your buttons."

*

Captain John sailed away up the lake to Holly Howe. It was a grim business this, of being unjustly suspected by Captain Flint, but at the same time he could not let Mother write to Mrs. Blackett about it. That might mean trouble for the Amazons. He found Mother writing letters in the Holly Howe garden.

"I say, Mother, you're not writing to Mrs. Blackett?"

"Not I," said Mother. "I wasn't going to write unless you wanted me to. That was why I rowed down to the island yesterday. What time did you get back last night? After I left Titty, Nurse and I kept a look-out for you by the boathouse, thinking I might stop you on your way back and ask you about writing."

John was a little taken aback. With Captain Flint in his mind, he had forgotten quite a number of other things.

"We didn't get back till this morning," he said.

"So the Blacketts made you stop the night," said Mother. "Poor Titty!"

"It wasn't poor Titty at all," said John. "Titty did better than any of us. She captured the *Amazon* all by herself."

"But then where were the Blacketts?"

"They were on Wild Cat Island."

"But where were you?"

"We were up the Amazon River, that's the river where they live, you know, and then it got too dark and we had to stop by the islands until it was light enough to see."

"Don't you think that was very nearly like being duffers?"

"Yes," said John, "it was rather. But you see it was war and it was our only chance. And I promise we shall never do it again. Stay out at night, I mean. There won't be any need. The Amazon pirates are coming to the island tomorrow to camp with us. The war between us is over. We've won. At least Titty won it. And Roger had two of everything on last night and slept in *Swallow*. And nobody has caught a cold or anything. But, I say, Mother."

"What?"

"All this is a most deadly secret, between you and me. I mean you mustn't talk about it, not to anybody." He had just remembered that the Amazons had escaped from their beds to make their night attack.

"All right," said Mother. "Mrs. Blackett seemed to know pretty well what sort of young women hers were. I shan't tell her. But all the same I'm glad it's over. There must be no more sailing at night. Promise?"

"I promise."

"You know you've only got about three days left. We are going home at the end of the week. It would be a pity if two or three of you were to get drowned first."

"Only three more days," said John.

"The weather can't keep on like this much longer and when it breaks you'll have to come away from the island anyhow. A camp of drowned rats is no fun for anyone. I've tried it. You make the most of your three days. We'll come again next year. You're sure you'd rather I didn't write to say you had never touched the houseboat?"

"Much rather."

"Very well. Come in and see Vicky and have some tea."

*

As soon as they had watched *Swallow*'s brown sail disappear beyond the look-out point and the north end of the island, Able-seaman Titty and the boy left the landing-place and went to the harbour.

"This isn't a secret place," said the boy.

"Any place is secret if nobody else is there," said Titty.

"Besides, we're going up on my rock, where I was when I saw the bird that bobbed and flew under water."

"Will the bird be there?"

"I don't know. He may be."

"Then it won't be secret."

"Yes it will. Birds don't count. There's nobody on the whole island except us and the mate, and she's sewing on buttons. How many buttons has she got to sew?"

"Dozens," said the boy. "One from each sleeve and then all the others came off the front when I tried to get both my shirts off at once."

"That'll take her a long time," said the able-seaman. "This

place will be as secret as any place could possibly be. Come on. Take your shoes and stockings off."

They took their shoes and stockings off and left them on the beach. Then they paddled across the shallow to the big rock at the side of the harbour, climbed up it and settled themselves on the top of it, dangling their legs in the sunlight and looking out over the rippled lake.

"Anybody could see us here," said the boy.

"Nobody could hear us," said the able-seaman.

"What is the plan?" said the boy.

"Treasure," said the able-seaman. "But I can't tell you unless you promise to come, all by yourself with me. . . ."

"Nobody else?"

"Nobody else."

"Not even Susan?"

"Nobody. We'll go to a desert island, a really desert island, not this one, and there we'll dig for treasure buried by pirates. For a long time we shan't find it. They never do. But then, at last, there will be a hollow sound under our pickaxes and thousands of gold pieces will be rolling about in the sand."

"But where is the island?"

"You haven't said you'll come. Treasure-seekers only tell each other. If I told you, you might go and let it out to a pirate or somebody."

"I wouldn't."

"Well, will you come?"

"All right," said the boy.

"You swear. Properly we ought to have a bit of paper and you ought to make a mark with your own blood. Can't you prick your finger?"

"No," said Roger.

"Well, you promise to come?"

"Yes."

"Then lean over a bit that way. Bend down so that you can see under that bough. That's the island."

"But that's Cormorant Island."

"It's Treasure Island too."

"How do you know?"

"I heard the pirates burying their treasure there last night when I was in *Amazon*."

"Real pirates?"

"Of course, real ones. They swore like anything."

"Real treasure?"

"Of course, real treasure. I heard them say how heavy it was."

"How shall we carry it if it's very heavy?"

"Bit by bit. Some of it will be in ingots of gold. And then there'll be lots of gold pieces, guineas and things. And precious stones. Diamonds. We'll carry away a little at a time."

The boy listened while the able-seaman told him all she knew about treasure islands. She knew a great deal. She told him how pirates captured ship after ship and took all the treasure out of each ship and made the crew walk the plank and fall into the sea to feed the sharks, and then how the pirates sank their prize and sailed on to capture another, to be emptied and sunk in the same way. She told him how, when the pirate ship was so crammed with treasure that there wasn't room for dancing on the decks and the pirates could hardly get into their own cabins when they wanted to go to sleep, they sailed to an island and buried all the treasure in a safe place. She told him how they made a chart so that they could come and find the treasure when they were tired of pirating and wanted to retire and live in a house by the seashore, where they could spend their days looking out to sea with a telescope and thinking of the wicked things they had done. ("Or live in a houseboat, like Captain Flint," said Roger.) She told him how the pirates always, or nearly always, lost the chart and how the treasure-seekers

("That's you and me") sometimes found the treasure instead of the pirates. She told him how sometimes the pirates fought among themselves till none were left, so that nobody knew where the treasure was. ("But we know, because I heard them putting it there.") She was still talking about it when they heard Susan calling from the camp and, paddling back to the island, put on their shoes and stockings and ran to the camp for tea.

*

Just when they were finishing washing up after a tea that had been very native, probably because Susan was still not feeling happy about having let them stay up until morning, Captain John came home.

His first words were, "I told Mother about our being out all last night and not coming home till today."

"Was she very upset about it?" said Susan.

"I think she was rather, inside. But she hid it, and it's all right now. Only, I've promised not to do it again."

After that, Susan cheered up and became much less like a native and more like a mate.

"The worst of it is," said John, "that Mother says we've only got another three days, even if the weather does hold out."

"We can do a lot in three days," said Susan.

"There's one thing we must do now," said John. "And that's make our chart. The Amazons will be here tomorrow, and they've got their own names for everywhere. We must make our chart today. Who's going to help?"

Everybody wanted to help. A few minutes later Captain John was lying flat on his stomach on the ground with the guide-book and its map open before him. The others squatted round him, watching him copy the outline of the lake on two pages of the big exercise book that had been brought for a log.

"There isn't room to do it here really properly," he said,

"but this is a sketch chart and we'll do a good one after we get home."

"A huge one," said Roger, "like Daddy's chart of the China Seas."

"And we'll hang it up on the schoolroom wall to show where we've been," said Susan.

"And to plan more explorings," said Titty.

"Will it have colours?" said Roger.

"Colours for the lights. We'll put a blob of yellow for our lighthouse and two little blobs for the leading lights."

"What colour will the land be?"

"They leave the land white on charts. It doesn't count, except where you can see it from a ship. And even then only bits of it count. They'd put in Darien, because it's a high point, but they wouldn't bother to mark Holly Howe."

"We will, won't we?"

"We'll put it in as a native settlement. They do that sometimes."

"With a little picture?"

John drew a tiny house with trees and three little figures, a quarter of an inch high, for the natives, Mother, Vicky and Nurse. Then, in Houseboat Bay, he wrote its name and made a picture of the houseboat. Then again there was Dixon's Farm, with a little figure and a cow, to show the produce of the country.

"Put in the savages with their wigwam and their snake," said Titty, and a snake, a three-cornered black mark for the hut, and a fire, showed the country of the charcoal-burners.

Rio was marked with little houses and landing stages. The islands off Rio Bay were drawn in, but only one of them had a name. John wrote "Landing Island" beside the one where landing was forbidden and the *Swallow* had rested, swinging from the wooden pier in the darkness of the night.

"You ought to put in my island," said Titty.

"Which island?"

"Where I watched for the Amazons that first day we saw them."

It went in and was marked "Titty's Island".

Wild Cat Island was marked, with its lighthouse tree, its landing-place, its harbour and camp. Then a fish was drawn in Shark Bay, where they went perch-fishing. Then the captain began putting in a dotted line to show the track of the *Swallow* from Wild Cat Island to the Amazon River and back again.

"How far up the river did you go?" asked Titty.

"As far as the lagoon," said John. "I've marked that."

"Put in the octopuses," said Roger.

"I'm no good at drawing octopuses," said John, when he had done his best.

The chart began really to look like a chart. North and south of the part of the lake they knew were dotted lines and the words "Uncharted waters" or "Unexplored". "It's no good putting in what we don't know," said John. "But of course we must put in mountains, where you can see them from the parts we have explored." John began drawing little anchors at all the ports where the *Swallow* had called. There was one by the island off Rio, and one at Rio itself, and one in the Holly Howe bay, and one in Shark Bay where Roger had hooked and lost his big fish, and one at the point where they had landed to visit the charcoal-burners, and one at the landing for Dixon's Farm.

"What about the place where I anchored in *Amazon*?" said Titty.

"Yes, that ought to go in," said John, and a little anchor was drawn close to the north end of Cormorant Island.

"There ought to be a Treasure Island," said Titty, "but the one that's got treasure on it has got a name already."

"Which?" said John.

"Cormorant Island."

"But there's nothing there but cormorants."

"It's a secret," said Titty, "but there is treasure there. Roger and I are going to discover it. The pirates put it there last night while I was anchored in *Amazon*."

"What pirates?"

"They came in the dark, rowing. I heard them."

"Fishermen, probably," said John.

"No, they weren't," said Titty. "They nearly smashed their boat and they swore."

"How you do romance," said Susan.

"You were asleep and dreaming," said John. "But, look here, we'll make one of the other islands a Treasure Island if you like. The biggest one off Rio hasn't got a name."

"But there really *is* treasure on Cormorant Island. Tons of Spanish gold. Roger and I are going to look for it. Let's go at once and make sure."

"Steady on, Titty," said Susan.

"It's too late to go tonight, anyhow," said John, "and there can't be any treasure there really."

"They put it there at dead of night," said Titty. "Tons and tons of it."

"Oh, look here, Titty," said Susan, almost turning native again. "Time to get supper now. All hands early to bed. Remember the Amazons are coming in the morning."

CHAPTER XXIV

GRAVE NEWS FROM HOUSEBOAT BAY

AFTER a good night's sleep the Swallows felt themselves again. They were up early and bathed. Then they went fishing for their breakfast and caught a dozen perch, for they wanted plenty of breakfast for the Amazons too in case they came early. "You never know when they might start," said Susan. "I don't suppose they'll be here in time, but if they are we've got enough for six. We'll cook the lot in case, and now somebody had better go up to the farm for the milk."

They had been anchored for the fishing in Shark Bay, not far from the Dixons' landing-place. They rowed ashore, and Roger and Titty went up the field with the milk-can, while the captain and the mate cleaned perch by the side of the lake.

"Titty'll be wanting to go off with Roger to look for her treasure," said the captain. "Of course there isn't any really, but she'll want to go."

"Sometimes she doesn't know what has happened and what hasn't," said the mate. "They can go this afternoon. But I expect she'll have forgotten all about it when the Amazon pirates come and Nancy and Peggy are putting up their tent and planning what to do next."

"We've got an awful lot to do this morning," said the captain. "I want to splice all the reef points before they come. I ought to have done it yesterday. And then *Swallow* really wants a scrub."

273

"And I want the camp to be like a new pin," said the mate. "My pots and pans are a disgrace."

By the time the perch were all cleaned and laid out in a neat row in the bottom of the boat, Roger and Titty came back with the milk.

"It's too bad," said Titty, as soon as she was near enough to talk. "Captain Flint's been at it again, worse than ever. We'd hardly said good morning to Mrs. Dixon before she said we ought never to have touched the houseboat. I told her we hadn't. She said, 'Well, somebody has.' Then she shut up and didn't say any more even when I said Captain Flint was a beast and I wished his houseboat was sunk."

"You oughtn't to have said that," said Susan.

"I forgot she was a native," said Titty.

"She didn't give us any cake or molasses. Not even an apple," said Roger.

"Why can't he leave us alone?" said John.

"Which perch did I catch?" asked Roger, looking at the row of cleaned perch in the bottom of the boat. "Was it this one? It wasn't the very little one. Susan caught that. I saw her."

They rowed back to Wild Cat Island. Susan stoked up her fire, put butter in the frying-pan and melted it for the frying of the perch. Roger watched her. John went up to the look-out point. Titty followed him.

"May Roger and I go and look for treasure after breakfast?" she said.

"The Amazons are coming today," said John. "We've got to scrub decks first and put everything shipshape before they come. But afterwards, perhaps. Hullo," he said. "Titty, skip down to my tent and get the telescope. That's the third boat I've seen go into Houseboat Bay."

"Aye, aye, sir," said the able-seaman, and ran down to the

camp. Here she was grabbed by the mate, who wanted someone to butter bread while she was looking after the perch.

"Captain wants the telescope," said the able-seaman.

"Tell him breakfast's practically ready," said the mate. "The telescope'll keep. Perch won't. They ought to be eaten hot."

Titty escaped with the telescope and gave her message.

"Coming in a minute," shouted John. He held the telescope to his eye. "There's something up in Houseboat Bay. There's a motor launch going in now with a lot of people in it."

The mate's whistle shrilled from the camp.

"Coming, coming," shouted the captain.

"If the natives are making an attack on Captain Flint," said Titty, "I wish we were there too."

The mate whistled again, and the captain and the able-seaman joined the others by the fire.

"Something's happening in Houseboat Bay," said John. "Boats going in one after another. I suppose he's telling them all that we have been touching his beastly houseboat."

"Don't think about Captain Flint," said Susan. "We can't help it if he thinks we have been at his boat. Nothing will stop his thinking it. Remember what Mother said. We know we haven't. Don't worry about him. I've put the sugar in your tea, and here's your perch. There's another one after that, and then one more if the Amazons aren't quick."

When each of the Swallows had eaten two perch, so that four were left in the frying-pan, Susan sent the boy up the look-out to see if the *Amazon* was in sight. He was back in a moment.

"No sail in sight," he said, "but there's a big boat going out of Houseboat Bay."

"They won't be here till after breakfast," said Susan. "That's another perch all round."

"I wonder what *is* happening," said John.

"Don't think about him," said Susan.

"All right. I won't," said John.

As soon as breakfast was over and done with, everybody set to work to tidy up. "I'll look after the camp," said the mate, "if you want to clean up *Swallow*. Take the boy and the able-seaman, and set them scrubbing decks and polishing up the brass-work."

"There isn't much brass-work," said Roger.

"There are the belaying-pins," said Titty.

"Well, go and polish them up," said the mate. "You can do a lot with sand and a damp rag. Here are two rags. Get along with you. Clear all the dirt out, and rub all over with a wet rag, and make her look like a new ship."

"I'm going to bring the sail up to the camp," said John. "It wants lacing again to the yard, and I can do the reef points best when the sail isn't bent."

"I don't care so long as you don't get in my way," said Susan. "I've got the pots to clean."

"We'll take *Swallow* round to the harbour and moor her so that she's all snug in her berth when the Amazons come," said John.

He went down to the landing-place with the able-seaman. The boy had run on before and was already aboard. They pushed off and paddled her round to the harbour, where they had left the mast and sail when they went fishing before breakfast. John stepped the mast and hoisted Titty's flag to the masthead. The boy and the able-seaman stayed aboard to do their polishing and cleaning. John moored *Swallow* with a warp over her stern and the painter from her bows, so that she floated at one side of the harbour, leaving room for the *Amazon* to come in.

"You can slack up the stern warps and haul on the painter when you want to come ashore," he said.

"Aye, aye, sir," said the able-seaman and the boy, already

busy scrubbing the thwarts and cleaning all the dirt from the bottom boards.

The captain took the rolled-up sail with its boom and yard, balanced them over his shoulder and carried them back to the camp. There he dumped them on the ground. Susan had just finished her washing up.

"I'll just go up to the look-out and see if those boats have gone," he said.

Susan looked up.

"It's no good thinking about him," she said. "Just don't think about him at all."

"That's all very well," said John, "but I can't help it."

"Come on and help me to hang out the blankets," said Susan.

"The Amazons may be in sight," said John.

"Never mind if they are," said Susan.

They took the blankets from the tents and hung them over the tent ropes that were stretched to the trees. Then they pummelled the haybags, which had got very lumpy. They shook them and pushed them and pulled them about until they were a little less like half-empty sacks of round Dutch cheeses and a little more like mattresses.

Then Susan started scraping the saucepan and the frying-pan and cleaning the black off them with fine sand. At least, it was not very fine sand, but it was the finest she could get.

"I'm going to leave the kettle just as black as it is," she said. "It looks fine."

John spread the sail flat out on the ground, undid the lacings and freed it from the yard and the boom. He settled down with some fine stuff, thin string, to finish of the ragged reef points with neat splices, cutting the frayed ends away with his knife.

This took a long time, and then he noticed that one of the seams in the sail was giving. An inch or two of stitching had come undone. John went into his tent and rummaged in his box.

"Lucky we brought a sailmaker's needle," he said as he came back.

"Luckier if you knew how to use it," said the mate a moment or two later, when she looked up and saw the captain sucking his thumb.

"Well, it isn't my fault," said the captain. "Real sailmakers push the needle through with a lump of leather in the palm of their hand."

"Let's have a look," said the mate.

Between them they made a pretty fair job of the seam. John's reef points were very good indeed. "If life was only splices," his father had said the year before, "you would have nothing left to learn."

With Susan's help he stretched the sail along the yard and began to lace it. They were both so intent on this that they saw nothing of a boat that pulled in to the landing-place until they heard it scrunch on the beach.

They looked up to see a large policeman, in his shirt-sleeves, pulling in his oars. He got up, balancing heavily, and stepped ashore. Then he picked up his coat, which was lying in the bows of his rowing boat, and walked straight up to the camp. He was very hot, and as he walked he struggled with his coat until at last he got out of it a big red handkerchief, with which he mopped his face. He looked down on the captain and the mate.

"Good morning," said John politely.

"Morning," said the big policeman. "Busy?"

"Yes, rather," said John.

"Cooler work than rowing in this weather."

"Have you come a long way?" asked Susan, who was wondering what she could give him to drink.

"Aye," said the policeman, "I have. And what might you be doing here, is what I want to know."

"This is our camp," said John. "Won't you sit down and rest yourself? I'm sorry we haven't any beer, but there are one or two bananas still left on that tree."

The policeman grunted and did not say "Thank you." With another struggle he pulled a notebook and a pencil out of his coat.

"Name and address, please," said the policeman.

"My name is John Walker," said John. "This is our address."

"Walker, John," said the policeman, writing. He mopped his face again. "Address?"

"Here."

"Where?"

"Here."

"That won't do," said the policeman. "Where do you live?"

"In these tents."

The policeman walked round to the tents and looked into them.

Susan protested.

"We haven't made our beds yet," she said.

Just then there was a cheerful noise of whistling from the other end of the island.

"Any more of you?" said the policeman.

"Lots," said John.

"Now, look here," said the policeman, "and answer me straight. When did you go aboard Mr. Turner's houseboat?"

"We've never been near it," said John, "except once when I went to talk to Mr. Turner."

"Come, come," said the policeman. "That won't wash at all. Why, the mess it's in . . ."

"Sammy!"

A clear, ringing voice made the policeman turn round sharp.

"Sammy, I'm ashamed of you. If you don't go away at once I'll tell your mother."

"I'm sure I beg pardon, Miss Ruth," said the policeman, turning redder than ever. "I thought they'd know something about the burglary if anybody did, seeing that they've been at the houseboat before. I had no sort of idea they were friends of yours."

"Of course they are," said Captain Nancy, coming into the camp and dumping a bundle of tent poles. "They've never had anything to do with Uncle Jim's houseboat. You go away back to Uncle Jim and tell him so. Or shall we take his boat and keep him prisoner?" she added, turning to John.

"No, don't do that, Miss Ruth," said the policeman. "Not today. I've got to row right down to the foot of the lake."

Peggy Blackett came along the path from the harbour, with a huge white bundle on her shoulder, followed by Titty and Roger with blankets and a bundle of fishing rods.

"Hullo, Sammy," she said. "What are you doing here?"

"It was all a mistake, miss," said the policeman.

"Run away, Sammy, and don't make those mistakes again," said Nancy.

The big policeman went down to his boat again and pushed off.

"Miss Ruth and Miss Peggy," he begged, "don't you say anything to Mother."

"All right, Sammy, not if you are good."

He rowed quickly away.

"What did he want?" said Titty.

"Why was he frightened?" said Roger.

"Did you know him?" said Susan.

"Of course we did," said Captain Nancy. "His mother used to be Mother's nurse, and she was our nurse too when we were very young. He's our policeman. He isn't afraid of anybody except his mother . . . and us, of course. I say, you know what's happened?"

"What?"

"You know that message the old Billies gave you to give to us, about telling Uncle Jim to put a padlock on his houseboat? Well, they were right."

"Uncle Jim's houseboat has been burgled," said Peggy.

"I knew something had happened when I saw all those boats there this morning," said John.

"The other pirates attacked Captain Flint's ship while he was away," said Captain Nancy. "He had gone, you know, when you said he had. We were wrong. Those lights we saw in the houseboat when we were sailing down here in the dark weren't his. They belonged to the burglars, to the other pirates. At that very moment they were about their fell work."

"Someone else saw those lights too," said Peggy. "The motor-man who knew that Uncle Jim was away. So in the morning he went to see and found the cabin door swinging open and the whole place upside down. He came over to tell Mother and Mother sent a telegram to Uncle Jim. He got here last night, and went to his houseboat, but everything was in such an awful mess that he came back with his parrot to our house to sleep."

"He was raging mad," said Nancy. "And the parrot was too cross to talk."

"Sometimes he was mad and sometimes just glumpy," said Peggy. "He said he wouldn't have minded if they'd taken everything he had except what they did take. They've taken his old cabin trunk, with his typewriter in it and the book he's been writing all summer, the book he's been writing so that he couldn't be one of us like he used to be. He said he supposed they took it because it was heavy. He didn't know what else they'd taken. But they'd emptied all the lockers out on the floor and pulled everything in the boat to pieces. Worse than a spring cleaning, he said it was. Sometimes he was just miserable and saying nothing at all, and then other times he would start raging away about the lake being covered with boys, and about you. . . ."

"He always thinks it's us," said John.

"I was just going to tell him that it couldn't have been you that night," said Nancy, "because you were up the Amazon River when we saw the light in his ship, but Peggy nudged me just in time and I remembered that we were in bed that night, so I shut up. I began to think it was a good thing we'd already got leave to camp with you. Any minute someone might have told us not to, they were all in such a stew. So we slipped off and stowed our things in *Amazon* last night and hid her up the river. And then this morning we lay low until Uncle Jim had rowed away back to the houseboat. When we did start there wasn't much wind, or we'd have been here before. We had to row through the islands, and then we waited for a bit watching all the boats taking people to Houseboat Bay to see the burglary."

"You got back in time yesterday morning?" said Susan.

"It was a near squeak, but we did," said Nancy.

"We just had time to get into bed with our clothes on when they came banging at the door," said Peggy.

"I say," said John. "Were they burgling the very night of our war?"

"Of course they were," said Nancy. "I told you. We saw their light in the houseboat. If we'd only known we could have captured the lot of them and made Uncle Jim our grateful slave for ever."

"Then perhaps Titty really did hear something that night," said John.

"Perhaps the pirates I heard were the very ones who had sacked Captain Flint's ship," said Titty.

"Did you hear any?" said Nancy.

"They were in a rowing boat," said Titty, "when I was anchored in *Amazon*."

"They probably were the burglars," said Nancy. "We saw their light and then you heard them. What beats me is why Uncle Jim should have got it into his head that you had anything to do with it."

"Of course we didn't," said Captain John.

"Gaskets and bowlines," said Captain Nancy, "you needn't tell me that. What puzzles me is why he should think you did."

Captain John was very uncomfortable.

"He didn't believe me when I told him I hadn't touched his houseboat, that time I went to tell him what the charcoal-burners had said."

"But why wouldn't he believe you?"

"Well," said Captain John. "Look here, Captain Nancy, it really doesn't matter."

"Of course it does," said Captain Nancy. "Old Sammy would never have come nosing round here if he hadn't heard something from Uncle Jim."

"It was that day we first saw you," said Captain John. "When we thought he'd fired at you. He saw us when we sailed up the lake to see where you went, and he thought it was us who put that firework on his cabin roof."

Captain Nancy turned very red, even through her sunburn.

"I'll put that matter right at once," she said. "Was he very beastly?"

"He did call me a liar," said John. "But it doesn't matter now, really."

"It does," said Captain Nancy. "Peggy!"

"Sir."

"Empty the rest of our stores out of *Amazon*, take the mast and sail out of her and bring her round to the landing-place.

Mister Mate, Captain John, have you got a pencil and a bit of paper in the camp? And I'll want a scrap of charcoal out of your fire."

Captain John went into his tent and brought out the exercise book and the pencil. Captain Nancy lay on the ground and wrote for some minutes, sucking her pencil between each word and pressing very hard. Twice she broke the point of her pencil and had to sharpen it again.

"I suck it to make it good and black," she explained, noticing that Susan watched her with surprise.

Titty and Roger stared at her open-mouthed.

When she had done she got up and took a bit of charred wood from the fire. She tore out the sheet on which she had been writing and smeared the back of it with burnt wood. Then she folded it up and put it in the pocket of her shirt.

"Boat ready, sir!" called Peggy from the landing-place.

"I'll be back soon," said Captain Nancy.

"But what are you going to do?" asked John as Nancy pushed off.

"Tip him the Black Spot," said Nancy and rowed, rather splashingly, away.

CHAPTER XXV

CAPTAIN FLINT GETS THE BLACK SPOT

THE houseboat man, Captain Flint, sometimes known as Uncle Jim, was alone with his green parrot in the cabin of his ship grimly trying to put things straight after his visitors. First there had been the burglars, and then this morning there had been all the people who wanted to see what damage had been done, besides Sammy and the other policeman and the sergeant from Rio, who had sent Sammy to the foot of the lake and the other policeman up to the other end to make inquiries. The burglars had turned everything upside down. Every one of the neat lockers and cupboards had its door swinging open and its contents raked out. The assegais and tomahawks and shark's-tooth necklaces and boomerangs and green and scarlet painted gourds, that were relics of Captain Flint's travels and had hung in honoured places on the cabin walls, had been torn down. It was like trying to tidy up after a whirlwind. Captain Flint trod on a little ebony elephant from Colombo. He picked it up, thinking of glue, but it had lost its tusks, its trunk and two of its legs, and he threw it desperately through the open cabin window.

The green parrot, perched on the edge of the cabin table, was trying to bite off the head of a little jade image of Buddha that Captain Flint had bought in Hong Kong.

"Go ahead, Polly," said Captain Flint, "smash it up."

"Pretty Polly," said the parrot, and holding the little idol in one claw twisted at it with its strong curved beak.

"Why on earth they couldn't have taken some of these things if they wanted them, beats me," said Captain Flint, who from living alone so much was accustomed to talk a good deal to himself and to the parrot. "And then they go and take the one thing that could be of no possible use to them but mattered a great deal to me. Never lock anything up, Polly, and you'll never lose it. Whoever the thief was, he took that box simply because it was heavy and he couldn't open it. If it was that boy he must be a strong one. But perhaps he had others to help him. Well, when he does open it he'll be sorry he didn't take something else. *Mixed Moss*, by 'A Rolling Stone', won't mean much to him, Polly, though it meant a lot of hard work to me."

"Pretty Polly," said the parrot, as the head of the idol dropped on the floor.

Captain Flint bent to pick up the fallen head, and a broken emu's egg cracked under his feet.

"All the king's horses and all the king's men," said Captain Flint, "won't put Humpty Dumpty together again and won't make me sit down to write *Mixed Moss* a second time."

The green parrot gave a loud, angry shriek when Captain Flint picked up the little jade head.

"Oh well, take it, then," said Captain Flint. The parrot waddled towards him along the table, and, gripping the edge of the table with one claw, took the head from him with the other.

"It's just a summer wasted," said Captain Flint. "And all my diaries gone too."

"Pretty Polly," said the parrot.

"There is one thing about it," said Captain Flint, picking up an armful of clothes and shoving them into one of the cupboards, "those nieces of mine had nothing to do with it. They do play the game, and they'd never have wrecked my cabin for me. But that boy. I didn't like his lying to me about his firework on my cabin roof. Boys are capable of anything,

Polly, even good ones. I was a bad one myself, so they say, but at least I didn't tell lies."

At that moment a small folded piece of paper flew through the cabin window and dropped on the table. The parrot shuffled towards it and picked it up. It seemed to be better material for beak work than the remains of the little jade image. Captain Flint looked out.

"Hullo, Nancy," he said. "Come to gloat?"

"I won't speak to you," said Nancy. "I've tipped you the Black Spot. Read it."

"What's the matter?"

"I won't speak to you till you've said you're sorry. Read the Black Spot and you'll see why."

Captain Flint was just in time to save the paper from the parrot. It was already in two pieces. Captain Flint untwisted them and put them together. On one side was a large round smudge made with the charred wood. On the other was a letter.

"To Captain Flint (*alias* Uncle Jim),

John never touched the houseboat. When you told him he was a liar, he wasn't. You were. He had come at risk of his life to warn you that savage natives were planning an attack on your houseboat. The Billies had given him a message for you. You wouldn't listen. Instead you called him a liar. Talk about being ungrateful. Now you've been burgled. I'm glad. Very glad. If you want to know who singed your beard (see Philip of Spain) by exploding a mine on your cabin roof, it was the undersigned. You deserved it. This is the Black Spot. You are deposed from being an uncle or anything decent.

NANCY BLACKETT (Amazon pirate)."

"Hi! Nancy!" shouted Captain Flint out of the cabin window.

But Captain Nancy, anxious to show the Swallows that she was holding no parley with the enemy, was already rowing out of the bay.

"By Jove!" said Captain Flint, "so it was those young harum-scarums all the time. What a brute that boy must have thought me. And I was a brute too. And now I've gone and told the police that I thought he might have something to do with this mess. Into your private cabin with you, Polly. There's too much about to leave you in charge here."

He put the parrot, squawking wildly, into its cage, ran up on deck, jumped down into his rowing boat, cast off the painter and set off after Captain Nancy, rowing as hard as he could. Whatever happened, he must see that boy at once and put things right.

CHAPTER XXVI

HE MAKES PEACE AND DECLARES WAR

For some moments after Nancy had rowed away Peggy and the Swallows stared after her in silence. No one knew exactly what she was going to do.

"Perhaps I ought not to have told her about it," John said at last.

"Rubbish," said Susan. "She'd have been bound to hear about it sooner or later. Let's get the Amazons' tent up before she comes back."

"Let's," said Peggy. "We've got all the things here. Nancy brought the poles."

"Oughtn't we to take *Swallow* and go and help her?" said Titty.

"Better not," said Peggy. "If she'd wanted help she wouldn't have gone alone."

She unrolled her big white bundle. It was a tent but not made like the tents of the Swallows.

"Where are those poles?" she said. "They're all in two pieces. You fit them together and get four all the same length. Then you push them into the hems at the corners of the tent. They're a horribly tight fit. The first two are easy enough, but after that it's awful, because it's so difficult to keep the hem straight for the pole to go in. I say, if your able-seaman and the boy will hang on to the other end and keep it stretched out, it'll be easier."

Everybody helped. The poles were put together, like fishing

rods, and pushed into the hems. At the top of the hems there were little bags for the ends of the poles, like fingers on a glove, and the ends of the poles, in their little bags, stuck out above the tent about six inches or so.

"They're just like ears," said Roger, "donkey's ears."

Then, when the poles were all in, Peggy gathered up the tent in a long bundle, or rather tried to. John took hold of one end of the bundle and she took hold of the other.

"This way," she said. "It's lucky you didn't pitch your tents on our place, or we really should have had to fight you for it. We couldn't put it up properly without these two stumps."

On the opposite side of the camp to the tents of the Swallows there were two stumps of trees that had been cut down. Between them, now that they looked, the Swallows saw the remains of a worn square patch. Peggy dug about with her fingers in the grass and found a hole at each corner of the square.

"The tent poles fit into those holes," she said. "Then these ropes go from the top of the tent to the old tree stumps and round them, and we tighten them up with these bits of wood."

The bits of wood had two holes in them, one at each end. The rope ran through one hole, then round the tree stump, then through the other hole, ending in a knot so that it would not pull out again. To tighten the rope, all you had to do was to pull the bit of wood up the rope, and then the other end, by pulling it sideways, stopped it from slipping when you let go.

"It's a lot easier with five to work at it," said Peggy, when the tent stood in its place, and the ropes from the donkey's ears at each end were properly tautened. "It takes us ages by ourselves. What did you do with that bundle of iron pegs that was with the blankets?"

"Here they are," said Titty.

"There are holes for them too," said Peggy, "but they have to be hammered in. Oh bother, I forgot our mallet."

"Skip for our hammer, Roger," said Mate Susan.

Along the bottom of the sides and back of the tent there were loops, and for each loop there was a peg with a crook at the top to hold it. Peggy found the holes that were left from the time of their last camping, and John drove the pegs home with the hammer.

"There's nothing else," said Peggy, "except the groundsheet, and that's at the harbour with our sleeping-bags, where I emptied them out of *Amazon*."

"It really is something like a camp now," said Titty, looking with pride at the three tents and the camp fire, and the kettle and Susan's newly cleaned frying-pan and saucepan. "Anybody would know it was a camp on a desert island, the moment they saw the sail."

"Let's finish lacing the sail," said Susan, but John had hurried off to the look-out point to see if he could see anything of Captain Nancy and the *Amazon*.

A moment later he came running back into the camp to fetch the telescope.

"I say, Susan," he shouted, "Captain Flint is coming after her."

"You're as bad as Titty with her treasure," said Susan. "Natives don't do things like that."

"But he is," said John.

"Uncle Jim isn't always very like a native," said Peggy.

"He's worse than any native," said Titty, over her shoulder, as she ran up to the look-out point. The others were close behind her.

Nancy had been nearly half-way back when Captain Flint in his rowing boat shot out of Houseboat Bay in pursuit of her. She was now close to the island, and Captain Flint, though he had gained a great deal, was still some little way behind her. His was a heavy boat.

"Well," said John, "he is coming after her, isn't he?"

"Perhaps she's invited him," said Susan.

"And she rowing fit to bust," said Peggy. "Not she. He's giving chase."

"And look how he's rowing," said John.

"Like a steam engine," said Roger.

"He's fairly lifting his boat along," said Peggy. "But Nancy'll beat him. She's got too much start. Go it, Nancy! Well rowed! Keep it up! Go it, Nancy!"

The little group on the look-out point shouted as if they were watching a race. Nancy heard them, and glanced once over her shoulder.

"Come on," yelled Peggy. "It's no good putting to sea to help her. But she'll get here first, and then we can all stop him from landing. Come on. Swallows and Amazons for ever!"

"And death to Captain Flint," shouted Titty.

They ran down to the landing-place. Nancy came rowing in, very much out of breath, but still six or seven lengths ahead of Captain Flint.

"We're in for it now, my lads," she panted, as she jumped ashore.

A few moments later Captain Flint's rowing boat grounded beside the *Amazon*. It was instantly seized and pushed off again by Nancy and Peggy.

Captain Flint had been laying his oars in. But feeling himself again afloat, he dipped his blades in the water again and turned to look at his enemies. His manner was not at all fierce. His face was red, but that was with the heat of rowing. His voice was mild. Almost, it might have been thought that he was shy.

"May I come ashore?" he said.

"Friend or enemy?" asked Nancy breathlessly.

"GO IT, NANCY!"

"Well, not an enemy," said Captain Flint. "Distressed British seaman, more like."

"You've had the Black Spot," said Nancy. "We've got nothing more to do with you."

"I've come to apologise," said Captain Flint, "Not to you, Nancy."

"Shall we let him land, Captain John?" asked Nancy. But John, at hearing Captain Flint's last words, had walked away.

"You have been an awful pig to him, you know," said Nancy, "but we'll let you land."

Captain Flint brought his boat in once more, stepped out of her, and taking no notice of anyone else, walked after Captain John.

Captain John was walking away along the path to the harbour. Captain Flint hurried after him.

"Young man," he said in a very friendly voice.

"Yes," said John.

"I've got something to say to you. Don't treat me in the way I treated you the other day and refuse to listen to me. I was altogether in the wrong. It was beastly of me even if I had been in the right. I ought to have known you were telling the truth. And I ought not to have called you a liar, anyway. I'm very sorry. Will you shake hands?"

There was a most unpleasant lump in Captain John's throat. He found that it was almost more upsetting to have things put right than it had been when they went wrong. Then at least he could be angry, and that was a help. This was worse. He swallowed twice, and he bit the inside of his lip pretty hard. He held out his hand. Captain Flint took it, and shook it firmly. John felt suddenly better.

"It's all right now," said he.

"I really am most awfully sorry," said Captain Flint. "You know I was quite sure it had been you because I saw your boat and you, and never saw my wretched nieces. Not that that is any excuse for the way I behaved."

"It's quite all right," said John.

They walked back towards the others.

"I've been paid for it in a way," said Captain Flint. "Nancy tells me you came to warn me, and give me a message or something. If I'd only listened to you instead of being a cross-grained curmudgeonly idiot, I shouldn't have lost my book. I'd have taken it with me. Nancy's told you what's happened?"

"Yes," said Captain John, "but I didn't come only to warn you. I was going to tell you what the charcoal-burners had asked us to tell Nancy and Peggy. Then I was going to tell you you were all wrong about that paper you put in my tent. Then I was going to tell you I'd never been near the houseboat. And then I was going to declare war."

"Well, I call that really friendly," said Captain Flint. "Do you hear that, Nancy?" he said, as they came back to the others who had come up to the camp. "Do you hear that? He was coming to declare war on me."

"Of course he was," said Nancy. "We all were. We have an offensive and defensive alliance against you. We were going to capture the houseboat ourselves, and give you your choice between walking the plank and throwing in your lot with us like last year. He was sick with you because you'd told the natives he'd been at the houseboat when he hadn't, and we were sick with you because of all this silly book-writing. But it's no good now, of course. You've had the Black Spot, and we won't have anything more to do with you."

"I don't know that it's too late," said Captain Flint. "There's no more of the book-writing, anyhow. The book's gone, and the typewriter with it, and I'm too old to start writing it all over again. I'm ready for a declaration of war whenever you like."

"I didn't want to capture the houseboat," Titty broke out.

"I wanted to sink her. I wish we'd sunk her at the very first."

"But why?"

"Titty!" said Susan, warningly.

"Because nobody could have been such a beastly enemy as you," said Titty. "We hadn't done anything to you, and you made the natives think we had, and then, when Captain John tried to help you . . ."

"Yes, I know," said Captain Flint. "I was a beast, but I can't do more than say I'm very sorry. And I really am."

"It's all right about that, Titty," said John. "It's all put right. It's over."

"Look here," said Captain Flint. "I'll do anything I can to make up. I've wasted my own summer, writing a book, and I've wasted some of yours too, Nancy's and Peggy's I mean, but I see their tent is here, so I suppose you are all together in things. Take back your Black Spot, and make peace with me, and we'll have a first-class war at once. If you want to capture the houseboat come and do your worst. I'll be ready for you. I've got nothing else to do now and I'll make up for lost time."

"Shall we forgive him?" said Peggy. "He's quite good at being one of us if he likes."

"We'll forgive him," said Nancy, "if it's to be war, and a real battle on the houseboat. We'll forgive him because he's ashamed, and because he's in trouble. He really has had his houseboat burgled."

"Well, he deserved it," said Titty.

"Yes," said Nancy, "but nobody ought to be allowed to burgle it except ourselves."

"Real battle," said Captain Flint. "At three o'clock tomorrow. I must tidy up below after those scoundrels. But at three o'clock tomorrow I'll be cleared for action."

"Really and truly?" said Peggy.

"Honest Pirate!" said Captain Flint.

"All right," said Nancy.

"Take back your Black Spot, then," said Captain Flint.

"You keep it," said Nancy, "to remind you never to turn native again."

"I will," he said. "But look here, I'd like to know the names of my enemies. And by the way, why in your Black Spot did you call me Captain Flint?"

"Because Titty, that's their able-seaman, said you were a retired pirate."

"Why, so I am. But which is Titty? Are you Titty?" he said to Susan.

"Of course she isn't," said Nancy. "She is the mate of the *Swallow*, and her name is Susan."

"How do you do, Mister Mate?" said Captain Flint.

"And this is Captain John of the *Swallow*."

"The skipper and I have met already. He's forgiven me, though I don't deserve it."

"This is Able-seaman Titty. Able-seaman Titty, Captain Flint."

"So it was you who knew the dark secret of my pirate past."

"I saw the parrot," said Titty.

"And this is Roger, their ship's boy."

"I've been a ship's boy myself," said Captain Flint. "It's a hard life."

"And we are the Amazon pirates."

"I know you two ruffians well enough," said Captain Flint.

"Do you really mean a battle on the houseboat tomorrow?" said Titty.

"Tomorrow as ever is," said Captain Flint.

"We'll take her," said the able-seaman. "Have you got a good plank?"

"What for?"

"To walk," said the able-seaman.

"Everything shall be in order," said the retired pirate, who, of course, knew just how things should be.

"What about dinner?" said Roger.

"If it's going to be war tomorrow," said Mate Susan to Captain Flint, "would you like to stop and have dinner with us today? I'll put the kettle on at once."

"There's nothing I should like better," he said. "I seem to be in the middle of an enemy camp . . ."

"Bang in the middle of it," said Nancy.

"But it's such a good one that I'd almost like to join you altogether."

"Too late," said Nancy. "They're going in two days. So are we. You're not the least use now except as an enemy. But we don't mind letting you be that, if you really want to be one of us again."

"Three o'clock tomorrow, and the scuppers will be red with blood," said Captain Flint. "But I suppose you don't mind my stopping to dinner today."

"Not a bit," said Nancy. "The mate's invited you. And there's lots to eat. We brought a plum pudding to cut up in pieces, and fry. Most luscious. Cook gave it us. And then afterwards we found a cold tongue. It had hardly been touched, so we brought it too. But we came away rather privately because we thought we might be stopped, and so we went and forgot the grog."

"I'll have the kettle boiling in a minute," said Susan. "You bring the plates out, Titty. Pick out some of the best potatoes, Roger, and we'll bake them. There's lots of hot ashes at the edge of the fire."

"Come on, Peggy, and we'll bring our stores into camp," said Captain Nancy.

"Can I give you a hand with that lacing?" said Captain Flint,

298

and in another moment he was sitting on the ground stretching out the sail while John reeved the lacing through the eyelet holes along the edge of the sail, and Susan was busy with the fire and the kettle, and Titty and the boy were bringing out plates and mugs and knives.

"This is a lot better than writing books," said Captain Flint presently. "Now, Skipper, if you'll take two turns there and hold fast, I'll show you a good way of finishing off."

Considering that Captain Flint was having dinner with his enemies, it was a very friendly meal. Even Titty softened towards him before the end of it. He never made the mistake of calling her anything but Able-seaman. The tongue that the Amazons had found and brought away with them was very good. So was the seed-cake of the Swallows. It was no good opening pemmican tins when there was nearly the whole of a tongue to be eaten. The plum pudding fried in slices would have come last, only the potatoes took a long time to get properly done, and in the end had to be used as a sort of hot dessert.

They were sitting round the fire, getting the insides out of the potatoes, which were almost too hot to touch, when they began to talk about the burglary.

"I wonder what made the Billies give you that message for me?" said Captain Flint.

"They said they'd heard something at Bigland," said John.

"That's away beyond the foot of the lake," said Captain Flint. "If we could only find out where the burglar came from, there might be some chance of getting my box back. But there was nothing to show who he was or what he was. My boat looked as if half a hundred wild cats had been having a general scrimmage in the cabin, and that was all, except that they took my old cabin trunk. But everything that mattered was in it."

"Was it a very heavy one?" said Titty.

"It was, rather."

"Were there ingots in it?"

Captain Flint laughed. "Afraid not," he said. "What there was was a typewriter, a lot of diaries, and old logs, and the book I've been writing all the summer. If they'd taken anything else I wouldn't have minded."

Thoughts struggled in Titty's mind, but she looked at Captain Flint more kindly than before.

"Was it a book you'd been writing yourself?" she asked.

"It was," said Captain Flint.

"About your pirate past?"

"Well, that came into it."

"Was it a very good book?"

"Come to think of it," said Captain Flint, "perhaps it wasn't. All the same, I'd like to get it back. You've no idea what a job it is writing a book. Keeping a log is bad enough."

"I know," said Titty.

"And now I might just as well not have written it."

"And been much nicer all the summer," said Nancy.

"Don't rub it in," said Captain Flint sadly.

There was a rapid secret talk between the Amazons, ending with Nancy saying, "Well, tell him if you like."

"Look here, Uncle Jim," said Peggy.

"I beg your pardon, I thought my name was Captain Flint."

"So it is. If you're really going to be one of us again, we've got something to tell you. We know just when the burglar was burgling your boat. We saw him do it."

"Did you, by Jove? Did you see which way he went?"

"At least we saw the light in the houseboat. We thought it was yours. We couldn't tell you yesterday, you know, because you weren't one of us, and when we saw that light we were in bed properly."

"Were you? And where were you improperly?"

"On the lake."

"So you were supposed to be in bed, and were really up to high jinks on the ocean wave?"

"It's a secret, of course," said Peggy.

"We were sailing down to Wild Cat Island in a private war," said Nancy.

"If the burglar had come this way, do you think you would have heard him?" said Captain Flint.

"We didn't. We only saw a light in the cabin, and thought it was you."

Then John spoke.

"Able-seaman Titty thinks she did hear something that night."

"Where was she?"

"In *Amazon*."

"What, with you two?"

"No. It was afterwards. We were on Wild Cat Island then. We were marooned."

"Who marooned you?"

"Titty did. She went off in *Amazon*, and left us to our cruel fate," said Peggy. "That's how the Swallows won the war."

"But where were the others?"

"We were up the Amazon River, or sailing back from it," said John.

"The lake seems to have been a lively place that night," said Captain Flint. "And what did you hear, Able-seaman?"

"I heard people rowing in a boat. They came close past me."

"And where were you?"

"I was anchored."

"Look here," said Captain John, "you'd better have a look at our chart. It shows just where she was."

He ran into his tent, and came out with the new chart and pointed to the little anchor that marked the place where Titty had lain in *Amazon* off the north end of Cormorant Island.

Captain Flint looked at it.

"Did they pass close to you?" he asked.

"Very close," said Titty.

"It's a funny course for them to steer from my houseboat if they were making for the foot of the lake. They must have nearly run into the island."

"They did run into it," said Titty.

"And then they went on?"

"They landed on the island," said Titty, "and they left their treasure there, or whatever it was they had with them. They said it was heavy. I heard them."

"Shiver my timbers!" said Nancy.

"Not really, Titty," said Susan.

Captain Flint jumped to his feet. "Able-seaman," he said, "if that box is there I'll give you anything you'd like to have. Come on, all of you, and we'll row across and look."

He grabbed Titty by the hand, and shook it. Titty, almost to her surprise, found herself smiling back at him. His hand was very large, and there could be no doubt about its friend-liness. And after all, even if her treasure was not Spanish gold, it was a book, and a pirate book. Her only regret was that the treasure-hunting expedition was to be so large. But that could not be helped.

"Look here," said Nancy, "if it's there, and you get your book back, you won't go and turn native again."

"Never," said Captain Flint. "Come on. Pile into my boat, all of you."

They ran down to the landing-place, and crowded in, the two Amazons, the four Swallows, and Captain Flint. In another moment, he was rowing round the island, and across to the island of the cormorants.

Captain Flint rowed as if he were still racing after Nancy. Every stroke jerked the boat forward and jerked his passengers backward. In a very few minutes he had reached Cormorant Island and found a place where he could pull his boat's nose up between two rocks. Everybody scrambled ashore.

But there was nothing to be seen on the island, except the bare tree and the white splashed rocks, and jetsam from the last flood, and big loose stones. They looked everywhere. Captain Flint climbed all round the island two or three times. He could find nothing.

"But I know they left it here," said Able-seaman Titty. "I heard them say they couldn't put it on a motor bicycle. And then they said they would come fishing and catch something worth catching."

"It was the middle of the night, you know, Titty," said Susan, "and you may have been mistaken."

"They may have changed their minds," said Captain Flint, "or they may have come for it already. Anyway it's something to know which end of the lake they came from. Not that I think I shall ever get it again," he added.

They rowed sadly back to Wild Cat Island.

The able-seaman did not weep, but she was very near it.

"I know they left it there," she said.

"Never mind," said Captain Flint. "We've had a good look."

"And perhaps, if you had found it, you'd have turned native again after all, and gone on bothering about publishers," said Nancy.

"Anyhow, I haven't found it," said Captain Flint, "so we'll think of something else. Three o'clock tomorrow, for example."

"Real war?" said Nancy.

"Blood and thunder," said Captain Flint. "Three o'clock tomorrow, and I'll be cleared for action. I'll be ready to repel boarders, or sink both your ships, or hang the lot of you at the yard-arm, or be captured as a Spanish brig or sunk as a Portuguese slaver . . . anything you like."

He put them ashore at Wild Cat Island, and rowed back to bring order into his wrecked cabin.

"Goodbye," they shouted after him in the friendliest manner.

"Goodbye," he shouted back. "Three o'clock sharp. Then Death or Glory!"

CHAPTER XXVII

THE BATTLE IN HOUSEBOAT BAY

"Then, having washed the blood away, we'd little else to do
Than to dance a quiet hornpipe as the old salts taught us to."
MASEFIELD.

THE Amazons were the first to wake in the morning, because
for some time they had been sleeping in a house, and had not
grown accustomed, like the Swallows, to the early morning
sunlight through the white tent walls. "Show a leg, show a leg,"
they shouted to the others and soon had the whole camp astir.
"Remember," they shouted, "battle at three o'clock sharp.
There's no time to lose." Really, in spite of bathing and fetching
the milk and having breakfast and dinner, it seemed a very long
time before the small hand of the chronometer crawled round
past the II, and nearly as far as the III, on the chronometer
face. A watched pot never boils, and a watched watch seems
to lag on purpose. But at last Captain John looked at it for the
last time, and gave the order. The Grand Fleet set sail.

*

"Shall we go in under sail or oars?" Captain John consulted
with Captain Nancy, as the *Amazon* and the *Swallow*, slipping
quietly along with a following wind, came near the point at the
southern side of Houseboat Bay.

"More seamanlike to do it under sail," said Captain Nancy.

"There won't be a leeside to him," said Captain John. "The
houseboat'll be lying head to wind. Our plan will be to reach

into the bay, and then come head to wind one on each side of him. If you'll lay yourself aboard his starboard side, I'll bring *Swallow* up on his port."

"Very good, sir," said Captain Nancy.

"Lower sail as we come alongside. Grapple, and board him. He'll go for one lot of us. He can't go for both. The others'll get aboard and take him in the rear."

"Hand-to-hand fighting from the very first," said Nancy.

"What about nailing our colours to our masts?" said Ableseaman Titty.

"Fasten the flag halyards with a clove hitch," said Captain Nancy. "That'll be as good."

"Just look at *his* flag," said Roger, who, as usual, was at his post in the bows.

They had passed the point, and could see into Houseboat Bay. There lay the houseboat, moored to her big barrel buoy, and on her little flagstaff of a mast, accustomed to carry the red ensign, was a large and most unusual flag, blowing out finely in the wind. It was a green flag, and in the middle of it, nearly filling it, was a huge white elephant. The Houseboat Man, Captain Flint, had dug it out for the occasion.

"I know what it is," said John. "It's the Siamese flag."

"I've seen it before," said Mate Peggy. "He brought it back from the East last year."

"Well, it's coming down in two shakes," said Captain Nancy. "As soon as ever we get aboard. Down with the Elephant! Swallows and Amazons for ever!"

"Blow your whistle, Mister Mate," said Captain John. "The fleet will now attack."

Susan blew her whistle.

"Blow it both loud and shrill like the man in the ballad," said Titty.

Susan was still blowing.

"Let me blow it," said Roger, and Susan, out of breath, gave it to the boy, who kept on blowing it till he nearly burst.

The two ships, the brown-sailed and the white, heeled over as their steersmen brought the wind on the beam to reach into the bay. For a minute or two the water foamed from under their bows. Then, as they came into the shelter of the point, the water quietened. Roger blew on, in gusts, whenever he had any breath to blow with. Suddenly a head in a huge white sun-helmet appeared out of the forehatch of the houseboat. Another whistle, louder than Mate Susan's, sounded over the water.

"Blow, blow, Roger!" said Titty.

The *Swallow* and the *Amazon* swept on towards the houseboat, the *Amazon* drawing a little ahead.

"Slacken away your mainsheet, *Amazon*," shouted Captain John. "Remember, I'm to board him on the port side. We ought to come alongside him at the same moment."

Captain Nancy let out her mainsheet, spilling the wind, and *Swallow* shot ahead.

"All right now," shouted Captain John.

The huge sun-helmet rose higher out of the forehatch of the houseboat, and Captain Flint, in a shirt and a pair of flannel trousers, with a big red handkerchief tied round his middle like a belt, struggled up on deck. He had some difficulty in getting through the hatch.

"He's rather a fat pirate," said Titty critically.

Captain Flint was bending over something on the foredeck that glittered in the sun. It was the little brass cannon.

"It's the cannon," said Roger. "He's going to fire."

Captain Flint straightened himself sharply. An enormous puff of blue smoke hid him for a moment, and there was a bang that echoed again and again between the hills on either side of the lake.

"Hurrah!" yelled Captain Nancy.

"Hurrah!" shouted Peggy.

"Hurrah!" shouted the whole ship's company in *Swallow*.

Captain Flint was busy again with the little cannon. He poured something into it out of a tin. Then he pushed something into it. Then he put it in its place, and took a pinch of something from the tin, and put it in the touch-hole of the little cannon. He lit a match, bent down once more over the cannon and again stood up sharply, this time putting his hands over his ears. There was another cloud of smoke, and a terrific bang. Something dropped in the water, between the houseboat and the advancing fleet.

"It's only the wad," shouted Nancy.

"At him before he can fire again," shouted John.

But Captain Flint was no mean gunner and, just as *Swallow* slipped by under the stern of the houseboat, there was another crash from the cannon, and the smoke and the smell of gunpowder drove over the little ship.

"Let go halyards," John and Nancy shouted almost at the same moment, as *Swallow* and *Amazon* shot up on opposite sides of the houseboat.

"Grab the yard, Susan," shouted John. "Down with it. Hang on to anything you can, Roger, and make the painter fast. Board!"

There was a railing round the houseboat's after-deck. Captain John swung himself up to the deck by it, climbed over it, and gave a hand to Susan. At that moment Captain Flint, roaring, "Death or Glory!" charged up the companion-way. He had gone down again through the forehatch and run through the cabin. He came up whirling two scarlet cushions round his head. But in hand-to-hand fighting like this it is not weapons that count, but hands. Captain Flint's were large, but he had only two of them. The Swallows' were small, but they had eight.

THERE WAS A BANG

One tremendous blow of a scarlet cushion caught Captain John on the side of the head, and sent him to the deck. But he was up again in a moment, and charged head down into Captain Flint. Mate Susan had got a good hold of one of the cushions. Titty and Roger, who had clambered aboard, took Captain Flint firmly round each leg and clung on like terriers so that as he moved they dragged with him. Even so, the battle might have ended with the complete defeat of the Swallows if Captain Nancy and her mate, Peggy, who had come aboard by the foredeck, had not rushed along the roof of the cabin and, with a wild yell, flung themselves into the struggle. Captain Nancy leapt from the roof of the cabin on to Captain Flint's back, and clasped him round the neck. Peggy joined John and Susan in pulling at him from in front, and, overwhelmed by numbers, Captain Flint came heavily down on the deck.

"Yield," shouted Nancy.

"Not while my flag flies," panted Captain Flint. "Elephants, Elephants, Elephants for ever!"

But Able-seaman Titty was already running forward along the narrow gangway outside the cabin. In another moment, the huge elephant flag came fluttering down to the foredeck.

"We've won," shouted John. "Your flag is struck."

"Why, so it is," said Captain Flint, struggling to a sitting position, and looking at the bare flagstaff. "Quick work. But very hot. I surrender." He lay down flat, puffing heavily.

"Bind him," said Captain Nancy.

Peggy picked up a coil of rope lying handy, and John and Peggy between them bound the prisoner's legs together. Then, with the help of the others, they rolled him over and bound his arms. Then, they tugged him along the deck, and lifted up the top part of him, so that he was sitting on the deck with his back leaning against the cabin. He fell over sideways. John pulled him up again, and he fell over on the other side. "I'll put you up once more," said Peggy, "but, if you roll over again, you shall lie there."

At that moment Titty came back.

"If we're going to make him walk the plank," she said, "there's one all ready on the foredeck."

"So there is," cried Nancy. "I'd forgotten about it. But how are we going to get him there?"

Captain Flint wriggled his feet, and wagged his head from side to side.

"I'm not a snake," he said, "I can't get along without feet."

"We must get him to the foredeck somehow," said Captain Nancy.

"Undo his legs and make him walk over the cabin," said Peggy.

"Cabin roof won't bear me," said the prisoner.

"It's not safe to let prisoners go below," said Titty. "They might set fire to the magazine and blow up the ship."

"We'll take him round by the gangway," said Captain Nancy. "He won't dare to struggle there while his arms are tied."

So they undid the rope from round his legs. With a good deal of difficulty they got him on his feet. He showed signs of sitting down again at once.

"None of that," said Captain Nancy, "or it'll be worse for you. Far worse."

One end of the rope was still wound round and round his arms and body. They made it fast, so that the other end served as a sort of painter or leading-string. Nancy and Peggy took hold of the rope, and went first along the narrow gangway. The prisoner, balancing himself as well as he could, walked next. John and Susan followed close behind him. Roger and Titty ran forward over the cabin roof.

On the foredeck there was a capstan, from which the chain

311

went to the big barrel buoy to which the houseboat was moored. There was the little brass cannon. There was the white sun-helmet lying by the forehatch. There was a locker close to the little mast at the foot of which on the deck lay the green and white elephant flag. On the starboard side of the deck there was a springboard, from which, on happier days, the owner of the houseboat was accustomed to take his morning dive. It might have been designed for the use of prisoners on their way to feed the sharks. At the sight of it Captain Flint shuddered so violently that he nearly upset the determined buccaneers who had captured him and his ship and were now holding him to prevent any attempt at escape.

"Belay that," growled Captain Nancy. Captain John was really commodore, but in some things Captain Nancy could not help taking the lead.

"Tie the prisoner to the mast," she said, and it was done.

"Don't laugh," she roared at the prisoner.

"Then help that pirate out of my sun-helmet," said Captain Flint.

Roger, the boy, had picked up the big sun-helmet, and put it on, and the whole of his head was inside it. There was a moment's pause while Mate Susan freed him from it.

"Would you mind putting it on my head," said the prisoner. "A last wish, you know. My bald head can't stand the sun."

Mate Susan put it on for him, and the prisoner, wagging his head, shook it into place.

"Now, Captain John," said Nancy. "We must consider his crimes. The worst is treachery. All this summer he has been in league with the natives."

"Desertion," said Peggy. "He deserted us."

"He came to Wild Cat Island, and went into our camp when we were not there," said Titty.

"He called Captain John a liar," said Nancy.

"That was a mistake," said Captain John hurriedly. "We've made peace over that."

"We can let him off that, then," said Captain Nancy. "But it doesn't matter. His other crimes are quite enough. Hands up for making him walk the plank!"

Her hand and Peggy's went up at once. So did Titty's. So did Roger's. John and Susan hesitated.

"Oh, look here," said Nancy, "no weakening. It's far too good a plank to waste."

"I think we ought to give him a chance," said John. "Untie his arms, and let him swim for it."

"Right," said Nancy. "We'll agree to that. All hands Up?"

All hands went up.

Roger was looking over the side.

"Are there plenty of sharks?" he said.

"Millions," groaned the prisoner.

"Bandage his eyes," said Captain Nancy. "Here's a handkerchief."

"A clean one?" asked the prisoner.

"Well, let him have Peggy's. Hers was clean yesterday," said Nancy.

Peggy's handkerchief had not even been unfolded. It was quickly made into a bandage, and tied over Captain Flint's eyes.

"Untie him from the mast, and get him on the plank," said Nancy.

Mate Susan and John loosed him from the mast. Then they unbound his arms. The prisoner swayed heavily this way and that. At last, with Titty and Roger pushing behind, Peggy, John, and Susan between them guided him to the plank. Captain Nancy watched with folded arms.

"Now walk!" she cried.

Captain Flint, blindfolded, moved his feet little by little

along the springboard. He stopped, shaking all over, while the springboard bent and quivered under his weight.

Captain Nancy stamped her foot. "Walk, you son of a sea-cook," she cried.

Captain Flint took another step or two, until he was at the very end of the plank, high over the water.

"Mercy," he begged. "Mercy!"

"Walk," shouted Nancy, "or . . . !"

Captain Flint stepped desperately forward, taking a long stride into thin air. Head over heels he fell. There was a colossal splash that even wetted the Swallows and Amazons on the deck of the houseboat. Captain Flint had disappeared, and the white sun-helmet floated alone, tossing lightly in the ripples.

"Perhaps he can't swim," said Titty. "I never thought of it."

But just then the big bald head of Captain Flint rose out of the water. He blew and spluttered mightily, tore the handkerchief from round his eyes, and sank again.

He came up once more, this time close to the sun-helmet. He grabbed it and threw it, spinning, up on the deck of his ship.

"He can swim all right," said Titty.

Suddenly he let loose a yell. "Sharks, sharks!" he shrieked, and, splashing as hard as he could, swam to the houseboat's big mooring buoy. He climbed on to it, though it upset him once or twice. At last he was sitting astride on the top of it.

"This place is stiff with sharks," he called. "One of them's nibbling at my foot."

He slipped sideways off the buoy, and swam to the side of the houseboat, splashing tremendously.

"A rope, a rope!" he shouted, bobbing in the water and splashing with his arms, while the Swallows and Amazons looked down at his struggles.

CAPTAIN FLINT WALKS THE PLANK

"Shall we let him have one?" said Susan. "He's been a good long time in the water."

"You'll never be in league with natives again?" said Nancy.

"Hard-hearted pirate, never," said Captain Flint, blowing like a walrus that has come up to breathe.

"We'll give you a rope," said Nancy.

"I'd much rather have a rope ladder," said Captain Flint. "At my age I'm getting too fat for ropes. There's a rope ladder just by the springboard, the plank, I mean. It's made fast. You've only got to throw the loose end overboard."

John threw over the rope ladder, and a moment later Captain Flint stood once more on the deck of his ship with the water pouring from him, and running away into the scuppers. He sat down on the capstan and swung his arms about his chest. "Well, that's that," he said. "Not even the Amazon pirates are ruthless enough to make a man walk the plank twice on one day. Hullo, Roger, looking for the sharks?"

Roger had been looking down into the water from the houseboat's deck.

"I don't believe there are any," he said. "None big enough, anyway."

"The young ruffian's sorry I haven't left a leg or an arm behind with them," said Captain Flint. "What are you going to do with me now?" he added. "You've captured my ship, you've hauled down my noble elephant, you've trussed me like a chicken, you've made me walk the plank. I've walked it, dodged the sharks, and come aboard to report for duty. Do you think my crimes are wiped out? Because if they are . . ." He paused.

"What?" said Captain Nancy.

"All the best sea fights end with a banquet," said Captain Flint. "And there's one waiting in the cabin and nobody but the parrot on guard there. Just let me go below and start the

Primus while I get into some dry things, and then there's nothing
to keep us from it."

Nobody had anything to say against that.

Captain Flint lowered himself through the forehatch. A
moment later he put his head out.

"By the way," he said, "I suppose you'll want to hoist the
Jolly Roger on your prize. You'll find one in the locker." He
bobbed down again, and they heard him bumping about below
deck. Peggy opened the locker by the mast, and there, on the
top, lay a black flag with a skull and crossbones on it as big as
the elephant. She and Titty took the elephant flag off the
halyards and fastened on the Black Jack. Then, with a cheer
from both ships' companies, Peggy ran it to the masthead.

Captain Flint's head bobbed up again through the hatch.

"What about going below?" he said. "You'd better come in
by the companion-way. And mind your heads, though I suppose
none of your heads are in as much danger as mine."

"Is yours really in danger?" said Titty, looking at it with
interest.

"Not for high treason," said Captain Flint. "Only of being
bumped on the way into the cabin."

Nancy was looking at a large burnt patch on the cabin roof.

"Well," she said to Captain Flint, "as one pirate to another,
I'm sorry it made such a mess. I never would have thought the
thing would have burnt both ways. But didn't it just bang?"

"It did, rather," said Captain Flint, as he disappeared once
more.

The Swallows and Amazons went aft to the companion to
go down into the cabin. The captains and the mates went by
the gangway outside, the able-seaman and the boy over the
cabin roof.

The cabin was all that the cabin of a retired pirate should
be. Captain Flint had been hard at work, tidying up after the

burglary, and the walls were hung once more with strange weapons and curiosities from all the seven seas. Everything that had not been broken and thrown overboard was back in its place. There was a long, narrow table down the middle of the cabin, with chairs set on each side of it. The green parrot was perched on the back of one of the chairs.

"Pieces of eight, pieces of eight, say pieces of eight!" said Nancy Blackett to the parrot.

"Pretty Polly," said the parrot.

"You're not fit to be a pirate's parrot," said Nancy.

"Are the chairs fixed to the floor?" asked Roger.

"No," said Peggy.

"They are in Daddy's ship," said Roger.

"We don't get a very high sea in this bay," said a voice from the doorway into the foc's'le.

The roar of a Primus stove came suddenly to an end. Captain Flint, changed and in dry clothes, came in with a big kettle.

"Sort yourselves," he said, and they sorted themselves, and the feast began. It was as good a feast as Captain Flint had been able to get sent from Rio. For example, there were ices, strawberry ones. There were parkins and bath buns and rock cakes and ginger nuts and chocolate biscuits. There were mountains of sandwiches to begin with. Then there was a cake with a paper cover over it. When the cover was lifted off, there was a picture of two little ships done in pink and white icing.

"The *Swallow* and the *Amazon*," said Roger.

"That's what they're meant for," said Captain Flint.

Friendliness between the Swallows and Amazons and the retired pirate grew rapidly as the feast went on. Indeed, when Captain Flint was going to help himself to a strawberry ice, Mate Susan stopped him.

"You mustn't have ices after walking the plank," she said.

"Mother says they give you a chill in the stomach if you eat them when you've just bathed."

"By Jove, I suppose I ought not," said Captain Flint, and took a piece of cake instead.

"You did walk the plank most awfully well," said Titty.

"Practice," Captain Flint replied.

The parrot had a bite of almost everything, but seemed to like lump sugar best. Titty put out her hand to it, and the parrot climbed on her wrist, and walked all the way up to her shoulder.

"Next year we'll make a voyage to a place where the trees are full of parrots," she said.

"We must think of something really good for next year," said Captain Flint. "Here and now I promise you that I shall be writing no more books. I shall have retired from everything except being a pirate. But, as for parrots, I'm going south for the winter, and I'll bring back parrots all round if you want them."

"Not really?" said Titty.

"Really," said Captain Flint.

"One that can really swear?" said Nancy.

"An out-and-out ruffian," said Captain Flint.

"What about monkeys?" said Roger.

Captain Flint pulled out a notebook and a pencil.

"Item. One monkey," he said, taking a note. "With or without a tail?"

"With a tail," said Roger. "The other sort are only apes."

"Don't bring green parrots for us," said Nancy. "Bring them grey with red tails. Then we can feather our arrows with red feathers instead of green ones."

Captain Flint opened his mouth and shut it again. He looked hard at Nancy Blackett, and then at a jam-pot on a shelf, in which there was a single green feather and some new pipe-cleaners. Nancy Blackett caught his eye.

"Your fault for being an enemy," she said. "And after all, we didn't take anything but a few feathers. We might have sunk the ship. And, anyway, you are in with us again now."

"True," said Captain Flint. "But I wonder how many burglaries there have really been."

"One," said Nancy. "Ours wasn't a burglary. It was honest revenge."

"What are you going to do tomorrow?" asked Captain Flint a little later. "It's your last day isn't it?"

"What about fishing?" said Peggy. "We haven't fished for ages. You can come too if you like."

"Yes," said Nancy. "Your boat is much better for fishing than ours are. Besides, you know the best places."

"Do come," said John.

"Please," said Susan.

"Well, if there's not too much wind, we might make a day of it. I'll come, but I can't start too early. And then we'll plan something tremendous for next year."

"I'm not going fishing tomorrow," said Able-seaman Titty.

"Why not?" said Susan.

"I'm going treasure-hunting."

"Where?"

"Cormorant Island. I'm sure it's still there. The sea-chest, I mean."

"Waste of time, Able-seaman," said Captain Flint.

"I know it's there," said Titty. "And Roger can come too if he likes."

"Then there'll be two expeditions tomorrow," said Captain Flint. "One treasure-hunting, and one whaling. What do you think about it, Roger?"

"I'm going with Titty," said Roger. And so it was settled, though Susan did say, "They can't go alone unless it's a calm day."

After the feasting had ended, and it lasted a long time, Peggy said, "I say, Uncle Jim."

"He's not Uncle Jim, you galoot," Nancy said.

"Of course not," said Peggy. "I say, Captain Flint, have you still got the accordion?"

"Tip us a stave," said Captain Nancy.

"If you'll dance the hornpipe, I will."

"There's no room in the cabin."

"On the poop then."

Captain Flint brought a huge accordion out of the fore-cabin.

"Lucky the burglar didn't find that," he said, "or he'd have taken it for certain. But perhaps he had no ear for music."

They all went up on the after-deck. Captain Flint sat on the rail and played the sailor's hornpipe, while Captain Nancy danced.

"That's not the way we do it," said Titty.

"Let's see your way," said Captain Flint.

He played on and on, and Nancy and Peggy danced their hornpipe and Captain John, Mate Susan, Able-seaman Titty, and the ship's boy danced theirs. The stamping on the deck could have been heard a mile away in the quiet evening. Faster and faster played Captain Flint. Faster and faster danced the Swallows and Amazons, until the tune went so fast that it stopped being a tune at all, and they all flung themselves on the deck, tired out.

"And to think how I've wasted this summer," said Captain Flint.

Then he played songs, and presently, when they had got their breath again, they sang. He played "Spanish Ladies", and

"The Whale", "Amsterdam", "Blow the Man Down", "Away to Rio", and many another.

At last it grew dusk.

"Our harbour lights are not lit," said Captain John.

"We must get back before dark," said Mate Susan.

"And there's hardly any wind left," said Captain Nancy. "Let's start while we can sail."

"Whaling tomorrow," said Captain Flint, as he said good-bye.

"Treasure-hunting," said Able-seaman Titty.

A few minutes later the *Swallow* and the *Amazon* were heading out of the bay.

Captain Flint leaned on the rail and watched them go. The sound of his playing reached them over the water until they cleared the point and met the wind.

"He made a jolly good pirate," said Captain John.

"It's a pity he's so old," said Roger.

"He isn't so awfully old," said Titty.

CHAPTER XXVIII

THE TREASURE ON CORMORANT ISLAND

TITTY had gone to sleep with one idea firm in her head, and she woke up next morning with it still there. She crawled out to see what sort of a day it was. It was a fine day without much wind, just what she wanted, for she knew that if there had been a strong wind she and Roger would not have been allowed to go off in *Swallow* by themselves, without the captain or the mate.

"Wake up, Roger," she called.

"What's the matter?" said Captain John.

"Somebody may get it first."

"Get what?"

"The treasure on Cormorant Island. Roger and I are going to look for it."

"But we've all looked once, and there's nothing there."

"It's our last day," said Titty obstinately, "and you and Susan said we might. And I'm sure it's there."

"But Captain Flint's coming, and we're all going fishing."

"Roger and I are going treasure-hunting. We settled it last night. And there's no wind."

"You'll be awfully disappointed, Titty," said Susan sleepily.

"Not when I find it," said Titty.

"Well, heave out, Roger," said Captain John, "you can go across and get the milk, anyhow, as soon as you've bathed."

"Double lot today because of the Amazons and Captain

323

Flint," called the mate. "We'll have to take some with us when we go whaling."

It was a quick bathe that morning for the boy and the able-seaman. The able-seaman did not bother about pearls, and she drove the boy out to dry as soon as he had shown that he could swim both ways, on his front and on his back. Then they hurried across for the milk. They came back to find everybody but the mate of the *Swallow* busy setting up fishing rods.

"You're not really going off to Cormorant Island, Able-seaman?" said Peggy. "You know there's nothing there. You'd much better come whaling with us."

But Able-seaman Titty was not to be persuaded, and the Boy Roger, though he thought rather well of whaling, made up his mind to follow the able-seaman.

After breakfast, while the others were busy catching minnows to be ready for Captain Flint, Mate Susan made them each a large packet of sandwiches and bunloaf, and gave them a bottle of milk.

"Now remember, Roger, Titty'll be in command, and you'll do just what she tells you."

"Aye, aye, sir," said the boy.

"What shall we have for a pickaxe?" said the able-seaman.

"You don't want a pickaxe," said the mate.

"Of course we do," said the able-seaman. "The treasure may be fathoms deep."

"Take the hammer," said John.

"We ought to have the compass too, and a chart with skeletons on it, and pictures of trees."

"You can have the compass, if you take care of it."

"Well, don't be too long, anyhow," said the mate. "You'll see where we go with Captain Flint, and when you're tired of the island, you can come. We'll take your fishing rods."

They walked down with their stores to the harbour. John

took the mast and sail out of *Swallow*. Everybody wished them good luck, and the able-seaman and the boy set off, Titty poling the *Swallow* out of the harbour.

"Don't stay there too long," Mate Susan called after them.

"Far better come whaling," called Captain Nancy.

There was too much in Titty's head to let her think of an answer.

*

As soon as they were clear of the island, Able-seaman Titty gave one of the oars to Roger. They sat side by side on the middle thwart.

"You keep time with me, Boy," said the able-seaman.

"All right."

Titty lifted her oar from the water. Roger gave one pull.

"Boy," said the able-seaman, "you mustn't say 'All right'."

"Aye, aye, sir," said the boy.

"We are going to land on a desert island, to look for pirate treasure – the treasure the pirates took from Captain Flint. There may be land crabs, or alligators, or enemies of all kinds. The treasure may be buried deep in dead men's bones. We may be all our lives finding it. . . ."

"Susan said we weren't to be long."

"The mate meant, don't waste time. We won't waste time, but looking for treasure you never can tell to a year or two. We must face our dangers. We must keep together. And you must do what you are told."

"Aye, aye, sir."

"Now then, at the same time as me . . . dig in."

They both dug in, and the *Swallow*, a heavy little ship to row, because of her shape and her ballast, moved on a zigzag course across the lake.

Able-seaman Titty knew that it was not the thing to keep

looking over your shoulder, but she was not very sure of how to manage without. Half-way across, she took both oars, and made Roger sit in the stern and steer.

Cormorant Island was little more than a heap of rocks and stones, sticking up out of the water. There was some heather on it, a little grass, but very little, and two trees, both dead. One of the trees was lying on the rocks. It had been uprooted a long time ago, and the ground about it was nothing but great stones. The other tree, gaunt and bare, splashed with the white droppings of the birds, was the perching place of the cormorants.

"We're quite near," said Roger. "I can see the birds."

Titty looked round. Two cormorants, black, long-necked, a patch of white at their beaks, flew away fast and low over the water. Two others waited on the topmost branch of the dead tree.

"They're guarding the treasure," said Titty.

"One of them's swallowing a fish," said Roger. "Now they've both gone."

The two last cormorants rose from the tree and flew after the others, swinging at first low, then high, over the lake, wheeling far away by Darien, and coming down to the water where neither Roger nor Titty could see them.

"There's Captain Flint," said Roger. They could see his big rowing boat between Houseboat Bay and Wild Cat Island. He was on his way to join in the whaling expedition.

They waved, but he was rowing with his back to them, and at the other side of the lake.

"This is the place where I was anchored in *Amazon*," said the able-seaman, "and I heard the pirates row past me, and then they crashed into the rocks."

"Real pirates?" said the boy.

"I couldn't see them," said Titty, "but I heard the oars of

their ship's gig, and I heard them talk. They swore like real ones. And then I heard them hit the rocks."

"It's all rocks on this side," said the boy.

Titty rowed slowly round the island. There was no good place for beaching *Swallow*.

"There's the place where we landed with Captain Flint," said Roger.

"His boat has narrow bows," said Titty. "We couldn't get *Swallow*'s nose in there."

She rowed nearer to the north end of the island.

"It looks as if we could come alongside that rock," she said, "but we won't try to beach her. Captain John said we were to be careful about landing. So look out."

There was just a little bump as the *Swallow* touched the rock, but it was not a bad one. The able-seaman scrambled out with the painter, and held the gunwale, while the boy followed.

"Shall I bring the compass?" he said.

"No," said the able-seaman, "we'll leave it in the ship until we need it. But bring the pickaxe and pass out the stores. Better leave the bottle."

The boy gave the packets of sandwiches to the able-seaman. Then he gave her the hammer and scrambled out.

"Now we'll fasten the painter round that rock, just the end of it. What wind there is is from the south, and she'll float off without touching anything. We'll leave the stores on the rock."

It was done, and for some minutes the able-seaman stood watching her ship, which rode quietly at the end of the long painter, clear of all danger.

"She's all right like that," she said at last. "Now for the treasure."

It was very hard going on those rocks, as everybody had found, even Captain Flint, when they had all come here to look for the stolen trunk, the day before the battle in Houseboat

Bay. For the boy and the able-seaman it was very hard indeed. The rocks stuck up at all angles. There were deep clefts between them, big enough to take a foot and small enough to make it difficult to get the foot out again. Then there were lots of loose stones which slipped all ways when you trod on them. It took the treasure-hunters a long time even to get from one end of the island to the other.

"I'm glad we live on Wild Cat Island and not here," said Roger.

"This is a real desert island," said Titty. "Keep a look-out for a skeleton."

"Here are lots of bones," said Roger a minute or two later.

"Real bones?" called Titty.

"Little ones," said Roger.

Titty climbed round a rock to where Roger was standing looking down at a little heap of white fishbones. She looked up at once and, sure enough, there was a small hole in the rocks above them, a hole big enough for a tennis ball to go into. The hole was splashed with greenish white, and so was the rock below it. Titty reached up towards it, but just at that moment something flew out with fast-moving down-turned wings, flashing brilliant blue in the sunlight.

"It's the kingfisher's nest," she said. "Those are the bones of the minnows he's eaten. Not pirate bones at all."

They went on with the search. There were many more bones on Cormorant Island, but they were all fishbones. When the boy and able-seaman scrambled along to the tree where the cormorants always perched, they found plenty of them, lying under it. But the rocks there were so dirty, and the smell there was so bad, that they were glad to get away. And they found no sign of anything that might be treasure.

Roger began to lose heart, and also to feel hungry. They sat down on the flat rock at the north end of the island where they had left their provisions. They got the bottle of milk out of *Swallow*, ate their sandwiches and took turns in bubbling the milk out of the bottle into their mouths.

"There's Captain Flint and the others," said Titty. "They're all in his boat. Over there. Not in Shark Bay. In the little bay we passed when we went to see the savages with the snake."

"I wonder how many whales they've caught," said Roger. "Sharks too, perhaps. Anyhow, lots of perch."

"It's much better to find treasure than just to sit catching fish," said Titty.

"But we haven't found any," said Roger.

"We haven't nearly looked everywhere yet. It must be here," said Titty. "Come on. You hunt one side, and I'll hunt the other. Shout if you find it."

Presently Roger shouted, but it was not because he had found the treasure. He had slipped on the stones and scraped his knee.

"Which knee is it?" called Titty.

"The one that wasn't scraped before," said Roger. "At least not the one that got scraped last, but the other one."

Able-seaman Titty, as surgeon to the expedition, washed the knee, and tied it up with Roger's handkerchief. Roger tried to blow his nose in the corner of it that was left after the tying up.

"You can have my handkerchief," said Titty. "It's my pink one."

Roger blew his nose loudly in the pink handkerchief, and cheered up again.

Time went on. The morning was gone, and the afternoon was going, and still there was no sign of anything that might mean treasure. Titty had worked at least twice right round the island. Roger stopped looking, and went and sat on the rock to which *Swallow*'s painter was tied. He pulled on the painter, and *Swallow* came obediently to his feet. He met her with a bare foot on her stern, and she slid back again.

"Let's row again," he said. "We could see just as well from *Swallow* as on these rocks. Then if we saw nothing we could go whaling."

There was no answer. He looked for Titty. She was crawling along the rocks at the very edge of the island, not far away. Suddenly he saw her jump up with something in her hand.

"Hi! Roger!" she called.

Roger stood up, and climbed along the rocks towards her.

"I've found a pipe," she shouted. "It must have belonged to one of the pirates. This must be the place where they landed."

It was an ordinary wooden pipe. She had found it between two stones close to the edge of the water. The finding of it made a great difference to the island. Even Titty had begun to think that perhaps she must have dreamed of the pirates landing here that night in the dark, but now she had in her hand a solid proof that someone had been there besides the cormorants and the kingfisher.

"If they landed here," said Titty, "the treasure must be close by. They didn't go far away, because I heard them banging about all the time."

They looked carefully about them. They were close to the place where the old tree had stood, the tree that was now lying on its side with its rotted dried roots straggling in the air. The ground was covered with big loose stones. Titty went carefully over them, and round the tree. She found nothing. She went round the tree again in a widening circle. Still nothing. She went back to her task of working right round the edge of the island.

Roger stayed where he was, and presently began to amuse himself by gathering small driftwood and dead reeds that were

"WE'VE FOUND IT!"

stuck among the rocks, and had been drying there since the last time the lake was high after the rains.

At last Titty began to lose hope again. She came back to the fallen tree and Roger with his growing pile of fuel.

"Do light it, Titty," said Roger.

The able-seaman looked at it.

"That's not the way," she said. "We'll make a fireplace like the one Susan made on the shore that day we saw the savages and the snake. Then we'll light a fire in it, and Captain Flint and the others will see the smoke of our fire on the desert island far away. Then they'll come, and there'll be a rescue."

She began building with small stones.

"We need a good big stone to go at the back," she said.

She pulled at a biggish flat stone close by the roots of the old tree. It moved easily, and as it moved all thought of making fireplaces flew out of Titty's mind.

"Help, Roger," she shouted. "Where's the pickaxe?"

She had put the hammer down when she began to build the fireplace. Roger picked it up and gave it to her. Titty tapped with it at a black corner of iron that showed under the stone she had moved. It rang of metal and wood. She pulled the stone further, and it was clear that she had uncovered the iron-bound corner of a box.

"We've found it, we've found it, we've found it," shouted Titty. She pulled the stone right away to one side, and there was a torn label on the corner of the box, a label with a picture of a camel and a pyramid, and the word Cairo, plain in big letters.

"Help, Roger," said the able-seaman, "get the stones off one by one."

They pulled off stone after stone, and with each stone that was removed the marvels of the box grew greater. It was entirely covered with labels. There were labels showing "P. and O. First Cabin". There were labels of the Bibby Line, of the

Dollar Line, of the Nippon Yusen Kaisha. There was a label with palm trees and camels and a river from some hotel in Upper Egypt. There were labels showing the blue bays and white houses of Mediterranean seaports. There was a label saying, "Wanted on the Voyage". There were labels with queer writing on them, and no English writing at all except the word Peking. There was a label of the Chinese Eastern Railway. There were labels of hotels in San Francisco, Buenos Ayres, London, Rangoon, Colombo, Melbourne, Hong Kong, New York, Moscow and Khartoum. Some of them were pasted over others. Some were scratched and torn. But each one delighted the able-seaman and the boy. In the middle of the lid were two letters, "J.T." Stone after stone was pulled away. The box had been put under the tree, in the hollow where the roots had been, and then covered with big loose stones, of which there were plenty on all sides. Some of the stones were so big that Titty and Roger both pulling together could hardly move them. As for shifting the box, it was like trying to move a house. They could not stir it a quarter of an inch.

"Let's get it open," said Roger.

It was heavily bound with big black angle irons. The able-seaman banged at them with the hammer. There were strange double clasps that met each other, and locked, and were as strong as the iron bindings. Titty and Roger banged away at them, but they might as well have been two flies trying to break into a steel safe.

CHAPTER XXIX

TWO SORTS OF FISH

"There's nothing for it," said the able-seaman. "We shall have to fetch the others and Captain Flint. It's his sea-chest. I'm sure it is, and it's got his pirate book in it."

"Let's take *Swallow* and row," said Roger.

But there was no need. For a long time the fish had not been biting, partly perhaps because there were too many fishermen in the boat, and partly, as Captain Flint said, because they knew there was a change coming in the weather. It was very hot, and the air was heavy, and though the wind had died away altogether there were big, hard-edged dark clouds lifting slowly over the hills in the south. The whaling party had decided it had done enough whaling, and was on its way home. Susan had said, "Those two have been on Cormorant Island long enough." And Captain Flint, who knew that they were looking for his chest, and was sure that they had been looking in vain, had said, "We'll row across there and give them a tow home." So when Titty and Roger looked across the lake expecting to find the others where they had last seen them, fishing south of the island near the opposite shore, the whaling party was already more than half-way across the lake and rowing steadily towards them.

Titty climbed up, and stood on the fallen trunk of the tree, and waved and shouted. There was a shout back from over the water, but at first neither the whalers nor the treasure-hunters could hear each other's words.

334

The first words the treasure-hunters heard showed how little what they had been shouting had been understood.

"Aren't you sick of it?" they heard in Captain Flint's cheerful voice. "Time to come home."

"We've found it," shouted Titty.

"Time to come home," shouted Captain Flint again. "Tea."

"We've found it," squealed Roger.

Suddenly Captain Flint heard. He bent to his oars and a few minutes later the whaling party reached Cormorant Island. Captain Flint was ashore in a moment, and jumping over the rocks. The others followed. "You haven't really found anything, have you?" he said, but before they could answer he had seen the box. "Well done, Able-seaman!" he shouted. "Shiver my timbers!" exclaimed Nancy. "Good for you, Titty," said Captain John. "Then you weren't dreaming after all," said Susan. "Who ever would have thought it?" said Peggy. "Why, Captain Nancy had looked for it herself, and never found it."

Captain Flint dropped on his knees beside the box, and pulled a bunch of keys from his pocket. "They don't seem to have opened it," he said, "but they've had a jolly good try."

"That was us," said the able-seaman.

Captain Flint unlocked it, threw back the clasps, and lifted the lid. Inside was a typewriter in a black case, a lot of canvas-bound diaries, and a huge bundle of typewritten paper.

"That's all right," said Captain Flint, fingering the bundle as if he loved it.

"It's very dull," said Roger. "Titty said it was treasure."

"There's treasure and treasure," said Captain Flint. "It takes all sorts to make a world. You know, Able-seaman, I can never say thank you enough to you. If I'd lost this, as I thought I had, I'd have lost all the diaries of my pirate past, and I've put all the best of my life into this book. It would have been gone for ever if it hadn't been for you."

"I heard them say they were coming back for it. So I knew it must be here," said Titty. "And it's just what pirates always do. They always mean to come back when they bury anything."

"Like dogs to a buried bone," said Captain Flint. "Well, they've lost this bone, though it wouldn't have been much use to them. I can't imagine them settling down to read *Mixed Moss*."

"What are you going to do about them?" said Captain Nancy. "Let's lie in wait for them and catch them."

Captain Flint thought for a moment. Then he said, "I'm not going to do anything at all. I told the police to inquire at the landing-places, because I wanted to take any chance there was of getting it back. But I don't want to send anyone to prison."

"Prison!" said Nancy. "They ought to be hanged in chains at Execution Dock, and rattle their bones in the wind."

"They only do that sort of thing to Amazon Pirates nowadays," said Captain Flint. "What did you hear them say, Ableseaman, about fetching their loot away?"

"They said, 'We'll come fishing and catch something worth having.'"

"And so they jolly well shall," said Captain Flint. "Let's see if we can find a bit of wood, a flat bit."

"We found their pipe," said Roger.

"Good," said Captain Flint. "We'll frighten them off burgling for the rest of their lives."

He found a flat piece of wood among the jetsam gathered by Roger for a fire. He sat down on a rock and pulled out a big knife. Chips of wood flew in all directions.

"What are you doing?" said Roger.

"Giving them something to catch," said Captain Flint.

He chopped away with the knife and presently the flat piece of wood had a narrow place at one end and a big forked tail beyond it. The rest of it was shaped like a melon, only flat, with a square piece sticking up from the edge of it, like a fin.

"It's a fish," said Roger.

"Didn't they say they were going to catch something?" said Captain Flint.

He carved the head of the fish, giving it big gill covers and a wide mouth and a large, round, staring eye.

"It's a very good fish," said Roger.

"They won't think so when they catch it," said Captain Flint. "Now," he said, pulling a bit of string from his pocket, "we'll tie their pipe to the fish's tail, and we'll bury them both under the stones where they hid my box. Then when they come on the lake pretending to be fishing, and land here to dig up their loot, they'll dig up the fish and find the pipe they lost; and if they put two and two together, as I expect they will, they will think that somebody was close at hand all the time and heard what they said and knows who they are and all about them, and I should think they'll go off in a hurry, wishing they'd stayed at home."

He hove up his box and put the fish and the pipe in the hole where the box had lain.

"Half a minute," he said. "They may as well have a sermon at the same time." Taking out his pencil he wrote in big letters along the side of the wooden fish, "HONESTY IS THE BEST POLICY." Then he put it back and covered the fish with stones. "Pile it up with stones," he said, "so it will take them some time to dig down to it." And the Amazons and Swallows piled in stones until the hole was filled up.

"Now it looks just like it did before I began to make a fireplace," said Titty.

"Well, that's that," said Captain Flint. "Good luck to them. And now," he said, "if all you people had not been doing exactly what you were doing that night (even if you were supposed to be in bed), I should never have got that box again. I should have been sorry to lose the old box, because it's been with me all over the world. And I should have lost the book I've been writing all summer in spite of the efforts of Nancy and Peggy to make any writing impossible. Never any of you start writing books. It isn't worth it. This summer has been harder work for me than all the thirty years of knocking up and down that went before it. And if those scoundrels had got away with the box I could never have done it again. I owe a great deal to all of you, and most of all to the able-seaman. Look here, Able-seaman, you tell me anything in the world that I can get for you and you shall have it."

"You did say that you were going to bring me back a parrot," said the able-seaman, "and there isn't anything in the world I'd rather have. If you really meant it," she added.

"Was it you who said you wanted a grey one?"

"I like green ones best."

"It's a long time to wait till next summer," said Captain Flint.

"I don't mind waiting," said the able-seaman.

Just then Captain Flint seemed to think of something suddenly.

"Look here," he said, "I must go off at once to tell the police to stop making inquiries. I'll take you across and drop you on your island."

"You'll come back for the shark steaks, won't you?" said Susan.

"Shark?" said Roger. "Did you get a shark?"

"A walloper," said Peggy.

"I'll do my best," said Captain Flint, "but don't wait for me. I've got a long way to row. Come along." He hove the big box on his shoulder and carried it to his boat. Roger was there before him, looking at a great green and white pike lying on the bottom boards.

"Did you catch him?"

"We caught him between us."

"He's nearly as big as the one I didn't catch. There aren't any like that in Houseboat Bay."

"Who's coming with me and who in *Swallow*?" asked Captain Flint.

"I'm going with the shark," said Roger.

"There's room for you all," said Captain Flint, "but someone ought to steer *Swallow* or she'll be all over the place."

"I'll steer *Swallow*," said Titty, really because she wanted to be alone. She had had one idea firm in her head and had held to it when everyone thought she was wrong; and now, when everybody knew she had been right, just for a minute or two she did not want to do any talking.

Everybody else crowded into the big rowing boat. Captain Flint rowed in the bows, looking at his old cabin trunk with its ancient labels. Roger sat on the cabin trunk, looking at the big jaws of the pike. John, Susan, Nancy and Peggy sat in the stern. John held the *Swallow*'s painter, and the *Swallow*, with the able-seaman happy at the tiller, slipped smoothly along in the rowing boat's wake.

*

When Captain Flint had rowed away, leaving the Swallows and Amazons on Wild Cat Island, they found a great deal to do. The fire was out and a new fire had to be made up and the kettle boiled for tea. The mates, Susan and Peggy, took charge of that. John and Nancy were busy taking down all the fishing rods and the fishing tackle. Roger was looking at the fish. Titty paddled *Swallow* round from the landing-place to the harbour. Then the two captains went to the harbour and joined the able-seaman, who was waiting for them. They stepped *Swallow*'s mast and then moored her side by side with *Amazon* but not so near that the two little ships could bump each other. From the harbour, when their work was done and *Swallow* and *Amazon* were both ready for the night, they looked out to sea, away to the southern end of the lake.

"Barometer's gone down two-tenths since morning," said Captain John.

"When it's as hot as this in the evening something always happens," said Captain Nancy. "Probably thunder."

"Don't like the look of it at all," said Captain John. "There's no wind to speak of, and yet look at that cloud."

Titty, too, was looking at the big dark cloud coming up in the south. If it was going to rain, she was thinking, what a good thing it had held off for today to let her find the treasure.

The mate's whistle sounded in the camp, and all three of them hurried back to a late tea of bunloaf and marmalade.

Almost as soon as tea was over and the mugs rinsed out Roger said, "Are we really going to have shark steaks for supper?"

"Why not?" said Mate Susan.

"Mister Mate," said Peggy, "have you ever scaled shark?"

"Not yet," said Susan.

"It's awful," said Peggy.

"We'd better start on it at once," said Susan. "It's late, anyway."

They went down to the landing-place where the great green and white mottled fish with its huge head and wicked eyes lay on the stones. They knelt beside it, each with a knife, and began scraping.

"You scrape from its middle to its tail, I'll scrape from its head to its middle," said Peggy.

The others watched. Roger hung round the mates as near as he could. He could not take his eyes off the fish.

"Whatever you do, don't get your hand into its mouth," said Peggy, when Roger tried to measure its head with his hand. "I did once, with a smaller one than this, and I couldn't hold a rope for a month."

"Why?" said Roger.

"Look at its teeth," said Peggy, and she stopped scraping and opened its huge jaws with a stone.

Roger looked in at the rows and rows of sharp teeth pointing backwards and the long teeth, like a dog's, in the lower jaw.

"Perhaps it's a good thing there were no sharks in Houseboat Bay," he said.

"Why?" said Peggy.

"Well, he's going to bring me a monkey," said Roger.

The scales came off easily enough, but flew in all directions. The arms of the two mates were covered with them. They even got scales in their hair. When one side of the fish was scraped they turned its slippery body over on the stones to scrape the other. Then the shark had to be cut open and cleaned, and that was even worse. It was done, and the mates washed the shark and their hands in the lake. Then they carried the great fish up to the camp and Mate Susan cut it into thick steaks, cutting it clean across from one side to the other and hacking through the backbone. She cut seven steaks, each about two inches thick. They put all that was left of the pike in the fire. Then, with plenty of butter in the frying-pan, they fried the steaks, turning them over and over, spooning up the butter when it ran down into the side of the pan and pouring it over the sizzling chunks of fish, until the butter turned dark and the steaks were nicely browned.

There was still no sign of Captain Flint in the distance when the shark steaks were ready for eating. And it was growing dusk. The sun had disappeared in clouds long before it set.

"Captain Flint did say we weren't to wait for him," said Susan, "and, anyhow, they smell too good to wait."

"Let's get at them," said Captain Nancy.

341

"I'm hungry," said Roger.

"We may as well begin," said John.

"We can keep his hot," said Titty.

"Pass your plates, then," said Susan, and the shark steak supper began.

It was found, by experiment, that fingers were a good deal better than forks. There are a lot of bones in fresh-water sharks and, though this was such a big one that the bones were easy to find, fingers were better than forks at pulling them out. So the Swallows and Amazons sat by their fire with a lot of salt in the lid of a tin and dipped their steaks in the salt and ate them, more like savages than explorers.

"I wish we weren't going tomorrow," said Titty. "We haven't had time for a furthest north expedition, or for a furthest south. There's lots of unexplored at both ends of our chart. I say," she turned suddenly to Captain John, remembering something important, "we can alter Cormorant Island to Treasure Island now, can't we?"

"Well, you did find the treasure there," said John.

"Oh, look here," Peggy objected. "We call it Cormorant Island too. And treasure is only there sometimes, but cormorants are there always."

"Cormorant Island is a very good name," said Captain John. "How would it be if we were to leave it Cormorant Island and put a cross on it to show where the treasure was and mark it 'Treasure found here'?"

Titty agreed.

"Let's do it at once," she said, and Captain John licked his fingers clean from the shark steak and went into his tent and came back with the chart. There and then "Treasure found here" was written in in small letters and a cross put on Cormorant Island to mark the place.

"Yes," said Titty, "now we've found the treasure it isn't

exactly a treasure island. It's an island where treasure was."

"The only treasure there now," said Roger, "is a wooden fish. When the burglars find it and dig it up they won't even be able to make steaks of it. Too tough."

"It's a jolly good chart," said Captain Nancy, looking at it with Peggy and holding it by the fire to see better. "But there are lots of names you haven't got."

"The savages are fine," said Peggy, "and so is the shark, but what have you put in our lagoon?"

"It's meant for an octopus," said John.

"Next year you can fill in a lot more," said Captain Nancy. "We'll do something splendid. We can plan it all winter. It'll be something to think about during lessons. Either Furthest North or Furthest South would be good. Going south, we should have to take a canoe to shoot the rapids in, and then we should come to the sea. Anything might happen. We could grab a ship."

"There must be something beyond the big mountains in the north." said Titty.

"You can get a long way into the hills, going up the river," said Peggy. "And then, in the mountains, we could walk. But there'd be the tents to carry."

"We could get a hill pony to carry the tents," said Nancy. "That's it. We'll go prospecting for gold."

"Beyond the ranges," said Titty.

"You can go for miles and miles up there and never see a single native," said Peggy.

"Captain Flint said he'd be one of us next year," said Nancy. "When he is, he makes things hum. He may charter a big ship, three or four times as big as *Amazon* and ship us all as crew. He's often said he would some day. Now that there are the Swallows as well, we could sail a really big one."

343

"What about his steak?" said Titty.

"I'm keeping it warm," said Susan, "but it's getting a bit dry."

"Stick another lump of butter on it," said Peggy.

It was nearly dark when at last they heard the sound of oars and then the scrunch of a boat on the shingle at the landing-place. A moment later Captain Flint walked into the firelight. He carried a large cage wrapped up in a blue cloth cover. You could see it was a cage by the bottom of it. The firelight glittered on the big brass knob that stuck out at the top above the cover. There was a ring in the knob to carry it by or for hanging it to a beam. Captain Flint put it on the ground by Titty. A big white label was fastened to the ring. Titty read it by the light of the fire:

"From Captain Flint to the able-seaman who saved his Life."

"But I didn't save your life," said Titty.

"I didn't write life. I wrote Life," said Captain Flint. "*Mixed Moss*. It's the same thing."

"Thank you very much indeed," said Titty. "I'll hang it up in the schoolroom, ready for the parrot."

But just then there was a noise of scraping from under the blue cover.

"Look inside," said Captain Flint. "I thought it would be rather a long time to wait till I come back from the south next spring."

Titty lifted the blue cloth cover and a loud cheerful voice, rather like the voice of Nancy Blackett, came from beneath it.

"Pieces of eight," said the green parrot, "pieces of eight!"

"It's never said it before," said Nancy. "And now it'll say it all the time."

"Am I really to have it?" said Titty.

"Of course you are," said Captain Flint. "You've earned it about ten thousand times."

"Mother will really believe we're back from the Pacific," said Titty. "Thank you very, very much indeed." She jumped up and put out her hand. Captain Flint shook it.

"It's me that ought to do the thanking," he said.

"My monkey will come next year," said Roger.

"If you can get your mother to say you may have it," said Captain Flint, "I'll see about it at once. There are monkeys nearer than Africa and I'm taking my book up to London now that I've got it again. I'll go and look at monkeys by way of a change from publishers. You shall have your monkey next week."

"With a tail?" asked Roger.

"A long one," said Captain Flint.

"Your steak's rather dry," said Mate Susan, "but it's still quite hot."

Captain Flint ate it in his fingers and said it was the best shark steak he had ever tasted.

After that they talked again of plans for next year, of climbing the ranges, of sailing to the Azores, or, better still, the Baltic, or of making a canoe voyage down to the sea.

"If we go up country," said Nancy, "do you think we could get a hill pony?"

"We could easily get a couple," said Captain Flint.

Everybody liked the idea of the shaggy hill ponies to carry the explorers' packs. But then, everybody liked the idea of sailing to the Baltic. So nothing was really decided.

"Whatever it is," said Captain Flint, "I'll be free next summer, and if you'll sign me on, I'll be glad to come. If we sail to the Baltic you'll want someone to haul up the anchor, and if we go prospecting it would be hard on a hill pony if he had to carry the gold as well as the tents."

"The monkey can come too," said Roger. "He can look out from the very top of the mast, or else he can ride on a hill pony."

At last Captain Flint said, "I must be getting back. Your camp fire is very jolly, but isn't it about time some of you people went to bed?"

"Won't you be lonely without the parrot?" said Titty.

"I must think of him too," said Captain Flint. "He's a young parrot and I'm a dull companion for him. He's in better hands now."

He got up to go down to his boat.

"By the way," he said, "are all your tents pretty strong? It looks to me as if we're in for bad weather before morning."

"Mother says ours are all right except in a high wind," said Captain John.

"H'm! It looks as if it's going to blow. Well, I don't suppose you'll come to much harm, even if it does."

He rowed away.

Not long afterwards, the Swallows and Amazons turned in. It was very hot and there were no stars.

"Pouf," said Nancy, "I can hardly breathe."

"Barometer's gone down another tenth," called Captain John. "That's three-tenths since this morning."

"Is that a lot?" asked Peggy.

"Rather a lot," said John. "Are you ready, Roger? I'm going to blow the candle out."

Titty had the parrot-cage close beside her in the mate's tent. She took the blue cover off. "He won't want it now," she said. "He'll be in the same dark as us. Good night, Polly!"

"Pieces of eight," rapped out the parrot, excited by the candlelight in the white tent. "Pieces of eight, pieces of eight, pieces of eight." It went on saying "Pieces of eight" as fast as if it were counting treasure.

Nancy Blackett's laugh sounded from the tent at the other side of the camp.

Then Mate Susan blew out the candle-lantern. There was

darkness in the tent and, in the sudden silence that came with the darkness, it was as if she had blown out the parrot.

"Good night," "Good night," the Swallows and Amazons called to each other. Their last night on the island had begun.

CHAPTER XXX

THE STORM

ALL this time the skies had smiled on the Swallows and the Amazons. There had been a few hours' drizzling rain, a few hours of fog and that dark night of sordid burglary and high adventure. But day after day had been dry and clear and, even when there had been clouds, there had also been sunshine and wind to drive their shadows, chasing each other, over the bright heather and bracken of the hills. Now that it was time for the Swallows to go, there came a sudden change of weather to remind them that the summer too was near its end. All that last day there had been the heaviness of thunder in the air. There had been a stormy sunset and, though there had been but little wind, dark, angry clouds had lifted in the south until at night they shut out all the stars.

*

The storm broke with a crash of thunder that woke the whole camp. With it came a flickering light as bright as day. There was the wild shriek of a parrot as if it were one of a flock screaming through the palm trees in a tropical hurricane. Then darkness and quiet. Then heavy drops of rain pattering down on the tents.

Titty woke, not comfortably, bit by bit, but with every bit of herself at once. She did not move, except to put out her hand and touch the parrot's cage. "Susan," she whispered.

"All right, Titty," said Susan.

Roger in the captain's tent sat up with a start and a shout. "He's firing! He's going to fire again!" He was back in the battle of Houseboat Bay and his voice died into a breathless "John!" as he woke to find himself in the dark.

"All right, Roger," said John, "it's only thunder."

"Where are you going, Nancy?" said Peggy. At hearing the first drops of rain, Nancy was up and lighting their lantern.

"To bring some firewood in, of course," said Nancy. "Don't you remember the last time it rained and all the wood got wet and we couldn't get our fire to light?"

She was back in a moment with a bundle of sticks from the pile.

"It's not raining much yet," she said, "but it's going to."

She wriggled back into her sleeping-bag.

There was another flash of lightning that lit the tents and threw leaping shadows on their white walls from the branches of the trees overhead.

"Never mind, Polly," said Titty, "it'll soon be over."

"Pretty Polly," said the parrot, now thoroughly awake.

One flash followed another and then there were three tremendous crashes of thunder and a lot of little ones as if the sky were breaking into solid bits and rattling down a steep iron roof.

"There's a broadside for you," called Nancy Blackett from her tent.

"Pieces of eight," said the parrot, and then, perhaps thinking of palm trees again, gave a long, wild shriek.

"Would you like me to put your cloth over you?" said Titty.

"What time is it, John?" called Susan.

"Four bells of the middle watch," said Captain John, who had looked at the chronometer with his pocket torch and had just put it into ship's time for himself.

"What is it in real time?" asked Peggy.

"Two o'clock in the morning," said Captain John. After all, there were some things these Amazons did not know.

There was a gust of wind and then a heavier pattering of rain on the tents and after that it was as if the rain were coming down in solid lumps of water that splashed and broke on the thin canvas.

"It's coming through," said Roger. "I can feel it."

"Don't touch the wall of the tent," said John.

"I'm not, but it's coming through all the same."

"It's coming through our tent too," said Susan "Titty, you'd better cover up the parrot."

"I have, but I don't believe he likes it."

There was more lightning and more thunder. The rain stopped for a moment and then poured down again.

"John," called Susan.

"Yes."

"Better get into our clothes and then we can keep them dry under the blankets. Have you got your oilies?"

"Yes. Have you?"

"I'll get them in a minute. I'm lighting our lantern. Spread your oilies over your blankets. Roger too."

Susan bustled Titty into her clothes and got into her own. Roger and John pulled on their knickerbockers. There was the sound of a squabble in the tent of the Amazons.

"Don't put your head under, Peggy. Get dressed like the others."

There was a glare of lightning and a crash of thunder all in one, and after that for a long time the thunder and lightning came so close one after the other that no one knew which flash belonged to which clap of thunder. The camp was full of light and the rolling, crashing thunder overhead made things seem hurried, as if there was something that ought to be done but no time in which to do it. The lanterns were lit but, though they were bright in the short moments of darkness, they seemed to give no light at all in the glare of the lightning flashes.

It was dark again and suddenly quiet. It was as if the storm were holding its breath. Then there was a deep, rushing noise, far away, louder and louder every moment.

"What's that?" said Titty.

"Wind," said Susan.

"I say," said Titty, "this *is* a storm."

As she said it the wind reached them.

There was a crash as a heavy branch fell somewhere at the low end of the island. There was a swishing noise as the trees swayed in the wind. Nor was the noise all. The tents of the Swallows were hung on ropes between trees and held down by stones in pockets along the bottom edges of the tent walls. The trees were blown this way and that and the rope now slackened, now tightened up again so hard that in the captain's tent the stones shifted and rattled in the pockets.

"Hullo, Susan," called John. "Have you got enough stones to hold your tent down? Our tent's getting smaller."

"Ours is all right," shouted Susan, "the stones haven't moved yet."

"What?" shouted John. "I can't hear."

"Our stones are all right," shouted Susan. But she spoke too soon. There was a loud crack. The stones had been heavy enough, but a furious jerk of the trees had snapped the wet taut rope on which her tent was hung. The whole tent flopped down, a mass of wet canvas, burying Susan and Titty and the parrot in its folds, knocking over their candle-lantern and putting it out.

From the other tents, they heard the crack, an angry scream from the parrot as its cage fell over, and then muffled shrieks of "Help! Help!"

John and Nancy were out of their tents in a moment. John had his torch, but there was no need to use it, for a long, flickering glare of lightning showed them the grey wet mass of the mate's tent on the ground with something struggling under it. They lifted the end of the tent where the door had been. Mate Susan and Able-seaman Titty crawled out on all fours, the able-seaman dragging the parrot's cage, which had lost its blue cloth.

"Come into our tent, quick," Nancy shouted in the roaring of the wind.

"What about our things?" shouted Susan.

"And Polly's blue cloak?" shouted Titty.

"Wet anyway. Leave them," shouted Nancy, and indeed it was the only thing to do.

Shielding the parrot from the wind and rain as best she could, Titty ran into the Amazons' tent, where she found Peggy, who was very glad to see her. Susan followed.

"We ought to have got our lantern out," she said. "You've only got a stump of a candle left."

"Do you think the trees are coming down?" said Peggy.

"They'd be down before now if they were coming," said Susan.

"Poor Polly," said Titty, but the parrot corrected her. He was smoothing down the feathers that had been fluffed out in the wind.

"Pretty Polly," he said.

"I don't believe he minds losing his blue cloak," said Titty.

"Is your tent going too?" shouted Captain Nancy in the wind.

"I hope not," said Captain John.

"What?"

"I hope not," he shouted in her ear.

The wind was blowing across the island in great gusts that shook the little trees like grass. Overhead the tall pine that was the lighthouse creaked and groaned. For a moment or two it was pitch dark, and then the lightning lit up the sky so that everything was as clear as in daylight. With each gust, Captain

John's tent clapped like a loose jib on a ship going about in a squall and there was a rattle of stones.

Roger crawled out into the rain.

"It's getting smaller and smaller," he said. "It's spilling the stones out of the pockets."

Nancy and John could not hear him, but they could see the tent thrashing about.

Nancy grabbed him by the scruff of the neck as he crawled out and ran him to the Amazons' tent and pushed him in. "You'll be dry, anyhow," she said. Then she went back to Captain John, who had struggled into his flapping tent and brought out the two things that mattered most, the chronometer and the barometer. In one of the lightning flashes he held up the barometer.

"It's gone down four-tenths," he shouted.

"Come along into our tent," shouted Nancy. "Bring the big lantern if you can get it."

Captain John gave her the barometer and put the chronometer in his pocket. He forced his way once more into the whirling jumble of canvas that had been his tent. He found the lantern and fought his way out again.

"There's nothing more to be done," shouted Nancy. "Come on."

They went into the Amazons' tent, where the candle-lantern was guttering out. John lit the big lantern and put it in the middle of the floor. Nancy hurried out again to slacken the ropes of her tent. Then she came in and closed the flaps of the door.

"Our tent has its back to the wind," she said. "All the big winds come from the south. That's why we chose this place for it. The poles at each end help it too. Our tent'll stand anything."

"Did you get very wet?" said Mate Susan.

"Rather," said Captain John.

"I'm soaked," said Nancy. "Lovely."

There was not much room for the six of them and the parrot-cage in the Amazons' tent. They sat three on each of the sleeping-bags. Between them right at the back of the tent was the bundle of dry firewood that Nancy had rescued for the morning. Then there was the parrot's cage, and then the farm lantern in the middle of the floor. It was a tight pack on each side, because they had to take care not to touch the tent walls. The weather outside seemed to matter less now that they were all together. Even Peggy, who really could not help not liking thunder, was cheerful again, partly because it would never do to show Roger that she was afraid. With Nancy it was different. Nancy knew, so that with her it was no use pretending. Susan was a little worried about the things getting wet, but glad that no worse had happened. John was thinking how lucky it was that the storm had waited till their last night. Nancy was proud of her strong tent and enjoyed the wind buffeting against it. Titty, with sparkling eyes, was thinking of typhoons. The parrot was putting his feathers to rights and now and then whistling cheerfully at the bright lantern so near him on the floor.

For some time they sat there, listening to the storm raging over the island. Then, ashamed that he had not remembered them earlier, John thought of the boats. "I'm going to have a look at *Swallow*," he said.

"Shiver my timbers," said Captain Nancy. "There's *Amazon* too. It's a good thing we moored them properly last night."

The two captains got on their feet. Nancy unfastened the tent flaps.

"Better fasten them up again when we're outside," she said.

"I'm coming too," said Titty. "The parrot'll be all right now."

"You'll only get wet," said Susan.

"I am wet," said Titty. "I couldn't be wetter. I want to see it. We may never have another storm as good as this one."

"I'm going too," said Roger.

WIND, RAIN AND LIGHTNING

"No, you are not," said the mate, "you're dry."

"I'll tell you what you can do, Roger," said John. "You can lend Captain Nancy your torch. Her lantern's no good and you'll want the big one in the tent."

"Aye, aye, sir," said Roger. If he could not go, at least his torch could, and that was better than nothing.

Titty, John, and Nancy slipped out of the tent into the storm. Using the torches and bending low against the wind and rain, they forced their way along the path to the harbour. There was a lot of water in the boats and the lake had already risen a little, but the *Swallow* and the *Amazon*, moored as they were, were quite all right.

"I'm going to slacken away my bow warp," said Captain John. "It's got very taut with all this wet."

"I'll do the same with mine."

They loosened the painters a little.

"It's a grand harbour, you know," shouted Nancy. "Just listen to it outside."

In the sheltered harbour there were waves, but nothing to matter. The big rocks on either side broke the waves before they could get in. But they could hear the crashing of breakers on the outer shoals and along the steep western shore. Titty slipped away from the others and crawled to the edge of the low cliff that ran along that shore, and crouched there, facing into the wind. Spray from the waves breaking beneath her was blown into her face. Flashes of lightning lit up the whole lake and showed great waves stretching right across it with white curling tops. Then it was dark again. Then more lightning showed her the fields and woods and hills on the other side of the lake, beyond the raging water.

The others missed her and would have gone back to the tent without her if Nancy had not seen the gleam of a torch away to the left of the path.

John found her and tugged at her sleeve.

"Come along," he shouted. "We thought you'd gone on already."

"Aye, aye, sir," said Titty, though John could not hear her, and they joined Nancy on the path and went back to the tent together.

"Well," said Susan, "if you were wet before, you're a lot wetter now. And nothing to change into."

"It was worth it," said Titty.

"Were the boats all right?" asked Roger.

"Couldn't be snugger," said Captain Nancy. "But their crews will have a lot of baling to do in the morning."

"What's the time now?" said Peggy. "Susan says it's only about three."

"It's nearly five," said John.

*

Nobody could go to sleep. They became shipwrecked sailors.

"Both our masts went by the board," said Captain Nancy.

"And before that the mizen was struck by lightning," said Captain John.

"Did you see the blue lights flickering on the ends of the spars?" said Nancy. "That was before the mizen was struck."

"Then we started a plank," said John, "and the water poured in."

"The mate came running on deck shouting, 'All hands to the pumps, five feet of water in the hold.' That was you, Susan," said Nancy.

"Why not me?" said Peggy.

"You were the second mate. You were cutting the wreckage adrift and making a raft. No, you weren't. We didn't make a raft. I forgot. You were cutting the wreckage adrift to clear the decks, and seeing to the lowering of the boats."

"One boat was called *Swallow* and the other was called *Amazon*," said Roger.

"And the waves were breaking over the ship," said Titty, "and she was going down by the head with every soul on board. Someone had killed an albatross."

"Pieces of eight, pieces of eight," shouted the parrot.

"Yes. She was full of them," said Titty. "That's what made her sink so fast."

"We launched the boats," said Nancy, "and then the ship went down and we were alone on the deep."

"Sometimes in the waves we could not see each other," said John, "but sometimes we could."

"We had no food in the boats but a biscuit each and a little water," said Susan.

"Day after day we ran before the storm," said Nancy. "North-west by north was our course. We had decided it before we left the ship."

"We ate the biscuits and drank the water," said Peggy.

"It blew and thundered and lightened and rained without stopping," said Titty, "and Roger and I were baling *Swallow* and Peggy was baling *Amazon*."

"Then the rain stopped, and for days and days we had nothing to eat and nothing to drink," said Nancy.

"In *Swallow* we were going to draw lots who was to be eaten first," said Titty.

"We were coming to that when we sighted land," said Nancy.

"We sighted land too, just in time," said Roger.

"There were great breakers on the beach," said Nancy.

"We only saw the land when there was a flash of lightning," said Titty. "Palm trees waving like anything."

"There was lightning all the time," said Nancy. "We ran on between the breakers. Our boats were capsized and we clung to them. They were thrown far up the beach by the waves. We were battered but saved."

"So was the parrot," said Titty. "And now we shall be here for twenty years. Every day we shall watch for a passing ship."

"But how have we got a tent?" said Roger.

"Luckily there was one in one of the boats," said Nancy. "I say, Peggy, what about a round of chocolate? There's still a lot left."

*

At last it began to grow light outside. For some time the thunder had been lagging after the lightning. After a flash it was a long time before the rumbling of the thunder began far away. The wind dropped. The noise of the rain on the tent grew less and less and came to an end. The dawn came up behind the eastern hills. The light of the lantern no longer filled the tent. Light was coming in from outside, through the canvas. The Swallows and Amazons went out into the early morning to look at the wreck of their camp. Patches of blue sky were showing overhead and patches of sunlight on the hills. Ragged clouds were blowing away. There was a wonderful smell of wet earth. The storm was over.

John went back into the tent to tap the barometer. It was going up.

Susan began raking the sodden ashes out of the fireplace. Nancy brought out her bundle of dry sticks. All the rest of the firewood was dripping wet, and it took them a long time to get their fire going. Without the dry sticks they could never have done it. Titty burrowed into what had been her tent and the mate's, and brought out the parrot's blue cloth and hung it on two sticks to dry.

CHAPTER XXXI

THE SAILORS' RETURN

A<small>ND</small> then came the natives.

The first to arrive was Mrs. Dixon. Just as the fire was beginning to burn the shipwrecked sailors saw her coming down the field from the farm above Shark Bay, with a milk-can in one hand and a big bucket in the other. And there was Mr. Dixon coming too, with a pair of oars over his shoulder. Mr. Dixon baled their boat and pushed it out and rowed Mrs. Dixon across to the island, splashing as he rowed. Though the wind had gone down there were still waves on the lake, even between the island and the shore.

"Whatever can they want?" said Nancy.

Peggy and Titty had gone up to the look-out point to look at the lake. They came running back into the camp.

"Captain Flint's coming," shouted Peggy. "He's nearly here, and there's another rowing boat, and there's a launch in the distance. I think it's ours."

"Mother's in the other rowing boat, with a native," said Titty.

"If it's the launch, our mother's in it, I bet you anything," said Nancy.

"There are still quite big waves down the lake," said Titty, "but Mother's got past them all right."

Everybody ran down to the landing-place, and got there just as Mr. Dixon stepped out and pulled his boat up. Mrs. Dixon clambered out with her big bucket and the milk-can. She had a tray over the top of the bucket for a lid, and steam was coming from under it.

"No. It isn't pigwash," she said, "though you might think it. It's porridge for drowned rats, which is what I reckoned you'd be. You've done well to get your fire lit at all. I could hardly rest for thinking of you in that storm. My word, how it did come down. And so you found Mr. Turner's box that was stolen. And I thought it was you that took it. Dixon told me the news when he came from the village last night."

The Swallows and Amazons looked at each other. Did everybody know everything?

"Porridge," said Roger.

"Aye, porridge," said Mrs. Dixon. "There's no room in anybody for a cold if they're full up with hot porridge, so I always say. Have you any spoons?"

"Lots."

"I'll just slop the milk into the bucket and give it a stir round. I put the sugar in up at the farm."

In another minute the four Swallows and the two Amazons were spooning hot porridge and milk out of the bucket and feeling each mouthful go scalding down their throats.

"This really is eating out of the common dish," said Titty.

Then came Captain Flint.

"Good for you, Mrs. Dixon," were his first words. "I ought to have thought of that. Porridge was the very thing. One, two, three, four, five, six. That's all right. Nobody washed away in the night."

"Seven," said Titty. "You've forgotten my parrot. He said 'Pretty Polly' at the lightning and 'Pieces of eight' when it thundered."

"Seven," said Captain Flint. "And two of the tents gone, I see. I was afraid they would. It was a wild go while it lasted. It was tough work bucketing into it even now, though the wind's dropped and the lake's nothing to what it was. It settles very quickly."

Then came Mother from Holly Howe, rowed by that powerful native, Mr. Jackson. She had brought three big thermos flasks full of boiling cocoa.

"Good morning, Mrs. Dixon," she said. "That was very kind of you, to think of coming across. I was afraid they'd not be able to get their fire lit."

"It's a wonder they have," said Mrs. Dixon.

"We haven't been able to boil a kettle yet," said Susan. "We couldn't have lit it at all if Nancy hadn't thought of keeping some sticks dry."

"And you are the Amazons?" said Mother, looking at Nancy and Peggy.

"Yes," said Nancy, "and this is Captain Flint. His other name is Turner."

"How do you do?" said Mother, and Captain Flint said how sorry he was he had not made friends with the Swallows before. "You don't know how much I owe to these children," he said.

"Children!" snorted Nancy Blackett.

"Explorers and pirates," Captain Flint corrected himself. "If it hadn't been for them I should have lost all the work I've done this summer."

"I heard something about it last night from Mrs. Jackson," said Mother. "I'm sure I'm very glad they've been of some use. Their father seems to think they are not duffers, but sometimes I'm not so sure."

"Mother!" said John, and Mother laughed.

"He's given me a parrot," said Able-seaman Titty, and Mother had to go and look at it.

"He's going to give me a monkey," said Roger.

"What?" said Mother.

Captain Flint explained, and Mother said that it must be a very little one.

"It shall be, ma'am," said Captain Flint.

Mother looked at the wrecked tents.

"They're no good in a wind," she said. "I remember once in the bush . . . I was in a tent like that and it ripped to ribbons and was blown clean away. . . . Well," she said, "it's a good thing you haven't got to sleep in them tonight, and a pity you didn't come home yesterday."

"I can hardly think so, ma'am," said Captain Flint.

"We wouldn't have found the treasure if we had," said Titty.

"The first thing to do is to put on some dry clothes," said Mother. "I've brought a dry change for each of you four."

"Roger never got wet," said Susan.

"That's a good thing," said Mother, "but you did, and so did John, and Titty looks like a dishcloth. Run down to the boat and ask Mr. Jackson for that bundle."

Then came the launch, chug, chugging in to the landing-place, and running its nose gently aground close by the three boats that were already there. The landing-place was so crowded that it was almost as bad as Rio Bay. Captain Flint ran down there to meet the launch, and Mrs. Blackett jumped ashore into her brother's arms. She was a very little woman, not really much bigger than Nancy, and very like her. In the native talk that followed, her tongue went fastest. Captain Flint and Mrs. Walker just put in a word sometimes.

"I'm so glad you're here," Mrs. Blackett said to Captain Flint. "Now then, Ruth . . ."

"Nancy, when she's a pirate, my dear," said Captain Flint. "Give her her right name."

"Nancy then, and Peggy, skip into the launch, you harum-scarums, and get into dry things. You'll find them in the cabin. How do you do, Mrs. Walker? You've met my brother, I see. And my wild young ones. And so these are the Swallows who turned out to be so much better than somebody thought they were."

She too had heard the news, even though she lived at the other side of the lake from Rio.

"Well," said Mrs. Dixon, "I think I'll be going now, if you've done with that bucket. I've the chickens to feed, and Dixon'll be wanting to get to his sheep."

Both the mothers and Captain Flint and all the Swallows and Amazons thanked her for bringing such a good breakfast.

"Aye, there's nothing like porridge," said Mrs. Dixon. "Well, I suppose I shan't be seeing any of you in the morning. I shall quite miss it. I've come to be in the way of looking for you. But perhaps you'll be coming again next year."

"Every year. For ever and ever," said Titty.

"Aye," said Mrs. Dixon, "we all think that when we're young."

Mr. Dixon, who was waiting down by the boat, had said "Good morning," when he came, and now he said "Good day to you," as he rowed Mrs. Dixon away. He was always a very silent native.

The others were not. They talked and talked, all native talk, about the storm and the burglary. Sometimes they asked questions which the Amazons found a little difficult to answer, though Captain Flint helped them out. Even Mr. Jackson, the powerful strong native from Holly Howe, wanted to know exactly how the Swallows had found the box.

At last the native talk began to slacken.

"What about packing up?" said Mrs. Blackett to the Amazons. "You can put everything in the launch, and come in it with me, and we can tow the *Amazon*."

"Tow *Amazon!*" said Nancy in horror. "We're coming home under sail. We want no salvage."

"Everything's so wet here," said the mother of the Swallows. "You'd better come back with me to Holly Howe."

"Not now," begged Titty. "We're quite dry, and we've got a whole tin of pemmican left, and lots of bunloaf, and it's our last day."

It would have been very dreadful to be swept home in a flood of natives, even of the nicest sort. Half the pleasure of visiting distant countries is sailing home afterwards. Besides, she had to say goodbye to the island. John, Susan, and Roger also begged to be allowed to stay. Nancy and Peggy flatly refused to go.

"What if it comes on to blow again?" said the Swallows' mother.

Here Captain Flint spoke.

"It's not going to do that," he said. "It was just the first of our autumn thunderstorms. It's blown itself out now, and I shouldn't be surprised if there's a dead calm before evening. It may rain again tomorrow, but I'll almost guarantee good weather for today."

And so it was agreed. Everything not wanted for the day was to be packed into Mr. Jackson's boat if it was to go to Holly Howe, and into the launch if it belonged to the Amazons. The launch would tow Mr. Jackson and his boat as far as the Holly Howe bay, so that the two mothers could be together in the cabin. "We have a lot more to say to each other," said Mrs. Blackett.

"About coming next year?" said Peggy and Titty together.

"Perhaps," said their mothers.

The packing of Mr. Jackson's boat came first. Captain Flint lent a hand, and it did not take long. The sodden tents were rolled up. "I'll spread them to dry after," said Mr. Jackson.

The blankets were stuffed into a sack. Nancy wanted to empty the hay out of the haybags to make a last blaze on the camp fire. "Nay," said Mr. Jackson, "it's good hay that." So it was spared to be eaten by cows. All the Swallows' things were stowed in Jackson's boat. Nothing was left but the big kettle, for making tea, stores for the day, the parrot-cage, and John's tin box.

"You don't want that," said Mother.

"It's got the ship's papers in it," said Captain John.

"We'll keep our tent," said Captain Nancy, "but we shan't want our sleeping-bags and things."

At last the natives were ready to go.

Captain Flint said "Goodbye."

"Are you going too?" said Titty.

"I'm going in the launch with the others," he said. "I've something to say to your mother about next year. And I've a lot to do, for I'm going to London tomorrow. There's that monkey to see about, you know. But I'll keep a look-out for you towards evening."

At last the launch chug, chugged away from the island, with the two rowing boats towing astern, Captain Flint's on a short painter, and Mr. Jackson's on a long one, from the port and starboard quarters. The natives waved as the launch moved off.

"Goodbye, Swallows," called Mrs. Blackett. "I shall expect you others when I see you."

"Don't be late," called Mother. "If you're home by seven, I'll bring Vicky down to the boathouse. She'd like to meet the sailors coming home from sea with a parrot. Goodbye, Amazons."

"Goodbye, goodbye," called Nancy and Peggy. "You will promise to come again next year?"

"We'll come," said Mother.

*

After they were gone the Swallows and Amazons looked at each other. They were rather glum.

"It's the natives," said Nancy. "Too many of them. They turn everything into a picnic."

"Mother doesn't," said Titty.

"Nor does ours when she's alone," said Nancy.

"And Captain Flint's not a bit like a native when he's by himself," said Titty.

"It's when they all get together," said Nancy. "They can't help themselves, poor things."

"Well, they've gone now," said Peggy. "Let's go on with the shipwreck. This is the day after we were thrown ashore. Now we've got to settle down for twenty years to watch for passing sails."

"But we're going home this afternoon," said Roger.

"You needn't say so," said Titty.

But it was no good. Everybody knew, and nobody could get back into the old mood.

"We ought to bale the ships," said John.

That was better. It was something that had to be done. There was a lot of water in both the ships. The wet thwarts were steaming and drying in the sun, which was already hot, but the sails were very wet. They hoisted the sails to dry them, and then went back to the camp.

The camp looked much smaller. There were pale, unhealthy patches where the Swallows' tents had stood and bleached the grass under the groundsheets by hiding it from the sun. The Amazons' tent stood alone and forlorn without its companions.

"Come on," said Nancy. "We've got to take it down anyway – to strike it, I mean – so we may as well set about it."

It was stiff work getting the poles out of the hems in the wet canvas, but everybody helped. The tent was loosely rolled up. The poles were taken to pieces, and made into a bundle, and wrapped in the groundsheet.

The Swallows and Amazons looked sadly round their camping ground. There was now nothing but the fireplace with its feebly burning fire, the square pale patches where the tents had been, the parrot's cage in a patch of sunlight, and Susan's kettle and a few mugs and the pemmican tin and the bunloaf and John's tin box, to show that it had ever been the home of the explorers and their pirate friends.

"When we've gone," said Titty, "someone else may discover it. They'll know it's a camp because of the fireplace, but they'll think the natives made it."

"If anybody takes it, we'll barbecue them," said Nancy Blackett. "It's our island, yours and ours, and we'll defend it against anybody."

"We're going to school at the end of the summer," said Peggy.

"So are we," said Susan.

"Well, we shan't be at school for ever," said Nancy. "We'll be grown up, and then we'll live here all the year round."

"So will we," said Titty, "and in the winter we'll fetch our food over the ice in sledges."

"I shall be going to sea some day," said John, "and so will Roger. But we'll always come back here on leave."

"I shall bring my monkey," said Roger.

"And the parrot shall always come," said Titty.

"Well, it's no good hanging about," said Nancy. "Let's put to sea."

Everything left was carried down to the harbour and stowed in the ships. Susan emptied the kettle on the fire. Titty took the parrot all over the island, so that when they got home it would remember her favourite places. At the last minute John thought of the rope for hoisting the lantern on the lighthouse tree. He ran back there and loosed one end of the rope, so that it ran over the bough high overhead and came down with a thump on the damp ground. He coiled it and brought it to the harbour.

Then they put to sea. The waves had gone down and so had the wind, but there was still a strong swell.

"Wind's from the south," said Captain Nancy. "We'll beat into it. We know a fine place for a landing down the lake. And then we'll have the wind with us for the run home."

"We'll follow you," said Captain John. He wanted *Swallow* to be the last to leave.

In *Swallow*, Roger was in the bows, Able-seaman Titty and the big parrot-cage in the bottom of the boat just aft of the mast, and Susan and John in the stern. John was steering.

Soon after they had worked *Swallow* out of the harbour and she was sailing on the port tack, Titty, who had been talking to the parrot, said, "Captain John, how are we to put Polly on the Ship's Articles?"

"We've got a captain and a mate, and an able-seaman and a boy. I'll sign him on as ship's parrot," said Captain John.

"Have you got the ship's papers here?" asked Titty. "It would never do for him to sign on after the voyage was over."

John handed the tiller to the mate, opened his tin box, and dug out the Articles that had been signed by everybody, so long ago, on the Peak of Darien. There was plenty of room for another hand. He wrote, "Polly, Ship's Parrot." Then he gave the paper to the able-seaman.

"You'll have to sign for him," he said.

But the able-seaman had opened the parrot's cage, and the parrot came out in a stately manner, as if he knew he was wanted on business.

"You can't exactly sign," said Titty. "But lots of sailors can't. You must wet your dirty claw and make your mark."

"Pieces of eight," said the parrot.

"He's asking about his pay," said John.

The able-seaman wetted the parrot's very dirty claw and put the paper under it. The parrot stepped firmly in the right place and left a good print of his claw, though he did put the point of one toe through the paper.

Titty wrote beside it, "Polly: his Mark."

"Ready about," cried Susan, and John and Titty ducked their heads as the boom came over, and *Swallow* slipped round and off on the other tack, hesitating for hardly a moment and then butting cheerfully through the waves.

"Doesn't *Amazon* look fine?" said Susan, looking at the little white-sailed boat ahead of them, with her fluttering black and white flag and her two red-capped sailors.

"*Swallow* must look just as fine," said Captain John.

"Finer," said Titty. "We've got a brown sail."

They sailed on, tacking from one side of the lake to the other and back again, till they were within a mile of the steamer pier at the foot of the lake.

Here they were passed by one of the big lake steamers, crowded with passengers, who came to the side and pointed. The captain, who was steering her, took out his binoculars, and looked through them at the little *Swallow*. By now the news had run all over Rio, and up and down the lake, about the way in which the Swallows had found the box that had been stolen from Mr. Turner's houseboat.

Suddenly a loud cheer sounded over the water, and again and again. The passengers waved their hats, and shouted.

"What *is* the matter with the natives in the steamer?" said Roger.

Then one of the sailors ran aft to the flagstaff at the steamer's

stern, and the big red ensign dropped to half-mast, and then
rose again.

"They're cheering at us," said Captain John, turning very
red. "How horrible."

"They've saluted," said Susan. "Oughtn't we to answer? The
Amazons are."

They could see Peggy at the halyards, busy dipping the Jolly
Roger.

Titty shut the parrot in his cage, and lowered *Swallow*'s flag,
and raised it again.

"It's a good thing we're going away," said Captain John.
"They'll have forgotten by next year."

The big steamer hurried on. The *Amazon* headed into a little
bay on the western shore of the lake. The *Swallow* followed her.
There were woods all round the little bay, and a small stream
ran into it. The Swallows and Amazons landed close by the
mouth of the stream.

"What a splendid cove," said Captain John.

"It's one of our most private haunts," said Captain Nancy.
"Altogether free from natives. The road's miles away on the
other side of the woods. No one ever comes here except us,
and no one can see we're here, even from the water, unless they
happen to look right in."

They made their fire and boiled their kettle by the side of
the little beck, noisy after the night's rain. The jetsam on the
shore was very wet, but in the wood they found a few dry sticks
here and there. They started the fire with a handful of dry
moss. It was not easy to get it going, but, once it was well lit,
the fire burned well enough to boil the kettle. Here, away from
the island, they spent their last day, until Captain Nancy noticed
that the lake was nearly calm.

"It's going to take us a long time to sail home," she said.
"What orders, Commodore?"

John started. He had been thinking of something else.

"The fleet sets sail and steers north," he said.

Very slowly the two little ships moved out of the bay into the open lake. There was very little wind, though now and again a catspaw hurrying from the south helped them on their way and darkened the smooth small waves.

"You'd never think it could have blown like it did in the night," said Roger.

They sailed up the lake with the booms well out. Up in the woods on the high hillside smoke was rising. They could hear the noise of the charcoal-burners' axes in the now quiet air.

"They'll still be here when we're gone," said Titty.

"Who?" said Susan.

"The savages," said Titty.

The wind was dropping. The boom swung aft, and the mainsheet now and then caught the water and trailed in it.

"Sit on the lee side, Able-seaman," said John. "That'll keep the boom out."

Nancy in *Amazon* was sitting on the lee side for the same reason.

"Hadn't we better row?" said Roger.

"You want a motor boat," said Captain John.

"No I don't," said Roger. "Sail is the thing."

Slowly the fleet slipped past Wild Cat Island. The island was once more the uninhabited island that Titty had watched for so many days from the Peak of Darien. And yet, it was not that island. John, looking at it, remembered the harbour and the leading lights and his swim all round it, and the climbing of the great tree. For Roger it would always be the place where he had swum for the first time. For Susan it was the camp and housekeeping and cooking for a large family. Titty thought of it as Robinson Crusoe's island. It was her island more than anyone's because she had been alone on it. She remembered

FAREWELL!

the path she had cleared, and waking in the dark, and hearing the owl. She remembered the dipper. She remembered getting *Amazon* out of the harbour. She looked suddenly across the lake to Cormorant Island and then at *Amazon* slipping silently through the water a cable's length away. Had she ever really been anchored in *Amazon* out there in the dark?

As they passed Houseboat Bay, Captain Flint rowed out to them to say goodbye once more.

"Goodbye," they shouted.

"Till next year," he shouted back, and rested on his oars and watched the fleet as it sailed slowly on towards the Peak of Darien.

Under the Peak of Darien the fleet broke up.

There were more shouts of "Goodbye," "Remember the Alliance," and "Come again next year." "Three cheers for Wild Cat Island," shouted John. They all cheered. "Three cheers for the Swallows," shouted Nancy. "And for the Amazons," they shouted back. John hauled his wind and stood in for the Holly Howe boathouse. *Amazon* held on her course. She was soon out of sight beyond the further point of the bay.

"I wish it wasn't over," said Roger.

"No more pemmican, anyway," said Susan.

"What about singing 'Salt Beef'?" said Titty. So they sang:

"Salt beef, salt beef, is our relief,
　　Salt beef and biscuit bread O!
Salt beef, salt beef, is our relief,
　　Salt beef and biscuit bread O!
While you on shore and a great many more
　　On dainty dishes fed O!
Don't forget your old shipmate,
　　Fol-de-rol-de-riddle, Fol-de-ri-do!"

"Susan is the old shipmate," said Roger.

"We all are," said John.

"What's the song they sing at the end of the voyage?" said Susan.

Titty began, and the others joined in at once, for they all knew it:

> "Oh, soon we'll hear the Old Man say,
>   Leave her, Johnny, leave her.
> You can go ashore and take your pay,
>   It's time for us to leave her.
> Leave her, Johnny, leave her like a man,
>   Leave her, Johnny, leave her.
> Oh leave her, Johnny, leave her when you can,
>   It's time for us to leave her."

"Who *was* Johnny?" said Roger. "Hullo, there's Mother and Vicky coming down the field."

SWALLOWS·AND·AMAZONS·FOR·EVER!

Also by
ARTHUR RANSOME

SWALLOWDALE

978 0 099 42715 5

'There was nothing of the Swallow *to be seen, except a couple of floating oars and one of the knapsacks, drifting in between Pike Rock and the island.'*

John, Susan, Titty and Roger return to the lake for another summer camping on their island with their old allies, Nancy and Peggy, otherwise known as the Amazon pirates. But immediately disaster strikes when the Swallows find themselves marooned ashore by the shipwreck of their boat. But if they can't have the island, there's always Swallowdale, the secret valley, hidden from the world and containing an extra secret concealed within it . . .

PETER DUCK

978 0 099 42716 2

The Swallows and Amazons are sailing with Captain Flint when they hear a tale to set their pulses racing and hopes shooting sky high. Soon their boat is on its way to a Caribbean treasure hunt and they find themselves up against sharks, storms and the vilest of pirates.

Winter Holiday

978 0 099 42717 9

When Dick and Dorothea meet up with the Swallows and
Amazons, they're soon swept into a wild adventure of
polar expeditions, mountain rescues, blizzards, igloos,
ice sailing and heroic work amidst the frozen wastes.

Coot Club

978 0 099 42718 6

Tom Dudgeon has cast off a motor cruiser from its moorings to
protect a coot's nest, but now the cruiser is searching high and
low for him – even offering a reward. Tom accepts an invitation
for a week's cruise to teach his new friends, Dick and Dorothea,
how to sail. You couldn't get a better sailor than Tom, but can
he really stay ahead of his pursuers long enough to complete
the voyage?

PIGEON POST

978 0 099 42719 3

Reunited for the summer, the Swallows and Amazons launch
a prospecting expedition to find the lost gold mine on the
high hills above the lake. But the mining camp runs into all
sorts of trouble: not only the danger of fire in the drought-
ridden countryside but also scary encounters with unsafe
tunnels. Worst of all is the sinister Squashy Hat, who appears
to be a rival prospector and a spy – how can they keep working
without him discovering what they've found?

WE DIDN'T MEAN TO GO TO SEA

978 0 099 42722 3

'Now, Susan,' Mother said, 'And you too, John.
No night sailing . . . No going outside the harbour . . .
And back the day after tomorrow . . . Promise.'

But promises can't always be kept. Within twenty-four hours
John, Susan, Titty and Roger find themselves fighting a night
gale in the treacherous waters of the North Sea, adrift and in
the main shipping lanes. Suddenly, it's a real adventure and
only their sailing skills can help them now . . .

SECRET WATER

978 0 099 42723 0

'You'll start with a blank map, that doesn't do more than show roughly what's water and what isn't. You'll have your tents, stores, everything we'd got ready. You'll be just a wee bit better off than Columbus. But you'll be marooned fair and square.'

John, Susan, Titty and Roger, the crew of the *Swallow*, take on the job of mapping the mass of small islands around Pin Mill while living on the biggest one. But who are the mysterious savages who lurk in the islands – and is the tribal totem they find in their campsite a threat of attack?

THE BIG SIX

978 0 099 42724 7

'But who are the Big Six?' asked Pete.
'It's the Big Five really,' said Dorothea. 'They are the greatest detectives in the world. They sit in the cubby holes at Scotland Yard and solve one mystery after another.'

It's great detective work that's needed now. Bill, Peter and Joe are falsely accused of setting boats adrift and the whole river is against them. Only Dick, Dorothea and Tom Dudgeon are there to stand by their friends and they soon set to work to investigate the crimes and trap the real criminals.

MISSEE LEE

978 0 099 42725 4

Miss Lee looked at John.
'Were you coming here when you lost your ship?'
'No,' said John.
'We jolly well would have if we'd known,' said Nancy.
'Why?' asked Miss Lee.
'Well, pirates,' said Nancy. 'Who wouldn't?'

Nancy Blackett, the terror of the seas, has finally met a real pirate – the tiny, pistol-carrying Missee Lee who has rescued them after their shipwreck off the coast of China. The only trouble is she wants to keep them . . . forever . . .

THE PICTS AND THE MARTYRS

978 0 099 42727 8

The dreaded Great-Aunt has come to stay with Nancy and Peggy just as their friends arrive for the summer holiday! Now Nancy and Peggy must wear dresses and read poetry by day. But at night they break out for wildness. It's a desperate gamble, but can it possibly work against the evil eyes of the fearsome Great-Aunt?

GREAT NORTHERN?

978 0 099 42726 1

'I was wrong,' said Captain Flint. 'He's not mad but bad. Rotten bad. It isn't only eggs he wants. He wants us to take the credit for it. You're quite right. It's up to us; it's up to the ship, to see he doesn't.'

Dick's birdwatching discovery turns the cruise of the *Sea Bear* into a desperate chase. Not only do the Swallows and Amazons have to solve the case, but they also have to dodge the savage natives and evade the ruthless pursuit of a fanatic egg collector, determined to kill a pair of rare birds. Fortunately, Nancy has a few plans . . .

THE ARTHUR RANSOME SOCIETY

The Arthur Ransome Society was formed in 1990 with the aim of celebrating Ransome's life and works, and of encouraging both children and adults to take part in outdoor pursuits – especially sailing and camping. It also seeks to sponsor research, to spread Ransome's ideas in the wider community and to bring together all those who share the values and the spirit that he fostered in his storytelling.

The Society is based at the Abbot Hall Museum of Lakeland Life and Industry in Kendal, where Ransome's desk, favourite books and some of his personal possessions are kept. There are also close links with the Ruskin Museum at Coniston, where the original Amazon is now kept. The Society keeps in touch with its members through its journal, *Mixed Moss*, and its newsletter, *Signals*.

Regional branches of the Society have been formed by members in various parts of the country, including Scotland, the Lake District and North, East Anglia, the Midlands, the South and South West Coast, and contacts are maintained with overseas groups in America, Australia and Japan. Membership fees are modest, and fall into four groups – for those under 18, for single adults, for whole families, and for those over 65. If you are interested in knowing more about the Society or would like to join, please write for a membership leaflet to The Secretary, The Arthur Ransome Society Ltd, The Abbot Hall Gallery, Kendal, Cumbria LA9 5AL, or email to memsec@arthur-ransome.org.

SWALLOWS·AND·AMAZONS·FOR·EVER!